SIN

———

EMMA HART

SIN

1

DAHLIA

It didn't feel real.

Staring at the book-themed bar that was now mine, I sighed. It was all I could think about. It wasn't real. It was a dumb dream that I'd wake up from if only someone would punch me in the face.

I'd always known that The Scarlet Letter would be mine. The bar was a love letter from my father to my mother, and today was the first time I'd stood in the building since my father's death. Seventeen years since my mom's murder had flown fast—but not as fast as the three months since my father's passing. I'd spent the weeks since his funeral staying with family in California, but two days ago, I'd gotten a call from the manager of the bar.

Someone wants to buy your bar, she'd said. He's offering a ton of money. You need to come and handle this.

Honestly, that was the polite version. Since the manager was my best friend, the exact words had been, "Dahlia Lloyd, that's enough of this. That cock Damien Fox wants to buy the bar and won't leave me alone. Get your ass back to Vegas to deal with your shit, because this is your problem, not mine. I won't fix anymore for you. Three months is long enough."

She wasn't wrong. She'd been running the bar in my absence, doing all the things that weren't in her job description because I'd been hiding from the reality of my situation.

Which was this. The Scarlet Letter, Las Vegas' most successful non-strip club, was mine.

This building with its book-nook booths and literary influence woven into every part of it was all mine.

I knew how to run it. I knew every inch of the building. I just didn't know what the hell I was supposed to do now.

"Well, hello, stranger." Abby, my best friend, strolled into the bar, cutting off my woeful and self-pitying inner-monologue. Her fiery auburn hair fell loosely around her shoulders, contrasting perfectly against her scarlet-red dress.

She pulled me into the tightest hug known to man, squeezing for all her worth. Which, thanks to her love of Pilates and yoga, was a lot.

"Hey. Can't breathe." I wriggled to extract myself from her tight grip.

"I don't care if you can't breathe." She squeezed one last time, as if to make her point, then let me go. "How dare you leave me here to deal with that insufferable man?"

I blinked at her. "I didn't even know you were dealing with him until two days ago."

"You should have known."

"With all my psychic powers?"

Abby pursed her glossy lips.

"I know, I know." I sighed. She could guilt-trip with the best of them. "I should have been here. I'm sorry, Abs. I just needed…"

"Time. I know. Four weeks from your dad's diagnosis wasn't enough time for you."

Swallowing hard, I carefully set my purse down on the table nearest to me. It was one of the one-legged ones that was fixed to the floor, and its lone leg was a stack of fake books. It was one of my favorite things about the bar.

"It wasn't," I agreed with her. "I still don't feel ready to be back here."

"You'll never be ready. You just have to do it. If we all waited until we were ready to do something, we'd do nothing but watch reruns on Netflix."

She had a point there, too. I hated it when she was wise like this. It made it hard for me to argue with her.

"Well, I'm back now. I dropped my stuff at the house earlier, and I'm not going anywhere." Somehow, saying the words made it feel more real. "You're right. Three months was too long."

And, if I was honest with myself, I was starting to get bored—and annoyed. I loved my family, but I had little tolerance for my soap-star cousin whose drama didn't stay on the set. I knew moping around wouldn't be something my dad wanted me to do. He'd made that abundantly clear the moment the doctor had looked at him and told him the tumors on his lung were cancerous and that treatment would only prolong his life.

"Don't cry for me, flower," he'd said, holding my hand. *"I've done my bit with you, now it's time for me to see your momma. It's all yours now."*

I took a deep breath and swatted the memory away. Holding onto it would do nothing but make me cry. It was still too raw—four weeks wasn't enough for anyone to find out they were losing a parent, especially not when that parent had raised you for almost your entire life.

Quite simply, I didn't really know how to live without my father. It was a world I was attempting to navigate, and most days, I felt like a newborn giraffe trying to walk for the first time. As lame as that sounded, it was the truth. That was why coming home was so scary.

I'd never been here without the knowledge I could call him. Now, I was, and it stung. All I wanted to do was grab my purse and get the hell out of here, but I couldn't. I'd neglected my duties long enough. It was time for me to pull up my big girl panties—but not too far, given that I was wearing a thong—and get the hell on with it.

"All right. What needs to be done?" I stepped up to the edge of the bar.

"Damien Fox needs to fuck off," Abby said it so simply, like it was nothing more or less than a fact. And I guess, to her, it was a fact. He needed to. "He said he'd wait for your call to discuss a meeting, and that his lawyer is on standby to draw up papers for the sale of the bar. But you can't call him before one p.m. because he's up late with the clubs some nights."

"Well, that's a surefire way to get me to call you before one o'clock." I rolled my eyes.

I didn't know much about Damien Fox except for the fact he lived up to his surname and owned half of the strip clubs in the city. My father had crossed paths with both him and his father on occasion, but from the rumors I'd heard, I went out of my way to avoid the entire family.

Now, it seemed that wasn't an option for me. I needed to confront the cunning, smug asshole myself.

"How do I contact him?"

"His card is in the register." Abby cocked a thumb over her shoulder and opened a folder.

Great.

I was hoping she'd say she didn't know.

Stepping behind the bar was strange. It'd been such a long time since I'd been there, yet at the same time, it felt right. I knew what Abby had said wasn't wrong—waiting until I was ready to come back would have resulted in me never doing it. I might have been throwing myself in at the deep end by calling Damien Fox immediately, but the situation needed handling.

I wasn't selling The Scarlet Letter. No matter how much money he tried to give me.

I opened the register and instantly found his card, the small, black rectangle obvious on the silver tray of the drawer. It wasn't hard, given that the register was empty because Abby hadn't put the cash tray in there yet. Knowing her, she'd deliberately dropped the card down the side of it so she didn't have to look at it.

Flipping the thick, dark card between my fingers and thumb, I glanced around for the phone. No way was I using my cell—I didn't want to invite Mr. Fox to call me on my personal time.

"Under the register," Abby said over her shoulder.

Sure enough, when I bent down to look, I found it. Each key beeped when I typed in the number on the card. I didn't know if this number was private, business, or to one of the clubs, so I ran the risk of not even getting through to him.

"Hi," a man's voice said.

"Hell—"

"You've reached Damien Fox. Please leave a message and I'll get back to you as soon as I can."

I was going to ignore the fact I'd just attempted a conversation with a phone recording.

The beep was long and loud, and I swallowed hard before speaking.

"Good morning, Mr. Fox. This is Dahlia Lloyd from The Scarlet Letter. Thank you for your interest in purchasing the bar, but the business is not for sale. Have a nice day."

The second I pushed the button to end the call, Abby burst out laughing.

"What the hell was so funny about that?" I frowned, staring at the phone. I glanced up in enough time to see her turn around and look at me.

"Really?" Her lower lip trembled. "You were so nice, then so mean, then so nice again."

"I wasn't mean." Was I?

"It's the way you said it. You were all, 'Good morning, Mr. Fox!'" she trilled her impression of me in a chirpy voice that made my skin crawl. "Then, you went, 'The business is not for sale,'" she continued in a sharper voice before going back to the chirpy sound again. "'Have a nice day!'"

Shaking my head, I put the phone back on the shelf where it belonged. "How else was I supposed to say it? I'm not a mean person, but obviously, the man doesn't take a hint."

"Have you ever known a man to take a hint?"

She had a good point.

"Well, no, but still. It was my first official act as the owner of the bar, and I wanted him to know I'm not a pushover."

"Just a little soft on the inside. Like a s'more."

I'd been called worse.

I rounded the bar and joined her at the table where she was sitting with her laptop open. "Can I help you with anything?"

She mock-gasped, pressing her hand to her chest as she looked at me. "Are you…working?"

I hit her with my best death stare.

"Kidding. *Boss.*" She grinned and handed me a folder. "I'll ease you back in gently."

"Are we using lube?" I asked, looking at the folder labeled 'Paychecks.' It was the one thing I'd done when I hadn't been here—but only because the accounts were all in my name and Abby physically couldn't sign off on anything.

"There's been a lot of overtime this month. Your bank account will probably need it."

It was good to be back.

Kinda.

Four hours sorting out my father's office, and I didn't feel like I was any closer to organization than I was when I'd walked through the door. I hadn't known it before, but he'd apparently favored a 'shove it in the folder' method of filing papers instead of using the filing cabinets along one wall.

All but one were empty. There were five.

I couldn't figure out how I'd never noticed it. Then again, I didn't have time to figure it out. I was too busy sorting out and correctly filing years of paperwork.

I'm sure this method worked for him and there were copies probably filed with the lawyers and bankers and accountants and everyone else, but it didn't for me. I needed some form of order.

And curtains. The office desperately needed new curtains, because the ones that were once dark red were so old, the color was now hinging on pink.

I sipped my iced tea and surveyed my work so far. The top of the desk was clear, and I'd already placed an order for a new desktop computer. Turning on the dinosaur that was currently atop the desk was probably going to be the most daunting task—who knew if it would even work? If it didn't, I'd have to find some tech genius to pull off all the data, and I didn't have time for that.

I didn't know where to look, either. Was that the kind of thing I could ask on Facebook? Maybe Craigslist?

Ugh.

Feeling sorry for myself again wasn't going to cut it. I needed to snap out of this and fast. I couldn't run a business as long as I had this woe-is-me attitude. If my dad could see and hear me, he'd laugh and tell me I was made of stronger stuff than fluff and self-pity, and he was right. He always was right.

Except about filing important papers. Then he was very, very wrong.

Another cursory glance around the office had me lamenting the fact I was an only child. This would be a lot easier if I had a sibling to share this with.

Not self-pity. Just a fact.

A knock sounded at the door right as I blew out a long breath. I used the desk to pull myself up off the floor before shouting a "Come in!" to whoever was on the other side of the door.

It creaked open to reveal twenty-four-year-old Rylie Fisher. My dad had hired the young redhead two months before he'd died. She was only part-time because she was still in school studying for her Masters, but from what I knew of her, she was pretty good at her job.

"Hey, Rylie. What's up?"

She returned the gesture and held up the phone. "Hey, Ms. Lloyd. You have a call. He's on hold."

A tingle ran over my skin when she said "he." There was only one man I'd called lately, besides my uncle. "It's Dahlia." I smiled. "Who is it?"

"Damien Fox. Again."

Well, shit. If even the part-time employee was saying it was him again, he must have been more persistent than Abby had given him credit for. "If you wanted to bring me a present, I recommend chocolate next time." I grinned and took the phone from her. "Thanks. I'll bring it out when I'm done."

Rylie laughed. "I'll keep it in mind."

I waited until the door had clicked shut behind her, dampening the noise of the music from the bar downstairs, and took the call off hold. "Dahlia Lloyd."

"Ms. Lloyd," came the answering voice. It was deep and smooth and very, very masculine. "Damien Fox. It's wonderful to finally talk to you."

I couldn't say the feeling was mutual. So, I didn't. "How are you, Mr. Fox?"

A light chuckle traveled down the line, and I had the feeling he knew exactly what I was thinking.

"I'm well, thank you. I'm sorry to hear about your father. How are you?"

"Better now I'm home," I answered. "I can't *possibly* imagine what you're calling about, so why don't we skip the rest of the pleasantries and get right to the point?"

"I received the message you left for me at some ungodly hour of the morning."

"Ten years of Bible class ensures me that even God is up and cooking his breakfast by ten a.m. I believe Satan is the lazy one."

Another laugh. Deep and rough. "I'd like to discuss it in person."

"I can assure you that my stance doesn't change regardless of how we have the conversation."

"I like to think I can convince you."

"You're welcome to think so."

"I rarely wake before midday, but as you so eloquently put it, even God is making breakfast by ten a.m. Can I assume you'll be in The Scarlet Letter at ten tomorrow?"

Blinking, I sputtered out, "Yes."

"I'll see you then, Ms. Lloyd."

I opened my mouth to tell him he most definitely will *not*, but the line clicked off.

It was dead. The call was over. He'd forced his way into my morning and, without waiting for me to respond, ended the call.

Understanding of why Abby hated him was quickly washing over me.

Who the hell did Damien Fox think he was?

2

DAHLIA

"What did one wear to meet an arrogant dick?" was the question of the day.

Thankfully, I hadn't packed most of my clothes before I'd left for California, so my 'work' clothes were still hanging, perfectly pressed, in my walk-in closet. Not that it made the choice any easier, mind you. Did I wear jeans and a smart shirt? A skirt? A dress?

Why did I care? I had no intention of spending any longer than five minutes with Damien Fox. I needed just enough time to tell him there was no chance in hell I was selling The Scarlet Letter and to get out of my bar.

I pulled a red dress off the rack and looked it over. It was one of my favorites, and the red-soled, black, Louboutin pumps I'd had my eye on since walking into the closet were the perfect match. I grabbed them before taking both the shoes and my dress into my bedroom to get ready.

I still didn't know who the hell Damien Fox thought he was. I'd replayed the phone call a hundred times, and I couldn't believe the audacity of him and his words. Was that how he conducted all his business? By ruthless, pushy tactics? Was anything he did honest or was it all underhand?

As far as I knew, the man had never been interested in buying Scarlet until my dad died. I was as deep in the running of it as he was, and I would have known if anyone had tried to buy it. That wasn't something Dad would have kept from me—he would have wanted me to be prepared for this exact situation.

SIN

As it was, I wasn't. Not even the tiniest bit. Was there a way to stop someone trying to buy your business when you didn't want to? I assumed I could eventually get a restraining order, but that seemed excessive. Even if the person in question was as persistent as a severe bout of vaginal thrush, just like Damien Fox seemed like.

I giggled at my own thoughts. Better the string of inappropriateness came out now, in private, inside my head. I doubted that particular thought would go down well if it came out of my mouth in his company.

Although, it would be worth it, just for the look on his face...

No. I was a business owner now, and I needed to be professional at all times.

I smoothed my dress down my stomach and looked in the mirror. Indigo-blue eyes partially hidden by dark-brown bangs blinked back at me. The red lipstick slicked across my lips matched the dress almost perfectly, but none of that hid the nerves that were rolling around in my stomach.

There was no difference between my nerves and an elephant doing a roly-poly. Both were as unsettling as the other. Not that I'd ever been in the presence of an elephant doing a roly-poly, but I could imagine how uncomfortable that would be to be around.

I stepped into my shoes and gave myself one more stare in the mirror.

Goddamn this, why was I nervous? I was Dahlia Lloyd. Despite my name, I was no shrinking flower. I never had been, and I wasn't going to start now just because a Fox wanted me to submit to his demands.

The sooner Damien Fox learned that, the better it would be for him.

I nodded at myself in the reflective surface, grabbed my purse, and went in search of my things.

And my bravado.

***

15

The Scarlet Letter was deathly quiet as I entered through the back door. It was so early that not even Abby was here yet, and that was for the best. She'd become fiercely protective of me after my dad's diagnosis, and I hadn't even told her about this meeting this morning.

If I had, I knew she'd march herself down here despite her late night just to make sure Damien Fox was handled.

He would be handled—by me. I'd become certain of that in my drive over here. He had no right to call me up and assume I'd meet with him, much less to assume that said meeting would lead to me selling him my bar.

He could go to Hell on a first-class ticket with a martini in hand for all I cared.

And I didn't. Care, that was. All I cared was that he took himself the hell out of my life and let me get on with getting back to my new normal. This wasn't what I'd planned on upon my return. Granted, I'd still be in Cali if it weren't for his constant going on, but still. Semantics.

It was whatever.

I locked the door behind me, grabbed the phone, and headed up to my office. I had a little time before Damien showed up, and all I could do with it was attempt to make my office a little tidier.

Not that it would make a big difference because not much could make this office tidier than it was. A hurricane could blow through this mess and make it better than it was right in that moment.

I'd barely put a stack of papers back in the right pile when the phone rang. The time flashed as nine-fifty, but the number was unknown. This was Damien, no doubt.

"The Scarlet Letter," I answered. "Dahlia speaking."

"Ms. Lloyd. I'm at the front of the building."

"You're—" my attempt at telling him he was early was cut off by what was quickly becoming his trademark hang-up move.

I slammed the phone down on the desk.

SIN

If I'd been in a better frame of mind, I'd have left him waiting for fifteen minutes. Unfortunately, I wasn't in that frame of mind. I wanted to get this crap over and done with so I could carry on with my life.

"Sonofabitch," I muttered, pushing off the desk.

At least I knew my makeup wasn't smudged. I hadn't had a chance to have coffee yet, and I paid good money to ensure that my lipstick didn't come off with the sip of a glass of water.

I tugged my dress down as I headed down to the bar. I had to walk through the entire bar to reach the front door where he was waiting for me. Keeping my temper in check was harder than I'd imagined it would be—annoyance crawled over my skin, twisting and turning it into goose bumps I couldn't will away.

Stopping in front of the double, wooden doors that made up the front doors to the bar, I did my best to school my expression into one that didn't give away how I was feeling. Judging by my inability to not purse my lips, I was failing.

Abysmally.

Whatever. If he didn't want to annoy me, he should try leaving me alone.

I unlocked the door and opened it. I'd seen Damien Fox before, but never in person, only in pictures. And in fact, that pissed me off even more, the photos I'd seen apparently didn't do the man justice.

He was devilishly handsome, from his dark hair to his dark, calculating eyes. The stubble that coated his strong jaw was trimmed short, but just long enough to be the perfect length to rub your fingers over.

Not that I wanted to rub my fingers over his anything. It was just an observation.

"Dahlia Lloyd, I presume?" His voice was just as deep and rumbly as it was on the phone. Better, actually. If horniness had a sound, it would be his voice.

Damn it. I was not one of those women.

17

I straightened my spine and met his gaze. "Were you expecting me to be anyone else?"

"A simple 'yes' or 'no' would have sufficed." His eyes glittered with amusement.

"Ask a stupid question and you'll get a stupid answer, Mr. Fox. Come on in." I stepped to the side for him to pass.

He joined me inside the bar. I locked the door behind him and waved him to follow me.

"Please excuse the mess in the office. I'm in the middle of sorting it out." I rounded my desk and offered him the seat on the other side.

His dark gaze cast around the room as he sat. A rectangle shape the size of a phone pressed against the fabric of his dark gray pants, and the matching jacket he wore seemed to stretch across his broad shoulders as he got comfortable.

I knew what he was seeing. Boxes upon boxes, random stacks of paper and folders, and an empty Coke bottle.

Whoops.

"Would you like a coffee?" Why was I offering him a drink? I didn't want him here long enough to finish one.

Thankfully, he shook his head. "I just had one, but thank you. I'd like to get straight to the point."

"I'm not selling The Scarlet Letter." What? He's the one who said we needed to get to it.

He arched one dark eyebrow. "You haven't heard what I have to say yet."

"Quite frankly, Mr. Fox," I said, resting my forearms on the desk in front of me, "I don't feel the need to hear it. I can't imagine that anything you say will make me change my mind."

"It's a deal that would benefit us both."

"The only thing that could benefit us both is you hearing what I'm saying."

"I'm hearing it, I just wonder if you know what you're doing."

My eyebrows shot up. Did he really just say that to me? Did he just imply that I don't know how to run a bar? "Excuse me?"

If he'd recognized my anger, he didn't let on. He rested his right foot on his left thigh and gripped his ankle. "You're awfully young to be running a bar. You're only twenty-five and barely out of college."

"That happens when you go back to complete your Masters."

"Fancy degrees don't run businesses, Ms. Lloyd."

"I didn't think dumb people could either, but here I am, looking at you."

He stared at me.

"I'm not quite sure who you think you are, Mr. Fox, but I can assure you, I'm sure as hell not who you think I am." The sharp edge to my voice made him sit up a little straighter. "While you seem pretty certain that a Masters in Business Studies won't run a business, you're neglecting to realize that I've been running this bar with and for my father for the past seven years while I've been studying. My age has nothing to do with my ability to keep this bar as successful as it is. I'm telling you that I'm not selling the bar, and even if I were, to sell it to someone who has zero respect for me would be an insult to my parents." Not to mention to myself. "I can't possibly see what else is there is to discuss, so I apologize for you wasting your time coming here this morning, but I think you should leave now."

I was furious. I'd known he was rude from the phone calls, but to sit in front of me in my building and tell me I was incapable of running the very thing I'd grown up being taught to run was beyond anything I'd ever known. The audacity of him was on another level.

He didn't move until I stood and held the door open pointedly. Then, in the same silence he'd adopted for the past few minutes, he followed me to the front doors where I unlocked them and held that one open, too.

Damien Fox stepped in front of me into the doorway and stopped. With his attention on me, he ran his gaze along the length of my body, not pausing to linger anywhere until our eyes met. Dark brown with hints of gold, his eyes were mesmerizing.

It was a shame his personality didn't match his looks.

"You're really quite fascinating, Ms. Lloyd," he said in a low voice that probably would have made me shiver if I weren't so angry.

"So is the Crime and Investigation channel," I shot back. "It would be a better choice of your time."

He laughed.

He actually laughed at me.

"You would think." A wry smile stretched across his full, pale pink lips. "I'll see you soon, Ms. Lloyd."

I sincerely hoped not. "We'll see." I returned the smile and was about to shut the door when I saw Abby heading our way.

A scowl formed on her face when she realized who was standing in front of me. Ignoring him completely, she said, "Morning, Dahlia."

"Morning, Abs. The coffee's on."

She gave me a thumb up before disappearing inside.

"Abs," Damien mused. "Abby, right? Your manager."

I couldn't help my smirk. "She doesn't like you much. And now, I understand why."

That smile reappeared on his face. It was a cross between a cocky grin and a sexy smirk, and I had a feeling it was one he saved for difficult people. "There's plenty to like about me, Ms. Lloyd. You'll find that out soon enough."

God, he was arrogant.

"Ten points for trying, but I have to get back to work now, so…" I trailed off and gave him a pointed look.

So, get lost now, please.

He inclined his head toward me, and then, I noticed something I'd missed before.

SIN

He had a scar, right beneath his right eye. It was faded, but it had caught in the sunlight that bounced off his face. About two inches long and relatively thin, it added a ruggedness to his overly-polished appearance.

How had he gotten that scar?

And why did I want to know?

"We'll speak soon." His voice pulled me out of my thoughts.

"No, we won't. We're done here."

"We're far from being done," he murmured, his eyes dropping to my lips.

My answer was to shut the door. Slam it, actually. In his face.

If only the door were soundproof, I wouldn't have to listen to that rich laugh of his through it.

I turned to find Abby standing next to the sweeping, circular bar, shaking her head.

"He's such a jerk."

It was hard to argue with the truth.

3

DAHLIA

I hefted the heavy box of paperwork off the desk of my dad's old office. The home office was just as bad as the one at the bar, and I felt like I'd already shredded an entire forest's worth of paper.

Unable to shake my annoyance from yesterday morning's meeting with Damien Fox, I had a permanent eye on my phone. He'd left too easily and too quietly. As much as I wanted to be done with this shitshow, I didn't need his promise that we weren't done to know that he was coming up with another plan to pry the bar from my hands.

Whatever his reason was for wanting The Scarlet Letter, I was more certain than I had been before that the only reason he was trying to buy it now was because he'd assumed I'd sell. He wrongly thought I'd be a pushover and that he'd own it by now.

He'd underestimated me, and I had a feeling that was why he'd left so easily. He needed to rethink his plan of attack. Going in, guns blazing and batting his stupidly long eyelashes at me hadn't worked the way he had hoped.

Was I entering a tactical war to keep hold of my bar? There was no way in hell that he was giving up that easily. Hell, he hadn't even acknowledged my mini-rant. He hadn't said a word until he decided to tell me I was fascinating.

A fact I, of course, already knew.

I wished he didn't, though. I couldn't shake the thought that the reason he was going to keep coming back was to find out more about me.

SIN

What if that was how he'd made his success? Was he the kind of person who tore apart your life to find your weakness to use against you?

The only weakness I thought I had was an enthusiastic love of chocolate ice cream.

He scared me.

I knew nothing about him, yet he knew a little about me. He knew I'd not long left college and how old I was. Neither of those things were something Abby would have told him, so he had to have found them out by himself.

I knew it was a common thing to do, but the fact he'd been looking me up made me shiver. What else did he know about me that I didn't know he knew?

Why didn't I know enough about him?

I needed to change that, and I needed to do it now.

I moved another box to the door for recycling—I'd had enough of shredding, it could go as it was—and looked at the clock on the wall. I didn't have to be at the bar until three, so I had time to do a little digging. And I knew exactly where to start.

I grabbed my phone and dialed my friend, Mia's, number as I walked to the kitchen. The sunlight almost blinded me as it streamed in through the vast, sliding glass doors, and I muttered a curse right before Mia picked up.

"Hi, stranger. A little birdie told me you're home."

I smiled. "I am. How's married life?"

"Same as it was before, except neither of us can decide what to do about the business." She laughed. "West wants me to rename it, but I don't know if I can be bothered to go through all the steps to change it from O'Halloran to Rykman. If I'm going to do that, I may as well name it something else altogether now there's a whole team of us."

"That would get my vote," I told her.

"But what?" I could almost hear her roll her eyes. "Never mind. I'm just going to ignore him until I can think up something. How are you holding up?"

"I'm doing good, actually. It's nice to be back and settling into work again. I'd be happier if I didn't have to sort through all dad's paperwork."

Mia laughed. "Remember when I did that small marketing campaign for him online? It took him two weeks to find the info from the last woman he hired to give to me. It was a good thing he booked me so far out."

I did remember, and she wasn't exaggerating. Maybe his filing system didn't work for him, either. "I do remember. I actually have a favor. I need some info."

"Fine, but it'll cost you a drink."

"Done. Do you know much about Damien Fox?"

She was quiet for a moment. "Not many people do, but I probably know the most. He's friends with West. Why do you need to know about him? I didn't think you knew each other."

I shook my head, even though she couldn't see it. "We didn't until his persistence brought me home."

"Are you...dating him?"

"If by dating you mean plotting his murder, then, yes, I am."

"Uh oh."

I gave her a quick rundown of the situation. "He seems to know a lot about me, and I get the feeling he isn't going to give up anytime soon. I need a head-start."

"Now that, I can help you with. I'll see you at seven."

I walked into the bar at two-thirty. The bar was dead. There was a group in the corner, a couple in a booth, and a table full of girlfriends who were laughing happily. The music was low and soothing, unlike later where it'd be turned right up in keeping with the party mood.

The versatility of the bar was why I loved it so much.

Charley, one of the waitresses, banged out of the doors that connected the bar to the kitchen with a tray resting on her shoulder. The smell of the cheesy-bacon stuffed potatoes we had on the appetizer menu made my nose twitch. They smelled so good, and now, I was hungry.

I'd skipped lunch to continue my Damien Fox information hunt. I hadn't found anything except the string of strip clubs he owned and articles about his charity and functions or some crap. I'd read one and given up. It was nothing but singing his praises, and I didn't give a shit about his praises. I gave a shit about something that would be useful to me.

I walked up to the bar and approached the giant bouquet of flowers. White and pink lilies stared out at me. "Hey, Abs." I softly ran a finger across the edge of a lily petal. "You got an admirer?"

She blinked at me and then the flowers. "Me? No. Those are yours."

I frowned. Mine?

"There should be a card in there somewhere. They were delivered about a half hour ago. I knew you would be here early so I didn't bother calling you."

"Yeah, the text of 'Are you getting your ass to work today?' covered that." I flashed her a smile before looking for the card. "Who sent them?"

She put down the glass she'd been cleaning and walked over to me. "Here." She bent and picked something off the floor. "It must have fallen out when I transferred them into the vase."

"Did you read it?" I took the small envelope from her and set down my purse.

"Nope. I can guess who they're from, though."

I stopped, mid-way through opening the envelope. "No."

Her grin was evil.

There was no way these flowers were from Damien Fox. Was there?

"Why would he send me flowers?" I blinked at Abby.

"I'm gonna go out on a limb here and say the answer to your question is in the card you're holding." That grin was still in place.

"What? Oh. Right. Of course." My cheeks heated.

"You're blushing." She dropped the grin—and her jaw. "Why are you blushing? He's a dick!"

"I'm blushing because I forgot I was holding the card. I'm shocked."

"Flustered. You're flustered."

"I'm shocked."

"Flustered."

"Ugh!" I ripped the envelope open the rest of the way. She was right—I was flustered. This didn't make any sense. Nobody had any reason to send me flowers. I'd had tons of them after my father's death, but they were all long dead.

I pulled the thick card from the envelope. It was plain white on the front, but inside, the note was written in clean, capital letters.

MS. LLOYD,
MY APOLOGIES.
DAMIEN FOX.

I stared at the card. That was it. That was all it said. Our names and the most half-assed apology I'd ever read in my life. Sure, it'd come with the flowers, but compared to the flowers…Who the fuck would send what had to be a hundred-dollar bouquet of flowers and combine it with this card?

I hadn't meant to call him dumb yesterday, but maybe I wasn't too far off the mark, after all.

"What?"

I looked up at Abby. Wordlessly, I held out the card for her to read.

She pulled it from between my fingers and read it. A loud laugh barked out of her, and she threw the card down on the bar with a shake of her head. "Just when I think he can't surprise me anymore, he does that."

That was one way to put it.

I dug around in my purse for my phone. Easier said than done. I had everything and its twin in there, so it took me a minute to clasp my fingers around the smooth Samsung and pull it out. Abs looked over at the screen as I pulled up my messages and started a new one with him as the recipient.

Me: *Why are you sorry?*

Someone came to the bar to order, so my best friend had to dart away, but not without snorting at my message to him.

What else was I supposed to say? Thanks for the flowers but your note was a pile of shit?

Well. Maybe that was the way to go.

Me: *The flowers are gorgeous. Thank you.*

There. Now I didn't look like I was ungrateful because I wasn't. They really were very pretty—the mix of red, white, and pink lilies and roses scattered with other flowers I didn't know the names of were the kind of flowers you could look at all day. He probably had an assistant pick them out and do the card, but whatever.

My phone buzzed in my hand, so I unlocked it.

Damien: *You're welcome.*

Another buzz.

Damien: *I apologized because I underestimated you.*

Well, *I* could have told him that.

It was interesting, though. Of all the things he could apologize for—there were many—he picked that. That told me he wasn't giving up. He wanted my bar, and for some reason, he wanted it badly.

Me: *I would have gone with being rude and pressuring as the reason for the apology, personally.*
Damien: *But I'd be lying.*
Me: *You're not sorry you were rude and borderline harassing with your behavior?*
Damien: *I'm trying to be sorry for that, but you're just too fucking hot when you get annoyed. It's endearing.*

What?

Me: *You know I'm torturing you in my mind when I'm angry with you, right? That's not typically hot.*
Damien: *Like I said, you're fascinating.*
Me: *Only because you assumed you could walk into my bar and purchase it without a fight once I'd seen you. I didn't drop to my knees and agree to let you buy it.*
Damien: *Touché.*
Damien: *Buying bars isn't usually what I'm doing when a woman is on her knees in front of me, though.*

He got worse and worse, didn't he?

Me: *Charming.*
Damien: *Come to dinner with me.*

My eyebrows shot up. Go to dinner with him? I'd rather sleep on hot coals and be sat on by a sumo wrestler. Not to mention his last text and the fact he didn't ask. He told me to go.

Me: *No.*

I put my phone back into my purse and zipped it up. Of course, the urge to see his response was overwhelming.

Because there would be one. A response. He was like a dog with a bone. I knew there wasn't a chance in hell that he'd take my answer and leave it.

It wasn't like I wouldn't go. I'm almost certain I would. I wanted to know why he wanted my bar as much as he did, so I couldn't not go. The only problem was, I didn't like to be dictated to, and Damien Fox was very, very good at dictating to me.

Case in point with the dinner message.

"He wants me to go to dinner with him." I picked up my purse. "He told me to go."

Abby coughed to hide her laughter. "Please tell me you told him what to do with that demand."

"I told him no, straight up. I'm going upstairs to do some more in dad's office and do some paperwork. Do you need me to do anything?"

She nodded. "The schedule for the next month. Finley leaves next week."

Damn. I'd forgotten that. Finley had worked here for five years but was opening a bar in Reno with a friend. He was damn good at his job, and I knew we'd struggle to replace him.

"All right. I'll get that done and put some ads out." I left her in the bar and headed up to the office. It was much quieter here, but there was a problem—no Abby.

Which meant the first thing I did as soon as I shut the door was check my phone like a loser.

Just like I knew there would be, there was a message from Damien, but it didn't say what I expected it to.

Damien: *You'll go to dinner with me. One day.*

I didn't respond. What was I supposed to say to that? It was obvious he was the kind of man who was used to getting his own way. He was essentially an adult-sized toddler. I was already getting fed up with his attitude, and unbelievably, every message he sent or word he spoke just made it even worse.

How could anyone be so cocksure of themselves? He was acting like he was the king of the universe or some other freaking bullshit.

How much longer was I going to have to put up with this?

I pinned the month's schedule to the board in the giant staff room and sent everyone a text letting them know to make sure to check the board in case anything needed to be changed. I hadn't made much headway in the office since phone calls came in left, right, and center, but I'd sent out the job advertisements so Abby could get to interviewing for Finley's replacement.

"Knock knock."

I turned at the sound of Mia's voice at the door. "Hey! Come in."

"Abby sent me back. Is that okay?" She tucked her auburn hair behind her ear.

"Sure. And she got you a drink." I grinned at the wine glass in her hand. "It's probably easier to talk back here anyway. I wouldn't be surprised if Damien Fox has someone stalking me."

She laughed and sat down with me on one of the large, squishy sofas. "Is it that bad?"

"He demanded me for dinner earlier."

Her raised eyebrow said it all.

"Yeah. And those are from him. An apology for underestimating me." I pointed to the flowers.

"Wow. I only know him as West's friend and even then, it's more business than anything, but that sounds exactly like the Damien I know."

I sighed. That wasn't what I wanted to hear. "I know nothing about him except that my father refused to do business with any of the Foxs. He wouldn't even talk about them, and I'd never spoken to him in my life until I got back."

"I'm not gonna lie, Dar, but this isn't the kind of place I expected him to try to buy. It's not exactly his usual business deal."

"Exactly. Aside from a couple restaurants, he exclusively operates strip clubs."

"Maybe he wants to turn this into a strip club."

"But, why? We run a crazy profit here because it's different. He has to know that."

Mia shrugged and sipped her wine. "Damien is used to getting what he wants. Kind of like you with your dad, he was groomed into taking over the family business. I think his dad is still involved, but only in ownership. From what West told me before, Damien's dad was pretty ruthless and had some less than legal dealings."

"The mob, you mean."

"I don't know for sure, and West didn't say, but I'd go with that. Something major happened that made Damien's dad change his ways, and as far as I know, as soon as the contracts ran out, that was the end of it. So, now the business is all clean, but the connections are still there on a personal level." She paused. "There's a rumor that when Billy Jo's shut down, that was because a friend of Damien's paid Billy a visit. Not long after that, Damien bought it and converted it into Dark House."

"I remember Billy Jo's shutting down." It was one of the most popular Western-style bars in the area, and it made no sense for it to shut down. It had shocked everyone, but now, it made a whole lot more sense. It was prime real estate, too. "Damn. Is that what I can expect if I don't sell out to him? A gun in my face?"

Mia smiled and shook her head. "He's an asshole, but he's not a bad guy. He's ruthless, but he cares a lot about his family. I don't think he'd send the mob around to get this place. West thinks he'll push his luck until he gets bored and then move on to something else."

"Great. I'm essentially a new toy for him to play with." Maybe my earlier toddler analogy wasn't too far off.

"You cannot just barge back here!" Abby shrieked from the other side of the door. "Mr. Fox!"

My eyes widened.

"Oh shit," Mia whispered, clutching her glass tightly.

Oh shit was pretty accurate, actually.

"Mr. Fox! This part of the bar is for staff members only. I won't ask you again to get back to the bar!" Abby was seconds away from having a heart attack.

I got up and yanked the door open. "What the hell is going on?"

Damien Fox stopped a few feet short of me, and Abby took her chance. She stepped around the side of him, squared up to him—which was pretty funny because she was at least eight inches shorter than him—and jabbed her finger in his chest.

"You aren't the exception to the rule, Mr. Fox. Staff only back here. Get back into the bar now before I call the police for your trespassing on private property."

That was a little extreme.

"What are you doing here?" I asked him, meeting his gaze. "I think I've made my stance very clear."

He held up his hands. "I came to talk to you."

"You wasted your time. I'm busy."

"Don't let me stop you." Mia got up and grabbed her purse. "Hi, Damien."

She was a traitor.

He did a double take between me and her. "Mia," he acknowledged. "I didn't know you were friends."

"Why would you?" she said brightly, coming up behind me. "I'll wait at the bar for you to get done here, Dahlia."

SIN

Me glaring daggers at her didn't diminish her bright smile at all. She simply grabbed Abby's arm, whispered in her ear, and dragged her away.

But not before Abby could shoot Damien a look so hard that if it could kill, he'd be dead on the spot.

I waited until they were both out of earshot and focused on the man standing in front of me. Today, his suit was navy blue, but it fit him just as well as the gray one had yesterday. I didn't let myself linger on that, though.

I swallowed. "What do you want to talk about?"

A slow, sexy smile tugged at the corners of his mouth. "You."

DAMIEN

Her indigo-blue eyes widened just slightly at my answer.

I had no fucking idea why she was shocked by that. I didn't come here to talk about the weather. Not that it would be a long conversation if I had—it was Vegas. It was hot. It was always fucking hot.

"Well?" I said after a moment of silence from her. "Are we having this conversation in the hallway or…?"

That seemed to shake her out of her daze. She blinked a few times before pursing her dark-red lips the way she did when she was annoyed. "You aren't supposed to be back here, so I should be telling you where to stick it."

My lips tugged to the side. "All you've gotta do is ask, sweetheart."

She clicked her tongue. Her gaze darkened ever so slightly as she held my eyes. "Try it, and you'll never be able to stick it anywhere ever again."

I chuckled and stepped past her. She wasn't going to move from this hallway by choice, so I forced her hand. I knew she'd follow me, even if it were only to tell me to get the hell out of the bar.

The bar that would be mine soon. One way or another—it would be.

"Take a seat," Dahlia said dryly as I dropped myself onto the soft, comfy sofa.

"Thanks. Fancy staff room." I cast my gaze around. Top of the line coffee machine, plush chairs, even a computer in the corner.

She swung the door shut and put her hands on her hips. "I take care of my staff."

The accusatory note darkened her tone.

I held up my hands. "Hey, I don't force anyone to do anything they don't want to. I take care of my girls just fine."

She side-eyed me as she walked to the coffee machine, her hips swaying in her tight, black dress.

Fuck, she had an ass that was made for slapping.

"Is that another innuendo?" She pulled a glass coffee mug down from the shelf and flicked on the coffee machine.

"I don't sleep with my staff." My jaw twitched. "People rarely strip for fun. They do it for money, and I have that in abundance, which makes me attractive to an awful lot of people."

"Well, look at that. We finally have something in common."

Her sarcasm wasn't lost on me, but I laughed anyway. She was right—I'd done my due diligence on this place. The Scarlet Letter turned a wild profit, and the woman standing in front of me was worth millions.

Not quite as many millions as I was, but enough.

"I'd love a coffee if you're making one." I smirked, even though her back was to me.

"Sorry, I was going to offer, but then I'd be worried that would make it look like I want you here."

I hadn't just underestimated Dahlia Lloyd—I'd *really* fucking underestimated her. Most people, men *or* women, would be giving me what I wanted by now, but she wasn't even close to stepping off the perch of resistance she was on.

She was strong. The kind of person you stood up and took notice of. Whose tenacity you admired, if you could watch it from a distance.

"I take my coffee black," I said, resting one arm along the back of the sofa. "No sugar."

She clicked her tongue again but pulled a second glass from the cupboard.

"Skip the fancy glass and use a real mug, would you?"

She slid a black coffee to the side, set the second mug to fill, then brought the first over to me. Her smile was saccharine. Too innocent. Too bright. Totally opposite to the dark glint of amusement that flashed in her eyes when she met my gaze.

I wasn't going to fool myself into thinking this was anything less than what it was: a power struggle.

She'd just made her move by giving in...defiantly.

Dahlia shut off the coffee machine, finished her coffee, and sat on the high-back chair. The glass clinked against the side table as she set the drink down. I didn't take my eyes off her as she smoothed out her dress, sitting down, and crossed one leg over the other. Slowly, she raised her attention to my face and met my eyes with a raise of her sleek brows.

"It looks like you're staying, so start talking," was all she said.

"You gave me the coffee and invited me to stay." I sipped it to make my point.

Her eyebrows went up even higher. "In my personal experience, you tend to beat the hell out of one line of conversation until you get what you want, so I figured it was easier to just give you the coffee. Sorry I couldn't accommodate the mug request."

Her politeness hid the bite of her words. Well, almost. I could hear the snark. Or maybe that was just the hint of laughter that made her eyes glitter.

I put my mug down and leaned back again. She was still staring at me, so I looked right back her. No denying, she was a beautiful woman. Her dark hair tumbled in loose waves to just below her breasts, and her bangs swept across her forehead, just long enough to brush the top of one of her eyebrows. Her dark-blue eyes were calculating yet warm, framed by thick eyelashes that only added to the drama of her expressions.

But it was her lips that made me linger. Full, pouty lips that were glossy and red parted so that she could flick her tongue against the corner of her mouth.

"If all you want to do is stare at me, Mr. Fox, can I suggest my Facebook page instead?"

I'd watched her lips as they formed the words, and now as my own formed into a tight smirk, I lifted my gaze back to hers. "Already tried. You're much prettier in person."

A light flush colored her cheeks.

So, she wasn't immune to a little sweet-talking.

"Flattery will get you nowhere." She tucked her hair behind her ear.

"The fact you're blushing tells me that's a lie."

"It won't get you what you want."

"Are you talking about the bar, or you being naked on your knees in front of me?"

Those shiny lips parted as my words hit her. She stared at me for a moment, mouth open, unblinking. I'd caught her off-guard, and I could almost see her mind whirring as she tried to come up with a suitable response.

Finally, she blinked.

But she kept staring. Didn't change her expression at all.

The grin that formed on my face was smug. I didn't have to look in the mirror to know that because I felt the smugness. She'd been almost unflappable until the moment those words left my mouth.

She closed her mouth, clearly still speechless. I raised an eyebrow as she sat there, unmoving, but still looking at me. It was as if she was frozen, caught in the aftershock of the words that had come so easily to me.

I did want her on her knees in front of me. Naked would be a bonus, but it wasn't like her being fully-clothed was a problem. I could work with either.

"Oh good," she finally said, her voice weaker than before. "You're a dating website come to life."

I bit back my laugh. "You refused my dinner invitation."

She sat up straighter. "That wasn't an invitation. That was a demand."

"Close enough to an invitation."

"You know that scene in *The Beauty and the Beast* where he demands she join him for dinner, and when she refuses because he didn't ask, he tells her to starve? I'd rather starve." Her smile was tight, and any embarrassment she'd felt was now hiding behind her bite.

No doubt, her bite was worse than her bark.

And I had no fucking idea what she was talking about.

"Never watched it," I said dismissively, ignoring her eye-roll. "I'll try it again. Join me for dinner?"

"That's still a demand."

"No, it's a shorthand version of '*will you* join me for dinner?' I asked it as a question."

Her face flushed, but this time, it wasn't a blush. "At this point, I don't care how you ask me, my answer is still no." She uncrossed her legs and stood. "If that's all you're here to talk about, we're done. I have work to do, and I'm sure you do, too."

Her hips swayed as she walked to the door.

How many spanks would it take to make her submit?

I wanted to find out.

I pushed myself up off the sofa as she opened the door. She refused to look at me, instead choosing to look at a spot on the wall behind me. If she thought she'd get the last word in this conversation, she could think again. It was bad enough that my cock was twitching inside my fucking pants at the thought of my handprint on her tight little ass.

I pushed the door closed with two fingers. She wasn't expecting it, so she dropped the handle, which brought her eyes back to mine. Her lips parted for her to speak, but I clasped her chin with my hand, still with the other against the door.

Her words died on her lips.

"One day," I said in a low voice, holding her harsh gaze. "One day, you'll have dinner with me, Dahlia. Just like one day I'll own this bar. One day, you'll be on your back, my handprint on your ass, and my cock buried right inside you."

She swallowed. "That's a fact, is it?"

"I'm used to getting what I want. Everyone gives in eventually."

"I'm not everyone. Sorry to say, you'll be disappointed when you finally realize that."

I moved closer to her. She took a step back and ended up against the door, a fact that only worked in my favor. I stepped right into her, just brushing my body against hers. My cock pulsed against my pants and the tiny gasp that she attempted to hide by clamping her mouth shut gave it away.

She'd felt it.

And now, she was blushing again. Only this time, it was furiously. She still held my gaze, despite the obviousness of her reaction to me.

I'd expected her to whimper, to drop her gaze, to do something other than stand there, her body a breath away from being pressed against mine, and hold her ground.

I ran the back of my fingers along the gentle curve of her jaw, not missing the way her chest heaved at the touch. I kept moving my hand until my fingertips toyed with her hair and her face was firmly in my grasp….Until she was cornered and unable to move until I let her.

"I'm well aware you aren't like everyone else," I murmured. My lips barely brushed her ear as I spoke. "Everyone else would be bent over that sofa by now, but if you think your defiance will put me off, you're wrong. I think it'll just make it so much sweeter when you give in."

"And even more satisfying for me when you leave me the fuck alone," she whispered, then cleared her throat.

"Not gonna happen, sweetheart."

"You need to leave now, Mr. Fox."

I pulled back and looked into her eyes, once more gripping her chin. "My name is Damien. Remember it. You'll need it when you beg me."

She slapped my hand away from her face, but she said nothing. Just the darkening of her glare and the tightening of her jaw was the answer.

I pushed off the door. Dahlia moved a second before I opened the door, and I gave her one last look before I turned and walked out of the room.

I felt her best friend's glare as I walked past the bar, but I ignored her. I was too wrapped up in the vixen I'd just left in the back room. The woman whose eyes sliced into me and whose lips haunted me.

The woman who would be mine—sooner or later.

SIN

5

DAHLIA

I slammed the door so hard the sharp bang echoed around the staff room.

My heart was racing. It pounded against my ribs doing double-time, and my chest was so tight I couldn't breathe steadily. Even my skin was on fire where he'd touched me.

Where he'd held my face, where he'd teased my hair, where he'd deliberately brushed his lips.

Damien Fox had taken hold of my personal space and ripped a hole for himself. And now, I couldn't kill the feeling of his body so close to mine.

Of his hard cock brushing against my hip.

Another deliberate move. Another seduction tactic. Another thing to attempt to make me break.

And goddamn my body, because it'd reacted to him. It'd given him what he wanted, and I knew it. I'd seen the hunger in his eyes at my gasp. The pleasure when I swallowed. The lust when I hadn't backed down.

I disliked him—severely. Maybe I almost even hated him just a little bit.

Or maybe I hated the way my body reacted despite the way I felt about him.

He was arrogant, rude, and cocky to the point of unbelievable. It was clear that he cared about one person in his life, and that was himself. His lack of respect for anyone infuriated me every single time he opened his mouth.

Nobody else mattered in the world of Damien Fox. He was its center and everything revolved around him.

I hated the way my clit still throbbed between my legs. *Hated it.*

I stormed over to the cabinets at the back. I knew there was a bottle of cherry vodka stashed in the back of one of the ground-level ones because I was the one who'd put it there.

While alcohol wasn't the answer, I needed something, anything, to distract me from the way I was feeling. The burn of the liquor against my throat was a damn good start.

I rifled through the cupboard until I found it. It clinked against some other things as I yanked it out, and when it was free, I instantly turned my attention to the cupboard where the shot glasses were.

Those were Abby.

The cherry vodka was stashed for situations like this where it was polite to use a shot glass but completely unnecessary.

The door clicked open.

I turned, yanking the cap off the bottle as I pointed it toward the person coming in.

Mia and Abby froze in the doorway.

"Oh dear," said Abby. "She's broken out the secret vodka."

"This vodka has never been secret. Everybody knows it's there, they're just not allowed to touch it." I sniffed and poured my shot. Keeping one hand on the bottle, I lifted the small glass and threw it back.

It burned as I swallowed it.

It felt good.

"I take it that didn't go well." Mia's heels clicked against the floor.

I shook my head and turned around, finally releasing the bottle. "How someone hasn't murdered him yet, I have no idea."

"He's hot," Abby said. "I assume he seduces people into what he wants."

I pursed my lips. "You assume correctly."

"He seduced you?"

"He attempted to." Almost successfully. "He has this stupid-ass entitlement that makes him think he can do anything he wants. Like he can have any woman—"

"Because he can and does," Mia interrupted.

"—and get everything he wants just because he's handsome and smooth with words. Well, he can kiss my ass, because I'm not any woman, and if he thinks he's going to get my bar by me jumping into bed with him, he needs to check himself."

Abby sidled up to me at the corner and poured a shot.

"Thank you." I swallowed it in one and slammed the glass against the countertop.

"What are you going to do now?" Abby asked, leaning against the side.

"There's only one thing you can do," Mia said before I could. "If you can't beat 'em, join 'em."

I gave her a sharp look. "I'm not playing games, Mia. I don't have the time for it. Hell, I don't have the patience for it."

"Have you ever seen her play Monopoly?" Abby raised her eyebrows. "I needed therapy after the first time."

She darted out of the way with a laugh when I moved to slap her arm.

Mia snorted. "No, but now, I'd like to see that."

"I'm not playing games," I repeated, folding my arms across my chest.

"Listen to me." She scooted forward on the sofa. "Damien is…persistent."

No shit.

"You want to know why he wants your bar so badly, and it's obvious he's going to use his…skills…to break you down. You know that, so just go along with it. Play along with him, still holding your ground, until he realizes seduction isn't going to get him what he wants."

"You want me to screw him to make my point?"

"Could be worse," Abby said. "At least you'll get an orgasm or two out of it."

"I fail to see how this conversation is helpful." I ran my hand through my hair. "I don't understand how giving Damien Fox part of what he wants will make him realize he won't get everything else. That's not how people learn to be reasonable human beings."

"He's already an unreasonable human being," Mia pointed out with a smile. "This is called a compromise."

"Is that what you did with West? Compromised?"

"Yes. It was enjoyable."

"And, now, you're married."

She opened her mouth, then paused. "Point taken. Maybe we need to rethink this."

Abby shook her head. "I'm going back out there. Thinking about having sex with him is starting to make me feel sick."

I stared after her. "You're the one who told me I'd get an orgasm out of it!"

She held her hands up as she disappeared.

I sighed and slumped against the counter.

"There are worse things you could get from a compromise than orgasms," Mia muttered.

"Yeah," I muttered right back. "Like herpes."

She laughed.

I laughed.

But it was hollow.

This sucked.

———

The cemetery where my mom was buried—and now my dad, too—was tucked away in a quiet corner of the city. I'd once found the distance a hardship, but over the years, as I'd gotten older, I'd come to appreciate it. It was almost always empty when I got there, and if I were unlucky, someone else would be there.

SIN

After my mom was murdered a month before my tenth birthday, I'd been completely lost. I had to stumble through my teenage years with the long-distance help of aunts and closer help with family friends who stepped in to be my female influence, including my mom's best friend, but it wasn't the same.

I didn't have anyone to help me choose a hairstyle. I had to buy my prom dress with my dad, and as great as he was, shopping wasn't his thing. Fights with my best friend, new bras, boys, starting my period—all the things I needed my mom for, all the things she should have been there for, were all struggles for me.

I remember the first time I spoke to her grave. I'd started my period that morning and I was using tissue. I was scared to tell my dad because it was *that* awkward topic, and so, I'd come to the cemetery for some comfort. I cried and told her everything I would have said to her if she'd been alive.

I'd left feeling weightless and with a sense of purpose. I'd shown up at her best friend's diner in the middle of the lunch rush. Paula had taken one look at my tear-stained face, taken me to the back, and wriggled it out of me. Then, she'd fed me a chocolate milkshake and a burger and handled everything— a sanitary pad from her purse and a trip to the store, plus that chat with my dad.

I'd realized then that my mom was still there, in a way. The act of talking and laying everything out without the fear or interruption or judgment had gotten me through my teen years. Before I'd left three months ago, the weekly trips had become updates on life in general, like I was writing a letter to a rarely-seen grandma who lived on the other side of the country.

It was soothing and cathartic.

Which was exactly what I needed right now.

I tugged up my yoga pants and pulled open the gate to the cemetery. The old hinges squeaked as it moved, and if I weren't used to it, the loudness of it would have probably freaked me out the way it used to. I was too familiar with everything.

I juggled the two small bunches of flowers and bottle of water as I closed the gate. My sneakers crunched along the gravel path as I walked to the back of the graveyard where my parents were buried right next to each other.

The lump in my throat was thick and almost painful. I hadn't been back here since the day I had buried Dad.

If I didn't need to let everything I was feeling out, I probably wouldn't have been there today, either.

As I approached the white, marble gravestones that marked their graves, I slowed down. It took everything I had not to burst into tears while I was still several feet away from them.

I managed to keep it in until I'd sat down. I arranged the small bunch of carnations in my dad's vase and then gave my mom the six red roses. The water inside the bottle fit both vases perfectly, and only then did I sit back in front of my mom's grave.

Glancing to the other headstone, I said, "Cover your ears, Dad." And then, I smiled.

The smile didn't linger long.

I ran my gaze over the headstone. *Melinda Lloyd, 07-29-1963 - 09-07-1998. Beloved mother, wife, and friend. Always loved.* I swallowed hard and rubbed my hand softly over the grass that covered the ground in front of me.

Like a tidal wave, everything came rushing out. All my inner thoughts from the past few days. My frustrations and my delights. My apologies and my promises. It left me quietly, not stopping until my eyes had dried and my throat was raw from the emotion I felt.

Yet, I was lighter. I could breathe again. There was no longer the crushing weight of confusion pressing down on my chest.

Sure, I didn't know what would happen now. I didn't know if I was making the right choice or if I was about to do the stupidest thing of my life.

SIN

Fact was, I had to go to dinner with Damien Fox.

I had too many questions not to. My father had always insisted that one day my curious nature would get me in trouble and I should have been a reporter, but maybe this was worth the risk.

Why did he want my bar?

Why was he so insistent he'd get me into bed?

And why had my father hated him?

Me: *I'm rethinking your offer of dinner.*

Damien's reply was almost instantaneous. I knew it would be. I'd waited until the middle of the afternoon before texting him, and something told me he'd been waiting for my message.

He knew it would come, after all.

Cue eye roll.

I hit CTRL-S on the document I was working on and unlocked my phone by tapping in the code.

Damien: *You are, are you?*

I smirked and picked up the phone to reply.

Me: *Are you surprised?*
Damien: *Not at all. It was only a matter of time.*
Me: *I haven't agreed to anything yet, you know.*
Damien: *But you will. There's no other reason for this conversation.*
Me: *Has anyone ever told you that you're kind of arrogant?*
Damien: *Some people think it's hot.*
Me: *Those people are idiots.*
Damien: *True.*

Damien: *Shall I pick you up at 7?*

Fucking hell—was that…a question mark?

Me: *Did you just…ASK?*
Damien: *Yes. Don't expect me to do it again. It was horrible.*
Me: *But I forgot the question.*
Damien: *Scroll up your phone, sweetheart. It's right there.*
Me: *I would, but I think making you ask again would be more fun.*
Damien: **picture attachment**
Damien: *There.*

I tapped the attachment to see it better and burst out laughing. He'd sent me a screenshot of the message where he'd asked me if he should pick me up. I didn't know if that was ridiculous and petulant or leaning toward freaking smart. I wanted him to ask again just to be a pain in the ass, and he totally found a loophole so he didn't have to ask again.

Because technically, he didn't.

I loathed to call him smart. So, I didn't.

Me: *LOL.*
Me: *No. Text me a time and place and I'll see you there.*
Damien: *You made me ask again just to say that, didn't you?*
Me: *Absolutely. Time and place, Mr. Fox. I don't have all day.*

Five minutes later, I got my response.

Damien: *7:30 at Figaro's. I'll be in the corner booth waiting for you. Don't be late.*
Me: *Bring your manners, and I'll be on time.*

DAHLIA

At seven forty-five, I got out of the cab outside Figaro's after paying and tipping the driver. My black and white lace dress had ridden up my thighs as I'd exited the car, so I pulled it down before approaching the doors to the restaurant.

I'd spent way too long getting dressed for this damn dinner. It wasn't a date, but business-smart wasn't classy enough for Figaro's. I could count on one hand the amount of times I'd eaten here, and there was no chance in hell this was where two people went for a business dinner.

Then again, I'd never said it wasn't a date, so Damien was perfectly within his rights to assume it was, even though I could almost guarantee that wasn't it at all. He probably just wanted me to think he thought it was a date, so I had to tread carefully. Unless the subject came up specifically, I had to play the line between professional and personal.

Thankfully, it was an invisible, metaphorical line. If it were real, I'd be screwed in my four-inch heels.

The line meant I had two rules for tonight: think before I speak, and no more freaking blushing.

The young guy at the door smiled at me and opened the glass-front door for me. "Ma'am." He dipped his head.

"Thank you." I shot him my best smile and stepped inside. The light was low, and I was only able to see thanks to the dim lights that hung over each table. "I'm here for Damien Fox," I said to the hostess.

She smiled and ran her finger down the list in front of her. "Follow me, Ms. Lloyd." She stepped out from behind the platform and guided me through the dimly-lit restaurant to the very back. The high-backed, black leather booths provided privacy from the other patrons, and I wasn't at all surprised that this was the table he'd booked.

I also knew that these particular tables booked out months in advance, so he'd pulled some serious strings for this.

A smile crossed his lips as he caught sight of me. He slid out of the booth, and I took the moment to admire the way his black shirt hugged his body. It fit him perfectly, like a second skin, and just gave the hint of solid muscles on his upper arms.

What? I was human. He might have been an arrogant ass, but he was a hot arrogant ass.

"Ms. Lloyd," he said in a low voice, taking my hand.

My skin tingled as he brushed his lips over my knuckles. "Mr. Fox. I see you're pulling out all the stops."

He ran his dark gaze over my body. "Speak for yourself, sweetheart."

I raised an eyebrow. I wanted to say, *What? This old thing?* but then he'd assume I'd bought it for him, and I'd owned it for nine months. I just hadn't worn it yet. "That sounded like a compliment."

"I am capable of such things." He kept hold of my hand until I was sitting down. Taking his own seat, he said, "Red or white?"

"Rosé."

He ran his tongue over his lower lip, hiding a smile, and turned to the hostess. "A bottle of your finest rosé for the lady."

With a nod, she disappeared.

Damien pulled his attention back to me. "I'm starting to think you do that to be awkward."

I had to fight my own smile. "Partially," I admitted. "But I do prefer rosé to the others."

"You don't drink red or white?"

"I'll drink Chardonnay if I can't get a rosé, but why would I choose to not drink my favorite wine in a place I know they serve it?"

"Especially when I'm the one asking you."

"Exactly."

His eyes shone with amusement. "You look beautiful."

He was taking the charm offensive route, obviously.

"Thank you. You don't look so bad yourself," I replied, crossing my legs under the table.

It was at that moment that a waitress returned with a bottle of wine. We went through the whole pour, sniff, sip, approve, pour some more routine before she set the bottle down and left us to look at the menu.

"That might be the nicest thing you've ever said to me," Damien said when we were alone. "Have you been drinking already?"

"No, but that doesn't mean I wasn't tempted." He didn't need to know about the vodka shot for some good old Dutch courage. That little moment was between me and Mr. Grey Goose.

He offered me a menu and, wordlessly, I took it. The leather-bound book was soft beneath my fingers as I opened it to the appetizers page. Minutes of silence passed while we both looked through the dishes on offer, but I wasn't really focused.

What was the purpose of this dinner?

What was his aim?

What was his *game*?

Surely, he had to know that on some level, there was no chance I'd sell to him. Was he really attempting the seduction technique to see if he could win that way? Would he give up when he didn't?

Why didn't I have any of these answers still? And why wasn't I bold enough to just ask all of them to his face?

I knew the answer to that last question; he'd have all the answers, but none of them would be genuine or true. They'd all be lies, fabricated to further whatever his agenda was.

I glanced at him over the top of my menu. He was focused on his own, his eyelashes casting shadows on his cheeks with his downward gaze.

He was smooth. Too smooth. Too handsome. Too sleek and perfect and untouchable.

And secretive.

Why didn't anybody know anything about him? Here I was, having dinner with him, and all I really knew about him was that he was relentless in his pursuit of the things he wanted, he owned a ton of business, and his dad potentially had contacts within the mafia.

It wasn't exactly a stunning character reference.

The waitress came back, breaking my inner monologue. It took me a few minutes to order given that I hadn't been paying attention to the menu. I ignored Damien's smirk as I placed my order and shut the menu for the waitress.

"I thought you'd at least order quickly since you kept me waiting." He lifted his glass of whiskey to his curved lips.

"Oh, please. Fifteen minutes isn't late. That's a minor delay."

"Was it accidental?"

"Define 'accidental.'" I grinned, unable to fight my amusement. It wasn't an accident. I knew it, he knew it. Hell, the freaking hostess who'd brought me to the table probably knew it, too.

"I'll take that as a no," he muttered into his glass.

One more thing to add to the list of things I knew about Damien Fox: he didn't like to be kept waiting.

Surprise, surprise.

I sipped my wine and twirled the stem between my fingers before saying, "Shall we get to the point of this dinner?"

Damien raised an eyebrow. "We will as soon as our food is brought out. Eating is the point of dinner."

Great. He was a smartass. Like me.

"I mean the reason for us coming here in the first place." It took everything I had not to roll my eyes. Did we have to be so literal, smartass or no? "There was a reason you asked me to dinner, and I want to know what it was."

"Do you often ask men who take you on dates for that reason?"

"This isn't a date."

"How do you know that?" He leaned forward with his forearm on the table, an action that made his shirt strain over the shape of his tensed bicep. "Maybe this is a date."

I twisted my lips to the side. "I'd be more inclined to believe that if you hadn't *told* me to come to dinner right after you attempted to buy the bar."

"Touché." His sexy, little half-smile made an appearance. "It's more of a business dinner, but I'd be lying if I said I didn't want to know more about you."

"Know more about me?" The man was still taking me for a fool. "Don't tell me you offered to buy Scarlet without finding out everything you could about me and the bar's history."

If he was sheepish or embarrassed I had him pegged, he didn't show it. I wasn't sure he was capable of such humble emotions, to be honest.

Instead, he laughed. Low and strangely seductive, it filled the small space between us, eliciting goose bumps along my bare skin.

It was one more unfair weapon in his charismatic arsenal.

"You're twenty-five-years-old and your birthday is June seventeenth. You graduated both high school and the University of Las Vegas a year early, opening you up to study for your Masters from home while working for your father. You were born here in Vegas and have lived in the same house your entire life. You have one parking ticket from nine years ago and are the sole owner of The Scarlet Letter." He picked up his glass and sipped, smugness radiating off him.

"That's pretty creepy." The words left my mouth before I could stop them. "You know it's not normal to know so much about someone you've only just met?"

"Not if you want to buy what they've got."

"Knowing about a parking ticket I got when I was sixteen is slightly excessive. So is knowing that much about my education."

He shrugged one shoulder. "To be fair, I didn't know you'd done your Masters until you mentioned it. I was interested. Looking you up on the university website wasn't hard."

That was slightly annoying.

All right, that was a lie. It was really freaking annoying.

"What does my parking ticket have to do with anything?" It was the lone blot on my record, a total mistake, and I hated it when it was brought up. I'd paid the damn thing within twelve hours, for goodness sake.

"Nothing. It came up when I checked your criminal record."

"I don't have a criminal record."

"The parking ticket says otherwise."

I went to respond, then stopped. He was grinning—he was freaking well goading me into annoyance. "You're the most annoying person I've ever had dinner with, and I've spent the past three months living in a house with four kids under the age of eight."

"Why, thank you." He grinned even as he took another sip of his drink. When I didn't back down from his amused stare, he sobered, a heavier look flashing in his eyes. "Listen to me, Dahlia."

Dear God, even the way he said my name was hot. Deeper and lower with a weirdly sexual inflection at the end.

Aside from his obvious personality flaws, was there anything wrong with this man?

"Yes, the point of this dinner was originally to discuss The Scarlet Letter." Damien twirled the glass between his fingers. "I'm not going to change that, but it's not a lie when

I tell you I want to know more about you. Like I've said a hundred times, you fascinate me."

"You know what else fascinates people? Serial killers." I paused. "Satanism. Scientology. Not all fascinating things are good."

"Did you mean to go for a bunch of 's' words there?"

"No, but it flowed." I shrugged a shoulder. "I don't know what else you possibly need to know about me when I know nothing at all about you."

So, that was a lie, but whatever. I was having dinner with Damien Fox—I either wanted a job or to get lucky, in the eyes of everyone else.

His dark eyes twinkled, and he leaned forward fully, shifting so both his arms were resting on the table. "My name is Damien Fox, I turned thirty in January, and I'm the CEO of Fox Enterprises. I co-own the company with my father who is almost retired, and while we primarily run strip clubs, we also own a restaurant in Vegas, one in Reno, and a cocktail bar on Lake Tahoe that's part of the Fox Casino there."

"If I did publicity, I'd be signing you right now."

"That wasn't what you hoped for, huh?"

I rested my chin on my hand and raised my eyebrows. "You're not the only person who can use Google." Even if Reno and Lake Tahoe were news to me. "Not to mention you sound like you're introducing yourself at a group therapy meeting."

He laughed again. "All right…I hate Jennifer Aniston, libraries, and Marvel."

I blinked at him. "I think we might be done here."

More laughter.

"What would possess you to buy a bar based on a book if you hate libraries?"

"I didn't say I hate books," Damien spoke slowly. "I said I hate libraries."

"They're one and the same."

"A book, a library." He motioned the book on his left hand and the library on his right. "Technically, different. One is a single book and the other is a lot of books."

I stared at him. I didn't know how I could be in the presence of someone who hated what was essentially, Rachel Green, escapism, and Thor.

That was it. I'd just found the biggest personality flaw of all.

"You do know that The Scarlet Letter has an almost-secret library-type function, don't you?" I blinked a few times.

He went to respond, but at that moment, our appetizers were brought out.

"A what?" he said when the server had disappeared.

I raised an eyebrow. So, he didn't know everything about the bar. Then again, I wasn't exaggerating when I said it was almost-secret. "You didn't find out everything in your little cyber-stalking mission then, huh?"

"I'm not dignifying that with a response."

I grinned as I stabbed a shrimp with my fork. "A lot of the books on the walls are real books. It doesn't operate like a library, per se, but similar. We have the check-out sheets at the front of the book, and the idea is that you write your name with the start and finish date."

He chewed slowly, studying me closely.

I ate my shrimp and continued. "The only rule is that you don't read a book someone else is reading unless it's been over four months since the start date and they haven't noted that it's finished. People come in, get their drinks, collect their book, and sit down."

"Social," Damien replied dryly. "Isn't that the opposite of what bars are about?"

Scratching my chin, I fought a smile. I ate a little before I replied. I needed to answer that carefully—because yes, it was, but we'd cultivated it so carefully, it wasn't what *my* bar was about.

"Social situations are stressful for introverts," I said carefully. "They don't like people and struggle to deal with the chaos Las Vegas brings—especially students. Before we started the library-style system, we did market research on the customers. Most of the introverts came to the bar because it was quiet and they liked the library theme because they were bookish kinds of people."

"It's still the opposite of what a bar is generally about."

"Which is why it's so successful." I gave him a tiny half-smile. "It gives the unsocial a place to be social. It gives introverts a place to feel like they still fit in with the club scene. And, it's the perfect place to meet people who are the same as you."

He raised his eyebrows in what was quickly becoming his signature look of disbelief. "What do you run there? Book Nerds Anonymous? Dating for Book Lovers?"

"No, but we do have a weekly book club who rent a back room on Monday evenings. Actually, they don't rent anything. They typically drink so many cocktails that it doesn't matter and they end up forgetting about what book they're reading." I paused. "Book Nerds Anonymous is a good group name. They were looking for one of those. Thanks." I flashed him a quick smile.

He tried not to, but he succumbed to temptation and smiled back. "You're welcome, sweetheart. Tell me more about these people who fall in love over books and booze."

"I should start a dating website type thing and use that as the tagline."

"Joint venture." He put his cutlery down. "We could go into business together."

"No offense, but I'm only here for my own curiosity. I can't imagine you running a dating service. Not to mention it wouldn't be good for business if I ended up murdering you."

"I'm the perfect gentleman."

It was my turn to quirk an eyebrow.

Damien held up his hands. "Have I tried to come onto you?"

I stared at him. Just stared. Now *that* was a statement not worth dignifying with a response.

"Never mind," he muttered.

I rolled my eyes. "Back to the bar."

"Yes. Let's go back to that. Good idea."

Was he...embarrassed?

He couldn't be. There was no way in hell he was even capable of feeling such an emotion, let alone showing it. But, he sure as hell wasn't comfortable.

I'd take discomfort, if only for my own amusement.

"Scarlet gives introverts a place to find like-minded people. I've seen people set dinner dates because of the book the other person is reading." I drew a circle on the table with my fingertip. "People are around others who understand them, and that's hard to find when you're an introvert. Besides, there's nothing better than making a date because of a book."

"Why?"

"Because books are easy to talk about."

"So are movies, and since they make movies about books..."

I shook my head. "They attempt to adapt books into movies, but anyone with half a brain cell knows the books are always better."

"I think you just called me stupid. Again."

I froze.

He grinned, his eyes twinkling with silent laughter. "Do you always get this passionate about books?"

Yes. "Not always. I just really like books."

"Interesting."

Was it?

7

DAHLIA

We fell into a companionable silence as our appetizers were cleared and our main dishes brought to the table. I didn't think my passion for books was necessarily interesting. It wasn't exactly a unique love, but somehow, I got the feeling that Damien didn't say "Interesting" and mean it in the traditional term.

Like, he didn't want to know more about it. He just wanted to slot that piece of knowledge into the puzzle of my life that he was clearly putting together.

The longer we sat in silence and ate, the more Mia's words from our conversation filtered through my thoughts. The man sitting opposite me was ruthless and determined, and perhaps, a little bit dangerous. It was a terrifying combination, but one that fit flawlessly with the thought I'd just had.

Damien Fox wasn't trying to win me over with seduction. He was using it as a sidebar to find out as much about me as possible. He was building a picture of my entire life, using mental note cards to put information into order until he found that one break in my life he could use to his advantage.

The problem was, I didn't think I had one. If the bar was struggling or I didn't want to run it, it would be an easy thing to exploit.

That was what he really wanted to do. He wanted to find a weakness and exploit it for his own good.

I knew he was underhanded, but I didn't know he'd be dirty about it.

No, that was a lie. I knew he'd be dirty about it, but for some reason, my conclusion sent a shiver of shock across my skin. How far would he go to get what he wanted? Would he create a situation I couldn't back out of? I had financial clout that others might not have had in the past, but I wasn't so naive as to think that I was richer than he was.

I could hold my own, that much was for sure. But if he did create a situation I couldn't get out of, would I be able to hold my reputation?

Of course, it was all theoretical at this point. Not that it mattered—I had to be ready for any situation. One thing was for sure, though. I'd spent all my time looking into him as a person, when I should have been looking deeper into how he runs his business.

He wasn't a stupid man, and there was no doubt that it wouldn't be easy to find that info, but unless he wanted to hand it over, I had no choice.

He wasn't letting the idea of owning my bar go away. He wasn't going to give up. Tonight had proved that. I needed to be prepared for who this man really was because my gut was telling me I hadn't scratched the surface of Damien Fox. For good or for bad, I wanted to be ready.

I would fight for The Scarlet Letter, even if it took everything I'd had. I'd go down swinging if it meant holding off his outrageous arrogance for just a little bit longer.

"You look like you're in deep thought." Damien's voice broke into my inner battle cry.

It was like I had a tiny Zelda in my head or something.

"Just thinking." I offered him a light smile and set down my fork. "Tell me about Fox Industries."

His hand, halfway to his glass, stilled. Something flitted across his features too quickly for me to discern, but he rapidly schooled his expression into one of mild surprise.

Mild, fake surprise.

"I thought this wasn't a date. It's starting to feel like one." He was deflecting.

I half-shrugged and tucked a loose lock of hair behind my ear. "You're the one who said you find me fascinating—I'm not going to tell you my life story without knowing anything about you in return."

"You know plenty about me."

"I know that you hate Jennifer Aniston, and honestly, I'm not sure how I'm sitting here after that revelation, never mind the libraries thing. You can redeem yourself now." I flashed him a playful smile to know I was joking.

But only a little.

"I've never killed a puppy?" he offered weakly.

"I should hope the majority of people I meet haven't."

"True." He pressed the glass to his lips but didn't sip. "I barely graduated high school. Didn't bother with college. I'm good with numbers, investments, and management, but not so much everything else."

Well, well, well. There was a surprise. "Really?"

"Really. Which is exactly how I know that fancy degrees don't run businesses."

"No, but they sure give you a bit of credibility to people who don't think you're up to the job."

"Low blow, Ms. Lloyd."

"Not low enough if you aren't on the floor, squealing." I picked up my wine glass and let it dangle between my fingers for a moment. "But, that still wasn't what I meant. I want to know more about your business."

He put his glass down and waved his hand in the air. "Did you want dessert?"

No. I wanted to know why he refused to discuss it.

I shook my head, and within seconds, our plates were cleared and a leather-bound booklet had been placed in front of him. He barely glanced at the total before he pulled out his card and signed the receipt.

"You're good at avoiding things you don't want to answer." I traced the line of his jaw with my eyes. "Too good."

"Some things shouldn't be discussed in public." He took the booklet back from the server, removed his card and receipt, and looked me in the eye. "Let's go."

"Go where?"

"I want to check out that library function you have. You can ask me questions on the way."

———

"Why would you want to check out the library function?" I asked once the door had been shut in the back of the sleek Bentley.

Damien ran his hand through his thick, dark hair and sat back against the black leather seats. His gaze swung from the closed partition between us and his driver to me. "I'm intrigued how it works."

"Even Satan would call bullshit on that."

He shrugged a shoulder. "It's true. I've never heard anything like that before."

Hmm.

The driver steered us into the slow-moving traffic. We were at least twenty minutes away from the bar without this speed of driving, so I had a chance to get some of the answers I wanted.

"Why wouldn't you talk about your work in the restaurant?" I set my purse on the floor by my feet and shifted to face him. "I've never seen anyone get out of a dinner so fast."

A small smile tugged the edge of his lips up. "Just like I said in there, some things shouldn't be discussed in public."

"Like politics and religion."

"You have a very smart mouth." He glanced down at said smart mouth. "Do you ever turn it off?"

"Never," I reassured him. "Now, we're no longer in public, so tell me about what you do."

He rested an arm along the back of the seats. His fingertips landed just inches from my hair, and I gave a cursory glance at their closeness.

Shivers tickled their way down my spine as he stared at me. He was entirely still except for the way his eyes flicked left and right repeatedly. It felt an awful lot like he was taking me in, committing me to memory for some strange reason.

"A lot of people don't like me. Pissing people off is part of business and I've done that a lot, so I try to keep my work private. It's that simple, sweetheart."

"I get it. But now, it is private." I wasn't going to let this drop. I'd quit reading before I did that. "I've told you a lot about my bar tonight, so now tell me something."

"You have the innate ability to make me feel like I'm back in high school and writing an essay about being reasonable."

"If you'd done that, you might know how to be reasonable." I paused when he laughed. It was low blow time again. "Look, Mr. Fox—"

"Damien."

"You don't have to tell me anything about your business and what you do, but given that you're failing embarrassingly in your attempt to buy *my* business, it's probably in your best interests to start talking."

He leaned forward and took my hair between his finger and thumb. Slowly, he twirled the strands around his finger, each twist lightly tugging against my scalp. "You should have been a cop. You're very persuasive."

"In that case, you could probably learn a thing or two from me. Your own skills are lacking."

"I don't know." He dropped his voice to a low murmur. "I think if I tried hard enough, I could persuade you into a few things."

I raised my eyebrows. We'd moved on from talking about business. Once again, the Master of Deflection was doing what he'd been doing for most of our evening together.

"I still haven't forgiven you for your antics yesterday, so I wouldn't even try it." I tapped his hand so he released his hold on my hair. It tumbled away from his finger so I could smooth the strands back down and gave him a pointed look.

"Forgiven me, or yourself?" His eyes glinted knowingly. Almost self-assuredly.

Hell, there was no almost about it. He knew exactly how I'd felt when he'd left me. He knew exactly what he'd done to me, and I did, too. Denying that I was annoyed at myself because I could still remember how it'd felt when he'd taken my chin in his hand was pointless.

"Both," I answered, sitting up a little straighter. "That doesn't invite you to exercise poor judgment and make another attempt to mix business with pleasure."

"Attempt? Sweetheart, if I'd attempted to do that, there would have been a lot less business and a lot more pleasure before I'd left you."

"You think I'd give in to you so easily?"

At those words, Damien slid smoothly across the leather seats. His arm, still resting along the back of them, hung down behind me, his thumb just brushing against my back. The rest of his body was mere inches from mine, and I bit the inside of my lip as he trailed his fingertips up my bare arm. My eyes followed his feather-light touch while his stayed fixated on my face.

He coasted his fingers over my shoulder where he touched them to my jaw. Lightly, he tilted my face around and up until I had no choice but to look him in the eyes again—to look right there where I could see exactly how much he wanted me.

Dark.

Hot.

Full of temptation.

Heavy and intense, his eyes screamed of raw lust and selfish need.

"I don't think you'd give in at all," he whispered. "I think your body would do that for you, and you'd be helpless to it."

"You think a lot of yourself, don't you?" I said quietly. I touched my finger to his belt, then ran it up the length of his torso, ghosting it over the solid packs of muscle that made up his body until I flicked the starchy collar of his shirt. "You think you can do this and I'll give in to what is essentially a biological reaction? I'm stronger than you take me for, you know."

He curled his fingers around my chin and dipped his face to mine. "She says with a racing heart."

I pressed one finger against his mouth and ran another along his strong thigh...right up to where his hard cock was straining against the soft material of his pants. "Don't you hate it when your attraction to someone is so obvious?"

His jaw clenched. "If you have any sense at all inside that gorgeous head of yours, you'll move your hand."

Now, who was the helpless one?

"I thought you'd make me give in," I said, trailing my nail down the length of his cock and back up again. He twitched beneath my touch. I was playing with fire, but it was too fun to stop. "Looks like I'm not the one struggling right now."

The hand that was just hanging limply clasped the back of my neck as Damien adjusted his body. His other grasped my hip. His fingers dug right into my skin, so hard it was almost painful, but it was the way he yanked me toward him that made me gasp.

My body was now flush against his. I wasn't even sure if I was sitting on the seat or if he was holding me just off of it, but heat spread through my body when my hand pressed hard against his cock.

"Struggling?" The word was husky in my ear. "I'm fucking struggling all right, Dahlia. I'm struggling not to roll that damn dress to your hips and fuck you stupid. Struggling not to make you pull my cock from my pants and play with it, since you touched it. Struggling not to find out what it would be like to see my dick in your mouth."

My clit throbbed, adding to the wetness between my legs. My hand was literally curved right around his cock, and he held on to me so tight that from the position I was in, rolling up my dress wouldn't be a hardship for him.

"Don't fucking challenge me on this, sweetheart, because you know as well as I do that I'll win."

"I don't think so," I whispered.

Lies, lies, lies.

He knew it, too.

"So, I could slip my hand between your legs and I wouldn't find a wet pussy?" His lips brushed my ear. "I wouldn't find your wet cunt half-ready to take my cock? Because your legs are clenched damn tight, and that tells me you're hiding something."

"It's telling you wrong." More lies. All lies.

Would he try to prove himself right?

I'd played with fire—was this where I got burned?

Damien swept one arm around my waist and pulled me on top of him. My squealed protest was fruitless. My hips were already nestled at his sides, and thanks to my dress rolling up as he'd moved me, my underwear was almost entirely exposed.

I glanced back at the partition.

"He can't see you. It's one-way." Damien kept one hand on the back of my neck. The other slowly, oh-so-slowly, crept up my now-bare thigh, edging ever closer to where my clit was aching beneath the lace of my thong.

"What are you doing?" My mouth was dry. Why was it so dry? Why wasn't I trying to get off him? Why was I letting him do this?

"Research," he whispered, pulling my head down to his. He dragged his lips across my jaw at the very same time his fingers probed my upper thigh.

As his thumb brushed the edge of my thong.

SIN

I pushed at his shoulders, shoving my body back despite the fact my hips were going in the opposite direction—toward him. I simultaneously wanted and didn't want his touch. I couldn't think clearly—this man was my rival, my enemy, and here I was, sitting on his lap, inches away from his thick, hard cock, and about to let him see if I was as wet as he thought I was.

I'd lost my damn mind, but yet...I stayed.

Maybe he was right. Maybe I would give into my basic urges.

Maybe I was wrong.

Maybe this was my weakness.

Maybe *he* would turn out to be my weakness.

DAMIEN

She shivered, her shaky exhale hot against my neck. My own breathing wasn't exactly normal—it wasn't shaky like hers, but it was fast, borderline uncontrolled. Just like my desire for her.

My hand inched closer to her wet pussy. I didn't need to touch her to know she was wet, but I wanted to. I wanted to push her, see how far she'd go before she realized I was right.

She would give in to her body. She already was. It was betraying her with how it responded to me, but she wasn't exactly fighting it. Her half-hearted attempt to get off me was just that—half-hearted.

She wanted this as much as I did in this moment. I wanted more. I wanted to free my cock and slip it inside her. She was right here on top of me after all. It would be easy. So fucking easy to fuck her wet little cunt until she screamed and told everyone inside and outside of this car what was going on.

Too easy.

Too. Easy.

I didn't want her easily. I wanted her on the brink and ready to take things into her own hand. I wanted her hovering on the brink of an orgasm before I finally gave in and let her have it.

I wanted her to need me the way I wanted her to.

I was selfish and greedy, and I didn't care one bit.

Dahlia swallowed. I brushed the backs of my fingers over the lace that covered the mound of skin just above her pussy. She took a sharp breath in, and her hips rocked, making my knuckles just ghost across the rough area where her clit was.

Wet.

I could feel it on the fabric.

"So much for not giving in," I murmured in her ear, slipping two fingers beneath her thong. "You can feel that, Dahlia. You can feel how much you want me."

She didn't respond. Her bravado was gone now that I had full control.

I liked having her at my mercy.

I eased my fingers across her pussy. Its wetness made it easy, and I adjusted myself so I could touch her properly.

She dropped her forehead to the back of the seats when my fingers found their way inside her. Her muscles clenched around my fingers. I moved them in and out of her a few times, slowly, teasingly, until the tiniest whimper of a sound escaped her flattened lips.

"But you don't want me," I whispered into her hair. "Right, Dahlia? You don't want to be sitting on top of me while I fuck your tight little cunt with my fingers, and you sure as hell don't want to sit on my cock so I can fuck you properly, do you? You said that. You won't give in easy."

Brushing my lips down her jaw, I eased my fingers out of her and set her underwear straight again.

"We're here," I added. "Shall I meet you inside?"

"Jesus Christ." She gasped, rolling off to the side. Frantically, she tugged at her dress, stretching it right down over her thighs until it was like it was supposed to be. "That wine must have been stronger than I thought."

"No," I said simply, eyeing her flushed cheeks and bright eyes. "You just stopped lying to yourself for a few minutes."

She took a deep breath and looked back at me. "Rain check."

With that, she snatched up her purse and got out of the car.

I adjusted my pants and leaned forward to open the partition. "Go home, could you, Will?"

The ever-silent man nodded, hit the blinker, and I sat back in the seat.

Dahlia Lloyd was a walking, talking, sin of a woman. One who had me going out of my fucking mind.

———

I finished the resume and threw it straight into the metal trashcan to the left of me.

My father's flagship strip club needed two new dancers, and so far, nobody had been a good enough fit. None of the girls in the other clubs wanted to move to Foxies, and I understood that. It was the first club, but not the best. Goldies was the number one bar we owned.

Dad rubbed his hand over his salt-and-pepper beard. "What kind of floozies are you interviewing?"

I gave him a dark look over the top of the newest resume. "None. Their resumes aren't good enough."

"They're swinging around a pole with their tits out. What kind of fucking resume do they need?"

"To not have a background in prostitution." I dropped the papers I was holding across the desk in front of him. Whoever Poppy was, she was the third woman in a row to have been a prostitute trying to "better herself."

I understood that, but the moment she got caught sucking some guy's dick in a private room for extra tips was the moment we got shut down.

Foxies wasn't that hard up to take the risk. Not yet.

"That complicates it." Dad folded the resume in two and handed it back to me to throw into the trash. "Did you put that on the advert?"

"Helena did it. She said she had a few places to advertise it as well as the usual ones." I filed the 'maybe' ones into a paper folder. "Face facts, Dad. We're not the only big competitor on the Strip now. Maybe we should put two clubs together. Less rent but more revenue."

His eyes, as dark as mine, glared at me. "You want to cut our portfolio?"

I sighed. I'd been dreading this conversation. "Listen to me, all right? I've been crunching the numbers and then some. If we consolidated Spark and Thunder, we'd pay thirty percent of the total rent we currently do. We can move Shawna and Darla to Swing since they're bi and that caters to the bi crowd with the mixed dancers. Alana and Marie have already expressed a desire to move to Passion since that's their crowd. We're mixing sexuality more than we need to. Take Alana and Marie from the straight club into the lesbian club, put the bi's into the bi club, and instantly, we have space to accommodate into Spark. Regina is quitting next month. Kaitlyn is pregnant, and Sally is going back to school. That's Thunder's staff who can't assimilate into Spark."

"The bar staff?"

"We split them between the others. They're always short. Play is understaffed four out of seven nights despite our best efforts, and Sugar's staff is overstretched. We're playing with the law with them because they need 'round the clock staffing." I tapped my fingers against the desk and passed him a financial breakdown for two months ago. "Dad, I know you don't want to sell, but Thunder just isn't as profitable as the others anymore. We're doing the staff a disservice by not putting them in front of the biggest audience."

A "hmph" escaped him, but he picked up the report anyway.

It'd been a long time since he'd been involved in the business. The last time was really seven years ago. Since then, he'd handed the control to me. He was still named as co-owner and president while I was co-owner, CEO, and COO, and I'd thought that'd been the shift in our power.

He'd always been my idol. The things we'd been through didn't bear speaking about, so we didn't. We kept them buried and ignored them as much as possible. Dad insisted that we moved on and focused on the present and the future, but that didn't stop me thinking about the past.

About Mom.

About Penelope.

About *him*.

Thirty-years-old and my demons still silenced me. Still controlled me. Still dictated happiness to me. I was thankful that the biggest demon was the man sitting opposite me, no matter that he wasn't evil.

No. Benedict Fox wasn't evil. He was heartbroken. Although, maybe, they were one and the same, especially as time passed.

I certainly felt the melding of the two emotions as time passed.

"Your idea holds merit," Dad grunted, dumping the report back on the desk. "What about The Scarlet Letter? Where are you with that?"

Fuck. I'd hoped we could avoid that vein of questioning for the day. It was only the third time he'd brought it up since Lennon Lloyd had died. The first time was mere days after his funeral. The second was the week before his daughter returned to town.

Today was the latest.

What did I tell him?

Did I ask him if he knew that Dahlia Lloyd was as intelligent as she was beautiful?

Did I ask him if he knew that Dahlia held the spirit of both her parents in the palm of her hand?

Did I ask him if he knew that Dahlia was compelling and fascinating? Educated yet fantastical? Wild and free? Careless yet disciplined?

I sure as hell couldn't tell him this, mostly because I know it to be fact. Dahlia was a dirty dream come to life, an infuriating daydream personified, an enigma that could never be decoded.

"Struggling," I answered honestly. "You were certain that she'd want to sell, but I fear you were wrong."

He rubbed his hand across his beard again. He always did that when he was thinking. He reminded me of an old wizard—Dumbledore or Gandalf. I wondered if he even realized he did it half the time.

"I wasn't certain." Dad leaned back as he admitted it. He slotted his fingers through the others as he leaned back and set his hands on his stomach. "I told you I was, but I never was. Lennon created the bar for Melinda. It was something they'd always wanted, and they built it together. I'm not surprised you're running into issues with Dahlia."

He had no fucking idea.

"So, why send me after it? Why do you want it? I couldn't care less." Annoyance bubbled up. This wasn't my fucking project, it was his. All this shit was doing was making me want a woman I had no place wanting.

"I want it for personal reasons."

I stared at him. "Why now? Why when her dad died? Why not before?"

"He would never have sold it."

"And you think she will?"

"I think she's more easily influenced."

I ran my hands through my hair. He was sending me on a wild fucking goose chase. He was assuming shit about a woman he knew nothing about. I'd been there just days ago. Dahlia Lloyd wasn't that person. She wasn't the rollover or the pushover or the fucking anything else anyone had her pegged as.

She was annoyingly strong and determined.

"She won't sell." That was no opinion.

Dad stared at the wall. He wasn't close to looking in my direction. He was stone cold still. Not even the fingers curled on his beard moved. "Try harder."

"You're wasting my time."

"She's a woman."

"A fierce woman."

"A woman all the same."

Anger twisted my stomach. "She's not defined by her gender."

Dad turned to look at me. His eyes were soulless, his lips thin, his expression emotionless. "She's a woman. She can be fierce and mouthy, but that doesn't make her comparable to you. She's a Lloyd. You're a Fox. Get that bar bought, Damien. No matter how."

I kicked my chair back as I got up. Dad's expression didn't change as I snatched up my phone and stormed out of the office. He'd clearly taken my response for frustration.

He could take it whatever fucking way he wanted. I didn't care.

Stealing The Scarlet Letter from beneath Dahlia's feet without a solid reason seemed unfair. Why the fuck did my father want that bar so bad? Why did he covet it the way he did? What the fuck had he done to deserve the mini-empire Lennon Lloyd had built?

Why did Dahlia deserve to lose all that just because my father wanted it?

One week ago, I didn't give a fuck about Dahlia Lloyd. She'd been a pretty woman with a pretty name and an education a pretty penny had bought. She'd been a pretty little easy target whose business had been easy pickings because her father had left. She'd been no more than a young woman with a broken heart, who'd bitten off more than she could chew.

Now, she was...I didn't want to think about that. She was under my goddamn skin, for a start. Every time I stopped to think, it was her that crossed my mind.

I felt like she was quickly becoming an obsession. With her dark eyes and bright lips, her smart mouth, and her tempting touch. She was everything a man like me could get addicted to quite easily.

Everything a man like me could break.

I knew it, and yet, I couldn't stay away. I couldn't keep behind the line of business. I had to take it personally every time for my own selfish needs. I was greedy and heartless, pushing her so I could know things.

SIN

Did I need to pull her on top of me in the car yesterday?
Did I need to touch her pussy to feel how wet she was?

No.

I didn't need to do either, yet I did, for no other reason
than I wanted to.

She was soft and gentle, a vulnerable young woman with
the weight of her world on her shoulders.

I was hard and brash, a total asshole, carrying the weight
of my own universe in my hands.

It didn't matter that my heart was just as broken as hers.
Didn't matter for a damn second that we shared a pain she
had no idea about.

All that mattered was that she was a wistful daydream to
me, yet to her, I was no more than a persistent nightmare.

9

DAHLIA

"I promise," I said to Patty, the cleaning lady. "I'm sending you home. Full pay."

The old woman sniffed and rubbed at her nose with a tissue. "You don't need to do that."

I touched her shoulder. "Go home, go to bed, and call your son to bring you some soup and tea, okay? You're sick, you crazy lady. Did you drive here?"

She shook her head.

"Let me get Fergus to take you home. Sit down." I directed her to a chair and walked back to where Fergus was rifling through resumes for Abby's perusal.

My assistant manager was a twenty-nine-year-old, blond, god of a man. He had muscles on every inch of his body thanks to a love affair with the gym, but it didn't look out of place on his tall, lean frame.

My favorite thing in the world was watching him get hit on at the bar. It happened five times a night and watching the look on women's faces when he said, "Sorry, darling, I'm gay," never, ever got old.

"Hey, Ferg?" I leaned against the doorframe. "Can you drive Patty home? She's sick."

He wrinkled his handsome face up as he lifted his attention from the desk to me. "I just got back from vacation. I don't have time to be sick."

"Nobody has time to be sick. Stop being a drama queen, or I'll make her sneeze on you."

He sighed, closed the folder, and stood. "Fine, but you know she lives only a block away from Reggie. If I see him and I cry the entire day, it's on you, and I'll need extra breaks."

I rolled my eyes so hard I saw my brain. He and his long-term boyfriend, Reggie, were constantly breaking up and getting back together. I had whiplash from the whole thing, honestly.

This time, they'd gone on vacation to the Bahamas for two weeks, and while there, Reggie had eyed up the cabana boys the night before they came home. If Fergus was to be believed—he had a flair for the dramatic—they'd fought the entire flight home to Vegas and promptly broken up the moment Fergus had taken him home yesterday afternoon.

That was twenty-four hours ago.

This morning, I'd texted Abby. I had fifty bucks that said they'd be back together in three days, and she said this one would be a week.

"I saw you rolling your eyes at me." He tucked his shirt back into his waistband as he followed me to the bar.

"Good. Then, maybe, you'll understand how ridiculous it is."

"He was eying up the cabana boy!"

I leaned against the bar, noting even Patty was covering a smile. "Honey, of course he was. He was bringing you drinks! Where else was he supposed to look?"

"At me." Fergus sniffed. "Come on, Patty, darling. Let's get you home." He went to put his arm around her before thinking better of it. "You're not contagious, are you?"

Patty answered with a cough. When he jumped away from her, she shot me a wink.

I dipped my head to hide my laughter, only letting it go when I heard the door shut behind them. If Fergus knew I'd laughed at him, I'd never hear the end of it.

Seriously, he'd be reminding me about it in ten years.

I pulled a packet of new coasters from beneath the bar with the intention to set them on every table, but the phone ringing beat me to it. Glancing at the clock, I picked up the phone and answered.

"Good morning, this is The Scarlet Letter, Dahlia speaking." I tucked the phone between my ear and shoulder. It was a little awkward, but it enabled me to tear the packaging on the coasters open.

"Good morning." The deep, now-familiar tone of Damien Fox stopped me in my tracks. "Are you able to talk?"

"I'm sorry, who is this?" I kept my tone light and airy.

"You know who it is."

"I know it's not Damien Fox. He doesn't do calls before one in the afternoon, and it's barely past eleven."

He laughed.

I shivered.

I suck.

"I'm his long-lost twin brother," he said.

"I hope you have better manners than he does, in that case." I grinned as I put three coasters down on a circular table.

Coughing came from his side. "Exponentially. Lunch, Ms. Lloyd?"

"My treat," I insisted.

"I can't."

"Then, I'm busy."

"Does twelve-forty-five work for you?"

"I'll see you at one." I clicked off the call.

I hated that I grinned like a wild child. I had no place smiling at that man. I was so mad at his earlier antics— madder still that I'd partaken in them—but still, here I was, grinning like a freaking idiot.

Then again, I'd just been really awkward. And awkward *was* my favorite thing to be.

I put the phone back on the bar and took a drink from my glass of lemonade just so I'd stop smiling. It worked, for the most part. I was able to kill the smiles and focus on setting out all the new coasters. Which was a good thing, because I didn't want to read into what it meant that I was smiling after a phone call with Damien.

As a rule, I'd been wildly pissed after every conversation we'd ever had. He could probably walk into the bar and walk right back out again and I'd still be annoyed.

He just had that effect on me.

Fergus returned thirty minutes later. I was humming along to Justin Bieber as I wiped down the leather menus from the tables along the back wall, and apparently, that was different enough that he came over, stopped me, and rested the backs of his fingers against my forehead.

"Oh. You don't have a fever." He dropped his hand. "You look happy."

"I'm wiping down menus. How can I possibly be happy?" I brushed off his words and moved to the next table with my damp cloth.

Fergus pursed his lips and leaned against one tall table, propping himself up by resting his forearm on the flat surface. He studied me, even when I turned away from him. Then, just as I flipped over a menu, he gasped so loudly I dropped it.

The slapping of the leather against the tiled floor made *me* gasp and jerk in response.

"What?" It came out snappier than I'd intended.

"Damien Fox called you!" Fergus jabbed a finger in my direction, accusation furrowing his brow. "And you're happy about it! You're a traitor."

I opened my mouth, but nothing came out, so I closed it again and settled for blinking aimlessly at him.

How did he get—*Abby*.

Abby had told him all about Damien at some point between him getting home and coming to work.

"Yes, he did, but I'm not happy about it," I answered, picking up the menu. "Believe it or not, I don't like the man."

"Then why did it take so long for you to respond, hmm?" He waggled his finger that was still pointing at me.

"I didn't know you knew anything about him."

Fergus sniffed. "More than you want to know, darling."

For the second time, I opened my mouth to speak, but this time, my silence wasn't from a lack of words.

It was from Fergus pushing off the table and disappearing into the back room, leaving me standing alone.

I inhaled deeply and let the breath go. If Abby had told him that Damien was interested in buying the bar, and Fergus knew him, it only stood to reason that they both knew something about the man that I didn't.

But what?

And why did it dilute Fergus' normally jubilant demeanor into something so flat?

⸻

I didn't see Fergus for the entire hour between his disappearing act and Damien's—early—arrival to the bar. We'd only just opened at twelve-thirty, so while I wasn't surprised at all that Damien was early, I wished the bar was still shut.

If it were, I wouldn't have to feel his eyes on me the entire time until I could leave at one.

He might have been early, but that didn't mean I would leave early for him.

Damien took a seat at one of the booths right as I fired up the coffee machine for a customer. I didn't often work behind the bar—people weren't exactly my favorite, well, people—but today was an exception. Not all the wait staff were trained, and getting Fergus out here before necessary seemed like a stupid idea.

He was on the emotional side of the scale today, after all. If he were a woman, I'd put a hundred bucks on him suffering from PMS.

"Ferg?" I lightly knocked on the door. "Are you done? I have a lunch meeting."

He looked up, flicking his hair away from his face. "Yeah. I'm coming." Standing up, he put his phone in his pocket and followed me out.

"I refilled the coffee machine, and Riley and Gia are working the floor. Sven's out in the kitchen terrifying poor Quinn." I snatched my purse up.

"That's nothing new," he grunted, slipping behind the bar.

"True." I checked my phone before tucking it inside my purse and slinging the strap over my shoulder. "I won't be more than an hour."

He waved me away with his hand. "Your date is here."

"He's not my date."

"You're dressed like he's your date."

"I'm dressed for work, you little douchebag." I tapped his upper arm. "And wipe that scowl off your face. I don't want this tantrum scaring off customers."

That only caused him to glare at me more. Something I wholeheartedly ignored as a customer came to the bar. The dark look on Fergus' face was quickly replaced by a wide, beaming smile that hid any trace of annoyance he was feeling.

If he weren't so good at his job...

I ran my hand through my hair as I approached Damien sitting in the mini booth. "Let's go. As you can see, I'm already working."

His full, pink lips curled to the side. The stubble that coated his strong jaw was thicker and more unruly than usual like he hadn't had a chance to shave this morning. "Efficient. Don't worry, sweetheart. I won't keep you long." He stood up with one smooth movement and raised his hand to Fergus.

Turning my head, I saw Fergus' barely-raised hand returning the acknowledgment.

Hmm.

Damien touched his hand to my lower back. "Come on. My car is waiting outside."

"Is there anyone you don't know?" I asked, stepping away from him. *And do you drive anywhere yourself?*

"I didn't have the pleasure of knowing you until a couple of weeks ago."

"That would be smooth if I didn't think you were avoiding the question."

He smirked and opened the door, spearing me with his dark eyes. "You're too smart for your own good."

"Ahh, but if I were any more stupid, you'd own *my* bar." I flashed him a grin right as I stepped onto the sidewalk.

He laughed. "That's exactly why you're too smart." He held the car door open for me the way he had the bar door. "How is Fergus?"

I slid inside the jet-black, shiny Bentley and eyed him speculatively. How did they know each other? My curiosity was spiking, nudging at me to ask that very question. So, of course, I did. "How do you know him?"

"The same way I know everyone else. Through business." He joined me in the backseat.

"Gee, that wasn't vague at all."

"Not everything needs a clear-cut answer, Dahlia."

"Only because you don't like to give them."

He sighed and leaned back in his seat. "Remind me why I asked you to lunch?"

Something tickled me in the pit of my stomach as I met his gaze. "Because I'm more fascinating than I am annoying."

"You think you're annoying?"

"No. I know I'm annoying—especially to you. I'm the puzzle you can't figure out, and it's driving you crazy."

The steadiness with which he held my gaze was all too intimate. Every blink seared the memory of his hypnotic stare deeper into my mind. Even the barest twitch of his lips that curled in amusement was all too familiar.

Too amusing.

Too endearing.

Too...*him.*

"You know what? You're right." He stretched his arms out in front of him and then shrugged. "I'm not even going to pretend that I don't want to figure you out, sweetheart, because I do. Believe me when I say, nobody is more annoyed about that than me. I tend to avoid people as a rule."

"The more time I spend with you, the more I realize we have in common. Not enough to be happy about this time with you, but enough that you're tolerable now."

"Good to know." His eyes sparkled. "I took the liberty of picking somewhere for lunch. Do you mind?"

"Actually, yes, but I suppose it's too late now."

A grin stretched across his face. "You can choose next time."

"You assume there will be a next time. Then again, given that you've picked both dinner and lunch, assumption seems to be a part of your character."

"Correct." The car came to a stop, and Damien opened the door. "Shall we?"

10

DAHLIA

We walked into a small sandwich bar tucked a few blocks away from the Strip. I hadn't been to Barny's since I was in college. It was far enough from the campus that it felt like a break but close enough that it didn't feel like you were crossing the entire desert for a sandwich.

Not to mention, they made the best sandwiches and subs in the entire city.

"I can afford more than a sandwich, you know." I eyed Damien as I pulled the door open and waited.

He stared at me flatly.

"What? I can't hold a door for you, too? Do I look like a damsel in distress at the top of her tower?"

He gripped the edge of the door, his knuckles whitening in the process. "I already agreed to let you buy lunch. Don't take it too far."

"How gracious of you." I let go of the handle with a flourish and stalked inside the busy sandwich shop. "God forbid your masculinity be threatened by a woman, of all things," I threw over my shoulder with a quick glare.

I'd barely turned my head when his hands were on my shoulders. He tugged me toward him, pulling my back flush against his toned body. My ass nestled against him, and his solid chest pressed against my shoulder blades, sending a shiver rocketing down my spine.

"I take it back," he murmured in my ear. "Take it as far as you like. Then, maybe, you'll see just how much my masculinity is *threatened* by you."

"Your masculinity can kiss my ass." I turned my face into his as we took a simultaneous step forward in the line. "Oh, wait. It pretty much *is*."

His cock was slowly hardening against my ass, pushing firmly against his zipper.

"It'll do more than kiss your ass, sweetheart."

"Not if I break it off."

"Are you gonna bite me? Seeing you choke on my cock might be worth the risk," he rumbled in a low tone, his lips now brushing my earlobe.

The people in front of us in line stepped up to order, and I shrugged myself out of his grip. No doubt, he could have kept me there against him if he really wanted to, but he let me go anyway.

What was with this newfound inability to have a conversation in person without it turning sexual?

He wasn't deprived, that much was sure. Handsome, rich, and charismatic, there was no doubt in my mind that he had sex virtually on tap. Thirty minutes in a bar would guarantee him company for the night. Yet, here he was, all up in my business with his dirty words all the damn time.

He couldn't be *that* hard-up.

Well.

Considering I'd felt his erection plenty of times, he was certainly able to get up and hard, but still.

I placed my order for a BLT with extra cheese and then, on no more than a complete whim, I pulled a Damien.

I ordered for him.

I handed over my credit card before he could protest. I'd ordered him exactly the same as mine, because who didn't like that? But, still, I could almost feel the annoyance as it radiated off of him. It was almost radioactive as he gripped the edge of the counter, leaning a little too close to me.

He stayed there, perfectly still, seethingly silent until our sandwiches were wrapped and handed to me. I took one in each hand and swept around him, turning toward the door. If he thought he was going to run the rest of this lunch, he had a thought or ten coming his way.

I tucked both sandwiches against me in one arm and opened the door. This time, I didn't even wait for him to walk through or grab it. I stalked outside without him and turned away from the car.

"Where are you going?"

I ignored his question and kept walking. More than anything, I was giving the man a taste of his own medicine. He'd done nothing but dictate to me since I'd met him, and he hadn't stopped for a second to actually realize something very important.

I wasn't the kind of woman you dictated to.

I followed rules well. I could take orders.

Demands were a whole other ball game.

I wove through the few blocks until I reached the small area of grass that was the park I'd spent a lot of my childhood in. And by childhood, I mean teenage years and evenings drinking vodka disguised inside Coca-Cola bottles.

"Oh, cute. A picnic," Damien muttered when I sat down not far from a flowerbed.

I glared and held out his sandwich. "You're not the only one who can assume and be a dick about it."

He sat down next to me and took the wrapped BLT from me. The paper crinkled as he gripped it, and he spared me a glance before he unwrapped it. "Is this how you feel when I picked Barny's without asking you?"

I said nothing. I simply unwrapped my sandwich and took a small bite out of the end without looking at him. Instead, I gazed out at the children's playground I'd been in so many times before, where so many of my youngest years had been spent with my parents pushing me on swings and catching me at the bottom of the slide.

He sighed.

I kept up my firm ignorance as the crinkling of his wrapper reached my ears. I didn't know if he looked at me—I didn't care to know. I wanted to make my point. Make the point that he couldn't keep steamrolling over me. It didn't matter how hard or how far he pushed me, I'd push right back, even if my back was against the wall and my arms were tied behind me.

I was Dahlia Freakin' Lloyd.

I submitted to *nobody*.

Sexually or otherwise.

I was, at the very least, an equal to everyone I crossed, because I was a goddamn human being. Very few things could push me off that pedestal of being equal to another person. Damien Fox's ego was not one of those things.

And damn it, I would take him down a peg or two. Even if it was only so nobody else had to put up with this shit.

I popped the last bite of my lunch into my mouth and crumpled up the wrapper. He was mere inches from me, and neither of us had spoken for at least ten minutes. Strangely, though, neither of us really needed to. My point was made. I didn't need to say anything else for that, but I did want him to realize something important.

That I wasn't just something he could play with.

That The Scarlet Letter was more than my business.

That I was a person who had a heart and feelings and who could be hurt.

"I used to come here as a kid," I said softly, still staring at the playground. One of the old swings creaked lightly as it swung seemingly by itself, but my eyes followed the young girl who'd just left it and was running toward her father's open arms.

Something tugged at my heart. Something strong and heavy.

I knew it well: it was grief.

"Really?" Damien's voice was just as quiet as mine.

I nodded. "Before my mom died. The last time I came here was the morning before…" I trailed off. *She was shot. The morning before someone shot her.*

It was obvious I'd left the sentence unfinished, but to my relief, he glossed over it. "What made you come back today?"

"I don't know," I said honestly. "I didn't really think about it. All I knew was that I wanted to show you that some things like lunch meetings are agreed between two people, not dictated by one."

"Fair enough." He fisted the wrapper into a ball. "I'm sorry. I keep forgetting that you're..." Now, he'd trailed off.

I wasn't going to let it go.

I turned my face until I was looking at his strong profile. At his thick brow and slightly-bumped nose and squared jaw. At the two-inch-long scar that glinted iridescently in the sunlight. "That I'm not the people you're used to associating with? That I'm not the pushover you'd prefer me to be? That I'm not the woman who'd sit and let you order dinner for her just to get the date over with?"

"Simply, yes. Although I'm glad you're not a pushover."

"Why? Because you'd be bored of me by now?"

His answer was a slow, slight smile as he turned and met my eyes. "Maybe, I would be. Maybe I'd have no reason to spend time with you if you were a pushover. I'd own your bar right now if you weren't you."

"You don't sound annoyed by that."

"How can I be? You love The Scarlet Letter. I think you're wrong for not selling to me, but at this point, my last hope is to keep bugging you enough until you give in just to make me leave you alone."

Despite my best effort, a laugh bubbled out of me. "I suppose I can appreciate your honesty."

That slight smile grew wider, reaching his eyes, and he nudged me with his elbow. "You're not laughing for no reason."

"Fine!" I let the laugh go and shoved him back. "Your honesty is, for once, refreshing. At least I know I need to get a lawyer on retainer to prepare a case for a restraining order."

"Fuck. I shouldn't have told you my plans, should I?"

"No way. I need a heads up. How else will I know who's throwing stones at my bedroom window?"

"You even know my next idea."

"I've watched a lot of movies." I shrugged a shoulder, grinning. "And for the record, yes. How you felt when I ordered for you was how I felt when you picked Barny's without asking me. The presumptuous acts are rude and unappreciated."

He rubbed his fingers along the stubble on his jaw. "For what it's worth, that was a damn good sandwich."

"And I didn't really care that you picked Barny's."

"But the principle is, it sucks," he finished the dual line of thought. "All right, all right. Next time, you can pick, as an apology."

"You assume I'll eat with you again."

"You will." Damien stood and offered me his hand. I raised an eyebrow but took it. He pulled me up and with a smirk, said, "Otherwise I'll keep throwing stones at your window until you agree."

I burst out laughing, stepping back from him. "I'm tempted to try that just to see if you will. I'd like to see you work out my bedroom window, first."

"I have my ways."

"Which are?"

He shrugged, adjusting the collar of his shirt. "Throw stones at every window until I get a response."

Don't smile again. Don't smile again.

Damn it.

I smiled.

"Apparently, you've seen your own fair share of movies," I said.

"Only the ones where the guy always gets the girl."

"Ah, now it makes sense. You're talking about porn."

He blinked at me. Then, a chuckle escaped his full, smiling lips. "Not really, but it's not wrong. Do you have to go back to work yet?"

"What time is it?"

He glanced at his watch. "One-thirty-five."

"I have a little time. Why?" I tucked my purse against my side, righting the strap on my shoulder, and looked up at him.

He motioned to the park before crossing his arms over his chest. "I want to show you something. Come back to the bar."

I narrowed my eyes. What was it? Did I trust him enough?

"You'll be back before you know it. It's only a couple minutes away. Please?"

I studied his face. His eyes almost pleaded with me, and I took a deep breath in.

Then, I agreed.

"Okay."

―――――

Foxies.

Anyone that knew anything about the Fox family knew that Foxies was their—aptly named—first strip club. It had, at one point, been the most popular strip club in the entire city. Hell, probably the state, if not the entire coast.

Most of how the club had opened was urban legend. Damien's father had appeared from nowhere with money coming out of his asshole, snapped up the building, and in three months, was a millionaire. Word had it that he had personal knowledge of the abilities of the girls who worked there. And by personal, I meant *personal*.

My dad had once told me that all the clubs under the business had been scouted and part of an undercover mission to locate brothels in the city, but despite the cops' best effort, the Fox clubs could never be linked to anything.

What I didn't know was why Damien had brought me here. What reason did he have? I wasn't a stripper. Hell, I could barely do the Macarena without falling on my ass. I was the furthest thing from a dancer in existence today.

"Foxies?" I asked him, standing beside him on the sidewalk.

He nodded, not answering me. He pushed open the front door and held it for me to pass through. When I did, I was only mildly surprised to see girls already at poles and men—and a couple women—sitting at the tables by the podiums. Pints of beer were already in front of those customers, and numerous dollar bills already dotted both the straps on the dancer's legs and the stage on which they danced.

"I'm confused," I said, leaning into him as we walked through the bar. "Why did you bring me here?"

He touched his hand to my lower back, but this time, I didn't shake him off. The music was too loud and in-your-face for this early in the day, and I was thankful when he took me out to the back rooms and away from the noise and the men.

He didn't release me until we were firmly inside the office. "Sit down." He motioned to a high-back leather chair behind a desk.

I raised an eyebrow, but I took the seat as he'd silently asked me to. I couldn't think why he'd brought me here, especially to the back rooms—an office, no less. "I have fifteen minutes to get back to work," I reminded him.

We'd had to take a detour thanks to the idiot who decided to wrap the front of their car around a streetlight.

Dark eyes surveyed me for a moment. "I've lost my damn mind."

"I'd argue you lost it before I ever met you."

His lips twitched. "I'd argue back you're the reason I've lost it."

I raised my eyebrow.

"I need your help." He sighed after a moment of silence. "I have business and marketing plans my father doesn't agree with."

Picking up a pen from the desk, I twirled it between my fingers. "Why are you telling me this?"

"I told you, I want your help." Damien perched on the edge of the desk and looked back at me. "A...what would you do, if you will."

I stared at him. His expression was flat—his jaw was a little tight, but other than that, his features were schooled into the perfect mask of uncaring, plain simplicity. He gained nothing from telling me this, so why was he?

I didn't understand this man. Not in the slightest.

"Why are you asking me? Mia is the marketing guru. I'm still remembering to get up with my alarm because nobody else will," I admitted. It wasn't exactly willingly, but hey, if he could admit he was having issues in his business, the least I could do was admit I struggled to wake up in the morning.

"You have a Masters in Business."

"That you said to me just a few days ago doesn't run a business."

He held his hands up. "I stand by that. It doesn't run a business, but you have a theoretical knowledge I might lack."

Was he admitting I knew more than him? "Are you admitting I know more than you?"

He scowled. "Don't push it."

"Fine, fine. You'll admit it one day." I paused, enjoying the dark flash of annoyance that danced through his eyes. "Spit it out. You're wasting time."

"One of our clubs is on the downward spiral. We have another that has never been one of our better ones, and I believe the staff could be better used in the failing club and others. They're too good to be stuck in one of the mediocre clubs, and the one that's losing its draw has staff openings." Damien paused, undoing a button on his shirt. "He isn't sure. The club falling down is one of his, not mine, and I think he's stuck in the years he ran this business."

I glanced around the office. "Foxies is falling apart, huh?"

He sat up straight.

"Oh, please. You bring me here for this story? Something we could have discussed in the park or even at

Scarlet?" I rolled my eyes. *Men.* Damien was sexy but dense. Like the guys who sent unsolicited dick pics. "I'm not surprised. It felt like I was in the nineties walking through there just then. It's outdated, Damien. I've seen grocery stores more stylish than this place."

"You're like a human Band-Aid, aren't you?"

"Ripping off the truth, one clear-cut statement at a time." I flashed him a grin. "If you're asking me if you think you would be better off bringing your staff to Foxies, the answer is yes. It's like your company's iconic club, right? But you have to update it or it's not going to make a difference. You can fix it if you play it right."

"Is that your professional opinion?"

"You don't wanna hear my personal one."

He stopped for a moment. Then, he burst out laughing. I struggled to contain my own smile as he stood up and held a hand to me for the second time today.

"Come on, sweetheart. I'll get you back to work now."

I placed my hand in his and let him pull me up. "This was a completely pointless conversation, you understand that, don't you?"

"Not entirely. I figured out that you and I agree on something else: what I should tell my father."

I twisted my lips to the side. "But why did you ask me? It's just an opinion. Not all opinions are right."

Damien pulled me closer to him, keeping his fingers wrapped cozily around my own. Our bodies were perilously close, and my gaze briefly dipped to the light smattering of chest hair that peeked out from just above the open buttons of his shirt.

"Because," he said, his lips bare centimeters from mine, "for some peculiar reason, I trust you."

"Why?"

"I'm easily waylaid by a pretty face."

I laughed, stepping back from him. His body emanated a warmth that seeped into my skin, that made me hyper aware of everything he was. "You're an idiot."

"I know. Dinner? Tomorrow?"

I met his eyes. "Are you asking me?"

With a nod, he said, "Yes. At my place. I'll pick you up, and you can leave whenever you want."

"Why?"

"Why, what?"

"Why are you asking?" I tilted my head to the side, picking up my purse from the desk. "That sounds a lot like a date to me."

"Maybe it is." He stuffed his hands in his pockets, seeming a lot younger than his thirty years, even as his dark eyes hinted desire. "Maybe I just want you all to myself for a couple of hours."

I stared at him.

"Seven?" he continued, his voice softer. "I'll pick you up at your place."

I didn't answer.

"Please?"

That undid me.

"Fine. But there better be wine if I'm going to spend an entire evening at your house."

His lips curled to the side. "There'll be wine."

SIN

11

DAHLIA

I'd made a horrible mistake.

It was becoming an even more horrible habit.

I tapped my fingers against the desk in a steady rhythm, one after the other.

Taptaptap.

Taptaptap.

Taptaptap.

Taptaptap.

My eyes stayed trained on the computer screen in front of me. The order form I was supposed to be filling out blurred together, the lines and items all mixing into one messy, unfocused fuzz of dots on the screen.

This was shit. I was shit. My life choices were shit.

And I couldn't even blame any of this on PMS. Nope, it was all me. Me and my bad choices.

What possessed me to say yes to having dinner with Damien? At his *house?* What in the ever-loving hell went through my damn mind when I said, "Sure, let's do that!" or whatever other stupid, stupid answer came out of my mouth.

Oh, I knew.

He'd looked me in the eye and played me like a goddamn violin. Worse—I'd let him. I'd let him tug on my strings and convince me that it was a good idea.

"Did you place that order yet?" Abby stuck her head inside my door. "If you don't do it by one, it won't be here tomorrow. That place is really awkward."

I glanced at the clock. I had thirty minutes. "I'm almost done," I lied. "Do we really need twenty cases of cranberry juice?"

"There's a cocktail special this weekend."

Of course there was. "Right—slipped my mind. I'll get twenty-five just in case. It'll keep."

She raised her expertly filled-in brown eyebrows. "What's up with you today? You're more scattered than a bath full of wet cats."

"But probably not quite as dangerous." I'd never been close to a bathtub full of wet cats, but I'd been near one wet cat, and that was enough for me. "I'm just tired and busy and overwhelmed," I lied.

I wasn't quite ready to admit to her what was really up. I was a shitty person lying to my best friend, but her dislike of Damien was something else. I was protecting him. Why? I hadn't worked that out yet.

I *was* working out that the professional front of Damien Fox was much different to the private man who crept out every now and then.

Much, much different.

And that was probably the reason why I'd said yes to dinner.

Except now, I was regretting it. It had nothing to do with the disbelieving, judgmental look on my best friend's face. It had everything to do with the fact that, while I had major issues with Professional Damien, I didn't have quite so many with Private Damien.

"I'd tell you that you need a break, but you just took one." Abby grinned. "I'll finish the order if you want to go."

I shook my head and grabbed my phone. "I'm fine. I just need to re-center myself. Eating helps."

She glanced at the dainty, silver watch on her wrist. "If Madison can handle the bar on her own, I'll go get us both lunch now."

"There's no 'if.' She asked me for more hours this morning, so she's gonna have to handle it to get that."

"Barny's?"

"A meatball sub," I answered with a nod.

"Gotcha. I'll be back soon." Abby disappeared, leaving the door slightly ajar.

I stared at the gap before looking down at my phone. Four taps on the screen for my code had the phone unlocked, and I brought up my messages app, clicking right on Damien's name. His was third from the top, bumped down by Mia and Abby.

Then, I gave the answer I should have given last night.

I didn't even stop to think about what I was doing.

I just did it. Just tapped out the message and hit send before the tiny niggle in the back of my mind could convince me otherwise.

Me: *Can't do tonight. Sorry.*

I put my phone face down and turned my attention back to the bumble of blurred lines and numbers on the screen. I knew what it all said, but that didn't mean any of it made any sense.

Regret tickled down my spine.

Why did I regret that text? Apart from the fact it was short notice, I had no reason to feel bad. I didn't owe the man dinner—I owed him nothing. I knew what he was doing, and yesterday, I'd allowed myself to be sucked in. That was all. Nothing more, nothing less.

It was a moment of weakness.

I had a lot of those around him.

The only way to stop them was to stop being around him. It was that simple, and knowing Damien—it was that hard, too.

There was no way he'd let it go easily. The second he saw that message, he'd be all over it, demanding to know why, being his usual, brash self. Or, just as likely, he'd show up at my house with dinner.

He knew everything about me. He sure as hell knew my address, too.

Finally, I managed to submit the order at twelve-fifty-five, right as Abby returned with our sandwiches. The moment she put mine down in front of me with a short, fat, bottle of water, my phone buzzed.

I hesitated.

"Aren't you going to get that?" She nodded toward the vibrating, slightly-moving phone.

I grimaced as I picked it up. Damien's name flashed on the screen. Abby peered over, snorted, and sat down.

"Hello?" I said tentatively, holding it to my ear.

"You canceled?" His voice was huskier and rougher than normal—like he'd just woken up.

"Yeah, sorry. Something came up."

If looks could kill, Abby would be murdering me right now. There was no way she couldn't hear this whole conversation.

"Bullshit," Damien muttered.

"It's true. Sorry, I can't make it." God, if words had a smell...He'd already described what mine would smell like.

The line crackled as—I assumed—he took a deep breath and let it out slowly. "All right. It's fine. I'll talk to you later."

Then, just like that, he hung up.

My mouth opened as I slowly pulled my phone from my ear and looked at it.

Silence lasted all of a second.

My best friend broke it by bursting out laughing so loudly a room full of five-year-olds would have taken it as a challenge.

I darted my attention from my phone to her before dropping the Samsung on the desk with a dull thud. "What the hell?"

"You," Abby sputtered. "Just got played."

"Got played? What is this, high school?"

"No, but you're the one who canceled something for no good reason."

Sighing, I said, "Dinner. I canceled dinner."

"Yeah, I would have reacted that way to you, too." She plucked a piece of tomato from her chicken sandwich and held it out while looking at me with arched eyebrows. "I don't know what the hell you're doing, but it's obvious you canceled on him out of principle."

"He's a business rival. It's not good business to mingle like that." There went my bullshit again.

"It doesn't matter why you think you did it, but it didn't work. I bet you thought he'd be all up in your business after that, right?"

"History dictates as much."

"But he blew you off." She shrugged a shoulder. "And now, you're pissed about it."

"I'm not pissed about it."

"You look pissed about it."

"I'm not pissed about it!"

"The lady doth protest way, way too fucking much."

"The lady thinks you're a dick. And put that tomato down." I huffed and tugged my sandwich right in front of me.

She leaned forward and waved the slice in my face. "Admit you're annoyed about it and I will."

"Fine. I'm annoyed." I batted her hand away. "I'm shock-annoyed, all right? I didn't think he'd do that. It goes against everything I know about the man."

"Everything you *think* you know," Abby paused, her fingers curling around her open water bottle. "Do you really know Damien Fox at all?"

———

Did I know Damien Fox at all?

If any question was ever worth a million bucks, it was that one.

I thought I did. Maybe it was a pre-conceived notion, sure. But it was an idea of the kind of person he was, at the very least. Sure, it was almost entirely made up of rumors and hearsay, of opinions from everyone other than myself, but was that a bad thing?

Rumors weren't always true, after all. Hearsay was generally just that.

The only person whose opinion I truly trusted where he was concerned was Mia's. Even then, by her own admission, she didn't know much about him at all.

Why did I care?

That was the second million-dollar question.

Why did I stop to think about who he really was? It didn't matter to me. Not really. It was nothing more than a fleeting, curious thought...That wasn't so fleeting at all.

It was more than that.

It was fleeting in its quickness—each and every time it passed my mind. The need to know who Damien truly was flashed like a bolt of lightning, consuming me for the split second it existed, only to peter out into the darkness once more.

The frequency of the thought was getting greater. The shout louder. The length longer.

It was becoming something more intriguing and consuming than I was prepared for.

Not that I was prepared for anything. The past several months had taught me to prepare for everything except what I expected.

I'd known that Damien Fox was a hard sell and that getting rid of him would be near to impossible, but I never thought it'd be anything like this.

I never thought he'd filter his way into my thoughts when I was in my own time...Like when I was sitting at the bar of Rock Solid, Mia's husband's bar.

I'd been staring at gyrating male bodies for at least thirty minutes, yet that's all they were. Hot guys moving their hips in a way that should be illegal.

SIN

West Rykman rested his forearms on the bar in front of me and slid me a small, clear shot with a deft flick of his finger. "Drink."

I didn't question it.

I threw it back and pushed the glass back toward him. "Is that it?"

He laughed, his handsome face crinkling. "Mia told me to give you something strong. She said if the words 'Dahlia' and 'Damien' were in the same sentence, it called for shots."

I couldn't imagine where she got that idea.

"History might support that," I admitted, staring at the empty glass. "But that was only one."

Wordlessly, he poured another and gave it to me.

I drank it with the finesse of the last one. I even dribbled a bit of the vodka and had to wipe my mouth, something that made West chuckle.

I flipped him the bird. "I'm too grown up for my age."

"Mia would agree with you," he called, pouring vodka into a tall glass. He added cranberry and handed it to me. "No ice, so you know I'm not screwing with you on the vodka."

I fought my smirk when he winked. "Mia is right."

"Mia's always right."

"Only because she's your wife."

"Shh. She might hear you." He grinned. "So, Damien Fox, huh."

"I did hear you," Mia said, slipping onto the seat next to me. "And I'm not sure she wants to hear what you have to say about him."

I glanced between my fiery-haired friend and her husband. "Actually..."

West sighed and reached for a wine glass. Less than a minute later, he'd handed Mia a glass of wine and we were following him upstairs to the office space that occupied the second floor of Rock Solid's building.

He sat on the large corner sofa and leaned back. "You have to know by now that not many people know much about Damien."

"But you're friends." I took a seat at the end, cradling my glass in my lap.

"That doesn't mean I know much."

Mia snorted. "You know more than you told me when I asked you."

"When you interrogated me, you mean." West glanced in her direction.

She sat on his desk and waved her hand. "Ask, interrogate…Po-tay-to, poh-tah-to."

He stared at her for a moment longer before flitting his attention to me. "There are a lot of rumors about the Fox family. Do you know many?"

I shook my head.

"I figured. Your dad wouldn't have told you unless you needed to know, which apparently, you didn't."

"You knew my dad?"

West nodded. "We did some business. Small things. He helped me with a supplier when mine went bust and took fifty grand of my money." His expression tightened. "I owe him a lot. Fifty grand to be exact, and now, you. If you need anything in the future…"

I swallowed. I hated talking money and hearing how much my dad used it to help others… "Donate it. I don't need it. Cancer charities need it more."

He stared at me for only a second before a slight smile touched his lips. "I'll write a check tonight."

Mia sniffed. "Sorry. Period."

West didn't bat an eyelid. "Rather you crying than shouting about the milk being on the wrong shelf."

"Everything has a place, West, even the milk."

I sipped to control my laughter.

"Anyway," West continued, turning so he was fully facing me. "The Fox family didn't become so predominant in Vegas without some scandal. It's been a generational thing, that's for sure. The...legend, if you call it that, says that Damien's grandfather screwed a casino out of half a million dollars. He used that to open a brothel operating as a dance show. He was caught and put in prison, but his son— Damien's dad—got control of the business. He was old enough to use it wisely and funneled it into strip clubs." He paused. "The next rumors are more personal, and while I don't feel entirely comfortable, you asked, and, well, he's never confirmed or denied them to me."

"Did you ever ask?"

"Once. Never again." He ran his hand through his hair. "When he was a child, his mom apparently left his dad. Some stuff happened, and then some tragedy followed it, and the family has never been the same since."

Hmm.

Now, I was the one who didn't feel entirely comfortable.

"That sounds like the makings of an HBO show," Mia noted, sipping her wine. "Nobody's life is that dramatic."

"Bravo would disagree with you," I replied.

She tilted her glass in deference.

"But what about him?" I asked West. "He's done nothing but annoy the crap out of me for a couple weeks now, and I know nothing about the man."

Except the fact he has a damn big cock and the filthy mouth to match it.

"He's a good guy," West said simply. "His business might not be totally above board, but we all break the rules once in a while. Personally, he's not a bad person. He's just private, and there's no crime in being private."

No, there wasn't.

But that was the problem, wasn't it?

12

DAMIEN

I leaned against the wall, barely ten feet from the pure black headstone with my mother's name on it.

Her name was engraved in white, but the morning sunlight glinted off it as if it were silver. It was almost blinding to look at the stone—but always painful. The stone was perfectly polished, but the grass was only barely trimmed. Weeds licked at the back and sides of the memorial, too leafy and green to be grass or wildflowers.

Not that wildflowers would grow here. It was a miracle the grass did.

She was closer to the desert than the city. Tucked out of the way, safely away from the hubbub and remembrance of the city she'd called home her entire life.

A glance to the headstone to her right reminded me that it didn't matter how far away she was; she was never alone.

I ignored it. That one hurt more than my mother's.

That stone belonged to the catalyst.

The person who, through no fault of their own, destroyed everything.

Who shredded my life as I once knew it.

Looking at their name was almost too much to bear. Sometimes, I could do it. Other times, it was unthinkable.

Today was one of those other days. It hurt too much. It was one of the days where I wish I had my mother here to talk to. It was a day where I wished I pay every cent I had just to get one answer from her. To hear her voice for a split second would be worth everything I owned. I'd sell my soul to feel her hug me again—to be wrapped in her warm embrace and be enveloped by the smell of warm vanilla and lavender.

The memory of my mother was more than my life was worth. I was sure of few things, but that was one of them.

Cold stone dug into my back through my t-shirt.

It was like ice, despite the blazing heat from the sun overhead.

My mom's name was still nothing but a mass of reflection from the light.

Yet, I stared.

I stared until I was blinded.

Until my phone buzzed in my pocket.

Until I turned out of the tucked-away cemetery and headed back to the city, ignoring the buzzing against my thigh.

My feet pounded against the asphalt rhythmically. I couldn't say that I liked running—I tolerated it. It was an excellent stress reliever. There was something soothing about the pounding of my feet against the concrete paths that lined the city that beat the emotion right out of me.

Emotion was easy to hold on to. It gripped hold of you like an icy winter, clinging until it was forced out by something stronger—something warmer.

Running was that for me.

A way of ridding myself, even momentarily, of the dark cloud that hung over me every day. Far from enjoyable but, dare I say it, now necessary. Necessary to shake off the occasional nightmare and more than occasional memory.

Maybe after all these years I should have been able to sleep better than I did. Maybe I should have been man enough to admit that the reason nobody was allowed to contact me before one p.m. wasn't because I was sleeping but because I was running. Because I was escaping, taking in the past so I could confront the present.

That was what grief was. Accepting the past and confronting the past. The future had jack-all to do with it. It was collateral damage to the pain that wavered daily.

At least, that's how it was to me.

Today, it was painful.

Mom's birthday always was.

I wanted—needed—to forget her. She'd been my Achilles heel when she was alive and now, even in her death, she was still. God only knew she'd put herself in some dumb situations, but it was the final one that always got me—the one where I wasn't able to help her.

Where I couldn't save her.

Where no amount of punches I took for her would have mattered.

I slowed outside the coffee shop I'd parked outside earlier and scrubbed my hand through my hair. Sweaty, dirty, dank—I was a sight and scent for sore eyes, but it was barely eight. The only people awake were those who ran, like me, and the ones who had a job to get to.

Entering the small shop, I was able to get straight to the counter. The blond behind the counter was the same young girl who served me at least five days a week, but I was fucked if I knew her name. She momentarily frowned when I ordered two coffees instead of one, but she recovered quickly enough that anybody else wouldn't notice the change in her demeanor.

Within seconds, she was back to her usual, flirtatious self. Usually, it wouldn't bother me. I'd welcome it. Relish it, even. It would be a regular part of my day.

Today, I wanted her to shut the hell up and make my fucking coffee.

The minutes felt like a goddamn hour, and I grunted my "Thank you" as I paid. Then, once she'd printed the receipt I didn't care about, I grabbed the cup holder and left.

SIN

If today were a few weeks ago, before I met Dahlia, I might have used the barista to make myself feel better. For my own selfish needs. There was no doubt she'd look damn pretty on her knees in front of me—but now, that thought mildly annoyed me.

The only person I wanted on their knees in front of me came with dark hair, blue eyes, and a cutting tongue.

I nestled the coffees onto the passenger seat before rounding the car and getting in the driver's side. I had no idea if the woman currently consuming my thoughts was even at home, but hell, I'd done the thing I never did and bought her a coffee, so I was gonna go there anyway.

Ten minutes later, I was permitted past the security that surrounded her estate and drove through the large, black gates. While I'd known her address the moment I'd looked her up, I'd assumed she lived inside a community and that the gates that surrounded her property were part of that, but I was wrong. They were personal—hers. The gates protected only her house.

I pulled up the gravel driveway at a snail's pace. I couldn't remember the last time I was nervous, but right now, as I put my car into park and twisted the key from the ignition, nerves tickled across my skin.

How would Dahlia react to me when, the last time we'd spoken, she'd blown me off and I'd been nothing but short and sharp with her?

In my defense—she'd pissed me off. While she was stern and organized professionally, she was the complete opposite personally. She was flaky and indecisive, the kind of person who needed corralling into just about everything.

Well, damn it.

The woman would have dinner with me at my house if it meant I had to throw her on my shoulder in her pajamas and fucking carry her there myself.

I gripped the coffee holder tight as I approached her front door. Wide, curved steps accented the rich, mahogany doors that were elaborately engraved, and my foot had barely hit the top step when one of those doors swung open.

Dahlia stood there in front of me, wearing a form-fitting, pale-pink dress and a scowl.

"Good morning, sunshine," I drawled. "Is that the expression you usually have when someone brings you coffee?"

"Actually," she said slowly, her eyes flitting between my t-shirt and the coffee, "I think it's one that only developed when I met you."

My lips tugged to one side. "Coffee?" I held the cups out to her.

"What's this? A peace offering?"

"I guess you could say that."

"Do you regularly turn up to women's houses post-workout with them?"

"I haven't given a peace offering since I was thirteen and ripped the head off my little sister's Barbie." The words slipped out of my mouth before I could stop them. I froze for the briefest moment, a nauseating feeling ripping through my stomach, but if she noticed, she didn't address it.

Instead, she shrugged a shoulder and pointed to the coffee on the left. "Mine?"

"Whichever. They're the same."

"I suppose I should let you in." She stepped back, pushing the door open a little more.

"Is the ice queen thawing this morning?"

"You brought coffee. If I were a tornado, I'd pause my destruction for coffee." Laughing, she turned, leaving me to close the door.

It clicked shut behind me, and I cast my attention over a surprisingly warm hallway. A curved staircase took up a good portion of the space to my right, and just below it to its left was a deep red chaise accented by a giant bouquet of white roses in a vase fit for a damn castle. Photos covered the walls. Dahlia's life was chronicled the way most people used photo albums and, these days, social media.

From newborn to kindergarten. There were parties and graduations and smiles and friends. Laughter and love practically fell out of the images. The only thing that said that this was a broken family was the fact that, about a third of the way along the wall, three family members became two.

Her mom disappeared.

Pausing, I stepped up to the last photo of her on the wall. It was of her and Dahlia, and if I didn't know better, I'd say I was staring at Dahlia as an adult herself. Her mom had the same, soft curves to her face. The same full lips that curved into a similar smile. The same thick, dark hair Dahlia did. The only difference was the eyes—her mom's were light where hers were indigo.

Dahlia cleared her throat, causing me to look in her direction. "You'd be a riot at a party."

I half-grinned as she approached me and took the coffees. Hesitating only a moment, I said softly, "You look just like her."

She took a deep breath and forced a smile.

It didn't reach her eyes.

Not even close.

She turned and led me into a spacious kitchen. The light-brown cupboards gave the open space a rustic, farmhouse feel, and that was only exaggerated by the vintage-looking table on the other side of the room and the homey decorations that adorned the walls.

She placed the coffees on the long, curved breakfast bar and pulled them both from the holder. I leaned against the countertop as she threw the holder in the trash.

"I'd rather I didn't," she replied, her voice barely above a whisper. "Look like my mom. It would easier if I didn't see her when I looked in the mirror." Sad eyes glanced at me, but before I could apologize, she chirped up, "Cream and sugar?"

"There's already cream in them. No sugars, because I didn't know how you like it." If she could gloss over my freezing at the mention of my sister, I wouldn't apologize for her pain.

What would I be apologizing for, anyway? I'd only be saying sorry that she'd been genetically blessed but that life hadn't blessed her the same way.

She slid a small pot of sugar toward me. "In case you want it. And, for future reference, should you need to make peace with coffee again, I take one sugar in my coffee, but two in my tea."

"Fancy." I grinned as I put two sugars in my cup. "But that information is noted. Whether I'll remember it or not is another matter entirely."

With a roll of her eyes, she dumped a heaped teaspoon of sugar into her coffee.

"Oh, come on. That was at least two teaspoons!"

A guilty smile crept over her face. "Technically speaking, it's one. It's just a big one."

"Is this like when women in the movies eat salads so their dates don't think they're greedy?"

"If it were, you'd be a serial killer in your sweaty, muddy t-shirt." She pointed her spoon toward a mark at the side of my shirt that I hadn't even noticed until now. "That, or a porn movie where a runner thinks they're being followed and knocks on the door of a random house."

"That would be more effective if our roles were reversed."

"True." She gave her coffee one final stir and threw the spoon behind her into the sink. "So. A peace offering, huh?"

I sipped my coffee. "Yep. For being rude on the phone to you yesterday."

"Who are you and what did you do with Damien Fox?"

"I told you—I'm his charming twin brother. I broke out of my cupboard under the stairs when he turned his back."

"There's a name for people who have voices in their heads, you know."

"Yeah, they're called authors. You have an entire bar based around them."

Dahlia paused. Then, she laughed. She threw her head back and she freaking laughed—gently yet loudly. "Well played, Mr. Fox," she managed to say through her giggles. "Apology accepted, by the way. I'm sorry for bailing on dinner."

"Nothing came up, did it?"

"Maybe."

I stared at her. She wasn't going to budge. "All right, but now, you owe me."

"I owe you?"

"You owe me. What are you doing right now?"

"Uhh." She paused, but she met my eyes. "Trying to think of literally anything I could be doing that doesn't involve you?"

Grinning, I said, "Come and have breakfast with me."

"At your house?"

I shook my head. "But I do need to go and get changed. I can pick you up here or at the bar."

She sighed. "I'll be here. Just don't take forever. I have to work."

I held my hands up. "I have an interview at eleven-thirty. Give me half an hour. I'll be right here."

13

DAHLIA

Apparently, my days were a string of bad decisions lately. The first? Agreeing to dinner with Damien. The second? Canceling that dinner. The third? Opening my front door to him this morning.

Well, maybe the last one wasn't. It wasn't like I didn't know it was him at my door—hell, when Dustin called me with his name, I could have had him send Damien away. The only reason I didn't was because I knew that I had to face him sooner or later, and the longer he was in my life, the more I realized that 'sooner' was the better option where he was concerned.

I had to be realistic. The more I put him off, the more persistent he'd become, and the more likely he ultimately was to drop into the bar, completely unannounced and on his own schedule.

Not to mention the fact I'd seen him on the camera as he'd approached the front door.

I'd watched as his car ambled up the driveway, as he'd slowly gotten out of it, as he'd grabbed the coffees and made his way to the door. The entire time, he'd had the saddest look on his face, made only more noticeable when he'd left his car. His lips had been turned down, his eyes hooded, his shoulders slumped…He was barely a shadow of the man who usually presented himself to me.

I couldn't put my finger on it, but there was just…something. Something about him and the way he held himself that was different. He'd tried to hide it, but he couldn't hide it in his eyes.

112

I wanted to know what was hiding behind that fake smile and those sad eyes. I wanted to know why, for a few minutes, he'd been so different to the controlled, unemotional man he appeared to be.

What was the pain he was hiding? What was buried beneath the cold, apparently unfeeling exterior?

I was curious by nature.

Curiosity killed the cat.

I was face-to-face with a Fox.

Inquisitiveness wasn't the best way to go about dealing with him, but hey. I was an idiot. That much was painfully obvious.

I snatched my purse up from the passenger seat and got out of my car. The place Damien had picked—and then asked my opinion on—was small and out of the way, tucked down a side road a thousand miles away from anywhere tourists would choose to go. I'd never been here, hell, I'd never heard of it, so I planned to step outside my comfort zone and defer to Damien on what to eat.

He was standing outside the door to the tiny bistro when I approached him. "You found it okay," he greeted me, hitting a button on a key fob. The lights on a sleek, black BMW blinked twice as it locked.

I glanced at the car. "You've driven yourself twice in one morning. Is it your chauffeur's day off?"

He laughed and opened the door. "I only use him when I need him. My morning run and breakfast with a beautiful woman aren't any of those times."

"But dinner is?"

"Of course. The back seat isn't fun by yourself, is it?"

He was back to his normal, sexy self, it seemed.

We sat at a small table in the back corner. It was well lit by the large window that allowed just enough sunlight through, and we both settled in with the menus.

"What do you recommend?" I peered up over the top of the foldout, cardboard menu.

Damien raised an eyebrow, meeting my gaze. "You can't decide?"

"I've never been here. I don't know what's good." I gave my most innocent, one-shouldered shrug.

"The California omelet with the French toast."

I waited for him to continue with another suggestion, but he didn't. "Just that?"

"I've never ordered anything else. I got it the first time I came here and it's too good to get anything else."

"Well, that was easy enough." I put my menu back into the holder and folded my hands on the table in front of me.

He stared at me for a moment before doing the same. "You look shocked."

"I didn't think you'd pay any attention to what I said." He scratched his jaw. "You generally do the exact opposite of what I recommend."

"You brought me coffee this morning. I'm feeling amicable." I half-smiled as the waitress came over.

We placed our order for the same thing, me adding an iced vanilla latte and him adding a regular coffee. Once she'd left after a lingering look at Damien, I suppressed my eye-roll and looked out the window. There was nothing to see, just the shops on the other side of the street slowly opening. Lights flicked on, shutters raised, and signs flipped in the window. They were more boutique stores, more catered to the individuals who dared walk down this out-of-the-way street than the kitschy, touristy ones I normally saw.

And of course, there were the people. The men in suits and women in smart dresses, not unlike the two of us at this table. Parents wrangled children, clutching at their hands to keep them out of the road. A young girl ran past in yoga pants with her headphones in, lips moving as she sang along.

I could watch people all day, and in this city, there was no shortage of diversity.

A fact that was proven as a gentleman teetered past the window in three-inch heels and a bright, red wig.

Ahh, Vegas.

"You know," Damien said, "if this were any other city, I'd be alarmed right now."

I peered over at him. He had a slight smile on his face as he looked out of the window, too.

"Me too. It's more normal than not."

"You've got something on your mind." He slowly turned back to face me, his expression unreadable.

I propped my chin up on my hand as our coffees were delivered. "I just inherited a multi-million-dollar business. I have a hell of a lot on my mind."

He inclined his head. "More than usual, then."

"I am wondering why you showed up at my house this morning."

"I'm wondering why you didn't have your guard turn me away at the gate."

"So am I." I fought a smile. "Color me intrigued. You generally blindside me at work—it's not like you to announce yourself."

"I was feeling generous this morning. Blindsiding you hasn't exactly worked in my favor so far, has it?"

"True." I sipped my coffee. "But neither has your attitude. Although, that does seem to have improved."

"I'm trying the charm offensive. Is this working?"

"Better than before. I might actually—shock horror—be starting to like you a little."

"Enough for dinner?"

"Enough that I might get through this breakfast without considering the quickest way to kill you."

"You're so delightful, Ms. Lloyd. This explains why I can't stay away from you."

"The reason you can't stay away, Mr. Fox, is because you still want to buy my bar," I drawled, not bothering to hide any of the dryness in my tone. "Don't think I've forgotten that fact."

He held his hands up, sitting back as a grin stretched across his face. "I'd be amiss in thinking you had."

"You continue to surprise me with your intelligence."

"I think that was a compliment."

I smiled. "It was the closest you'll get to one today."

Damien laughed and adjusted his sleeve. "I'll take it."

Then, our breakfast arrived, cutting short our conversation. We ate in a somewhat awkward silence, except for him asking me if the food was good. It was—of course it was, and he knew that. The question was whether or not he meant it or whether he'd asked just to break up the awkwardness for a second. Either one, I didn't care, because it *had* broken the silence and the awkwardness, and for that, I was thankful.

I hated silence around him. I never knew what he was thinking. When he knew you were watching, he clammed up. That was something I'd slowly realized over the past several days. He played his cards close to his chest, and he was exactly who I'd want on my poker team, that was for sure. Emotion and feelings were shared as and when he deemed fit.

Otherwise, he was the human version of Pandora's box. Who the fuck knew what was going on behind those dark, brown eyes?

Not me.

Sometimes, I didn't want to know.

No, I used to not want to know. I simply wanted to rid him from my life.

While I didn't necessarily want to keep him in my life, I wanted to know everything about him before he disappeared.

If he did.

I was spending too much time with him for him to disappear easily.

My phone rang when I was halfway through eating. I hesitated, but Damien motioned for me to get it with a wave of his finger, so I pulled my phone from my purse and excused myself from the table.

Stepping outside into the already sweltering heat, I answered Abby's call. "Hey. What's up?"

"Fergus is dying," she drawled. "Barry is sleeping in the back. I forgot to tell him that Fergus was in early today so he had to leave early."

I rubbed my hand across my head. Barry wasn't a bad guy—he was just homeless. I knew nothing about him except he sometimes helped out in the basement hauling stuff around for a cup of coffee, fifty dollars, and permission to sleep on the step of the back door. Like my father, I'd once tried to offer him a place to stay, but he accepted a shower and simply moved on. He was happy, and who was I to judge that?

Fergus, however…

Well, he was a bitch.

"Give him a Xanax and a shot of vodka and tell him you've moved the scary man on," I answered.

"Tried it. Except it was ibuprofen, and that was for me because his scream has given me a headache. I'm going to fire him if he doesn't stop breathing into that paper bag in a minute."

I had an assistant manager who was a diva and a manager who didn't suffer fools.

I needed to rethink my staffing.

"I'll be right there." I sighed. There was no way of getting out of this. I had no doubts she would fire him—and despite the fact I was the one who had the final say, it would do nothing but cause Fergus to need an ambulance. "Avoid Fergus. Give Barry his coffee and have him help you do the order when it gets there."

"Gotcha." She hung up.

I headed back inside. "I'm sorry," I said to Damien. "I have to go. Fergus is having a breakdown."

He raised his eyebrows, more in amusement than in shock if the slight curve of his lips was anything to go by. "I don't envy you that."

I paused. "Right. You know each other." How well did they know each other? And why didn't I know more about that? "How do you know each other?"

"His story, not mine." He chuckled and threw fifty dollars down on the table. Way too much for the breakfast, even with the tip. "I'll come with you. I've seen one or two of those from him. What set him off?"

I grabbed my purse. "We have a homeless man who comes around every now and then—sleeps on the back steps. He does some odd jobs and stuff for us. Totally harmless. The first time Fergus saw him, he freaked out, so now we've got a system. I don't even see him half the time, but this morning, Fergus took the early shift with Abby and Barry was sleeping outside."

Damien chuckled, opening the door for me. "I know Barry. He does the same for most of us on the Strip. He's a good guy."

"Do you know why he's homeless?"

"Not a clue, but then again, I've never asked." He pulled his car keys out of his pocket. "I'll see you at the bar?"

It sounded like a question. Like he was asking my permission to come with me, although he'd already said he'd come.

I hesitated for a moment, flicking my gaze over his face. "All right. Just don't kill my manager."

He smiled slowly and stepped toward his car. "No promises."

———

I pulled up to The Scarlet Letter just seconds before Damien did. By the time I had my key out, he was standing right behind me, close enough that I could feel his breath on my shoulder.

I needed to wear a dress with sleeves thicker than a spaghetti strap around him.

I bit the inside of my cheek at his closeness and, in a show of control, dropped my keys to the ground.

Awesome.

He laughed, bending to pick them up. "Here," he said in a low tone, straightening. "Let me." He touched one hand to my waist and leaned around me, smoothly inserting the key into the keyhole and twisting.

"Thank you." My throat and mouth were both dry, so the words came out croakily. I swiped my tongue across my lips and took the keys when he offered them to me.

"You're welcome," he said into my hair. His lips brushed my hair, and in one less-than-graceful motion, I yanked open the door and threw myself through it into the bar.

His laughter was just loud enough for me to catch it.

I hated that he knew that he affected me like this.

Attraction was such a bitch.

"I hate you," I hissed back over my shoulder.

"But you'd still fuck me." He laughed, pushing me inside and closing the door.

I shook off his hands and stalked through the bar. Fergus' wailing traveled down the back hall from the staffroom, and Abby popped up from behind the bar. Her hair was scrunched into a bun on top of her head, her mascara was smudged beneath her left eye, and her eyes said she wanted to kill me.

"You've got a little…" Damien rubbed under his left eye.

She turned her death glare on him. "I was doing my makeup when Fergus screamed. I poked myself in the eye with the mascara wand. Would you like me to show you how that feels?"

"Let's not," I jumped in, shooting Damien a glare of my own before he said something else to deliberately piss her off. "Waterproof mascara?"

"Mhmm," she hummed in reply.

"Where is Fergus?"

"Locked in the staff room. I tried to put him in the corner, but he wouldn't stay there."

Damien burst out laughing.

"The corner? Dear God, Abs. He's not a damn toddler."

119

She stared at me, expressionless. "Watch his tantrum on the security tapes and tell me different."

Chalk and cheese. They made chalk and cheese look like friends.

I shook my head and headed back to the staff room. She tried to put him in the corner? How had they co-existed running this place while I was in California? In hindsight, I should have expected to come back to the building burnt down. Or one of their houses at the very least.

Hmm.

Maybe that was how I got Damien to leave me alone.

No.

Arson was not the answer. The idea of it was pretty fun, though.

I unlocked the staff room door and pushed it open. "What the hell?"

Fergus was sitting on the sofa, wide-eyed. "There was a homeless man sleeping on the step."

"Did he touch you?"

"No."

"Did he speak to you?"

"No."

"Did he do anything even remotely human toward you?"

"No."

"Then this is ridiculous." I planted my hands on my hips. "You know Barry helps us out. Or is this just because you and Reggie are still fighting?"

He burst into tears.

This wasn't in my job description.

"That was insensitive," Damien murmured, leaning in close to me. "You could have been a little nicer."

What?

"What else am I supposed to do? Hug him? This is his own fault," I muttered right back. I was fully aware that I sounded like a petulant child, but whatever.

"I'm just saying, you could have been a little nicer to him. He's obviously hurt."

SIN

"Oh, so you're all for being nice to him, but you'll asshole your way through life around me?"

"Pretty much."

"Do you mind?" Fergus wailed, throwing himself forward and hitting the coffee table. "I am having a crisis! Can you have your lover's spat later?"

Damien tilted his head to the side. "If he were a woman, I'd be blaming PMS right now."

"I may as well be a woman!" Fergus flung his arm through the air, falling back against the sofa cushions. "No man wants me! If I were a woman, I could be a lesbian!"

"Or you could, you know. Just be straight," I pointed out.

"Just be straight, she says!"

Oh, God. *What have I done?*

"You know what else isn't straight? Roundabouts! Would you walk up to a roundabout and ask why it isn't a square? No, you wouldn't. You'd accept its bentness and embrace it."

"You're the one who said you wanted to date women."

"Only if I were a woman. Then I'd still be gay. But you're judging me!"

Damien coughed. Hard.

If he was smothering a laugh, I would kill him.

"Fergus." He stepped forward and crouched in front of my hysterical employee. "You've gotta calm down, man. I know you're upset, but shrieking isn't getting us anywhere. Is it Reggie?"

"It's always Reggie! Do you know what he said?" Fergus blinked at Damien in earnest. "He said we need a break because I'm dramatic. Dramatic! How could he say that?"

I leaned against the doorframe. "I can't possibly imagine."

Both Fergus and Damien turned to me. One was scowling and the other was fighting a smirk.

It wasn't hard to guess who was who.

"I can't believe you're so flippant about this. I'm heartbroken, Dahlia."

"You're also a thirty-two-year-old man who's crying over a homeless guy sleeping on the step and being called dramatic. Take a look at yourself, Ferg. This is dramatic. I'm gonna get Bravo on the phone and see if they can get you into a Real Housewives of Las Vegas or something."

He opened his mouth as if he were going to gasp, then, he froze. What left him was a sigh, and he slumped right back into himself. "You're right. I'm a mess."

"I wouldn't say a total mess, but you're definitely leaking around the edges."

He sniffed. "Can we talk about something else? Like when you two are going to go away and fuck?"

14

DAHLIA

"Never. There, conversation closed." I pushed off the doorframe and crossed to the coffee machine. "Let's talk about how you're going to get Reggie back."

"Not calling Bravo would be a good start," Damien suggested, getting up from his crouched position.

"I don't want to talk about it. I need to do something useful." Fergus flicked a bit of lint from his jeans. "Something else. Let's talk about something else."

"Like how you two know each other?" I smiled innocently, looking at both men.

Fergus pouted.

"That's the second time today," Damien said, looking at Fergus. "I'm surprised she doesn't already know."

"Well, I didn't exactly put you down as a reference," Fergus snapped.

My jaw dropped. "Oh my God! You—holy shit!"

He rolled his eyes. "Oh, please. Now who's being dramatic? I stripped. Started in college and left when I got this job."

"I'm not being dramatic, I'm just surprised."

Damien choked back a laugh. "How else do you think we know each other? No offense," he said, glancing at Fergus, "but he's not someone I'd generally meet in a bar."

I opened my mouth and closed it. God, I had to look like a thirsty fish doing that, but I was shocked. I couldn't imagine Fergus naked and dancing on a pole. More to the point, I didn't *want* to imagine Fergus naked and dancing on a pole.

"None taken," Fergus said. "I wouldn't want to meet you in a bar either."

Damien grinned.

"Wait! Is that how you met Reggie?" I asked, gripping the edge of the counter.

Fergus nodded. "He was only at the bar three weeks when I asked him out. He thought I was joking—a lot of the guys who work in the gay bars aren't gay, you know? And he was in the closet, so it was a long process."

As much as I loved him, and I did, I didn't want to hear about his dating exploits with Reggie, given the current state of that relationship. Fergus had a tendency to over-share. Not that his dramatic streak made that obvious at all.

"Right, yeah, well." I scratched the side of my neck. "Barry is helping Abby with the order. Do you think you can control yourself now?"

He sighed. "I didn't recognize him without his beard. If someone had told me…"

"We try to make sure he's not around when you are. For this reason."

If he was offended, he didn't show it. "Well, thanks. Maybe if he were around, I would have noticed."

I couldn't win with him. "Fergus?"

"Yeah?"

"Go work, would you? The books all need checking to make sure they're in right places."

"But—"

I stared at him flatly. I wasn't interested in his displeasure in the job, because it was part of all our jobs, and I'd just done it last week. The schedule said it was his turn, so it was his turn.

He got up from the sofa with a sigh so loud it was as if I'd just asked him to birth a baby giraffe from his asshole. Thankfully, he didn't complain as he left the room. I was pretty sure he mumbled under his breath as he went, but hey. He went. And that was all I cared about.

Double bonus because he shut the door behind him.

"I'm exhausted." I slumped against the counter. "It's like looking after a child when he gets like that."

"Try running a bar full of them," Damien drawled. "That looks like heaven after some of the scenes I've witnessed."

"Try being a girl in high school." It was all I had to shoot back. Also, it probably wasn't that far off the mark in general.

"I'd rather not. I much preferred looking at the girls in high school."

"Cute. You think you grew out of that."

"I did. I look at women now."

"Good for you."

He grinned, his eyes finding mine. "It sure is when you're the woman I'm looking at."

I pursed my lips. "You've gone from tolerable to annoying real quick."

"I take that as a compliment," he said quietly, closing the distance between us in a split second. "Annoying you works in my favor often."

"It really doesn't." I straightened, turning to face him fully. "And to think, this morning, I almost liked you."

Damien planted his hands on the counter on either side of me. Dark eyes met mine for the briefest second before he dipped his face, rubbing his stubbled jaw against my cheek as his lips found my ear. "You like me a lot more than you pretend to," he whispered. "A hell of a lot more, Dahlia. Your pretense is nothing more than amusing now."

"My pretense? The only thing I'm pretending against is my desire to kick you straight in the balls."

"I like you." His lips never left my earlobe, his hands never moving from their position on the counter on either side of me. "I like you a lot, sweetheart. I like the way you purse those pretty, red lips of yours. I like the way you hate me so much with your eyes. I like the way you shiver when I touch you, the way you pretend I don't affect you and carry on. But I do, don't I? I affect you more than you care to admit, which is why you fight it so much. You don't hate me because I'm an asshole—you hate me because you like the fact I'm an asshole."

"You sound like a dick jock from a teen movie."

"You think you disprove my point by saying that."

"I think you're an overgrown douchebag who left his adulting at his high school graduation."

"I think you'd still fuck me if you had the chance."

"I think you're the most insufferably arrogant human being I've ever had a conversation with." I smacked his arm away from the counter, but my pathetic attempt didn't even buckle his elbow. "Just when I think you might be halfway decent, you open your mouth and prove me wrong yet again."

He leaned in, cupping my jaw. "There are other things I could do with my mouth that would prove you right."

"I doubt it. I'm sure they'd all prove you to be a dick."

"If you want a dick, I can oblige there, too."

"Not yours," I snapped.

"Dahlia." His fingers tightened, splaying from my chin to my neck, holding my face perfectly in position. His lips were inches from mine when he spoke again. "Sweetheart, if you had any idea what I could do with my mouth, you'd be on your back with my face between your legs."

A shiver rushed down my spine.

"I did gymnastics for fifteen years. Put your face between my legs and I'll crush your skull."

He laughed low. "You were a gymnast? That doesn't make me less attracted to you. That tells me you're flexible."

"You're right, I am. I can suck your dick and kick you in the head at the same time."

"That defies physics."

"So does the fact you won't shut the fuck up."

More laughter. More spine-tingling laughter combined with a heart pounding tightening of his fingers as they slid along my skin.

SIN

He gripped his fingers into my hair, wrapping his strong hand around the base of my skull and pulling me closer to him. A breath of air separated our lips, and I knew that my strong exhale danced across his lips the way every one of his breaths did to mine. "There are plenty of things I can do that are better than shutting up. I could talk, read you a story, quote Shakespeare…"

His eyes met mine.

"Kiss the fuck out of you."

The deep breath I'd been missing came hard.

"Don't you—"

"Dare?" he breathed in response. "Why? You gonna stop me, sweetheart? If I hoisted you onto that counter and kissed you, you'd push me away? Try again—tell me another fucking fairytale, because you'd melt."

"Once upon a time, the princess knight met an asshole masquerading as a prince. She kicked his ass," I snapped, once again pushing his arm out of the way.

This time, it worked.

His arm buckled, freeing enough space for me to scoot aside.

I failed in my escape.

Damien gripped my wrist.

Tugged.

Yanked.

Pushed.

Shoved.

My ass pressed against the counter behind me.

His chest slammed to mine.

My heart pounded.

His fingers slipped between mine.

My hands pressed to the cold stone.

His knee pushed through my thighs.

My stomach flipped.

His lips touched mine.

Firmly.

Fearlessly.

127

Ferociously.

I breathed him in.

Gasped.

Faltered.

Sighed.

I melted into him. Into the way his fingers wove through my hair. Into the way his body fit against mine. Into the way I slipped my hands up his firm body and gripped onto his collar like nothing else mattered but that.

Because, maybe, nothing else did.

Maybe in that moment, all that mattered was the way Damien Fox's lips felt as they explored my own.

As he gripped me so tightly I was sure I'd have bruises from his fingertips.

As I slid fully onto the counter with the help of his deft fingers, my dress inching up the more my legs opened for him to slip between my thighs.

As I took his kiss, as smooth as silk.

His hands explored my thighs as I wrapped my arms around his neck and pulled him into me, forgoing common sense for hormones, intuition for impulse. He felt so right as our bodies connected; his hot skin against mine as his tongue battled mine and our limbs entangled on top of the counter I was still perched upon.

It was all so right.

So free.

So exhilarating.

So reckless.

So wildly wrong.

Because this was wrong. I knew it. Every brush of his fingers and every pinch of his fingers was wrong, yet I couldn't stop. He was Heaven and Hell and all the sins in between.

This kiss wasn't just a sin, and neither was he.

It was the sin.

He was the ultimate sin.

And against everything I believed, I was indulging. Carelessly indulging despite all the reasons I needed to stop.

Damien cupped the back of my head, sliding his tongue over my tender lower lip. The scratchy stubble on his jaw rubbed against my chin as he kissed me slower, moving his lips almost lazily over mine.

Savoring it, almost. Tasting me softly. Teasing me slowly.

If a kiss could be used as a weapon in battle, his fighting ability would be unparalleled.

And the fact that he'd been right about me melting under his kiss was really, really fucking annoying, I realized as he pulled his lips from mine.

Yet, I couldn't speak. Through the racing of my heart, I couldn't breathe easily. Regulating each breath was a chore, a fight against the desire that had gripped hold of my entire body and demanded that I kiss him again—that I take more than just a kiss.

The inner battle that waged as it raced through my blood tied me up in knots. One minute I had to kiss him again, the other I wanted to shove him away from me for taking that kiss without asking me. Not that he *had* to ask me, and it wasn't like I objected to being kissed like, well, *that*, but still.

He was a man who took what he wanted without reproach.

I was a woman who hated giving people like him what they wanted.

Damien slid his hand around to my face, cupping the side of my jaw. His thumb brushed over my cheek, sweeping over my flushed skin until I opened my eyes, only to look straight into the dark abyss of his gaze.

The dark, lusty, restrained stare that almost glared back at me.

"Dinner. Tonight," he said in a low voice that gave no room for arguments. "I'll pick you up at six-thirty."

I darted my tongue out and wet my lower lip. "I'm working."

"Until when?"

"Eight."

"Then I'll be here at eight." He pressed a firm yet hasty kiss to my lips, released me, and stalked across the room.

I didn't know if that kiss was to annoy me or shut me up, but it served to do both.

"You forgot to ask me, asshole!" I shouted when he shut the door behind him.

He opened it and poked his head through. His hair was a scruffy mess where I'd sunk my fingers into its thickness and gripped it. "Do you mind?"

I blinked. "Yes, actually. I do."

"You'll get over it."

The door clicked shut behind him.

"*You'll get over it?*"

We'd see about that.

"Fergus! You're a man!" I stomped into the bar and leaned on the end of the bar.

He stopped, towel stuffed inside a glass jug. He slid his gaze toward me the way a child would if they'd been caught with their hand in the cookie jar. At least he appeared to be over this morning's drama. "Well spotted, darling."

"Thank you. I'm on the ball today." I half-smiled.

"Don't forget that I'm a rather feminine man."

"That's what I'm hoping will work in my favor."

He raised his eyebrows and slowly put down the jug. "Do tell."

"If you wanted to piss off a man, what would you wear?"

"By piss off, I assume you mean to sexually frustrate while you play hard to get?"

"You're the woman whisperer. If you could bottle that, you'd make a fortune."

He grinned. "I'm just waiting for science to catch up to me."

"I hope it doesn't. Your knowledge could be dangerous. I don't know what I'd do if men understood me."

He sighed. "You and me both."

With anyone else, that would be worthy of an eye roll. With him, after this morning? Not out of place at all.

"Stockings and something flirty." Fergus tapped his finger against his chin. "Heels high enough to do some penile damage and low enough you can run away. And take a rape alarm on your keys...Just so he knows you have his number."

"I'm not sure a rape alarm says 'hard to get.'"

"No, but it does say, 'Touch me and everyone will know about it.'"

"I'm not going to set it off in the middle of a restaurant, Ferg."

He held a finger up to serve a customer. I waited, drilling my own fingers against the shiny bar so many times I was probably wearing the lacquered surface down.

"Dinner?" He finally joined me at the end of the bar. "Tell me more."

"There's nothing to tell," I lied. "I was informed I'd be joining Damien for dinner after work tonight."

"Do you want to finish early?"

"I want to work all night."

He laughed, folding his arms so his biceps pushed against the short white sleeves of his shirt. "Damien Fox does tend to have that effect on people. And his lack of being able to ask anyone anything is quite alarming."

Alarming, annoying...Same difference as far as I was concerned.

"So, flirty dress, reasonable heels, and stockings." That was a strong summary of what he'd said to me.

"Tan ones with a black lace top," he answered.

"I don't know if I have any."

He glanced at the chunky, silver watch on his wrist. "I have a break in thirty minutes. I can buy some." He took a few steps back and looked at my legs, his lips pursed as he glanced up and down. "Medium? Hmm, maybe large. You've got long legs. That might be more comfortable."

I blinked. Too many times.

"Definitely large to be on the safe side. What about your bra? What size are you?"

"I'm not telling you my bra size!" I sputtered out, much to the amusement of the young guy who appeared at the bar at that very second.

"Sure you can," Fergus said.

"I'm not telling you my bra size," I repeated.

"They're a solid D. I'd start there," the guy standing a few feet away from me said, his eyes fixed firmly on my chest.

"You know what else starts with a D?" I stared at him. "Drop that attitude or get out of my bar."

He held his hands up. "Just trying to help."

Fergus clucked his tongue. "There are strip clubs for that. What can I get you, apart from some manners?"

"Behave yourself, Fergus," I sighed, pushing off the bar and turning to the back.

"I always do!"

———

Unfortunately for me, Fergus hadn't been lying about buying me a bra.

In related news, I had an opening for a new best friend, because I'd just fired Abby for telling him my bra size.

At least he didn't buy me panties. That would have been a step or ten too far.

I wasn't happy about the bra, but according to Fergus, it screamed sex kitten. Given that the only person who would see the bra on was me, I didn't see that I needed to be a sex anything.

At least, that was my plan.

I hadn't planned on being kissed either...Or seeing Damien...Or basically anything that had happened today.

SIN

If I'd learned one thing today, it was to quit making plans, because mine apparently sucked. And, no matter what I planned, it was going to go to shit anyway.

Funny how that never happened with Damien's plans.

I adjusted the top of my stockings and looked at myself in the mirror of the staff room. I felt ridiculous—I wasn't really a stockings kind of girl. I couldn't remember a time in my life when I'd ever worn them, but I only had myself to blame. Asking Fergus was the quickest way to clothing styles I had no interest in; although I had to admit that the bra he'd bought made my boobs look good with the sweetheart neckline of my dress.

Really, really good.

I put my hands on my hips with a huff. How had I gotten talked into this? How was I standing in the back room of my bar, wearing stockings and a bra bought by my gay employee, while waiting to go to dinner with a man who was as attractive as he was infuriating?

If you'd asked me ten years ago where I thought my life would be at twenty-five, it sure as hell wouldn't have been this.

Hell, if you'd asked me a year ago, it wouldn't have been this.

In that instance, my father's illness was still nothing but a situation I hoped we never found ourselves in, Damien Fox was no more than a guy who owned strip clubs, and I was just Dahlia. I worked. I spent time with my friends. Then, I worked some more.

I didn't have time to date.

I still don't. I have even less time. But the only way to get out of this was to go into the witness protection scheme or something equally like that, and that seemed a little drastic.

I slipped my feet into my favorite, shiny, black heels. They were my 'comfort' shoes and added a good four inches to my height, but I still felt stupid.

This whole thing was stupid.

I knew it.

Yet I couldn't put a stop to it. I could if I really wanted to. Despite how annoying Damien's persistence was, something told me that if I put my foot down once and for all, I'd never see him again.

So, why couldn't I do that?

Why couldn't I use tonight to tell him that I wasn't interested in whatever game this was? Why couldn't I put an end to this once and for all? There was nothing he could do to convince me to sell to him. This game was for his own amusement, to see if he could play me into giving him what he wanted.

My reflection stared back at me with the answer.

Because I wanted to play his game. I wanted to know about him, to break beneath the surface and figure out all the things that made him tick. I wanted his secrets and his lies. I wanted to know everything, and the only way to get what I wanted was to make him think he was getting what he wanted.

And, I wanted more.

I wanted him.

I wanted his mouth on mine again. I wanted his hands and his body. I wanted to see if he was as good as he said he was—if his words were empty or understatements.

I wanted to fuck Damien Fox. I had since we'd had dinner and he'd pulled me on top of him and slipped his fingers inside me.

It was that simple.

But, maybe, the best way to play his game was to bend the rules.

Just a little.

15

DAHLIA

He wore all black.

Jacket, shirt, pants, shoes. If it weren't for the light behind the bar illuminating the different fabrics, they'd have all blended in together.

Damien Fox was the definition of tall, dark, and handsome. At least he would be until he opened his mouth, then there would be several adjectives one could replace 'handsome' with.

I'd taken up position behind the bar when I'd finally emerged from the staff room half an hour ago. It was nothing more than a stall for time. I'd hoped we'd be busy enough at this point that I'd have to cancel to work, but apparently, Abby and Fergus had seen right through that and had called in reinforcements.

Abby nudged me. "Go."

I made a face at her. "I thought you didn't like him."

"I don't. That's why I'm making you go. I'm getting annoyed being in the same building as him."

I rolled my eyes. "You know I'm being forced into this."

"Yes, your ability to say 'no' has mysteriously disappeared," she replied dryly.

She wasn't wrong there.

"Go, Dahlia. He's only going to sit there all night if you don't."

That much was true. As much as I wish it weren't, I knew better.

"Fine." I grabbed my purse from beneath the bar. "You'll call me if there's a problem?"

"As always. What can I get for you?" She turned her body away from me and toward the customer she was about to serve.

Sighing, I tucked my purse against my body and stepped out from behind the bar. Damien was perched at a tall table and the center of attention for every woman within ten feet of him. If he noticed, he didn't show it. His eyes were fixed firmly on me as I approached him.

His gaze was as compellingly intense as always, even as he dropped it to my feet and slowly crawled it up my body with obvious appreciation.

I stopped in front of the table. "Do you want me to take a step back so you can undress me with your eyes again?"

He tugged his lips up to one side. "It's not my eyes I want to undress you with."

"Carry on making promises you don't keep, and I'll start thinking you're full of hot air."

He stood, taking a step toward me, and reached for my face. He trailed his thumb along the curve of my bottom lip, his eyes darting to my mouth for a moment. "Well then, I feel obliged to tell you that after dinner, I'm going to take you home and fuck you 'til you scream."

I looked him dead in the eye and said, "You better eat quickly, then."

His eyes widened. They went back to normal so quickly it could have been a twitch, but the slow way his lips formed a smirk told me it was deliberate. "Are you being...agreeable, Ms. Lloyd?"

"Are you talking shit again, Mr. Fox? Because we're still standing here."

"I have a better idea." He dropped his hand to my waist and pulled me against him. "I'll cook at my place. Then you'll already be where I need you to be."

SIN

"Then let's go."

Damien took my hand in a firm grip, and we wove our way through the crowds building in the bar.

I'd lost my damn mind, because despite my resolve earlier this evening, now I felt sick. Butterflies swarmed in my stomach, flipping it this way and that, yet there was a fission of excitement, too. One that danced its way through my veins and sent goose bumps up my arms. One that tickled its way down my spine until I had to hide a smile by dipping my head.

We stepped outside into the evening warmth. It was still too hot to be entirely comfortable, and if I was hot in a dress, God knows how he was cool wearing all black.

Even his fucking car was black, for the love of God.

"How are you not too hot?" I asked as he reached for the back door. "Does your clothing match your soul?"

He looked back at me, still gripping my hand, and half-smiled. "They say dress for the job you want."

"Judging by your all-black attire, you either want to be a pimp or Satan."

"I'd take Satan," he said, his eyes crinkling as he fought a laugh. "The power to make people do what I want would be fun."

"By that logic, you're already the devil."

"Says the one wearing red."

"It's my color." I flashed him a smile and got in the car.

He leaned forward to the front window before joining me in the back. The partition between the front and back of the car was closed, and the black, tinted glass afforded us almost complete privacy.

My cheeks heated at the memory of what happened last time we were in the back of this car. It wasn't just my cheeks that got warm—my clit ached at the memory of how easily he'd turned me on without kissing me. The firm way he'd touched my body and pushed his fingers inside me flashed in the forefront of my mind, prompting me to reach for the seatbelt in an effort to shake it away.

137

Damien was staring at me.

Was he thinking the same thing I was?

Was he remembering, too?

Did I want to know what he was thinking?

Why did any of it matter?

He turned away without speaking, but a smile played on his lips. Silence descended between us, but it was less awkward, more…comfortable.

I didn't know what to think about that. Just this morning, it'd been strange to be silent together. Yet now…the only thing that had changed was my willingness to accept my attraction to him.

I refused to believe that was the reason for this newfound comfort. It couldn't be that simple. Deciding to fuck someone didn't equal this strange kind of peace that hovered between us.

Or did it?

I'd stopped fighting him. Was that it? Was that the key to this? The fact I'd decided to go with this? Maybe it was. I'd stopped fighting and because of that, I'd all but stopped caring about the things I couldn't control. My attraction to him being one of them.

Or maybe it just *was*. Maybe I was overthinking it. I did tend to do that, after all.

Over-thinking was exactly why I was in this situation.

I should have been born with an 'off' switch.

"You get this little twitch in your eyebrow when you're thinking really hard about stuff. Did anyone ever tell you that?"

I turned to face Damien. "How do you know I'm thinking really hard?"

"You have a little twitch in your eyebrow." Laughter twinkled in his eyes.

My eyebrow twitched when I thought hard? I didn't know that. Why had nobody else ever told me that?

"It's twitching again. Are you thinking about thinking?"

I blinked at him. "I didn't know that. Nobody's ever mentioned it before."

"Then it's likely nobody has ever paid as much attention to you as I do. Which is a damn shame."

Self-consciousness washed over me. I covered my eyebrows with my fingers, just in case they decided to twitch again, because what did he mean by that?

"Dahlia." He leaned over the seat and gently wrapping his fingers around my wrists, lowered my hands. "Don't. It's cute."

"Great," I said, letting my hands fall. "That's what every self-respecting businesswoman wants to be called. *Cute.*"

"What's wrong with cute?"

"Is anything right with it?"

"Kittens are fine with it."

"You've probably only talked to male kittens, then."

He laughed, resting his elbow on the back of the seat and leaning his head against his hand. "You're probably right. Although past you, I can't say I talk to many women, either."

I raised my eyebrows.

"I don't talk to many people in general," he clarified. "And the women who are worthy of conversation make it known relatively quickly."

"That's the most chauvinistic—"

"Ah, good. We're here."

"—sexist, bullshit thing I've ever heard you utter, and that's saying something," I finished. Annoyance prickled at my skin, making me sit bolt upright.

Damien unclipped his seatbelt, apparently unfazed by my miniature rant. "Are you coming or not?"

"Certainly not now."

"I didn't mean it like that and you know it," he replied, opening the door and getting out. He bent down, one hand on the top of the door and the other on the car. "Are you coming to continue this conversation, or are you going to go home and stew, only to ultimately realize we should have carried on, if only for you to get justification for what you're pissed off about?"

Goddamn it, I really hated him sometimes.

"Motherfucker," I muttered, unclipping my own belt and shoving it off me. I scooted over the seat to the tune of his laughter. My dress rode up my thighs as I did, getting caught under my ass, and as I stood, Damien reached for my leg.

"I like these," he murmured in my ear, fingering the lace top of one of the stockings. "Bet it'll feel even better when your legs are around my neck."

"Right now, it'll be the stocking sans leg around your neck," I shot back, pushing at his chest so he moved. "Until you justify that ridiculous comment, they're my potential murder weapon."

"You watch a lot of TV, don't you?" He smiled, closing the car door.

I glanced at the car as it rolled away. "Where does he go? Don't you ever invite him in?"

"Would you like me to invite him in? It's not usually my thing, but if you'd like someone to watch you come on my cock..."

"I shouldn't have gotten out of the car."

He laughed. "Maybe not, but you did, and you're here, so come inside." He grabbed my hand and pulled me up the wide driveway to the front door.

His house wasn't huge, but it was well secluded, and I recognized it as one of the houses in a gated community not far from my home. Damien fumbled with the key for a second and moved to an alarm box as soon as the door was open. It beeped a few times, and he flicked on the hallway light.

Bare.

That was the first word that sprung to mind. Not in a judgmental way, but as a general observation. Despite the fluffy rug on the tiled black floor and one mirror on the plain white walls of the entryway, there was nothing else. A stark contrast to my own warm entrance.

"Wine?" Damien asked, touching his hand to my back and guiding me into the kitchen.

He flicked another light switch, and the room lit up thanks to several spotlights spread across the ceiling. A few were concentrated over the large, rectangular island in the middle of the room, their brightness glinting off the shiny marble countertop.

"There's rosé in the fridge," he continued, motioning to a backed stool at the island.

I arched my eyebrows. "You remembered. I'm impressed."

A tiny twitch caught the corner of his mouth. His eyes flashed with something genuine—something I couldn't quite pinpoint because he turned around. "Of course I remembered." He pulled the bottle out from a rack inside the fridge and shut the door. "Like I said in the car...I pay a ridiculous amount of attention to you, Dahlia. It's an easy thing to do."

I didn't know how to respond to that, so I swallowed and watched as he poured the pink wine into a glass. He followed up by placing the bottle back in the fridge and pulling out a beer. Popping off the top with a satisfying hiss using an opener attached to the side of his fridge, he caught the cap and threw it into the trashcan.

"Do you want to eat before or after I justify my perfectly sane comments to you?" he asked, wiping the side of his bottle.

"Oh, the one where you deemed women unworthy of your conversation?"

"If it were women in general, you wouldn't be putting wine in your mouth. You'd be putting *me* in it."

I took a big mouthful of wine and glared as I swallowed it.

He sighed, despite the smile playing with the corners of his mouth. "It's so fun to mess with you."

141

I carried on glaring at him. He may have thought so, but I couldn't say I agreed. Messing with him was probably way more fun.

"There are three types of women in my world." Damien held up three fingers, leaning back against the kitchen counter, before bending two down so only one was up. "One: the types who come to me for a job. They do it for fun, for college, or for their kids. Maybe even for their parents. Mostly, they're good people, stuck in a tough place. Our conversations are short and sweet." He flipped up a second finger. "Two: the types who get dollar signs in their eyes when they look at me. You'll know them as gold diggers, and I bet you've seen your fair share of male ones. They don't care about me or my business. They care about my car, my bank, and whether or not I'll spend fifty grand on a fucking handbag for their birthday or not." The third finger went up. "Three: the very rare women who actually give a shit about me. Maybe we're colleagues, family friends, or we have business to do. Those are the two-way relationships and the conversations I have time for."

All right.

"Your explanation is spot on, but your original delivery needs some work." I leaned onto the counter and propped my chin up on my hand. "And yes, I have seen my fair share of gold diggers who see money when they look at me. That doesn't mean they aren't worthy of my conversation. I can't adequately tell them where to go if I don't talk to them."

"You tell one to fuck off and you're feisty. I do it and I'm an asshole."

"A label that shouldn't bother you, given that you are. Mine doesn't bother me." I grinned.

Damien smiled behind the rim of his beer. "I forgot the fourth type of woman."

I watched him expectantly, twisting my glass in my hand.

"The business rival who drives me crazy." His smile twisted into a dirty smirk. "She goes by Dahlia Lloyd, but I prefer to refer to her as my little pain in the ass."

"I can be a pain in a whole lot more." I blinked at him innocently, lifting my glass to my mouth.

He put his bottle down on the island and rounded it. His eyes were fixed on mine as he approached with slow, calculated steps that made a shiver run down my spine. His dark eyelashes fanned across his cheeks every time he blinked, and the closer he came to me, the more the memory of his kiss tingled across my lips.

He stopped right in front of me.

Pulled me up.

Held me against him.

Ran his lips across my jaw.

"My sanity?" His lips brushed across my earlobe as he spoke. "My resistance? My common sense? My ability to make good decisions? My ability to leave you the fuck alone, Dahlia? 'Cause I can assure you, you're a pain in all of those. In fact, they're all non-existent where you're concerned."

My heart thumped.

"You make me insane. I can't fight you. You kill my common sense. I make nothing but bad choices around you. And you're sure as shit too damn irresistible for me to leave you alone for a single day." Damien dug his fingers into my skin, shooting thrills throughout my body. He dipped his face right against mine. His stubble scrubbed across my jaw, rough and tough, tickling as the hairs flicked across my face. "I want you," he breathed, lips barely a heartbeat from mine. "And if you had any fucking idea how badly, you'd run into the wind."

His shirt was as smooth as silk, flawless beneath my fingers as they mapped their way across his muscular body. The fabric rippled and slipped beneath my touch, and that smoothness only stopped when my fingertips left the material and fell upon his neck. Hot yet rough courtesy of his trimmed stubble, his skin sent tingles across mine, starting from where we touched until I felt them all over my entire body.

"This is a bad idea," I said breathlessly, hand on the side of his neck.

"Good things come from bad ideas." His eyes bore into mine, a raging inferno of want and lust that burned. "Didn't you know that?"

"I don't think I've ever really carried out any of my bad ideas before." My voice gave out on the final word as the truth hit me.

I hadn't.

Not ever.

Except him—except every idea I'd ever had that he was involved in.

"Then," his voice was low, and he slid one hand down my back, holding me tighter against him. "I'll be the first."

His mouth covered mine before I could think of a response. Not that I had one—hell, if I had to make a really bad decision, it might as well have been this. I'd already made it, too. After that kiss this morning, there was no way I'd be ending this evening without sleeping with him.

I'd come here to do that, hadn't I?

I shut off the voice inside my head and fully gave myself over to the man in front of me. His lips were hot but slow, moving over mine in a way that was firm yet easy—that put him in control. It was a kiss that laid out his intentions.

His intentions to control this, to dominate me, to own this entire thing.

I had no chance of taking any of that away from him, so I rolled with it. I let him think he did, even as he broke the kiss, clasped my hand, and pulled me toward the stairs. I paused at the bottom to remove my heels, but he stopped me.

Damien shook his head. "Don't even think about taking those off."

I raised my eyebrows but said nothing. I wasn't against it or anything...

We carried on up the stairs until we reached the upstairs hallway. Like the one downstairs, it was plain and clean, almost clinical in its appearance. But I didn't have a whole lot of time to focus on it, because Damien dragged me down the hall to a door at the end. All the doors were ajar except this one, and when he opened it, I saw why.

"This is your room," I said, not bothering to hide my surprise.

He rolled his head to the side and looked back over his shoulder. "What were you expecting? A sex dungeon?"

"Now that you mention it…"

He laughed and pulled me inside, pushing the door shut behind me. He walked backward as he guided me into the room with slow steps. "No dungeon, no special room, no sordid basement…I promise. I don't usually…entertain…at my house."

"Then why am I here?"

He stepped toward me, slipping his fingers between mine and holding me close. "I make exceptions for exceptions."

"What does—"

He silenced me with a kiss. His fingers slid into my hair, easing to the back of my head and cupping it. I gripped his shirt, leaning into him. A shiver raced across my skin when he flicked his tongue across my lower lip, and my toes twitched as if they wanted to curl. Just when I thought he'd deepen it, he released me.

My lips parted. I drew in a deep breath, my lame attempt at hiding the desire that was building.

Damien's footsteps were silent on the plush carpet. He came behind me and rested his hands on my waist, stopping me from moving, and reached up. Hair rose across my skin as he ghosted his fingers over my shoulder to my hair. He swept it to the side, brushing it over my other shoulder, exposing the curve of my neck and top of my dress.

His fingers closed around the zipper pull.

Warmth flushed through me.

With my harsh breathing as the only sound for it to contend with, the deep buzz of the zip as he undid it seemed unnaturally loud. The brush of his knuckle following the zip down my spine only heightened the sound—heightened the way my heart beat a little too fast. But then—then, he touched his lips to the base of my neck, and I shivered, my entire body feeling the effects of just one touch.

He smiled, mouth still against my skin. "It's coming off."

Working the sleeves over my shoulders, he peeled the fabric down my body, bending his knees and crouching until it was pooled at my feet. I closed my eyes. I was wearing nothing but my heels, the new bra, and one of my sexiest thongs.

"Out," he said, tugging at the fabric.

I stepped out, squeezing my eyes shut. A swish sounded, and then Damien's hands were on my legs, fingers splayed as he ran them up my calves, over my knees, up the backs of my thighs until he cupped the curves of my ass cheeks.

"Can't imagine why you wore these." His lips brushed my skin, just next to the band of my underwear, and stood, gripping my hips. He spun me, nothing but carefully controlled restraint in his eyes.

"You're overdressed." I popped open the top button of his shirt and moved to the next one. I did them all in seconds and yanked on the material to free it from his belted pants.

His body was rock solid, packed tight with muscle that just begged me to touch it. I glided my fingers over his enviable stomach lazily, teasing him back the way he had when he undid my dress.

I could take it. I didn't think he could. He wasn't great at patience, after all.

I used that to my advantage, exploring his body entirely at my leisure. From his hard chest to the tempting 'v' that curved over his hips and disappeared beneath his pants, pointing right at the hard bulge against the zipper. I even brushed my baby finger over his cock once or twice before I finally grabbed his shirt and tugged it over his shoulders.

"Oh for fuck's sake." Damien's tone was deep and guttural, so husky that my heart thumped at the frustration in his voice.

He yanked himself away from me.

SIN

Ripped off his shirt.

Threw it down.

Grabbed me around the waist. Threw me back onto the bed. Pounced on me.

Immediately fisting my hair, he leaned over me and kissed me. He didn't mess around this time. His tongue found mine in an instant, the ferocity of his kiss wiping all thoughts from my head and replacing it all with him.

With how his toned body burned against mine.

With how my scalp stung from his tight grip.

With how my fingers dragged over his skin, my nails lightly scratching him.

There was nothing but Damien and the lust that pooled between my legs, making my clit ache.

He tugged my head back and kissed down my neck, his cock pressed between my legs. I gasped when he shifted, pressing harder against my clit. Relief washed over me when he released my hair to undo my bra, but within seconds, he had his mouth over my nipple.

Nibble, suck, graze, lick—he alternated between mild pain and wild pleasure. I wanted more and wanted him to stop. It was a crazy sensation, needing to get both closer and further away at the same time. It didn't stop as he turned his attention to my other breast where he did the same thing until I whimpered.

Pain? Pleasure? I didn't know.

He leaned back up over me, kissing me again. The light smattering of hair over his chest rubbed against my tender nipples, and he flexed his hips, once again teasing my clit with his cock. I reached between us, desperately trying to get hold of his belt, and felt his grin against my lips when I finally made contact with the cold metal of the buckle.

He laughed quietly into my neck.

"You're wearing too many pants," I murmured, breathless from the kiss.

He laughed a little louder and got up. I propped myself up on my elbows and watched as he undid the buckle, then the button, then the zipper. My mouth went dry as he bent over and pulled off his pants, but that was because he didn't stop there.

He pulled his boxer briefs off, too.

I took a deep breath in as he wrapped his fingers around his cock and gently stroked it. He kept his hand there as he opened a drawer in the nightstand and pulled out a condom. He kept it there as he climbed back up onto the bed, positioning his body over mine, between my legs, and kissed me again. The corner of the foil packet tickled my hair, and I wrapped my arms around his neck, pulling myself up to kiss him deeper

Using his legs to open mine further, he released his cock and brushed his thumb over my thong. My clit throbbed beneath the light touch, and I gasped when he moved my underwear to the side and pushed one finger inside me. I was already wet—wet enough to take him, and that was all I wanted to do. I didn't want to mess around with foreplay any longer.

I wanted his cock inside me, and I wanted it now.

He grazed his teeth over my lower lip, breaking the kiss. As if he'd heard my inner thoughts—or my moans against his tongue—he pulled back and ripped open the condom. My entire body jolted into high alert, tingling with anticipation.

My legs drifted shut as he grabbed his cock at the base and rolled the condom on in one smooth motion. His gaze traveled hotly from his cock to me, and he knelt with one leg on the bed reaching for my thong. The lace tickled as he peeled it down my legs and over my heels, dropping it on the floor.

"Open your legs," he demanded hoarsely.

I clenched them together and drew in a deep breath.

"Dahlia."

That sent a jolt of desire straight down my spine.

"Open. Your. Legs."

I clenched them even tighter.

SIN

Damien gripped my knees and shoved my legs open, unwilling to wait for me any longer. My muscles were still tight, so he ran his hands up the insides of my thighs, digging his fingertips into me, applying enough pressure that I couldn't move against him.

Then, he dipped his head and ran his tongue along my pussy, pausing at my clit and closing his lips around it. He sucked, pulsing his tongue against the taut bundle of nerves.

I gasped, grabbing the sheets as an uncontrollable burn of pleasure flushed through me.

He moved, laughing breathlessly, and covered my body with his. His hand between us, he guided the head of his cock to my pussy and lightly pushed himself inside me. He eased in, inch by inch, my muscles clenching and hugging his hardness. Heat washed over me. I cupped the back of his neck and his shoulder, closing my eyes.

Slowly, he moved, pulling out almost entirely before he buried himself back inside me.

The slowness didn't last long. I wrapped my legs around his waist and crossed my ankles, basically curling myself around him as he found a rhythm. He picked up speed, our skin slapping together as he fucked me harder, deeper, faster.

My heart pounded. Sweat slicked across my body as he moved. I grasped and grabbed, digging my fingers into his back and his shoulders, scratching at his neck, arching my body and taking all of him.

He paused, sitting up. His fingers were hot against my legs as he unwound them from his waist, and the question of what he was doing died on my tongue as he slid off the bed, yanked me by my thighs to the edge, and guided himself inside me again. At the apex of my thighs, he splayed his fingers, holding my legs wide open.

If I thought he was fucking me hard a moment ago, I was wrong.

This was hard.

It was rough. Relentless. Greedy. Each thrust of his hips slapped his skin against mine and forced pleasure onto me.

His grip meant I could do nothing but lie there and take it. Arch my back and writhe as the heat of an impending orgasm swamped me, tickling my skin, tugging at my senses, drying out my throat as moans escaped my parted lips.

My fingers dug into the sheets, gripping desperately. Something had to ground me, hold me here, because the sensations wracking my body were overwhelming. Blinding, almost. It built and built and built and built until the gentle rise of pleasure mounted and slammed into me, taking me over the edge into an orgasm that had bright spots dancing behind the lids of my closed eyes, that had all my muscles clenched, that had my entire body trembling with its strength.

And somewhere through it was Damien, releasing my legs, bending over me, groaning. Groaning my name…Clutching the back of my neck…Buried so far inside me that, for the barest moment, in the middle of heightened senses and wild pleasure, we were a whole lot more than two pawns in a game.

16

DAMIEN

My cock twitched every time I looked at her.

Like right now. She was sitting cross-legged at my breakfast table, wearing one of my white shirts that swamped her body, and she was struggling to suck up a piece of spaghetti from her fork. The strand flicked up and got sauce on her nose, which only made her half-snort with amusement and wipe the sauce away.

She didn't get it all.

I leaned over and wiped it away with the pad of my thumb. "You're hot even when you eat like a three-year-old."

Dahlia pointed her fork at me. "Until I get it on your shirt, you can't say that."

I cleared my throat and looked at the pocket. It was barely noticeable, but there it was. A tiny bit of sauce, vibrantly red against the stark whiteness of the shirt.

"God fucking damn it," she muttered, swiping at it.

It only made it worse.

It was my turn to snort. "Like I said: Three-year-old."

"Bite me." She sipped her wine.

"You want round two?" I raised my eyebrow in question, a flash of lust prompting my cock to twitch yet again.

She put down her fork and reached for a bit of pizza. "Now, it makes sense. You brought me here to fuck me, knowing you could entrap me with food after so I'd have the energy to do it all again. I bet you weren't really planning on dinner or cooking, were you?"

"Sweetheart, you're lucky I like you as much as I do. Or we'd be at your house and I'd have already crept out."

"You're such a gentleman."

I motioned to the spread of Italian food on the table in front of us. "Did I or did I not order seven different dishes from the restaurant because you couldn't decide?"

She opened her mouth, paused, and sighed. "You did."

"Right, so let's summarize the evening: I made good on my promise to fuck you blind, fed you, wined you, and didn't complain when you got sauce on my shirt." I looked pointedly at the pocket. It didn't help matters that she was braless and I could see her hardened nipple through the fabric.

She looked around, nibbling on the pizza. "That's what happens when you let a three-year-old wear your clothes."

I laughed, leaning back and swinging my feet up onto the chair between us. "A grown ass woman with the habit of eating like a three-year-old."

"Got any cookies?" she asked, mouth full.

"You're such a lady."

She clapped her hand over her mouth and dropped the pizza. She did a strange half-laugh, half-choke, that wasn't even remotely close to ladylike, but was highly amusing. I sipped my beer as she smacked herself in the chest and reached for her wine with her eyes watering.

She'd already dirtied one of my washcloths by removing her makeup. Both beige and black was smeared all over a white washcloth, and there was even a little on the towel she'd used to dry her face.

Except the lipstick. Somehow that godforsaken red lipstick was still perfectly in place, bar one tiny fleck on her lower lip. It had to have glue as a main fucking ingredient, because the way I kissed her earlier, I should have kissed it all off.

I didn't think I'd ever seen her without that lipstick on. As much as I loved it, now I was looking at her without makeup on, I wanted to see her completely bare faced.

SIN

Her lashes were just as dark and long as they were with mascara, if a little less curled. Her skin wasn't as flawless as the makeup made it look; a tiny mole hid on her hairline, and freckles dotted over her nose and upper cheeks, making her seem even more beautiful than she normally was.

What color were her lips under that war paint? Were they light pink? Rosy and dark? Somewhere in the middle?

Would they be just as tempting?

Would they feel just as soft against mine?

Why the fuck did I care?

I didn't have a place caring. Shit, I didn't have a place giving her my shirt so we could order food and talk. I had no damn place sitting opposite her at my fucking table in nothing but sweatpants while examining her clean face.

Had no fucking business thinking about anything *but* business.

I should have been thinking about one thing: how to use this newfound relationship to my advantage. To wrench that damn bar from her grip. I should have been thinking about how I could use this to manipulate her into getting what I wanted, but I wasn't.

I was thinking she looked damn cute sucking up spaghetti and getting the sauce all over her. That she was fucking adorable sitting cross-legged at a table wearing nothing but a shirt because she'd informed me in no uncertain terms that she was *not* putting that dirty underwear back on.

I was thinking that I didn't care much about the fact that dirty underwear had been cleaned in my bathroom sink and was now hanging off the shower door to dry.

And I also didn't give much of a fuck that it probably meant she wouldn't be going anywhere anytime soon…Like until tomorrow morning.

"How are you so messy when you eat? And why do you not get this messy in public?" I darted my gaze over her face. There was now pizza sauce on the collar, she had some sauce up by her *eye*, and I'm pretty sure there was cheese in her hair.

"I eat very, very carefully when I'm in public," Dahlia answered, noticing the cheese. She peered down and pinched it, pulling it out with her bright, red nails.

I stared at her, expressionless. It still didn't answer my question. The last person I'd seen eat like that was my niece, and I hadn't seen her for three years.

She sighed and grabbed her wine glass. "Look," she said, focusing on me with those big, blue eyes, "I can't be everything. I can't be smart, rich, and a clean eater, too."

"You forgot beautiful."

"Huh?"

"You said you 'can't be smart, rich, and a clean eater, too.' I'm telling you that you missed out beautiful."

She blinked at me. "Okay, fine. I can't be smart, rich, damn beautiful, and a clean eater. Nobody is that perfect."

I grinned at her taking my words and going to the next level. Nobody could accuse her of lacking confidence, that's for sure. "You're right, nobody is that perfect. And I guess there are worse things a woman could be."

"Like sarcastic, a bitch, snarky, independent…"

"Did you finish listing your good qualities, so you moved to your bad ones?"

"You think those are my bad qualities? Oh, boy, you're in for a shock if you're still annoying me when the Great White stops by."

I stilled. "One: no, not at all. I happen to like those qualities on you. You wear them well."

"Thank you."

"Second: what the hell are you talking about?"

"The Great White. The shark. Shark week. You know, the five days every month I'm guaranteed to hinge upon clinically insane, cry at pet food commercials, and eat my body weight in carbs and candy?"

"That was more than I ever needed to know about a woman's menstrual cycle."

"I can get more detailed if you'd like."

"Please don't. I don't like."

She grinned. Crazily. Her eyes even fucking crinkled, lighting up with barely restrained laughter that had her shoulders lightly shaking. She looked soft and innocent and playful—all the things I'd never seen before, all the things she kept hidden beneath that icy, independent exterior she portrayed to the world.

And fuck if I didn't like this side of her.

"Can I ask you a question?" she said, tucking her hair behind her ear and dropping her smile.

"Is it more about periods?"

"No." More restrained laughter.

"Aren't you supposed to be working right now?"

I shook my head, resting my beer in my lap.

"Why not?" She blinked at me earnestly, leaning forward on her table. Her chin was now propped up on her hand, and she tapped her fingertips against her cheek.

Tilting my head to the side, I weighed up my two answers. The arrogant one that said I had people to do it for me, or the second one—the honest one.

"I don't really run the clubs," I said, my mouth choosing the answer for me. "My dad still stops in and does a lot of that. I'm more the mind behind it all now. I keep it running smoothly. I guess I'm the oil for the cogs of the business. Without me, the entire thing would collapse."

Lines appeared on her forehead as she pulled her brows together. "So when you say you're up until stupid times in the morning…"

"Nope."

"And the sleeping in all morning thing? Wait, that can't be true. You were at my house stupidly early today."

"Yesterday. It's after midnight." My lips pulled to the side as I deflected. She didn't need to know about yesterday. Not yet. Not ever. "It's a lie. I wake up early, work out, and go straight to work. I say nobody can call me until one because then I'm not interrupted when I'm busy and I can get a ton more done."

Her jaw dropped. As much as it could, encased in her palm. "That's a brilliant idea."

"I'm not just a handsome face and huge cock, you know."

"Clearly. You're modest, too."

"At least I can eat without covering myself in my dinner."

"Damien?"

"Yes?"

"Shut up."

———

I opened my eyes to darkness.

The room was lit up only by the light glare from the clock on my nightstand. Most of it was swallowed by the wall it faced, so I rolled over and reached out toward it.

Five a.m.

I'd barely slept for four hours, yet I felt wide awake. Dahlia's breathing was soft and shallow beside me, and a glance over my shoulder told me she was still asleep. My bladder screamed at me, so I carefully slid out of the bed, tugging at the waistband of my boxers, and headed across the room to my bathroom. So I didn't wake her with the light, I waited until I'd closed the door behind me before flicking the switch.

I blinked to adjust my eyes and walked over to the sink. My reflection in the mirror that hung on the wall above it showed tired eyes still full of sleep, imprints from my pillowcase on my cheek, and a scar by my eye that seemed too white. It was too bright in the harsh light, and I gripped the edge of the counter and dropped my head forward so I wasn't looking at it anymore.

My eyes fluttered shut. I needed a vacation, but I wasn't sure there was a way to vacation from the heartbreak of your past. It was the kind of thing that followed you no matter where you went or what you did. I knew. I was an expert. Mine had followed me for years.

The tap creaked as I turned it on to splash cold water on my face. I was awake anyway so all the damn water would do was make me focus a little more. I glanced back up into the mirror as I turned off the tap. My eyes were brighter and my cheeks were more flushed, making me look a bit more human than the pale figure I'd cut moments ago. It would do. I'd be able to creep through the bedroom to head downstairs and do some work.

There was always work that needed doing. Always an order or an email or a phone call. A check in or a resume or a marketing strategy. Accountants and bankers and deliveries. It was never ending, and while I was almost always thankful for that, right now, my motivation was nowhere to be found.

I didn't fucking *care*.

I stared at myself in the mirror. I knew exactly why I didn't care. I didn't have to be a fucking Mensa member to figure it out.

The woman sleeping in my bed was the fucking reason.

Last night had started one way and finished another. It was supposed to be dinner and a fuck—night over. Instead it was fuck, food, sleep. I could see her sexy ass thong hanging off the shower door in the mirror behind me, for the love of God. Right there, clear as day, as obvious as a toothbrush but without the significance.

"Damn things must be dry," I muttered, hitting the light switch before opening the door. There was no fabric to them, so they had to be. I just wasn't going to touch them to find out. I didn't care that much.

Not to mention there was the chance she was awake. I didn't lock the door. I didn't want to think of a scenario where I was gripping her fucking panties to check their dryness and she walked in.

I felt around the floor for the sweatpants I'd ditched last night. I found them half under my side of the bed and tugged them out.

Dahlia shrieked, the sharp noise slicing through the silent darkness.

I jumped off the bed I'd just perched on and reached for the lamp. I missed the switch by a mile, instead hitting the shade. It crashed back against the wall and down onto the floor. "Shit!" I grabbed it, hit the switch, and set it back on the nightstand. "What?"

She blinked at me, her lips parted, fear in her eyes. "Jesus," she whispered, clutching the sheets to her chest. "You scared the life out of me."

"Out of you? You screamed."

"Because you scared me!" She rubbed her hand down her face, pausing at her lips that were now half-free of the lipstick she couldn't get off. "What time is it?"

I turned the clock around and sat on the bed. "Five-thirty."

"Why are you awake?"

I shrugged as I stood and tugged my pants over my ass. "I wake up early sometimes. Today is one of those days. Go back to sleep, okay?"

She narrowed her eyes, her gaze following me as I headed for the door. "What if I wake up early sometimes, too?"

And the sweet Dahlia of last night had disappeared. "You're awake because I woke you up. You're being awkward."

"Maybe I am."

I paused at the door, looking back with a slight smile on my face. "Go back to sleep. I'm just gonna work."

She harrumphed, then leaned over the bed to switch off the light. The room flooded with darkness once more, and I shook my head as I left, closing the door behind me. I didn't expect her to stay there for long. The way she'd looked at me said she knew I was lying—that I didn't wake up for just no reason. And I hadn't, of course. Memories that filtered their way into my dreams were the culprits of my early awakening.

Unfortunately for my subconscious, I wasn't prepared to deal with the things it wanted me to.

I padded down the stairs silently. The early morning sun filtered in through the vast windows that illuminated the entryway. I made my way into the kitchen to escape the glare from the bright orange sunrise, thankful that the sunset was always the view from the vast windows that made up the back wall overlooking my backyard.

I set the coffee machine going and leaned back against the island. The silence of my house had never bothered me before, but this morning, knowing that someone else was asleep upstairs, it was eerie. It seemed to wrap around every wall and slipped through every doorway, hanging thick in the air. A shiver ran over my skin, making me shudder, and I grabbed my coffee cup from the machine when it was done.

Finished making it, I put it on the island and went to fetch my laptop. I didn't want to work in my office. I had a feeling that Dahlia would come looking for me sooner rather than later, and her in my office would invite questions I wasn't ready to answer.

Hell, her lying in my bed invited questions I wasn't ready to answer.

I fired up my computer and settled in at the island, ready to work. I dealt with the seemingly endless stream of emails, contacted the web designer to make amends to the Fox parent website, and even sent an email to Mia Rykman about another marketing campaign. An hour passed before I heard the telltale creaking of the bottom stairs, telling me that Dahlia had probably waited as long as she possibly could before coming down.

"I'm surprised," I said, typing while staring at the screen. "I thought you'd have been down here forty-five minutes ago."

"I tried to show some restraint," she replied. "I lost my lives three times over on Candy Crush, found out what kind of pizza I'd be, and read about five Buzzfeed articles based on Kardashian memes."

"Sounds like a solid way for a businesswoman to pass an hour." I smirked, turning to look at her.

Fuck.

She was wearing another one of my white shirts. It swamped her, skimming her thighs, and was just thin enough that I could see she was wearing her underwear again. Still no bra, but she didn't need it in that. Hell, she probably didn't need a bra at all. She had perky, round tits, and right now, I wanted to pull her over against me, tear open the shirt, and tease her with my mouth until she begged me for more.

"It is. Even I need downtime. And stop looking at me like I'm your breakfast."

"It's time for breakfast," I said, following her with my eyes when she sat down.

"It's way too early for breakfast." She leaned forward on the counter and rested her chin on top of her hands. Hesitating for a moment, she said softly, "Can I ask you a question?"

I dropped my attention back to my screen. The gentle tone of her voice told me I probably wasn't going to like what she had to ask. "Mmm," I replied noncommittally.

"Is that a yes or a no?"

"That's a 'you might as well because I know that if you don't ask me now, you'll ask me later.' Since there's a good chance I'm not going to like your question, you may as well get it over and done with."

"You're too observant."

"Perhaps you're too easy to read." I glanced up with a pointed look.

"Next time, I won't bother asking you anything."

"You still haven't, unless you're counting your question about the question. Next time, sweetheart, don't ask if you can ask. Just ask it."

Silence.

And then, "Why don't you have any pictures? Anywhere?"

I wasn't surprised at all.

160

SIN

My fingers stilled, hovering just above the keys in front of me. "Am I supposed to have pictures anywhere?"

"Answering a question with a question. Cute," she muttered, getting up. "Can I make a coffee?"

"Go wild." I typed again.

She fidgeted around the kitchen behind me. A few huffs and puffs exaggerated her movements, and after one particularly loud, grating sigh, I saved what I was working on and turned around.

"What are you doing?"

She pointed at the machine. "What is this thing? How do you work it?"

I rolled my eyes and got up. Within seconds, I had the machine spitting coffee out into the cup beneath it and had even retrieved the milk for her. "You're welcome." I sat back down and got back to work.

I'd barely typed out a paragraph when she sat down and stared at me.

Stared was the wrong word.

She glared at me, hitting me with a look that could melt an iceberg.

"Any reason you're looking at me as though I've grown two heads?" I asked, pausing yet again in my work. Why I didn't stop, I didn't know.

"You didn't answer my question."

"You didn't answer mine."

"That's because yours was a rhetorical question and total bullshit," she said firmly, taking her seat again. She tugged at the collar of the shirt, a hint of awkwardness settling over her expression briefly before disappearing. "I'm just wondering, that's all. You don't have to answer...I just assumed you would have some family photos or something somewhere."

I remembered why I didn't bring anyone to my house. Ever.

"Nope," was my answer.

Just nope.

DAHLIA

I waited for him to elaborate, but he didn't. The tap-tap of his typing filled the air in the kitchen as bright rays filtered in from the hallway, lighting up the space behind him. His lightly tanned skin was almost golden against the orangey hue of the sunrise that was taking over the sky outside. His hair was messy and unkempt, a mixture of sex, sleep, and what looked an awful lot like stress.

Stress I was getting the feeling I was the cause of.

Damien didn't look up from his laptop despite my gaze being fixed on him. This conversation was apparently over when it had barely begun, and whatever it was that had woken him up so early—and by default, me—was apparently related to my question, judging by the way his attitude had changed. Gone was the relaxed, teasing man I'd enjoyed food with late last night. He'd been replaced by the Damien Fox I knew well.

Cold. Icy. Closed-off.

Even more so than I was.

I did my best to keep my sigh under wraps and grabbed my coffee. I glanced back as I left the room, but he didn't pay the blindest bit of attention to me. He stayed where he was, fingers moving quickly over the keyboard, eyes focused wholly on the screen. I went back upstairs to his room where my purse and my clothes were. I had makeup in my purse, and if I caught a cab to the bar where my car was, I knew I'd find a change of clothes in my office.

I knew there was a reason I kept sweats and sneakers there. Apparently, this was it.

SIN

I set my coffee on the nightstand and grabbed the small pouch holding my makeup out of my purse. I didn't need much, just enough to look human, so a brush of powder and lick of mascara later, I was heading back into the bedroom and grabbing my clothes. I dressed quickly, even with the move of a contortionist to do the zipper up in my dress. Perching on the edge of the bed with my coffee in one hand, I called my preferred cab company and had a car come to Damien's.

I was ready to go home. If I was honest with myself, I didn't know why I was still here. I should have gone home last night—heck, I shouldn't have come here last night.

My attempt to play his game had backfired on me. My curiosity had done the same thing. Both had led me close to emotional danger, because last night, he'd been more than the man I knew him to be. He was funny and relaxed and playful. Warm and teasing and the kind of person I liked to be around.

I'd assumed that last night had changed our relationship.

I was wrong.

A fact that was proven when I went downstairs to a silent house.

He hadn't left, so he was somewhere here, basically hiding.

I didn't care to look for him.

With my purse on my shoulder and my heels in my hand, I walked outside, barefoot, closing the door loudly behind me.

"He's offered a significant amount," my lawyer said down the line.

I balanced the phone between my ear and shoulder, dumping a stack of papers into a box. I was finally done organizing all Dad's stuff, and I didn't want to be dealing with

163

another offer from the Fox family, especially after last night and this morning. It'd been eight long-ass hours since I'd left Damien's house, and now, I was on the phone with my lawyer because his father had put in another offer for my *not-for-sale* business.

"I don't care, Geoff," I said, grabbing the phone and perching on the edge of the desk. "I'm not selling. I don't care if he offers me his entire savings. You know that."

"I know, but I am obligated to tell you."

"Well, in the future, it's an automatic refusal of any and all offers unless I tell you otherwise." I paused. "And you can send Benedict Fox and his son a Cease and Desist for their offers on any of my property unless they're notified of an intent to sell."

Geoff coughed. "If you're sure."

"Perfectly."

"They'll have it within the hour."

I ended the call and sighed, pressing my hand against my face. I slid it up over my forehead and into my hair, sweeping it back from my face before running my fingers completely through it.

Anger fizzled in the pit of my belly.

I was beyond frustrated. Humiliated. I'd never felt anything close to this before in my entire life. My entire body burned with embarrassment as the realization that my attempt to play along with his plan had backfired more spectacularly than I'd ever imagined it could.

Mia had told me that Damien Fox used people to get what he wanted.

That was all last night had been.

I knew that. Deep down, I knew that. So why did I pick up my phone to see if he'd called or texted me even though I knew he hadn't?

Because I was an idiot of the highest level. I was a freaking idiot who had an angel on her shoulder telling her last night had been real and the devil telling her it wasn't.

Two sides of me warred, both of them right and wrong at the same time.

Last night had been real if only a little bit. At least, for me. I'd felt it. Felt the moment I saw the real side of Damien for a few, short hours. Not that the time made it any less important to me.

That was also the reason it was wrong. Wrong because I'd wanted to know about him, not know him specifically. Knowing someone for who they really were was dangerous, and the longer I thought about last night, the more I realized I'd underestimated Damien's powers of…whatever the hell they were.

In a time where I should have been angry at him, I was angry at myself.

Angry because I saw his fleeting, genuine smile that teased a dimple.

Angry because I saw a softness in his eyes when he saw me getting spaghetti all over myself.

Angry because I'd felt him stroke my hair just before I fell asleep. Because I'd felt the heat of his body next to mine all night and felt nothing less than completely comfortable.

I was angry because despite it all, I couldn't stop thinking about the man I'd been with all night. I couldn't stop thinking about the way it'd felt to just be with him. How very easy it'd been to sit half-naked in his kitchen, eating food at stupid o'clock at night.

Most of all, I was angry because I couldn't shake all those feelings. I didn't want to be thinking about them or remembering anything. I wanted to grip onto my anger toward him and stew in it until it consumed me because then it would be easier to tell him that I never wanted to see him again and mean it.

It would be easier to tell him never to call me or text me. Never to email me. Never to show up. Never to touch me. Never to kiss me ever fucking ever again.

It would be easier to believe it.

Dear God, I'd crossed the line from hating him to wanting him, and then I'd stepped a little further into my own personal hell, wanting him even more than that. Through all the anger and the annoyance, he'd slowly become a part of my life—a part that a small bit of me was getting attached to.

More than curiosity.

More than a to and fro of wills.

More than business rivals.

More than people with the upper hand, sneaky tricks and whatever else we'd been doing for the last couple of weeks.

I wanted him in a way that I couldn't pinpoint.

I wanted him in a way that scared the life out of me. In a way I couldn't control.

I didn't know what to do about any of that. So, I sat down behind my desk, propped my elbows on the top, sunk my fingers into my hair, and dropped my head.

"Never trust a Fox," Dad had said, looking at me earnestly. "They live up to their name. They're sly, Dahlia. Cruel and cunning. Whatever you do, never, ever trust them."

The memory of his words spun around and around in my head. That was just it—I didn't think I did trust a Fox. I wanted one, but I didn't trust him. I didn't think I did. I wouldn't trust him to catch me jumping off a six-foot-high wall, let alone anything else.

I dropped my hands to the desk and tapped my nails against it. I needed a brain cleanse to be able to do anything today. Finishing tidying the office was all I'd successfully managed.

Even then, 'successful' was a matter of opinion.

The office door opened, making way for Abby's vibrant hair that, today, was twisted on top of her head in a ballerina bun. "These are yours," she said slowly, handing me five envelopes. "The mail guy was running late today."

"I don't think he can call it running late when it's the regular time he always shows up." I took the envelopes from her and flipped through them. None looked important.

"I know, but I humor him." She shrugged and gripped the edge of my desk, leaning forward. "So…what's up?"

"I can see down your shirt." I put the envelopes in a mail holder on the shelf next to me. "Nothing. I just finished up here and got off the phone with Geoff."

"What did he want?"

Sighing, I said, "Benedict Fox made another offer."

She wrinkled her face, pulling all her features together in an expression of disgust. "What did you say?"

"I responded with a Cease and Desist. To both him *and* Damien."

"Dinner didn't go well, then."

"It has nothing to do with this." It came out sharper than I'd intended.

"Good, because he's called the bar twice to see if you're here."

I blinked. Why not call me? "What did you say?"

She straightened, twisted, and perched on the corner, looking back at me. "I figured if he was calling the bar and not you, last night had gone about as well as a sandstorm, so you weren't available today."

And just like that, she was off the hook for telling Fergus my bra size.

I grabbed my phone and checked my notifications again. I definitely had no missed calls or messages from Damien, so why was he calling the main phone here? "I don't get why he's calling here and not me."

Abby tapped her finger against her lips. "Did he do something to piss you off?"

"Yes. No. Maybe? Ohhh," I groaned and sat back. "I did kinda leave and slam his door on my way out."

"Last night or this morning?"

"Does it matter?"

She grinned. "This morning it was."

"I don't know why you're so happy. You don't like him, remember?"

"I don't, but I like the fact you got you some."

I cleared my throat. I didn't want to talk about it. At all. Not even gossip. "Can we move on?"

"Yes, but now I have to know what he did to make you storm out. Is he selfish?"

"Um, no." My cheeks flushed.

"Well, then, I'm out, because there's gotta be something wrong with you."

I rested my head on my hand again. "I kinda asked him a stupid question and didn't drop it when I should have. He got pissed off, I got pissed off, so I left."

Abby frowned, and then, "Oh God. You didn't ask him if it was in yet, did you? Jesus—is that it? Does his ego make up for his dick? I knew it."

"Um, well, no," I choked out. "The ego…matches…his dick."

"What the hell did you do?"

"Whose side are you on here?"

"Right now? His." She wiggled her fingers and ticked things off. "Hot. Rich. Big dick. Sexually generous. What the hell is wrong with you, girl?"

Who was this person, and where was my best friend? There was no way in hell she'd say this about Damien. Any other guy, sure. But him?

"I'm not saying I was right in leaving, but he made it perfectly clear the conversation was over." Why the hell was I justifying myself? "I went upstairs to get changed, and when I got back down, he'd disappeared. I took that as my cue to leave, so I did." She didn't need to know I'd already called a cab.

"Did you look for him?"

"No. Would you have?"

She paused, pouted, and tilted her head as if she was thinking about it. "Honestly, it depends how good the sex was."

I said nothing. My blush said it for me.

A slow grin eased across her face. "Was it dirty?"

"I'm not talking about this!"

"It was dirty. I can tell. Does he fuck like a porn star?"

"Abby!" Oh my God, why wouldn't my cheeks stop burning? Even my stomach was clenching with embarrassment. I was seconds from going up in flames, I was sure of it.

"What are—why are you blushing? Oooh!" Fergus clapped his hands together, appearing in my doorway. "Mhmm," he hummed knowingly, looking me over. "The eggplant met the taco, didn't it?"

Abby burst into hysterical laughter.

I stared at him, half-hyperventilating, half-trying not to laugh. What? What did I just hear?

What was happening?

Fergus made a circle with his left hand and poked his right pointer finger through the open space. His lips were pursed and his eyebrows arched so high, he could have given teenage girls a run for their money in the smug, sarcastic expression fight.

"What is happening?" I whispered.

"The. Egg. Plant," Fergus said oh-so-slowly, "Met. The. Taco."

I was going to be traumatized beyond belief when this conversation sunk in.

"I'm not doing this anymore." I stood and grabbed both of them. Then, with all my might—and no resistance from them, I might add—I dragged them to the door, shoved them in the hall, and slammed the door behind them. And I freaking well locked it. "Go away!"

I have no idea what just happened, why Abby did a one-eighty on Damien, or why Fergus was talking about eggplants and tacos. I was still stuck with my cheeks burning like I was fifteen after my first kiss, except it was times a hundred in the embarrassment.

I pressed my hands to my cheeks and closed my eyes, ignoring their laughter on the other side of the door.

Assholes.

"Uh, Dahlia?" Fergus managed through his giggles. He knocked three times.

"What?" I snapped, my humiliation now at its highest level. Ever. In my life.

"Damien is at the bar, waiting for you."

I turned so quickly I almost fell over. I yanked at the door, but of course, I'd fucking locked it, so I turned the key and tried again. "What do you mean," I said, glaring at them, "he's at the bar? Abby! You said you told him I wasn't here!"

"I did," she answered, not caring. "I didn't say Fergus didn't."

"I'm not here." I grabbed the door to slam it again.

"Too late." Fergus grinned. "I already told him you were."

"You're fired."

18

DAHLIA

His raucous laughter answered me. We all knew I didn't mean it. It was my knee-jerk reaction to what he'd said. I wasn't happy, but I also knew that Fergus had thrown me under the bus and just driven the damn thing right on over me.

So, I did the only thing I could.

I shut the door.

Of course, that only made them laugh again. Abby was seriously on the way to having her best friend card revoked again, and Fergus and I were gonna have to have a little chat about how I was never to be in the bar when Damien showed up.

I took a deep breath and placed my hand over my eyes. A deep ache throbbed behind them. Was it stress or tiredness? I couldn't tell. Both were completely viable.

"Dahlia?"

The laughter gave way to Damien's deep voice.

"Dahlia isn't here," I replied, dropping my hand.

"You sound like her."

"I'm her unreasonable twin." I bit down on my lower lip and looked up to the ceiling. Had I just thrown his stupid line back at him? God, I had. I was a mess.

"There are a lot of these twins around, huh?"

The laughter that he was hiding in his voice was the thing that made me turn and open the door. Only by an inch, though.

I poked my head into the gap and peered up at him through my eyelashes. He smelled like coffee and fresh air. His hair was brushed and slicked back in its normal style, a far cry from the messy mop it was this morning.

I was kinda sad about that. There was something so freeing about him when his hair wasn't tightly styled back. This one made him look…uptight.

"Have you ever considered not slicking your hair back like Gomez Addams?" The words all but fell from my lips, much to Abby and Fergus' amusement and my mortification.

Yep. Abby and Fergus were still hanging around like a pair of bad rashes.

Damien's lips twitched to the side. His eyes twinkled in that annoyingly charming way of his, and he skipped right over my question. "Can we talk?"

"We *can*. I think the question you're looking for is *could* we talk."

"We *could*, but by this logic, my question should be *would* you talk to me." His amusement was mounting. "So, would you talk to me?"

"I'm so awkward," I muttered, stepping to the side and opening the door for him.

He joined me inside as I shut the door on Abby and Fergus waggling their eyebrows.

"I wouldn't have ever pegged you as awkward," Damien said, meeting my gaze. "But, that said, ever since last night, I'm starting to see that you can be awkward."

"We've all got our bad qual—" A bang interrupted me.

I pinched the bridge of my nose and reached for the door handle. One quick tug later and the eavesdroppers were struggling to stay on their feet.

"I forgot my—" Fergus started.

"Buttplug!" Abby finished, clapping her hand over her mouth. "Wait. Was that stereotypical?" she asked him.

"Little bit." He grimaced.

I cleared my throat and hit them with a look that said it wasn't cute anymore. "Don't the two of you have work to be doing? Like managing the bar, Fergus? And an interview in fifteen, Abby?"

Abby glanced at her watch. "Oh, shit!" She grabbed Fergus' shirt and dragged him after her down the hallway.

"There are a few times," Damien began, looking after their retreating figures, "that I've thought you're lucky to work with your closest friends. Today is not one of those times."

"You're preaching to the damn choir," I muttered to myself. "Let's go. Fergus is great at delegating stuff and a terrible gossiper." I snatched my purse and phone up from the desk.

"Where are we going?"

"Somewhere the nosy neighbors can't see or hear us." I locked the office door behind me and led him into the bar. I stopped by the end of it—I had to let someone know I was leaving, even though I didn't think I'd be gone that long—and saw my favorite thing.

Fergus being chatted up by a woman.

I nudged Damien in the stomach lightly. "Watch this."

"Is she—ohh." He leaned forward a little, his fingers brushing across my hip as he went to grip the edge of the bar.

A flash of heat spread over my skin where he'd touched me.

The girl opposite Fergus bent right over the bar, squeezing her boobs together. I glanced up, but Damien didn't react. Well, he reacted with amusement when Fergus slid her drink across to her, leaned in, and her expression changed to one of embarrassed shock.

"Never gets old," I mused, catching Fergus' eye and nodding toward the door. He shot me a thumbs up. "Come on. Before he decides to take his break and follow us."

"He'd do tha—never mind."

I laughed. "Of course he would. I might be his boss, but he's still older than me. He plays the elders card on a semi-regular basis."

"Have you reminded him what happens when you get old?" Damien held the door open for me.

"Yes. He's more bothered about the wrinkles than anything else."

It was his turn to laugh. He pulled his sunglasses from where they'd been hanging at the collar of his shirt and put them on. I had to dig in my purse for mine, but we'd only taken a few steps when I had mine on, too.

"Where are we going?" he looked down at me.

I glanced at my feet encased in my white, lace flats. "We can just walk."

"All right…" Skepticism tinged his voice. "Are you sure?"

"Yep." I was wearing a skirt and spaghetti-strapped shirt with ruffles around the v-neck, so I wasn't worried about getting hot. "It's not my fault if you always wear black shirts."

"I don't always wear them."

"You have at least twenty white shirts, and I don't know if I've ever seen you in one."

"I like black."

"I suppose it matches your soul."

He smirked, his head twitching in my direction. "And my heart. It's a curse."

I ignored the implications of that given my earlier thoughts about my growing feelings toward him and stuck my hands into the pockets of my floaty skirt. "So, you want to talk."

He adjusted the collar of his shirt. "You disappeared this morning."

"Uh…You disappeared, actually."

Lines formed on his forehead. "No, you went upstairs and I used the downstairs bathroom to shower. I figured you needed a few minutes after I was short with you."

Oh, good. My entire day had been based on what was apparently a misunderstanding between two grown adults, and we were going to deal with it the long-ass way around.

Just fabulous.

Fuck.

"I didn't—I'm going to need a drink for this conversation." I turned right immediately into one of my favorite cocktail bars.

I loved it when that happened.

"Fun. Cocktails are my favorite," he drawled, catching the door just before it could shut after someone left. He motioned for me to go in first, and I did so, ignoring his snark to remove my glasses.

I grabbed a tall table in the back corner, hung my purse on the hook beneath the table, and sighed. "Get the Hickey Mickey," I said.

"What the hell is a Hickey Mickey?"

"Makers on ice."

"Is that the best they have?"

"I'm sorry, Your Highness. Too common for you?"

He half-smiled, sitting down. "Just asking."

I rolled my eyes and placed our order the moment the server came over. We sat in silence as we waited for our drinks to be brought over—his whiskey and my frozen strawberry mojito. I peered into the frozen, red drink, mixing the ice with my straw, and quietly said, "I'm sorry for asking something that's obviously uncomfortable for you."

"Don't be." He reached over the small table and brushed his thumb over my cheek. It was such a tender touch, so out of place for him. "You were just asking, and I had a feeling you would. I probably shouldn't have been as sharp as I was. It was just a question."

I glanced up at him. His hand was still resting on my jaw, and there was a slight smile playing at his lips.

Lowering his hand, he said, "My family is a tough topic for me." His voice was slightly strained as if the admission was hard for him to make. "It's not a great situation. It's hard to explain and—"

"It's complicated," I finished for him with a slight smile.

"Yeah. Complicated. That's one word for it." He let go of a long breath before wiping the hint of frustration from his features with the hand that was just touching my face. "So, what happened to you this morning? You disappeared into nowhere."

"I didn't disappear." I tapped my finger against the tabletop. "I went upstairs to get dressed because you were obviously in a terrible mood and decided it was best if I left. So, I called a cab, and then when I got back down, you were gone. It was silent."

"And you decided to go instead of trying to find me?"

"What was it? A game of hide-and-seek?"

"No, good manners."

I pursed my lips. "If you were in the shower, why didn't I hear it?"

"I'm assuming," he said slowly, "it's one of those wonderful coincidences where I'd just turned it off and was still in the bathroom. I heard a door shut, but I thought it came from upstairs."

Wrong. "That would have been me leaving."

"Coincidence it is, then."

I sipped my drink with a huff. "Coincidences like that don't happen in real life. What bullshit."

He arched an eyebrow. "Is that because you've been in a horrible mood all day or because you didn't get to see me wet and naked?"

I paused. Actually, now that he mentioned it...

"You're considering your answer very carefully, aren't you?"

"Am I that obvious?" I twisted my mouth to the side. "Damn it," I said at his nod.

He chuckled, the low laugh sending a tickle of happiness down my spine.

I reached back and scratched it. *Damn it again.*

"Both," I finally answered, seeing his smile around his glass. "There's no use lying about it."

More low laughter.

That laugh was really starting to get on my nerves. Specifically a bundle of them. Between my legs.

I squirmed and sat up straight. "Okay, so now we've both apologized and agreed we were wrong—"

"I didn't say wrong."

"I'm saying it for you. You don't need to. You know I'm right."

He lifted his glass back to his lips and peered at me. "Of course, you are."

I stared at him flatly. I saw that lame attempt at placation for exactly what it was. Entirely ridiculous at best. Insulting at worst. "We both agreed we were wrong," I continued. I was going to take the high road here. "We're back at our original impasse."

"Of mutual dislike and attraction."

"Oh, please. You never disliked me."

"So humble and modest," he said right as his phone rang. He pulled it out from his pocket and glanced at the screen. "It's my father. I have to get this—do you mind?"

Oh.

Shit.

I opened my mouth to tell him not to answer that call because *uhhelloawkward*. Instead, I shook my head that I didn't, and tried not to lose my mind entirely as he held the phone to his ear.

This day just went from bad to worse.

I must've really pissed someone off in a past life.

———

By the time Damien walked back through the door with a frown on his face, I'd finished my drink, called and paid for the check, and finally beaten my nemesis level on Candy Crush.

He slowly walked up to the table, staring down at his phone like he'd just gotten terrible news.

Which, if that conversation was about what I thought it was, he hadn't exactly received great news…

He stopped right in front of me. Very carefully, he dragged his gaze from his screen and up to my face. Our eyes met, and where I expected to see annoyance or frustration, maybe even anger, I saw a mixture of bemusement and confusion.

"Did you…" he trailed off, then rubbed his hand over his mouth. "Did you send my father a Cease and Desist?"

"Yes." I nodded to punctuate it. "I sent you one, too, if you didn't check your email yet."

What the hell? Might as well put it out there.

His mouth opened and closed. Dropping his attention to his phone, he licked his lips and swiped at the screen with his thumb. "So you did," he said, surprise flitting across his face. "That's…random? Strange? Confusing?"

It was?

"It is?" Now, I was frowning.

"Yes." He looked back at the email as if he didn't understand what he was reading. "What is it for? Is this because—Dahlia, I'm lost. Completely lost."

Confused.

I was very, very confused.

Did he—oh my God. Didn't he know his dad had been offering formally for the bar?

What the hell?

"I don't think this is the right place for this conversation." I hopped off my high seat, clutching my purse, and reached for his hand. It felt so natural, that even as I pulled him along, it didn't seem right to let go.

Apparently, he felt the same, because he adjusted his hand to wrap his fingers around mine.

I pulled him right out onto the sidewalk and down a few buildings to where a quiet—thankfully clean—alleyway was tucked away. It was the back route to Scarlet, and one I'd taken as a teen when I'd crept out during some of my office work shifts during my one-month-long rebellious phase.

"Did you drive here?" I asked Damien, letting go of his hand when we reached the tiny parking lot tucked behind the bar. Parking lot was generous—it was four spaces.

"No. I walked over from Goldies."

"Get in." I nodded toward my car and unlocked it. My red Jaguar was sleek and shiny thanks to a valet while I'd been working.

Damien got in the car after me. I waited until he'd buckled up before pulling away and sliding into the Vegas traffic.

"All right," he said when we came to a traffic standstill. "What's going on?"

I took a deep breath and tapped a light beat to the bottom of the steering wheel. "Those notices weren't random, Damien." I glanced at him. "My lawyer called me about half an hour before Fergus told me you were at the bar. Your father made a formal offer for The Scarlet Letter. His second one today."

"His *second* one today?"

"Mhmm." I couldn't help the pursing of my lips. "The first I was notified of via email at eight this morning. The second warranted a phone call. That's four formal offers altogether from him alone and not counting the calls and inquiries, according to my lawyer. So, now, if he makes a *fifth* offer..." I left him to finish that sentence.

"Right. I understand that, but I haven't made any formal offers. So, why did you send *me* a Cease and Desist?"

I shrugged my shoulder. "Killed two birds with one stone. Now, legally, you've been warned against talking about buying my business." My smile was a little too gleeful, but I couldn't help it.

"I might as well get out of the car now. What else are we supposed to talk about? Apart from me pinning you down and putting my face between your legs, of course."

"Wait, why do I have to be pinned down? Can't I pin you down instead?"

"Only if you're willing to sit on my face." He paused. "And then slide right down to my cock."

I swallowed hard and gripped the steering wheel, turning my knuckles white. "I can't help but feel we're off-topic."

"Again, what else are we supposed to talk about?" His hot gaze flicked up and down my body before he settled on tracing my profile. "The weather? Football? Shoes or some shit?"

"We could talk about football." I moved the car forward a few feet.

He did a double take. "You want to talk about football?"

"I didn't say I wanted to, I said we could. I used to watch it with my dad, so it's not like I don't know anything about it." I looked at him out of the corner of my eye. Bewilderment contorted his features, from his one raised eyebrow to his parted lips. "What? Don't look so shocked."

"I just don't peg you for a woman interested in football. Then again, I didn't think you had the eating habits of a three-year-old, either. You continue to surprise me."

"I'm like a Russian doll. Just when you think you've gotten to the middle of me, boom. I throw a curveball your way." I moved the car a little more.

"You really watched football?"

I sighed, briefly meeting his eye. "That's how my parents met," I said it slowly so the pang that always accompanied talking about them together wasn't so strong.

I had to say it slowly. If I said it too quick, I'd choke up.

Damien opened his mouth, but I spoke again before he could.

"Dad played football in both high school and college. Mom made the cheer team when he was in his junior year. She said it was love at first sight. He said it was the start of a six-month long attempt by him to get her to pay him the blindest bit of attention."

"Was it?"

"Love at first sight or a long attempt at getting her attention?"

"Either."

"Both." I laughed quietly, moving the car a little more. "She told me once that it didn't matter if she liked him or not. He had to prove to her that he was worth her time, but she had to prove it to him, too. She was absolutely certain that the key to their relationship was the fact they both knew the other was worth whatever hard times would be thrown their way. He felt the same."

Damien said nothing.

"They would watch football together. Every game of the season as long as I could remember, and they got tickets to the UNLV games whenever they could. I didn't care about it until she died." The traffic moved forward several feet, so I moved with it. "Dad tried to watch the first game of the season after, but he couldn't. I'd never watched a damn game, but I did then, just so he didn't have to watch it alone." I swallowed as the pain clogged in my throat. "After that, I watched every game I could with him." I slid my hand around the steering wheel just to feel the softness of the leather against my skin. So I could focus on the stitching where the leather joined. Anything but the sadness that was taking hold of my body in the wake of the memories.

"She really made him work for her attention for *six months*?" he asked, shaking his head.

The exaggeration in the way he said "six months" pulled a laugh from me instead of the sob I feared was coming.

"Something tells me he wasn't as persistent as someone else I know." I slid him a knowing look, hitting my blinker to move into the lane one over. I slipped into an empty space when the car behind didn't move into it. He flashed his lights and beeped, so I reached back between our seats and stuck my middle finger up at him through the back window. "Ass."

"Road rage," Damien said dryly. "Awesome. You're a box of tricks, aren't you?"

"Not for much longer. There's a great ice cream place a few blocks off the Strip if this traffic will just start moving." I punctuated my last few words with a few beeps on my own horn.

"A cocktail bar and an ice cream parlor. Is this how I get my girl card?" he asked, deadly serious, his expression void of all emotion.

"No," I said, trying to look past the car in front of me. "Cocktails and ice cream is how you increase the likelihood of me sitting on your face."

Damien leaned over the car and rammed the heel of his hand into the horn. "Come on, assholes!"

Well.

His opinion changed pretty quickly.

19

DAHLIA

"An emotional talk about feelings, cocktails, and ice-cream." Damien shoved his hands in his pockets, stretching his legs right out in front of him and tilting his face up to the sun. "This is the most feminine day I've ever had, and I have two sisters."

"You do?" The question escaped before I had a chance to hide the surprise in my voice. Did I know that? Had it ever been mentioned?

He paused for a moment, something that looked familiarly like pain turning his lips down before he regained control of it. "Yep. I'm the eldest of three. Two younger sisters."

Hmm.

Were they the complicated part he spoke about when he talked about his family? Obviously, I was an only child, but I'd experienced enough sibling rivalries growing up around Abby and her siblings.

"Oh," I said. I wouldn't push it further—hell, it was the most information he'd ever willingly offered me. I'd been given more personal info from my pet rock when I was seven.

I pulled a hair tie from my purse and swept my hair back into a ponytail. The sun was falling lower in the sky, but it hadn't cooled down any from earlier this afternoon. The traffic had reached a crazy level, too, so we'd left my car in the shaded parking lot and once again taken to the streets of the city by foot.

Damien had even stopped to buy a short-sleeved shirt. Of course, it was black, but the damn thing fit him like a glove, even though it'd come right off the hanger.

"Can I ask—"

He jerked his head toward me with a firm look.

Right. Don't ask if I can ask. Just do it.

Like *Nike*. Except I usually put those yoga pants on to watch Netflix, so maybe not that kind of just do it.

"Do you ever take a day off?" I turned to face him.

His eyebrows raised, and pleasant surprise shone out of his dark eyes, twisting his lips up slightly. "From what? Work, or annoying you?"

I was tempted.

I settled for saying, "Work."

Damien stared at me for a moment before he responded. "No. Not really. I don't have much of a reason to. What would I do? Wander around my empty house? Sleep? Play video games?"

"Do you have a video game console?"

"No."

"Well, then, that was a stupid idea."

His mouth twitched to one side before he started laughing. "I didn't mean it literally. It was just an idea. But, literally: the answer is no. I don't take time off. Something always needs to be done, no matter where I am or what I'm doing. My attention is always required."

"Wow."

"What?"

"I just…I can't imagine doing all the things that you do all by myself." The admission had me tearing my gaze from him and looking at a tree on the opposite side of the street. "How do you not go crazy? There are so many different clubs and staff members and managers. The mere thought makes my head spin."

"I've learned to delegate," he said slowly. "I deal with the, shall we say, broader picture of things. A lot of the stuff you deal with is probably far more personal than I ever will.

That's the manager's job. Mine to make sure everything lines up."

"But there's nobody to take your place. If I need a break, I know I can count on Abby. Hell, she just did it for months when I left."

"You were grieving. There's a difference."

"It doesn't mean I was right to leave." I sighed and sat up straight, looking down at my feet. "The longer I'm here, the more I know I was wrong to go for three months, no matter how much I was hurting. But I could, so I did. I had someone here who could take up the slack for me. I could have a breakdown tomorrow and my business would be okay. Do you have that? Do you have anyone who would do the same thing for you if you broke?"

Damien slid his hands from his pockets and clasped his fingers behind his head. "No."

He didn't go on.

"Just no?" I asked.

"Just no," he confirmed. "I have nobody. My father could do it for a few days, but he's worked his entire life and shouldn't have to. Otherwise, I have nobody who could or would do this for me."

"Not even...your sisters?"

"Neither of them are able to." Vagueness surrounded his answer, as simple as it was. "Even if they could, they probably wouldn't."

"That's sad. I like to think that if I had a brother or sister, they'd help me."

"If you had a brother or sister, your life would be very different," Damien said quietly. He dropped his arms, laying one along the back of the bench. His fingers brushed my hair as his hand fell down next to my shoulder. "Your childhood would be filled with memories of fighting for attention and never being good enough unless you were the princess. Which, honestly, you probably would've been."

I would've argued that, but it was true.

"There was always something." He stared out in the same direction I'd been looking for the past few minutes. "Whose turn it was in the bath, why was there no hot water, where the hell was the TV remote, why was there no space on the DVR, why didn't you get off the phone…It was an endless stream of bullshit that, given the chance, I'd probably take back. Not all of it. They deserved the shit occasionally. But sometimes, I would."

I said nothing. I didn't even move when he brushed his fingers through the end of my ponytail that hung over my shoulder.

"I'd give them the phone or shorten my shower. I'd delete a show from the DVR or *not* hide the TV remote in my laundry basket. Actually, no. I'd never not do that last one because that was too evil to not ever be fun."

Laughter bubbled out of me. "That's such a guy thing to do. And the grossest thing ever."

"Depends if you're the one getting the remote or not."

"Didn't you have to take it out?"

"No. My mom learned pretty quick to empty my basket without stuffing the clothes in the washer first." He laughed quietly, if a little sadly. "Then she stopped washing my clothes until I learned *my* lesson."

"Did you?"

"Of course. I put the controller in their laundry baskets instead."

Resting my foot on the edge of the seat and hugging my knee to my chest, I looked over at him with a smile. "I feel like young Damien was really fun."

"He was." His laugh was louder, brighter, more infectious than normal. The laugh of a man who, just for a moment, had been able to let go of just enough pain to let it go free. "*I* was. I guess I grew up and amongst all the bullshit, forgot how to be him."

What bullshit?

What happened to change him this way?

I wanted to know.

I had to know.

Just...not today.

"So, take a day off," I said, resting my cheek on my knee as I looked at him. "Take a day off and do something totally stupid. Wake up at ten in the morning, shout at the TV, eat junk food, screw around... do anything but work. It'll be good for you. You're pretty uptight."

His eyebrows shot up. "I'm uptight," he said flatly.

"You're more uptight than a nunnery full of rejected virgins."

"Sounds like my kinda place."

I shoved him in the arm, laughing. "Do it. Take a day off."

Damien stared at me. Dark eyes flitted across my face, shining with skepticism. His jaw clenched in a random way, probably aligning with the same thoughts that clouded his expression with conflicting darkness.

He looked at me as though the idea was foreign.

Ridiculous.

Unthinkable.

Yet, he wanted to. I could see it. It was hanging in his silence, dancing in his stillness, screaming in his hesitation. He wanted to do it, to breathe, to separate himself from the business that controlled his life so staunchly. Could he do it, though? He was a workaholic. I didn't know if the way he worked was healthy. Then again, I was still settling into it fully myself.

"All right," he said after a minute or two of silence. "I'll take a day off. Tomorrow. If you take one with me."

I knew there'd be a catch.

Lie. I didn't. But it makes perfect sense.

"And do what?" I asked, hugging my leg a little tighter.

"Wake up at ten in the morning, shout at stupid TV, eat junk food, screw around...with each other."

"You always have to make sex part of the equation, don't you?"

"Yes. Why wouldn't I?"

187

I sighed and dropped my foot back to the floor. "Fine. I'll take tomorrow off, but you will, too."

"Tomorrow?"

"No, let's plan this in six months time," I scoffed. "Tomorrow, Damien. You have…" I glanced at my watch. "Enough hours left today to let all your minions know."

He twirled a lock of my hair around his finger. "You underestimate how angry my father is going to be."

"And you're a thirty-year-old man without the dramatic flair of Fergus," I replied dryly. "Perhaps you should not be worried about your father because he doesn't run the business anymore, you do."

"He still owns it."

"So do you."

"Stop making so much sense."

I grinned. "It's a female thing. I can't help it."

He met my eyes, then turned, rolling his. He stretched his hands far above his head and said, "Tomorrow, then. We'll both take a day off and you'll show me how to relax."

"In a way that isn't sex."

"I'm not agreeing to that."

Of course, he wasn't. "Well, if you're good, I'll drop you on the Strip and you can pick up a friend."

He shook his head, briefly closing his eyes. When he opened them again, he stood, stopped, then turned to lean over me. His hands gripped the back of the bench on either side of me. The tightness of his grip radiated up his arms, exaggerating the veins that trailed up his forearms and the muscles that bulged on his biceps. "No need," he said in a low voice, face inches from mine. He reached for my jaw and cupped it, tilting my face up toward it. "The only picking up I'll be doing will be when I pick you up to fuck you against the wall."

"You sound pretty certain of that."

His fingers dug into my jaw and—

Just like that—

He kissed me.

SIN

One kiss. Firm. Confident. Hot.

His lips pressed against mine with the certainty of a man who had every intention of following through with the words he'd just said.

While my mind protested, my body did not.

"See you tonight," he said, lips still touching mine. "When you'll be against that wall."

"Tonight?" I jolted back, swallowing.

"Day off starts at midnight." He pushed off the back of the bench to stand up straight. His upper body blocked out the sun, and the light streamed around him as if it were framing an angel.

The glint in his eyes told a different story.

The sun wasn't even highlighting a devil.

It was highlighting a walking, talking, sin.

One I should be saying no to.

One I couldn't say no to.

One who enthralled me and held my attention in the palm of his head, who distracted me at every possible turn.

If I had to compare him to something, it'd be a romance novel. One that was deep and dark and questionable, full of secrets and twisty-turns layered under lies and sex and lust.

"Midnight, then," I said, my voice barely louder than a whisper.

"Midnight." He winked and turned, and as he disappeared from my view, I didn't have the words to ask him where he was going.

But me…I had to go home.

I had to think about what the hell was going on and what the ever-loving hell I was doing, playing with fire the way I was.

DAMIEN

"Cease and Desist!" Dad roared, throwing the sheets of paper down onto the desk between us. "A fucking Cease and Desist, Damien!"

"I got one, too."

"The offer was one and a half times what that shithole is worth!"

The smell of hard rum permeated the air.

Once a year, it took over.

Numbed the pain, he said. Of her birthday. Of their deaths. Of the loss of more than them. Of everything. As if it didn't hurt for the rest of the year, too. Like it didn't hurt worse when it was ignored.

"Her father was a nightmare, but this girl is something else. She learned from the worst," Dad went on, kicking a chair under the desk. "I'm surprised she hasn't gone out of business already. Fucking hell, it's a miracle that her old man managed to keep the business going. I give her six months before she fucks it all up and—"

"You know nothing about her." I stood, shoving my chair away from me. "I have no idea what your fucking obsession with that bar is, but you have no idea what kind of a businesswoman she is."

He hit me with a dark stare. "What kind of businesswoman is she, Damien? She ruthless? Harsh? Cutting?"

"She's honest." I rubbed my hand across my forehead, pulling my chair back beneath me.

My father's laugh was cruel as it sliced through the air. "Honest? Honest works when you're sixteen, son. Not in business."

"I said she was honest, I didn't say she was weak."

"You mistake those for being different things."

"Do I? Because the way I see it, Dad, she's the furthest thing from weak. She's one of the strongest people I've ever met. She's twenty-five and just got an entire business dumped on her shoulders. Have you considered the kind of pressure she's under right now?"

"Strong?" That cold laugh echoed again as he reached forward and grabbed the cigarette box from the desk. He tapped one of the long, white sticks out and placed it between his lips to light it.

I wrinkled my face as he lit a match and held it up to the end. It glowed bright orange in the dim light, the smoke from the dying match swirling through the air in front of Dad's face.

"She just ran away for three months," Dad said, silvery smoke escaping his lips with each word. "She hid and left the running of her bar up to someone else. That's not strong, son."

"She was strong enough to realize she needed time." I stared up at him.

He cut a cold, heartless figure, one that was hard to love—that had been hard to love for the past few years. Every ounce of ability to feel emotion he'd once had, had died with the two people he loved most in this world. That much was painfully true, and it was a fact I was reminded of every time I opened my mouth.

I might have been the prodigal son, the heir to the Fox empire, his visual double, but I was the furthest thing from perfect. I'd always been third-best to him. I always would be.

"And for you to talk about strength is rich," I said in a low voice, unmoving. "You've drunk your way through their deaths each year. You hide every time they're mentioned and refuse to talk about them. You avoid it as if it never happened and they'll walk through the door any minute. When you accept the fact that Mom and Penelope—"

"Don't!"

"—are never coming back, then you can stand on your fucking pedestal and criticize other people for being what you perceive as weak. At least she's brave enough to stand up and take responsibility for her business, even if that means telling you to go and fuck yourself. And you know what? She isn't wrong."

His cigarette burned brightly as it hung out of the corner of his mouth. "If you weren't my son—"

"You'd be fucked," I replied flatly. "Because without me, this business would have gone under the day they died. You tell me Dahlia is weak, yet I've been running this for the past eight years. You slapped this on my shoulders at twenty-two. I've lived and breathed this company that entire time, doing whatever the fuck you wanted me to. I haven't seen my sister in six years. We lost more than Mom and Penelope that day if only you'd open your fucking eyes and see it. I lost my entire family."

Dad took a long drag on the cigarette, then violently stubbed it out in the glass ashtray in front of him. The smoke wisped up into the air in a long line before it finally died, disappearing into the tense silence that enveloped us.

"I don't know what you're doing with that girl," he said in a tight voice. Planting his hands flat on the desk, he leaned forward until only inches separated the tips of our noses. "But it's all a bad fuckin' idea. Those Lloyds ain't nothin' but trouble."

I said nothing. I couldn't honestly tell him what I was doing with Dahlia because I didn't know either. At least not enough to be able to tell him honestly. Until I figured that shit out myself, it was a topic of conversation off-bounds.

Just like my mother and sister were for him.

After a few minutes of strained, angry silence, my father pushed up off the desk. As he left the room, slamming the door behind him, so did the chill that accompanied his presence. The room warmed as if I'd just opened the curtains and direct sunlight was glaring in through the window.

The worst part was that the blinds were open and the sunlight was already streaming through the windows.

The echo of the slammed door receded, leaving me sitting in complete silence. Emotion churned inside of me. Anger, frustration, grief—it all tickled at my skin, forcing the hair on my arms to stand on end until I was forced to fight off a shiver.

Discomfort.

That was the lingering, strengthening feeling that hugged me as I sat in the quietness of my office. My father would be long gone, off to do whatever it was he did when he was confronted with shit he didn't want to face up to. I wouldn't see him for a few days now. That was the way it worked.

He'd get annoyed. I'd piss him off more. He'd disappear.

I didn't know why I still cared. I was fucking thirty-years-old. I wasn't a child desperate for his approval anymore, yet here I was, caring as though his opinion was the be-all and end-all of the purpose of my life.

It wouldn't just be the mention of my mom and sister that pushed him over the edge. My defense of Dahlia would have angered him just as much. I'd asked him many times why he had such a dislike of her family, but he'd never told me. I doubted he ever would.

For the life of me, I couldn't think why he hated them.

If her parents were anything like she was, and for the little I knew, they were, there was no way any rationally minded person could hate them.

Of course, my father wasn't rationally minded. He wasn't rational in anything. Cold and heartless and broken, yes. But not rational.

I looked up and stared at the closed door.

So many secrets. So many lies.

Would I ever know the fucking truth?

***

Little lights illuminated the dark, metal gates that separated Dahlia's house from the rest of the city. The yellow-white glow they gave off bounced off the shiniest parts of the gate.

I glanced around as I pulled my car to a stop. I expected to see the guy who guarded it, but there was nobody around. After a moment of waiting in the car, I got out.

Nothing.

Nothing except the tiny blinking light on the intercom. I stepped forward and pressed the button, and right at that moment, something snapped behind me.

I turned and jumped.

The figure of a well-built man stepped out from behind a small, dark building. The cigarette between his lips pulsed and glowed as he broke through the darkness. Momentarily, panic jolted through my stomach.

It receded when the man drew level with the lights on the gates.

"Dustin." I chuckled nervously. "You scared the shit out of me there."

He laughed back, smoke swirling around his head. "Sorry 'bout that, Mr. Fox. Ms. Lloyd doesn't like me smoking in the building, so I just stepped out for a moment." He held the cigarette up. "Let me get the gates for you. She told me you'd be by late."

He retreated into the building, leaving his cigarette perched on an ashtray just outside the door. There was no judgment or question in his voice about why I'd be here so late, just matter-of-fact that I would be.

That was appreciated. I wasn't in the mood for endless questions. I'd had enough of those in the past few hours. Dad had been MIA since our conversation, and the thought of my still-living sister had plagued me since that moment.

The gates creaked open, swinging inward.

"Thanks, Dustin," I called, opening my car door again.

"Anytime, Mr. Fox." He stepped back out of the building and raised a hand to me, bending down for his cigarette.

I started my engine and drove through the gates. The driveway was long and badly lit, but my headlights guided me safely down to the house.

Lights blared out from the windows downstairs. Curtains twitched as I got out of the car and locked it. The beep echoed through the night, seeming too loud. It'd wake the dead if there were any around here.

I raised my hand to knock on the door, but it swung open before my fist could connect with the wood.

"I have to admit to being surprised," Dahlia said, standing there in nothing but a long tank top with a low neckline. "I didn't think you'd actually show up at midnight."

I glanced at my watch. "Technically speaking, I'm late. And if you didn't think I'd show up, why are you awake."

She waved a book at me.

Stepping inside, I glanced at her shirt. It read 'Boys in books are better.' I raised an eyebrow. "I didn't take you for a graphic tee kind of person."

She looked down at it. "I'm sorry—should I be wearing lingerie just as expensive as my car?"

"Would you like to be?"

"Are you here for a day off or to annoy me?"

"You seem to be confusing those things for being different."

She groaned, shutting the door. "Whose idea was this?"

Grinning, I reached for her and pulled her close. I had to laugh when she held her arm out so her book didn't get crushed between our bodies. "Yours," I said, still chuckling. "But, don't worry. Your book is safe."

"Oh, well, thank goodness. This is turning out well already." She rolled her eyes and extracted herself from my arms. "Hold this so I can set the alarm."

She shoved the book at me before I could answer. Somehow, I managed to keep the page she was on, and I flipped it so I could take a look at the cover. There was a man in a suit in a very—ahem—compromising picture with a woman in not a lot of clothing at all. He was grasping her ass and she had her head thrown back in pleasure.

Dahlia cleared her throat. I peered up at her standing in front of me, hand outstretched for the book, eyebrows raised expectantly.

"What is this?" I asked, showing her the cover.

"A book," she answered smartly.

"It looks like a guide to porn."

"I'd be hard-pressed to disagree with you. Can I have my book back now, please?"

I looked at the book and then her.

"Fine, then put it back on the shelf. Insufferable man." The last two words were said entirely to herself, muttered under her breath as she spun on the balls of her feet and headed down the hall.

I followed her. Why was she so bothered about me examining her book? It was just a damn story. I turned my attention back down to the book in my hand. *The Virgin Billionaire.*

Huh?

"*The Virgin Billionaire,*" I read slowly, a few feet behind her. "Interesting."

"My God," she breathed, clapping her hands to her face. "Why did I bring the book? Of all the things, I brought the book."

"I'm quite interested in this. Who's the virgin billionaire?"

"Damien."

"Why are they a virgin if they're a billionaire? Do they know you can pay people to help you with that?"

She whispered something to herself, turning and walking into a dimly-lit room. The walls were lined with bookshelves. Books were stacked in order in places, haphazardly in others. I couldn't see any of the titles, but I had a good feeling some of them matched the book I was currently holding.

"The Virgin Billionaire," I said again, rolling the words around my mouth.

"Oh my God." Dahlia threw herself down on the sofa and covered her face with her hands. "This is the most embarrassing day of my life."

I grinned and sat next to her. "Are you reading a dirty bit?" I opened the book and looked down at the pages.

She was reading a dirty bit.

"Well," I said, clearing my throat. "Is this boy in this book better?"

"All right, that's enough. I like dirty books. I'm not ashamed of that!" She rolled to face me and made a grab for the book.

I held my arm out so the book was out of her reach and read, "*He pulled her close with a tug on her arm. Her knees buckled, sending her flying down on top of him.*"

"Stop!" Dahlia swung for it again.

"*A little adjustment was all it took for her to be straddling him, pushing her hot center against his cock. His erection bulged against his tight pants, and instantly, he regretted putting them on that morning.*"

"Stop it!" She covered her face again.

"*She whimpered at the contact, but she didn't push him away. She had no reason to—she knew what it felt like when he was inside her.*" I paused, pursing my lips to hold back my laughter. "'*And she wanted nothing more than to feel his pulsing cock burying itself in her slick wetness once again.*' This chick is no virgin," I added.

"Oh my God. They fucked already. Give me the damn book!" She dropped her hands with such vigor that they slapped against her thighs. "You're being ridiculous."

"You're the one reading trashy novels about a 'pulsing cock' and 'slick wetness.'"

"And this is why boys are better in books."

"Why? Because their cocks pulse? What are they—set to fucking vibrate?"

She blinked at me with those wide eyes. Her shoulders trembled, and her lips twitched with the effort to keep her obvious amusement at bay. "Damien," she said, voice quivering with laughter. "Give me back my book."

"No. I want to know more about this pulsing cock of…" I scanned the page. "Matt's. I'm intrigued. What else does he do to her?"

"Dami—"

"*With just a breath of air separating their lips, Matt said, 'I want you, Lily. Once wasn't enough.'*"

"*I can't,*" *she replied, breathless.* "*You work for me, Matt. I promised myself it couldn't happen again.*"

"*Frustration coiled in his stomach. She had no idea how badly he wanted her—how much he needed her. He had an ache only she could fill, and that would only be filled if he could fill her.*" I slapped the book shut and gave her a flat look. "Oh, come on. It would only be filled if he could fill her? Is she a fucking grocery bag?"

Dahlia launched herself at me. This time, she put her entire body into it, and she threw herself on top of me, stretching her arm out for the book. Her fingers brushed it, and I held it out as far as I possibly could without her being able to actually grab it.

"Give me the book!" She reached out further, climbing more and more on top of me.

My cock twitched.

"Sweetheart, if you have an ounce of sense left after reading this crap, you'll get off me right now."

"Why?" She tilted her head to meet my eyes, arm still outstretched. "Is your cock pulsing?"

"I never want to hear those two words together again."

She grinned wickedly. "It's funny. You say you hate those words, but your cock actually does pulse when you come."

"Been thinking about that, have you?"

"Only when I wonder who's better in bed—you or Matt."

I dropped the book onto the table next to the sofa and pulled her onto my lap. She slipped her legs on either side of me, straddling me exactly how I'd just read in the book. My cock was even hard and straining against my zipper. Never mind that the thought she'd been comparing me to a fictional person was enough to make me shudder—the thought we were recreating that scene was terrifying.

Or was it?

Her cheeks were flushed. Her eyes shone. And where she could have climbed off me, she was still, looking into my eyes.

Had that book turned her on? Was it a coincidence? It had to be—she had no way to know that I'd be taking the book from her and would read it.

"Is that what you think of when you read? If I'm better than the guy who doesn't exist?" I asked in a low voice, spreading my fingers across the small of her back.

"Maybe I do."

"Shall we finish reading how good Matt is and then I'll show you?" I snatched up the book and flicked back to the slightly-bent page before she could say a word. "Here we go. *'Despite her insistences otherwise, Lily didn't protest when Matt stripped off her shirt and kissed down her chest. He fondled her breasts, taking her nipples into his mouth, gripping her ass like if he let go, she'd run. Maybe she would. She didn't know what she was doing and she couldn't think as he ran a finger along the inside of her thigh, up to the quivering bundle of nerves that was her clitoris.'"*

"Oh God," Dahlia whispered.

"Does your clitoris quiver?" I asked, deadly serious.

She opened her mouth to speak, then closed it. She did that a couple times before her throat bobbed and she said, "I've never particularly associated those words with one another, no."

"So, there's a pulsating cock and a quivering clitoris. Excellent. One is set to vibrate and the other is terrified."

This time, she couldn't contain her laughter. She dropped her head down onto my shoulder. Her entire body shook as she fought the giggles that vibrated through my shirt and onto my skin. They ultimately won out, and each little laugh was sweet and low as they escaped her.

"How do you read this?" I closed the book—for the final time because I wasn't going to traumatize myself further—and turned my head toward hers. "It's all flowery, girly shit."

"I like it, okay?" She sat back upright. "You're reading a very tiny part of a book. And yeah, some of the sex scenes might be a little cringey, but you're missing the bigger picture."

"Don't tell me his friend has a pulsating cock, too."

"The love story." She tapped her fingers against my shoulder. "The sex scenes are probably five percent of the book. The rest is all about they fall in love, and that's what really matters."

My stomach tightened. "That so? Love over sex?"

Dahlia glanced at the book and then back at me. Except on me, her gaze lingered, deep and dark and soulful, swirling with uncertainty. "Well, yeah. Isn't that what it's all about? If I wanted to read books about sex over love, I would. But I don't. I want to read about two people overcoming obstacles and falling in love despite all the odds."

The way her voice dipped at the end had me freezing.

She looked away, dropping her eyes to the arm of the sofa.

But still, she didn't move.

I did, though.

I reached up, cupping her soft cheek, and turned her face back to mine. I traced over the freckles that decorated her nose and upper cheeks with my gaze. She was makeup free. So fucking beautiful it almost hurt to look at her. To look at someone so unfairly perfect with such hesitance in her eyes.

She believed in love—unequivocally.

I…My jury was out on it, but if pushed, I didn't.

She believed it brought happiness.

I believed it brought nothing but pain.

Yet, I kissed her. I pulled her face to mine and brushed my lips against hers. Tenderly and thoughtfully. So fucking softly my entire body screamed at me to press harder, kiss her deeper, take her to desperation.

I didn't. I waited. Waited until the tingles from the touch of her lips against mine had subsided and given way to unfightable desire.

She should have fought. Should have pushed me away.

But she didn't. She leaned in, kissing *me* harder, wrapping her hands around the back of my neck until her body was pressed flat against mine. She spread her legs, pushing her wet little cunt against my cock, melding herself into me as much as she could.

It wasn't, though. She wasn't as close against me as she could have been. We both knew it, so when she flicked her tongue against the seam of my mouth in a silent plea for more, I took the opportunity she offered me.

I gripped her tight ass, holding her against me so that she couldn't move away, and I kissed her properly. I kissed her, tongue against tongue until her hips gyrated and begged. I kissed the fucking hell out of her until she dragged her hands down to the buttons of my shirt and undid them, one by torturous one.

Her hands across my skin were hot and teasing, exploring my body with the ease of a woman who knew what she wanted. She was irresistible and undeniable, poison in a person.

I ran my hands over her body, sliding them up and down her bare thighs, reaching beneath the hem of her tank that had barely skimmed beneath the curve of her ass. Her skin was smooth and hot. Her muscles clenched as my fingers edged ever closer to her pussy.

She gasped into my mouth as my thumb made contact with her clit. She was wet, slick beneath my touch, and she moved her hips, pressing her clit into my thumb further.

Her nails dug into my shoulders as she flexed. My teeth dragged across her lower lips. I wanted to be an ass, to ask her a stupid question in relation to that goddamn book, but I couldn't. She was on top of me, half naked as she'd been when she'd opened the door, and my hand was uncomfortably between us, my fingers finding their way through the wetness of her pussy.

Dahlia leaned up, putting space between her pussy and my cock. Tilting my head back to kiss her, I reached further between her legs.

She beat me to it.

Propping herself up with one arm on the back of the sofa, she slid the other between us and undid my pants. Button, zipper, then, underwear. She moved her hand right in and freed my rock hard cock, her soft fingers wrapping around it.

My entire body clenched when she rubbed her thumb over the head of my cock. It throbbed, my balls tightening when she gripped me tightly.

Then, she moved her hips right over me, positioning her pussy just inches above the tip of my dick. Her hand was still wrapped around me, hugging me tight, just waiting for the moment when she could lower herself onto me.

"Wait." I held onto her hips, pulling my mouth away from hers. I dug into my pocket and pulled out my wallet. A condom was tucked into it, and I extracted it quickly. Within seconds, I had it open and was rolling it onto my cock.

Dahlia took over, pushing it down as far as it would go before she kissed me again. This assertive side of her sent both frustration and thrills through my body, but I took it. I took whatever I could get because I knew it wouldn't last.

The second she slid that wet pussy onto my cock, she'd be at my mercy. She'd belong to me, if only for an hour, if only for moments or minutes.

And that was what I wanted.

Her to belong to me.

She grabbed my cock. Positioned her hips above me. Lowered herself.

SIN

Pushed her tight, wet, cunt down onto my throbbing, hard cock.

She took me deep. Her muscles clenched as she stretched for me. Heat throbbed through my body like an otherworldly feeling. There was nothing like being buried deep inside her. Nothing.

It was an escape and torture at the same time.

I gripped the back of her neck and pressed my mouth against hers. My scalp tingled when she gripped her fingers into my hair and held onto me tight.

She moved against me.

Rocked her hips.

Flexed her body.

Took my cock like it was second nature.

Like it didn't make a difference.

She rode me like she was made for me.

I gripped her ass and fucked her like I owned her.

Fucked her 'til she couldn't take it anymore and cried out, her lips by my ear. Until I was ready. Until her wet pussy was pleasure and beyond. Until her tight little fucking pussy was clenching for all she was worth and her moans were nothing but ecstasy in my ears.

Until her moans mingled with my groans.

Until I held her so hard I bruised her skin with my fingers, fucking her, pleasing her, pleasing me.

And she owned me.

Until, for mere moments, I owned her, too.

21

DAHLIA

I tiptoed across the bedroom to the door. Damien was sleeping soundly in the bed, and I didn't want to be the reason he woke up, but thirty minutes of lying in bed in silence was enough for me.

I took a deep breath and crept through the doorway into the hall. I had to grab my boobs with my hand given the fact I was naked except for my panties. I held on tight as I made my way downstairs and into the utility room. Grabbing a bra and long shirt, I dressed, walking into the kitchen.

It wasn't early by any means. Ten-thirty blinked the clock on the oven. It glared at me as I started the coffee machine with a yawn. I'd had eight hours of sleep, but it felt like I'd had about two. My head was so damn foggy I was going to need at least three cups of coffee just to get through to the afternoon.

I yawned again.

I had to figure out what to do today since the whole day-off thing was my idea. Unfortunately, I was regretting it. What kind of thing was I meant to do? Should we go swimming? Bake cakes? Swan around doing whatever?

Ugh.

I hadn't thought this through, clearly.

What the hell was I doing?

The coffee machine sputtered into silence, pulling my attention to my now full mug. I grabbed it with a clink and reached to the fridge for the milk.

I had no idea what I was doing.

When the milk was back in the fridge, I reached for my phone and texted Mia. I knew all about the tempestuous beginning to her relationship with West—in fact, she'd all but admitted he was as much of a pain for her then as Damien was for me now.

Me: *What do you do with a workaholic who's taking his first day off in forever?*

I'd barely put my phone down when it buzzed with her reply.

Mia: *Have sex with him.*
Me: *I don't know why I asked you.*
Mia: *Are you with Damien?????????*
Me: *I plead the Fifth.*
Mia: *Girl Code says that's a yes.*
Me: *Eh, Girl Code is ridiculous.*
Mia: *Are you having sex with Damien?*

I pinched the bridge of my nose.

Me: *Yes. Right now, in fact. I'm on my knees with the phone under my pillow.*
Mia: *Smartass.*

I laughed, putting my phone down again. That conversation wasn't going to give me any serious answers. Some people—cough, Mia, cough—could have sex over and over. Abby was another one of those people.

I wasn't.

At least, I didn't think I was. I guessed I'd never really had time to find out. Besides, what was better? Lots of quick, sub-par sex, or less of long, earth-shattering sex?

Definitely the earth-shattering sex.

If I wanted quick and unexciting sex, I'd use my fingers.

I sighed heavily and sat down. I felt deflated, like the slip of the moment conversation had been a giant mistake.

Right then, sitting in the middle of my kitchen in total silence, the weight of my emotions was crushing. It lasted only a second, a sick mixture of grief and confusion and frustration before it disappeared again. But the second was long enough. Too long. Too strong.

My laptop was sitting closed just a couple of feet away from me. I reached over and slid it toward me to start it up. While I wasn't aiming to work, I knew I was falling into the rabbit hole by just turning the thing on.

Sure enough, the moment I logged in and opened the browser, my email loaded up.

Three hundred unread emails. All right—they weren't all work. I had a terrible habit of subscribing to websites using my work email, not my personal one because who had time for more than one email?

Not me, evidently.

I scrolled to the last read email, deciding that working forward was my best bet. I moved the website emails into another folder to check, deleted some spam, and then…moved into the folder where I'd just put the sales emails.

Was shopping for new shoes for work, working?

I tapped my nails against the laptop for a moment, lips pursed.

No.

Not this morning, at least.

I didn't need more shoes, but I wanted them. Or rather, I wanted something to do, and if there was one thing I knew, it was that buying shoes was always a good idea.

I sipped my coffee as the website loaded. I'd been awake now for an hour. Damien said he always woke up early, but here I was, waiting for him to wake up.

Was he that exhausted?

Was he maybe naked in my shower?

Damn it, no. I didn't need to think about him naked in my shower, but if I followed my shoe analogy…No, no. I wasn't going to do that. The jury was still out on how freaking crazy I was. I didn't need to add fuel to the mental fire I had for that.

What I wanted to do was wake him up and ask him a ton of questions. I had so many I probably needed a notebook to write them all down so I wouldn't forget. I had so many that I was afraid to ask.

Why don't you talk about your sisters? What about your mom? What happened to make your family so awkward and complicated? What did life do to you to make you so closed-off?

Where did the scar by your eye come from?

That was one was the most terrifying. Would he tell me? Did I have a right to know? To *ask*? Was it really any of my business?

The answer, of course, was no. I didn't have any rights and it was none of my business. If it were me, I'd be telling him where to stick it.

I guess what I hated more than anything was that he knew so much about me, yet in the grand scheme of everything, I knew so little about him.

Sure. I knew that he was handsome and cocky and, sometimes, he made me laugh. He was tempting and sexy and a walking sin. Firm and strong, his body was a walking wet dream, and his mouth was so dirty, he could probably make a woman come with just words.

I knew that he had a pain buried somewhere. That sometimes, his eyes belied his words and gave me a peek at that pain. That it was one he carried heavily, tucking it away behind a poker face.

I also knew that somewhere, deep down inside, he was capable of emotion so strong it could bring a person to their knees. There was no doubt about it—I'd barely scratched the surface of the man, and that was both exhilarating and terrifying.

Maybe I'd never really make a dent. Maybe this was all convenient, still part of the grand plan to take what was mine.

Maybe he was so good at hiding emotion that he could pretend it, too.

I was either reading too deep or not deep enough. I was either a fool or, well, a fool. Either one was dangerous.

Fools rushed in.

Fools fell in love.

Fools kept the scars.

I didn't want to be a fool. Not for him.

Anyone but him.

Yet, there I was. Shopping, wearing little clothing, waiting for him to wake up. Waiting to see him walk through the door into the kitchen and smile at me.

Like a fool.

Like I wasn't vulnerable and a little lost. Like my heart still wasn't shattered irreparably.

Like he could fucking *fix* the ache that followed me around constantly. The same ache I now recognized for what it was—loneliness.

I was lonely.

My house was huge and empty, filled with ghosts around every corner. The pictures that had hung in the entryway for years did nothing but remind me of the time in my life when my mom was killed, of when everything changed and I learned that a skinned knee was the least painful thing that would ever happen to me.

The only person I'd ever trusted and loved in my life who hadn't left me was Abby.

The idea that I was learning to trust and feel for Damien Fox was the most frightening thing I could think of.

But I was.

The stairs creaked, slicing through my self-pity. The uncontrollable thoughts disappeared, locking back away in the back of my mind. Where they belonged.

I minimized the Internet screen when he walked in, filling the doorway with his presence. His hair, wet and sticking up, almost touched the frame, while his shoulders filled out a good portion of the rest of it. A water droplet trickled down the side of his abs and melted into the waistband of his sweatpants.

I stared there a little too long. It wasn't my fault—another bit of water slipped down his tanned skin into the low-slung band that hugged exactly the part of him that I wanted to touch.

"Are you working?"

I snapped out of my trance. I wasn't going to acknowledge the way my heart beat a little faster, either. Nope. Not for a second.

"No," I said when he rounded and came behind me. "I'm shopping."

"What are you buying?"

"Shoes." The word was a mumble. I had pairs upon pairs.

"Why is the browser closed?"

"Habit. My dad used to tell me I had enough shoes, so I used to hide it when I was supposed to be working."

He leaned in, laughing quietly. "Sweetheart, you do have enough shoes. I just counted ninety-nine pairs in your closet. You may as well make it a round hundred."

"I don't have ninety-nine pairs of shoes!" I turned my face to him.

That was ridiculous. Wasn't it?

"You sure do." His lips tugged up on one side, and the rightness in his usually stern gaze made a tickle tease down the back of my neck. "Like I said, what's one more pair?"

"I…Well…I…Um. Never mind." I knew a futile attempt as denial when I tried it.

He laughed again, gripped the edge of the counter, and opened the Internet browser for me. His body was still a little damp, but it was hot, and his chest pressed against my shoulder blades as he leaned right in and scrolled down the website.

"You're pretty into shoe shopping," I said when he hummed.

"I'm pretty into you wearing these shoes while I fuck you."

Fair enough.

"These." He stopped and clicked on a lace-up pair of scarlet red heels. They had a pretty price tag but at the same time… They were oh-so-pretty.

"I can't possibly imagine where I'll wear them. I was looking for a pair for work."

Damien tapped a finger to the screen. "Scarlet heels. Scarlet Letter. Problem solved." He hit 'Add to Cart' and slid my laptop over in front of the next stool. "And I have plenty of imagination for where you can wear them."

"What are you doing?" I blinked at him as he perched on the seat.

"I'm buying you shoes."

More blinking. "I can buy my own shoes."

"No, really?" His tone was flat. "I thought you were dirt poor and living in this palace by accident."

"I can buy my own shoes."

"You're mistaking me for someone who cares."

I reached for the laptop, but he knocked my hand away. His finger flew over the number pad on the right. I stared, slightly horrified, as he entered his card numbers and his address, then hit 'Process.'

Oh my God.

The confirmation page flashed up.

"There. Problem solved." He closed my laptop and gave it back to me. Then, without looking at me, got up and walked over to my coffee machine.

He'd just spent a little under fifteen-hundred dollars on a pair of shoes for me and not blinked at it.

"I mean. Sure. If you say so." Great. Now I felt like I owed him.

Also, why was he buying me shoes?

"Why did you buy the shoes?"

"Because you weren't going to. Like one more pair would matter." He laughed and made his coffee. When it was done pouring and he'd turned around to me, I raised my eyebrows.

He promptly ignored my annoyed look.

"What are we doing today?"

"Ummm." Great question.

"You have no idea, do you?" He smiled behind his mug.

Again, denial would be futile. "Not a damn clue."

"Let's go for a run."

I eeked out a strangled noise that was a little too alike a choir of alleycats at midnight. "Running? It's hot as Hades out there."

He shrugged. "I'll buy you chocolate after."

"Chocolate? Really? Am I five?"

"No. You're a very beautiful twenty-five, but if you don't want the chocolate…"

"I can buy my own."

"I know. But I'll probably run shirtless."

I hit him with a firm stare that completely expressed my displeasure at the idea, but damn if he didn't talk me into it. I could deal with him shirtless and running.

Maybe.

22

DAHLIA

"I hate you!" I shouted, running several feet behind him. "I hope you break your knee!"

His laughter echoed through the desert air.

"I hope you choke on your laughter, you sick bastard!"

More laughter.

"Sadist! Satan is your friend, you shit!"

That did it. Damien stopped and bent over, hands on his knees. His arms were tensed, and the utter bastard didn't have as much as a roll of fat on his stomach, even bent forward.

The worst part was his laughter.

I'd died at least five times. I'd visited Hell each and every time, and Satan had laughed at—wait, no. That wasn't Satan. It was his long-lost cousin, Damien freaking Fox.

"Stop laughing at me." I was aware I was whining. But, I was also wheezing, and I couldn't stop. My lungs were on fire. My hair was plastered to my skin. My skin was weeping sweat the way teenage girls wept when One Direction broke up.

I hated my life.

I wanted to kill the hot, shirtless asshole who'd made me do this.

I collapsed onto the ground. It was dirty and sandy and dusty, but I was already looking like something out of a junkyard, so who cared? Not me. That much I knew.

"You don't run, do you?" Damien asked through his laughter.

Gritting my teeth, I answered, "No. I cycle. I do yoga. Pilates. Spin class. I don't run."

"That was a rhetorical question."

"The only appropriate rhetorical question right now is me asking you how painful you'd like your death to be. If I'm going, you're coming with me."

"The only place you're going is back to the car. We're back where we started."

"Then I suggest you find water while I attempt to regain control of my breathing."

He half-grinned and jogged over to the dusty parking area where his now not-shiny car was. Dust had decorated the front and sides the moment we'd arrived, and all I could think was that at least I matched the car.

I didn't think he'd appreciate the dirt inside it very much but never mind.

Damien returned, carrying two of the towels from my closet and two bottles of water. Without speaking, he handed me one of each.

I drank that water faster than I'd ever drunk anything in my life.

I still felt like hell.

Ugh.

"Better?" Damien eyed me.

"No. I still hate you."

"Some things never change." He was fighting a grin if the twitching in his cheeks was anything to go by.

He came over, the towel around his neck, and held a hand out to me. Reluctantly, I took it. He heaved me up with a firm grip and a giant tug, right against his body, where he pressed a hard kiss against my mouth before dragging me after him.

"Let's go," he said. "But wipe your legs...Or sit on the towel."

"No. I plan to smear dirt all over the inside of your car. It's your punishment."

He winced, his fingers momentarily tightening around mine. "Please don't."

"You owe me so much chocolate right now."

"I'll buy you an M&M factory. Will that suffice?"

"The entire factory? I'll take a weekly subscription."

Laughing, he unlocked the car and reached for the door. "Duly noted. Shower, then food?"

I peered back at him as I got into the car. "Yes, but you're cooking."

Even as he shut the door, his groan was audible.

And oh-so-satisfying.

The drive back to my house was taken in silence. I had to exchange several messages with Abby about a mistake in the order that meant my shower was delayed by fifteen minutes while I called the supplier to fix it.

They did, not without moaning, but my entirely bullshit threat to change suppliers soon changed their tune.

Now, I was thankfully, blissfully, in the shower. I planned to stay for at least an hour to make sure I washed off every inch of this damn dust. I was grimy and dirty, and those were two things I wasn't used to being.

The water beat down on me. It was so refreshing, and I spent a good few minutes alternating between hot and cold water. The extremes were wildly refreshing against my dirty skin, and I felt cleaner than I had all day.

Dust and sweat were not a good combination. Ever.

I ran my hands through my wet hair, squeezing my eyes shut and screwing up my face as the water hit it.

The fact I was half drowning in hot water was the only explanation for why I realized I wasn't alone until I felt hands grasping my hips.

"What are you doing?" I gasped and stepped out of the water.

Damien spun us both, putting himself under the showerhead so the water trickled over me, just enough to keep me warm. His fingers tightened on my skin as he pulled me back against him, tucking me against his body.

His cock hardened when it pressed against my ass and lower back. The heat that flushed through me had nothing to do with the water. Uncontrollable and feverish, desire swamped me, tingling through me until all I felt was want for him.

"Showering with you," Damien murmured, his lips in my hair. "I'm killing two birds with one stone."

"What birds are they?"

"Where I get clean and fuck you at the same time."

My heart went crazy. It thumped furiously against my ribs, and I clenched my thighs together as his hands crept over my hips and closer to the apex of my thighs.

"It's slippery in here." My attempt at a refusal was laughable. My clit was aching, throbbing, begging me to give in to what he wanted.

"Turn around." He brushed his lips over my earlobe.

With a deep, shuddering breath, I spun, pressing my bare body against his, turning into the stream of the hot water that cascaded over his body.

He slipped his hand up my back, cupping the side of my face. His fingers brushed my hair. His thumb pressed against my jaw as his lips found mine, taking my mouth in a sweet yet suggestive kiss that had his tongue sweeping across the seam of my mouth.

"Open your legs," he said against my lips. "Let me touch that tight little cunt of yours."

My thighs clenched again, this time, tighter than before.

"Dahlia." His voice was smooth, sexy, deep. An order and a plea, all wrapped into my name, making it impossible to deny his demand. "I love when you do what I say."

His hand found its way between my legs as he kissed me once more. His thumb circled my clit in seconds, pushing pleasure through my body easily. I was already turned on and ready for him, but a part of me wanted to make him work for it.

Make him want it like I wanted him.

Make him need it more than I did.

Moving away from him, I reached between us. My fingers trailed across his skin, searching for his cock. His wet, hot skin was smooth beneath my touch and there was nothing comparable to the way he twitched and flexed against my hand.

Slowly, I wrapped my fingers around his cock, grasping him gently but firmly. His cock throbbed against my grip, his fingers tightening on my neck and now, my hip.

The water was a lubricant, and slowly, I moved. Up and down, playing with him, rubbing my thumb over the head of his cock, relishing the way that one, thick vein that traveled the length of his shaft pulsed against my fingers.

I squeezed.

He snapped.

Damien pushed me against the cold, wet tiles. He ripped my hand from his cock and grasped my thighs, lifting me, bringing my pussy level with his erection.

The word "condom" flashed through my mind as he kissed me and pushed himself inside.

It was desperate and unapologetic, panic mostly canceled out by my own knowledge of my contraception. A fizzle of fear held, but there was something about the way his hot skin felt against my pussy, about the way his bare skin slid against mine, nothing but my wetness separating us.

I gripped him tightly. My fingers dug into his shoulder and upper back, but he made no complaints. My back slid against the wet wall, but he unfairly kept his balance, fucking me harder as my body succumbed to the pleasure he gave me.

His grip on me tightened.

My legs wrapped harder around his waist.

The water fell over us, closing my eyes, dampening the kiss in texture but not in passion.

Nothing mattered but the way he fucked me.

Grasped me.

Kissed me.

Pleaded me.

Held me.

SIN

Wanted me.

Needed me.

Begged me.

Nothing.

Not a fucking thing. Not even as I came, clenching and moaning and holding him.

Not even as he came, mouth on my neck, fingers grabbing my ass, and my name rasping from his lips.

It didn't even matter that as I fell down the wall, I fell for him.

For the addiction that was Damien Fox.

For the one man I feared I would never get enough of.

It didn't even matter that, after he pulled out of me, he softly lowered my feet to the ground. He still held me against him, but this time, more gently.

What did matter was the way he squeezed shampoo into his hands. The way he massaged my scalp as he lathered it in my hair and washed it out. The way he rubbed the sponge over my body, filling the air with the scent of hot steam and rich cranberry.

The way, after a hard, rough fuck against a solid wall, he treated me as though I were fragile and breakable—someone who could break at any second.

And the worst part?

I was.

Just as I feared, he held me together.

Just when I thought I'd break, he held my cracks together, far more tenderly than I'd ever imagined he was capable of.

Just when I thought it was done, I knew I was fucked.

Physically. Mentally. Emotionally.

As he ran his hands over my skin, across my shoulders and down the curves of my sides, he stole a piece of me like the thief I feared he was.

Stole it.

Hid it.

Somewhere I'd never find it.

He had to steal it.
Giving it to him freely…that scared me.
So much more than I could ever put into words.

23

DAHLIA

"So." I leaned back on the sofa, bag of the promised M&M's on my lap, and rested my lower legs on Damien's lap. And then, I forgot what the hell it was I was going to say.

"Hmm?" He peered at me sideways like he knew. He probably did—he knew everything else.

I sighed. "Never mind. I forgot."

He reached over and snatched a handful of the candy-coated chocolate from the packet before I could protest against it.

Damn it. He was quick.

"Did you actually forget, or have you just decided that it's a bad question?"

"You're wasted as a business owner. You should be a cop." I threw a lone candy into my mouth. "But for the record, I did actually forget. I've still forgotten. Hell, twenty minutes ago, I opened the fridge and stared at into it until you scared me into stopping. Is me forgetting really that unbelievable?"

"Not in the slightest. I was just keeping you on your toes...Like I was when I watched you looking at the fridge for five minutes."

Hmph.

"I didn't even need anything from the fridge," I muttered.

Damien nodded toward the ice water on the coffee table in front of us. "You're right. You needed the water from the dispenser in the door, which makes it all the more puzzling why you opened the thing at all."

"All right, give it a break. You made me run today. Running makes me forgetful."

"And here I was thinking I'd fucked the coherent thought out of you."

"You probably could if you tried hard enough."

"There's no probably about it. I absolutely could. If I weren't so good in bed, you wouldn't have screamed my name."

"Ah, the master of the motion of the ocean. You're humble, too."

He grinned. It was so wide and infectious that it made his eyes smile, too. "Humility is one of my better qualities. It's right up there with modesty, the occasional bout of self-doubt."

"Is that a yearly event? Can we buy tickets for it?"

"You can see it for free." He traced light circles around my kneecap, his expression now solemn and almost apprehensive.

I twitched as his finger tickled me. "That sounds perilous."

"Why? You think I don't get any self-doubts like other people?"

"I didn't say that, but all the things I know about you point to 'no.'"

The sofa cushions shifted as he did, resting his head back comfortably. "Right now, I'm sitting here wondering what the hell I did to deserve sitting here with you."

"Shower sex is a good place to start." I started to smile, but when he didn't move, I stopped. "What do you mean by that?"

"It means that you're an incredible person, and I'm...not."

That was the most cliché thing I'd ever heard. "I thought we agreed that you hadn't killed any puppies."

That made him crack a smile. A small smile, but a smile all the same. "I haven't, and I have to admit it's not on a bucket list." He stopped circling my knee and stroked his hand up my leg until his fingers were curved around my thigh. "But I do wonder why I'm here. Why you're here. Why you've gone from hating me so much to being in my company regularly."

"The first answer is because you wouldn't leave me alone," I said honestly. "The second is because you're not such a bad person after all. You're just not so good at the first impressions."

"Or in your case, the second, or the third, or the fourth…"

Laughter escaped me. "Or the fifth or sixth," I continued, nodding my head. "But that doesn't mean I don't like you because I do."

"But do you trust me?"

"Like I know you'd save me from a burning building kind of trust? Or I'd trust you to tell me that my skirt is caught in my underwear?"

He stared at me for a moment, blinking. "Correct me if I'm wrong, but aren't they up there on the same level?"

"Well…Perhaps. There's a chance."

Slowly, he nodded, but he still didn't elaborate. He stayed silent, holding my leg, looking at me. I didn't know what he meant when he asked if I trusted him, mostly because I hadn't exactly figured it out in the past few hours since I'd asked myself that.

"Do you trust *me*?" I asked, holding his intense gaze with one of my own.

"To save me from a burning building or to tell me if my fly is undone?" Mild humor peeked out from the restrained emotion that had filled his eyes.

"I'd call nine-one-one. Does that count? As for the other…eventually."

"I trust you, Dahlia. Although, I'm not quite sure why."

"You don't trust anyone, do you?" My voice was soft. I didn't need to ask—I knew the answer. It was plain to see thanks to the hurt that flashed in his eyes. "I mean, I know that, but I just…"

He let go of a long, heavy breath that was deeper than a sigh. "No. I did, once upon a time. Just not anymore." He picked up the controller and started the movie we'd planned to watch when we sat down.

The opening credits rang out, and Damien smiled at me.

But this wasn't the smile I was used to.

This was shallow and barely-there, singing with the sadness he'd concealed from his voice.

Whatever had stopped him trusting people, it ran deep. Maybe right down to his very bones where he'd never be able to get rid of it.

As I ran my gaze over his strong portrait, lingering a little too long on his full lips and stubbled jaw, the realization came at me like a bullet.

Instantly. Clearly. Silently.

For what it was worth, for all that it mattered…Damien and I were a hell of a lot more alike than I'd ever truly believed.

———

I'd barely watched any of the movie. Not because I didn't care, but because I struggled to make myself care about it. I'd glanced at him the entire time, and even now, with it almost done, I was looking at him again.

He knew it. He had to know it. I'd stared at him while we ate pizza and while he poured drinks. I'd stared as he'd sat back down. As he'd left for the bathroom. As he'd scratched the side of his nose.

Like I could stare at him hard enough and he'd tell me everything. He'd tell me all the answers to the questions I was too afraid to ask.

Maybe it was time to be brave. He trusted me—there was a whole lot more to this than met the eye. At least, that's what I believed. That was what I wanted to believe.

What I had to believe.

So, I did it. As I traced my gaze across the silver-white scar that seemed to explode with light every time the movie flashed through the darkness, I asked the one thing I wanted to know more than anything.

"How did you get it?" The volume of my question was barely above a whisper, but that was all it needed to be. He'd heard me, even through the bass booms of the TV.

"Get what?" he asked weakly, not looking at me.

I didn't answer. Instead, I swung my legs down from his lap and crawled across the large sofa until I was next to him.

He sat frozen as I reached up.

The moment my fingertip touched the edge of the scar, he winced.

"I don't..." He covered the side of his face with his hand. "I don't really think about it anymore. I don't notice it. It's been there long enough now."

"But why? How?"

"Dahlia."

"Sorry." The sharper way he'd said my name had me shuffling back to where I'd been sitting a few minutes ago.

If there was any wonder into why I was afraid to ask questions, I'd just wiped it out. That—the sharp, almost venomous way he responded when I'd gone too far. It was as if he were slamming the door down on the way he really felt.

I knew the method well. Shut it out. Take it out on another person.

I'd coped that way enough times in my life.

I wished it didn't hurt. Wished it didn't slice through me in the way it was but shouldn't have.

It stung.

Like hell.

It obviously showed on my face, because even though I wasn't looking at him, he sighed and moved closer to me.

"Dahlia," he said softly, brushing my hair from my face. "Damn it. I'm sorry. I didn't mean to upset you."

"I'm not upset."

"Then, I'd love to play you at poker."

I pursed my lips and faced him. "I'm not upset," I half-lied. "It's obviously something you don't want to talk about, and I get it. I used to push people away when it hurt too much, too."

"You think I'm pushing you away?" He arched his eyebrows. "By not sharing how I got the damn thing?"

"No. You're pushing me away with your harsh response. You do it every time." I shifted and faced him. "It's like you're afraid to talk about the things that hurt you. What are you so scared of? It's not going to make it hurt more."

"Then what will it do? Take away the pain like it's a fucking bribe?"

"Make you face up to it! Stop you burying it away where you can't live your life because it's consuming."

He shook his head. "I'm not having a fucking therapy session with you, Dahlia. If I wanted to talk about my life, I'd pay some shrink an extortionate amount of money to tell me all the things that are wrong with my refusal to talk about it."

"You don't need to. I'll do it for you. You'll never move on. You'll never be able to be happy because you'll always be caught up in it."

"Thanks, Dr. Lloyd," he said bitterly, moving away from me. "You want me to pay you fifty bucks for that insight, or can I go now?"

He stood without waiting for my response.

I jumped off the sofa and ran in front of him. He towered over me, our normally fair height difference drastically changed by the fact I was barefoot.

He stepped to the side, and I did, too.

"No." I shook my head and pointed to the sofa. "Sit down."

His jaw clenched. "I'm done."

"Well, I'm not." I stepped closer to him.

He dipped his head so his face was inches from mine. Until I could read the anger on the lines on his forehead and in the depths of his eyes.

Until I didn't give a crap any longer.

Annoyance boiled, catching and flaring like a flame on a gas station floor. It burned red-hot inside me, tickling my skin and filling me with adrenaline.

It pumped through my heart. Wildly and harshly.

"I don't care if you think you're done just because you don't like the truth. Ever since I met you, you never have liked the truth. It doesn't play in your little world." The words burst out of me like poison.

If it stung him, he didn't show it.

"You'd rather live in a web of lies and sit on a throne of bullshit if it means you can do it easily and without that pesky thing called emotion. But I'm not that person. If you had any idea just how many things I'm terrified of right now, you'd shut your mouth and listen." I jabbed him in the chest. "I'm not done talking to—"

He grabbed my wrist, peeling my finger away from his chest. "I am."

Yanking my wrist from his grip, I stared at him, and in a deathly quiet voice, I said, "Damien Fox, you sit your ass back on that sofa right the fuck now."

He didn't move.

"I don't know why I care, but I do, and that's one of the things I'm scared about right now. So help me, you will sit back down and listen to me until I say I'm done talking."

My stomach clenched.

His throat bobbed as he swallowed.

Then, he moved.

Back.

To the sofa.

And he sat down.

I bit the inside of my cheek and joined him back on the sofa. He rubbed his hand down his face, pinching his nose. The end credits of the movie filled the tense silence that hung in the air between us.

There were many things I wanted to say, I just didn't know how. All the words seemed to disappear from my mind, but the silence was welcoming at the same time. It added a lull to the flash of high emotion we'd just shared. It brought it from boiling to a soft simmer.

"I know that you're doing it to hide some kind of pain because I did it, too." The first admission was said softly. "When I was ten."

He drew in a quiet breath. "When your mom…"

"Disappeared from the pictures in the hallway?" I finished for him, meeting those devastating, dark eyes of his. "When she died, yeah. I remember everything. I was in school, my dad was at work, and my mom was running errands. Getting things ready for my grandfather's birthday a few days later, stuff like that."

I picked at a loose thread on the bottom of my old, NKOTB concert tee.

Had I ever told the story in its entirety?

No. Not once.

So why am I now?

"She was driving when someone shot at her in her car. It was a drive-by. Two bullets went straight through her window and into her. Nobody else was shot, and the car disappeared, so the police said it was an arranged hit. We found out after it had all been a mistake. It was a planned hit, but not for her. The gunman had fucked up and shot her instead of the person he was supposed to shoot."

The lump in my throat. God, it hurt. I couldn't breathe through it and I couldn't swallow it. Nothing worked. It was lodged there, absorbing my pain, swelling with every word I spoke.

"They rushed her to the hospital and into surgery. I remember coming out of school to my mom's best friend who took me to the hospital to tell me. I thought it was my grandfather who was sick. Then my dad told me. Someone had deliberately shot my mom, and the surgeons didn't know if she would survive it."

Eyes.

My eyes stung, and it took everything I had to blink it back. It all flashed through my head on an endless loop leaving me to pick and change the scenes as I relived them, over and over and over again.

"The details are where I'm fuzzy. I was too young to understand, but her lungs had blood in them where one bullet had hit her and there was swelling and water in her brain or something. I can't really remember, but they told us that we needed to be prepared for the worst. That she probably wasn't going to last the night."

My vision blurred so badly with tears I could barely see.

"She proved them wrong. I wish she hadn't. It would have been easier if she'd died there and then. Every day she didn't was another day I hoped she'd wake up. Because she got better. Slowly. So they took her in for another surgery. The tests said she'd make it. They wheeled her into recovery and she went."

My voice cracked.

"She wasn't strong enough. And I hated it. I was so angry. I didn't speak to anyone for two weeks, and then when I did, it was all the things I hated about the world. I hated God for being a horrible person and taking my mom. I hated the people who shot her. Hated that she wasn't strong enough to fight because I needed her. I hated my dad because he was alive and she wasn't. But I never spoke about her. Not until I found her best friend crying. About two months after Mom died, I found her crying in Mom's reading room because she couldn't help me. She couldn't make it better for me. And that's all she wanted to do."

Thick.

Tears.

Lump.

Pain.

It was a whirlwind of emotion in one package.

"Because I was being so horrible to everybody. I couldn't cope with the hurt of losing her, but that was the first time I realized I wasn't alone. I wasn't the only one who missed her and wanted her back. I wasn't the only person who was angry—at life, at God, at the injustice of the whole thing. She was, and my dad was, too."

I looked up, finally. I could barely see Damien through my tears, but I was glad of that. I didn't talk about that time and I sure as hell never cried in front of anyone else.

"It's been fifteen years and I'm still angry. Every day. I'm angry right now. But it doesn't consume me anymore because I won't let it, because I know I can talk about it. I know that not holding onto it makes it easier to live and be happy. Mom wouldn't want me to hold onto that anger. She wouldn't want me to do anything but be happy and live and find someone to love me the way my father loved her."

That was it.

The moment I broke.

The moment it all burst out of me, and the silent tears became heaving sobs that took over my entire body.

It was the moment Damien framed my face with his hands and pressed his mouth to my forehead.

And I cried a little harder.

24

DAMIEN

She was shaking. I'd never seen a person shake as much as she was beneath my touch. Her crying filled the entire living room cutting through the now-silent air.

The loss she cried for was monumental. The pain and hurt that fueled every sob was palpable. If I tried hard enough, I could have plucked it out of the air and destroyed it.

I couldn't.

I wanted to reach inside her and rip it away from her. Make it so that she never had to feel this kind of ache in her life ever again, because I knew how much she hurt.

I knew the loss. I knew that pain. I knew how it consumed you and reminded you of all the things you'll never have again.

I pulled her into my chest. My arms wrapped around her tightly, and the urge to swallow her pain and feel it twice for myself was overwhelming.

I'd never cared before.

I'd never wanted to care. I'd never wanted to do anything to stop another person's heartbreak, but I'd take hers in a fucking heartbeat if I could.

In this moment, her heartbreak was my heartbreak.

Seeing her cry was nothing short of gut-wrenchingly devastating.

This woman was a marvel—strong and smart and beautiful, fearless and unrestrained. I respected her, I trusted her, and I wanted her beyond belief.

Nothing. Nothing mattered more than making her stop hurting. Nothing mattered more than holding her and rocking her and smoothing her hair until she was all cried out. I didn't shh her or try to stop her.

I held her.

Kissed her hair.

Squeezed her tighter.

Breathed her in.

Wiped her cheeks.

And she held me back. She buried her face into the curve of my neck, soaking me with her tears. She was nestled onto my lap, pressed so firm against my body that guilt licked at me everywhere we touched.

As her fingers twitched against my skin, the guilt flinched.

As her tears rolled down my chest, the guilt followed.

As she calmed every few minutes, whimpering, only to cry again, the guilt ebbed and flowed through me until it mirrored her grief.

I made her hurt tonight.

My refusal to tell her the truth about my life, about that fucking scar, about my fucked up, broken family, had driven her to relive her own hurt to the point she couldn't breathe.

I had self-doubt. I had self-doubt, all right, even if she never believed it. I doubted I'd ever be good enough for her. My selfishness would always mirror her selflessness. We both knew loss and pain and loneliness.

We were two peas in a pod.

Except one was rotten.

And it wasn't her.

I was the master of lies and manipulation. She was the master of kindness and truth. I breathed in deceit and exhaled hatred. She inhaled love and sighed out laughter.

If it weren't for me, she'd be laughing now.

She'd given in to her hurt. For me. For someone who didn't deserve her kindness.

She was afraid of caring about me.

I was afraid of her.

Terrified.

More than anything else in this world, I was afraid of falling for the woman in my arms.

Because I knew. I knew, deep down, that she deserved more. More than the person who'd lied and tricked his way into her life, even if I would eventually leave with honesty.

The biggest problem with that was that I was even more afraid of leaving her and going back to life before Dahlia.

To life without her eyes or her laughter or her smile. Without her wit or her sarcasm or her smartass comments.

Loving her terrified me.

Never being able to try, scared me even more than that.

"I'm sorry," I whispered into her hair, stroking it. "I'm so sorry."

Over and over.

I said it again and again. The guilt drowned me. The anger stabbed at me. But I could block that out.

For now.

For right now, because she was more important. I would face it, though. I would be her kind of brave and tell her everything. I owed her that, even if I never uttered any of the words again.

I would tell her about the destruction of my family. Of the lies. The hurting. The secrets. The deception. The fixing. The happiness.

I would tell her about the final breakdown that shattered it—and me—forever.

And then, maybe, I would be strong enough to leave her so she could be happy.

I pressed my lips to her forehead in a kiss that screamed to me I'd never be able to. Even squeezing my fucking eyes shut didn't beat that thought from my brain.

"I'm so sorry, sweetheart," I whispered.

She was finally silent, the only tears remaining completely noiseless.

"Why?" she rasped, her voice cracked and broken and hoarse. She tilted her head back and looked up at me. "You didn't do it."

"I know." I cupped her cheek and brushed my thumb beneath her eye. "But right now, all I want to do is suck the pain right out of you, and I can't do that."

"That's okay. It's mine."

"It shouldn't have to be."

"I know," she whispered, tucking her face back into my neck.

I shut my eyes and rested my cheek against her head. "I'm sorry I made you relive it."

A moment passed before she said, "I've never done it before. Not like that."

Guilt. It hit me hard once again

"Maybe I should put you to bed and then go."

"No!" She scrambled on me, twisting and turning, her knee narrowly missing ramming into my cock.

Not that I didn't deserve it.

Dahlia grasped my face, laying her hands on my cheeks, and looked into my eyes. Her skin was red and puffy, blotchy right down to her neck. She focused her swollen eyes on me and shook her head with such vehemence, it was shocking.

"I didn't tell you to make you go. I told you so you'd understand. So you'd get it, Damien." Her soft, earnest voice twisted my heart. "I don't...Please don't..." She took a deep breath. "Stay. Please stay."

I gently took her hand and kissed the center of her palm. "You want me to stay?"

She nodded.

"Then, I'll stay." I kissed her hand again, then scooted forward on the sofa. She wrapped her arms and legs around my neck and waist when I stood, lifting her up. The TV was already blinking to go off, and I paused for her to turn off the light.

I wouldn't sleep, but she was exhausted. A part of me wanted to lie next to her in bed and watch her sleep. Watch her at peace.

Did it hit her when she slept, like it did to me? Or was she spared it?

SIN

I hoped she was spared it. I hoped like fucking hell she didn't endure the subconscious terrors and reminders that I did in the middle of some nights.

I carried her into her room and gently set her on the bed. When I tried to let go, she tightened her grip on me, bringing her lips to mine. It was little more than a comfort, something to hold onto, but that didn't mean I would pull away. I wouldn't give her more, but I'd give her this. I'd give her a thousand soft kisses if it made her happy for even a split second.

After a minute, she released me, twisting so she could take off her t-shirt. By the time I'd brushed my teeth and returned in nothing more than my underwear, she'd already crawled into the bed.

I joined her. Immediately, she snuggled against me. She was still trembling, so I wrapped myself around her, cocooning her with my body and the sheets as much as I could without her being uncomfortable.

"Sweetheart?" I whispered, touching my lips to her hair.

"Mm?"

"I understand. And...I promise. I'll tell you. Just not tonight."

She shifted so she could tilt her head back and look at me. "You don't have to."

"I do." I brushed a kiss over her mouth. "Trust me."

"I do. Trust you. For both the skirt in my panties and the burning building thing."

We shared a smile.

One that was warm and genuine and punched me in the fucking heart with its intimacy.

"Go to sleep. You need to." I kissed her once more and wriggled.

She did the same, except she closed her eyes as she adjusted herself in my arms.

Minutes later, her breathing shallowed, and her heartbeat slowed against my chest.

233

I stared into the darkness of her bedroom. I could do nothing but let reality wash over me, because fuck.

Fuck.

Dahlia Lloyd owned me.

My mind. My body.

Everything but my goddamn soul.

For now.

———

She was so hot when she slept. If there was any doubt in my mind that she was a red-blooded woman, one night of having Dahlia Lloyd pinned against me for hours on end would have killed them.

She was a human sauna.

It'd been three hours since I'd left her at her house and I could still feel the heat of her skin against mine. She'd insisted she had to get to work, completely refusing to acknowledge her emotions from last night.

I wasn't going to push. I wanted to, though. I wanted so fucking bad to know even more about her.

Now, I knew how she felt.

I hadn't known a thing about her mom, but I'd always wondered how she'd died. I'd always wanted to know that one thing—when, how, why? All those questions had quietly bugged me for the last few weeks.

Now, it didn't feel good to know.

Seeing her pain had drummed home how I felt about her. How much I truly wanted her—how badly I wanted a little piece of her heart for myself.

How selfishly I wanted all those things.

Nothing good would come of that. Even if I snuck through the darkness and stole a piece, it wouldn't change that.

So different. We were so fucking different, even though we were so similar. I had to remember that. I had to remind myself of all the reasons why we wouldn't work. Thinking about the reasons we would…

I shook my head and ran my fingers through my hair. The stone wall behind me pressed through my shorts and into my ass, so firmly it was stinging across my skin.

This morning was the first morning that running hadn't helped. It'd done nothing to beat out the frustration that clung to me. It'd done sweet fuck all to push away my feelings for Dahlia.

I traced my mom's name on her midnight-black headstone like I always did. Except this time, it was slower. I took in every sleek curve of the blocky, bright-white font, from beginning to end.

Her name.

Her birthday.

Her death day.

The line that said she was loved.

The one that said she was a cherished wife and mother.

The final words that proclaimed her death to be an irreparable hole in the lives of all who knew her.

If I knew the day she died how true that final statement would be, I would have created the biggest goddamn fuss of my life.

It seemed like a fucking eternity since she'd died. Eight years wasn't that long, not really, but it was still as raw to me now as it was back then.

I shifted my gaze to the stone next to my mother's. *Penelope Fox.*

My heart clenched. Pain radiated throughout my entire body. I didn't think about her. I'd blocked her out. All the memories had been firmly locked away from my life because thinking of her as a real, living person was too excruciating.

Maybe I missed her more than I missed my mom. It was an incomparable ache, I knew that much, but Penny had been so much more.

My baby sister had been the glue that was destined to hold our family together.

In a sick twist of fate, she was the explosion who'd shattered us.

I should have been thankful. Thankful she only took my mom. Thankful my dad felt a sense of duty to me and Perrie. Not that it had mattered for Perrie—she'd been the burden and I'd been the failure.

Penelope had always been the golden one.

The irony of that wasn't lost on me either.

I'd been the failure, and now, I'd succeeded. Penny had been Miss Perfect, and she'd fucked up so monumentally, she'd ruined all our lives with her choices.

She'd fucked it all up, broken our family in more ways than one, and she wasn't the one who didn't have to live with it.

When she died, her pain died with her.

Not that I gave a fuck about her self-inflicted pain. I gave a fuck about her actions, about the way she'd stolen life, about the hurt she'd forced on the people who once idolized her.

I took a deep breath.

Dahlia's words—her decision to tell me what she had—made sense. Hit me like a motherfucking freight train going faster than it should.

Anger.

I was fucking *angry*, even that description wasn't enough. I didn't think the pure frustration and fury that rolled inside me was describable. It burned and it stung, consuming me one heartbeat at a time.

Yet, at the same time, it was freeing. Something inside me gave out, moving aside for a fucked-up form of acceptance.

Acceptance that it had happened.

That my baby sister was the cause.

That my mom had responsibility, too.

That there was nothing wrong with me.

SIN

But most of all, acceptance that this anger, this gut-wrenching sickness I'd been holding onto for the best part of the last ten years, was o-fucking-kay.

———

My dad was waiting for me in my driveway when I got home. I was sick and sweaty, covered in dirt and dust from the graveyard. The first thing he did when I walked in was to take a good, long look at the grass stuck to my sneakers.

His nostrils flared as he did so, and the downturn of his lips proved something else to me—in his eyes, I'd never be the success who'd kept his business up on cloud nine.

I'd always be the little failure, paling in comparison to my perfect sister.

My perfect, dead, addict sister.

My father said nothing, so I turned upstairs before he could change his mind over his silence. He knew exactly where I'd been from the grass on my sneakers, so there was no doubt he was furious.

He hadn't been in years. Not that I knew of, anyway. I didn't want to know. I was pretty sure that, by this point, whatever heart he'd once had, had died with my mother.

In reality, Penny hadn't stolen just one of my parents.

She'd stolen them both.

My hand went to the scar that curved around my eye. I rubbed, the sting in it brought to life by the thoughts that'd been streaming through my mind for hours.

That night. I remembered it.

All too well.

I pushed it back—temporarily—and got into the shower. I had work to do after this. There were emails and phone calls, plus two interviews. I had to contact the realtor to set up a surveyor for one of the club buildings because I'd made up my mind.

We would distribute the strippers in the failing club. We'd send them where they'd be happier. We'd put the building up for sale and plow the money from it into the other clubs.

My father had been living in the past, and so had I. Except, he'd lived it over and over, and I'd ignored it. Either way, the result had been the same.

I got out of the shower and dressed.

I found him in the kitchen, nursing a hot cup of coffee, sitting at the marble-topped island. No doubt the coffee was laced. A glance toward the liquor cabinet confirmed that suspicion. The door was ajar.

I kicked it shut and leaned back against the side. He barely glanced up before taking a big gulp of his coffee.

Tension tightened in the air between us.

"You went to see them," he said gruffly.

"I go more than you realize. Just because you've forgotten them, doesn't mean I have."

He snorted, putting the mug down with a clink. "I haven't forgotten them. I just choose to think about them differently."

"I'd say that by the time you reach the bottom of the bottle, you don't possess the mental ability to remember your own name, much less two people who died eight years ago."

Another snort. Another swig of coffee.

"I'm calling the realtor today. It's time we sold Thunder. I already have it planned out. I'll be running it by the staff today and rearranging everything through the rest of the week. The building isn't prime real estate compared to Spark and all the others." I folded my arms across my chest. "It'll be quick and painless, and you won't have to do a thing."

"Is that a fact?"

"Isn't that how you want it?"

He grunted.

Apparently, he'd already exhausted his conversation for the day.

"You got that fucking bar yet?"

SIN

I should have known that was coming. "No."

He drained the rest of the coffee, which I was sure was actually more alcohol, judging by the fact that smell outweighed the one of caffeine. "Why not?"

I rubbed my hand over my jaw, wondering how to break it to him. Had I decided fully? Had I made a decision to stop, to let her keep it?

Why was she so determined to keep it?

"Because I haven't." On that final note, I pushed away from the kitchen counter and headed for the front door.

He had a key.

With any luck, he'd lock the door on his way out...then put the damn key through the mail slot.

DAHLIA

Books.

There were books everywhere. Books on the chairs, books on the tables, books on the bar.

I delayed opening. I didn't want anyone to come in here while books took over almost the entire bar. That was asking for careless little bastards to spill stuff on them, and they were too precious for that.

They were my mom's, and they'd been on those shelves for too long.

I'd updated them occasionally. Of course, I had. I didn't have a choice. Books were timeless, but patience wasn't.

The books were a symbol of my mom, of the legacy she'd left behind. I'd never wanted to remove them, but it was time. Time to replace the battered corners and folded pages with sharp, crisp edges. Time to replace the cracked and wrinkled spines with flat, shiny ones.

They were all special. Every last book. Beloved tales from fictional lands that told of mystical creatures, past decades, and everlasting loves. But still, it was about time it changed.

These books belonged on my shelves at home where I could see them every day. My mom would still live on in this bar because at its core, it was hers. Built for her love of books and literature and love itself.

Taking the books she reread more times than I could ever count wouldn't hurt it.

The bonus? I got to go shopping for more.

SIN

I wasn't going to lie to myself and say that idea was terrible. There was no place like a bookstore. Multiple bookstores were even better. Kind of like orgasms.

Happiness was where the books—and orgasms—were, after all.

I stroked the spine of *Little Women* before I tucked it into the box next to an old book of classic poetry. I folded the corners of the box flaps until they were steady, taped the top, and then shoved it over to the side of the thankfully empty table.

Then, I reached for another box. More books. More packing. More tape. More boxes. More books. More packing. More tape.

It was oddly therapeutic. As if I were packing a piece of the past away, but not in a bad way. As if I was making the bar mine in the simplest way possible.

Knocks at the door broke through my rhythmic movements.

"Sorry, we're closed until later!" My voice echoed through the empty bar.

"It's me," Damien's gruff reply came.

I held the old copy of *Outlander* to my chest and walked to the door. I unlocked it with a click and opened it.

He stood there wearing dark jeans, a white shirt, and a light blue jacket. One of these days I'd figure out how he constantly coped wearing those damn jackets, but today was not that day.

I dragged my gaze up over his body to where the tiniest amount of short hair peeked out through the open collar. "Yes?" I said, finally meeting his dark gaze.

His lips twitched up. "Good afternoon to you, too."

"Good afternoon?"

Damien held out his hand, pulling his sleeve up, and showed me his watch.

Afternoon it was.

"Then, good afternoon," I said with a smile. "Can I help you?"

His eyes twinkled. "In more ways than one. Are you busy?"

"Er…" Looking over my shoulder at the mess of the bar, I sighed. "You could say that."

He leaned to the side and looked past me. "What the— what the hell are you doing in there?"

"A re-do?" was my lame answer.

"A re-do," he said flatly.

"A re-do."

"You've got to explain better than that."

I sighed and dragged him inside. "You're letting all the cold air out. Plus, I feel hot just looking at you."

"If you want me, all you have to do is ask."

"Not right now. Just wear some climate-appropriate clothes, you lunatic. This isn't Canada, it's Vegas." I put the book I was holding into a box while he laughed. "And I'm replacing the books."

His laughter cut short. "You're replacing the books? Why?"

I shrugged a shoulder and picked up a few more. "I feel like it's time. These books have been collected over the years. They're all my mom's favorite books or authors. It's time to replace them with mine."

"You're not keeping any of them?" His eyebrows shot up and he picked up a Jackie Collins book. "You're starting completely fresh?"

"Yep." Slowly, I nodded. "This was her bar until my dad died. Now it's mine. Everything they created won't change. Just the books. And the lights in the ladies' bathroom."

Damien put down the book he was holding. His fingertips trailed over the covers of the books on top of each stack. Every few steps he paused to read the titles, moving the odd ones out the way so he could see what was underneath.

"I didn't realize there were so many books here." He swept a finger over the cover of *A Game of Thrones*. "Your mom read this?"

"Dad. He loved the whole series. I think he might have trolled the author on Facebook once for taking so long to write the next book."

"Did you watch the TV show?"

"We tried. It got banned a couple seasons in. Something about too many changes." I shrugged, finishing packing up another box. "He snuck a few in that he liked."

"Why don't you keep some? Buy the books again, just newer. There are so many…" He trailed off, picking up book after book. "You know I always hated reading?"

"I think you mentioned a hatred of books once before. Right along with Jennifer Aniston."

He pointed a book at me. "An episode of *Friends* came on. They *were* on a break, and I still can't stand her."

"I'm not getting into that, and you're an idiot."

He laughed. "Still—my mom used to make us read every night. It was the worst thing ever. Perrie would read out loud, and Penelope would scream and laugh at the dumbest things, even when she stopped reading picture books. She once re-read the same page over and over just because she thought it was funny. That thirty minutes each night before bedtime was the noisiest part of my day and I hated it."

Oh my God. He's talking about his family.

"Perrie and Penelope are your sisters, right?"

He nodded.

"I used to do that, too. I stopped reading out loud once Mom died. There was nobody left who had the time to listen to it." I sighed and smiled sadly. "Until you started reading my book out loud, of course."

"Are any of these filled with pulsating cocks and quivering vaginas?"

"I don't know. I haven't read them all. There are a few suspicious looking ones on the far table. I'm not even sure I can bring myself to donate them. I think they might be dino-porn crept onto the shelves by idiot students."

"Dino-porn?" Disbelief flashed across his face, but so did curiosity, so I wasn't surprised when he walked over and picked one up. "*Taken by the T-Rex.* So, that's a thing."

The laughter crept out of me. "That's a thing."

He dropped the book with a shudder. "Are you taking all of these home? To the library?"

"Yep. That's where they belong. Then, I'm going shopping."

"Today? You're running out of time."

"Today, tomorrow…Whatever." I shrugged and packed another box. "There's no rush."

Damien shrugged off his jacket and unbuttoned a sleeve. "Got more boxes?"

"What are you—you don't have to help me." I blinked at him, holding the edge of the box. "It's just me being crazy. In fact, I'm pretty sure I have serious bookworm regret right now."

He finished folding his sleeves up and walked around the edge of the table to me. His hands framed my face, their warmth skittering across my skin as he looked right into my eyes. "The crazy makes sense. If you want help, I'll give it."

He was so earnest, so open, so…so *dangerous*. This was the side of him that, if I had any sense left, I'd avoid.

But I didn't have sense left.

"That would be great. Thank you." I gave him a tiny smile, one that he gently kissed before he released me.

"I'll pack the human-porn books, but I'm not touching the dino-porn."

I rolled my eyes. Human-porn my ass.

***

"Grab a cart!"

"A cart? They have shopping carts at the bookstore?" His eyes bugged as I skipped toward the front of the store. "Why the hell would you need a cart at a bookstore?"

I stopped on the sidewalk and turned. Blinking innocently, I replied, "Why the hell wouldn't you?"

"I'm not going to go there." He rubbed his hand over his mouth and did as I'd asked by grabbing a cart. "There's no way anyone can fill this with books."

"That sounds like a challenge." I grinned, setting my purse in the child seat. "Watch and learn, Mr. Fox."

"This was a horrible idea. Why did I offer to help again?"

I glanced over my shoulder and shrugged. "You probably want in my pants again."

"Sweetheart, as a rule, I *always* want in your pants." He stepped into the vast store with me and paused. "Does following you around make it more likely?"

Hmm. That was a loaded question. At this point, he could take his shirt off and I'd probably let him do whatever he wanted to me.

"That depends on your behavior while we shop."

"What am I, five? And what do you mean, we?"

I beelined straight for the romance aisle, hooking my fingers through the spaces at the end of the cart so Damien had to follow me. "We. Just that. You're helping me shop for books for the bar."

"I don't read." He said it slowly, enunciating all three syllables as though he were speaking to a complete idiot.

"You don't have to read them." I rolled my eyes, turning left into the romance aisle. "You just have to pretend like you want to."

He stopped the cart—and me, in the process—and faced a shelf. I spun around in just enough time to see him reaching for a bodice-ripping, historical novel. He gave the cover the most pathetic excuse for a cursory glance before he dropped the book into the cart.

"There." He moved his gaze from the book to me. "Did that help?"

"Oh, yeah. What did you just buy?"

He leaned over to see the title. "*The Countess' Lover.*"

"Is it good?"

Retrieving it from the cart, he showed me the front and pointed to the bottom. "The cover is a little kinky. Did you see all that ankle on show?"

Damn it. I was not going to laugh.

I was going to laugh.

My flat expression broke in less than ten seconds, and as I replaced the book back on the shelf, I giggled. "Ankle was a taboo thing back then. It wasn't ladylike."

"How big of a heart attack would these people have if they came to Las Vegas?" He picked up a book through his musing. "It would be quite fun to take one of these stuffy men to a strip club."

I swiped the new book from him and replaced it on the shelf. "They weren't stuffy. They were…proper. There were rules for dating. Well, it was courting then, but still." I ran my fingertip along the shelf. I hadn't read many historicals in my life, but I knew a few names, thanks to the Internet. "It was all very prim and proper and, most of the time, the women were virgins."

"They were virgins?"

I nodded, pulling a few books off the shelf and depositing them into the cart. "No sex until after marriage."

"Imagine being a man with a three-inch cock and knowing your future wife was going to hate you after your wedding."

"That's pretty shallow."

"I'm only thinking about how gutted I'd be if I were six inches smaller."

"Is it the bookstore, or do you default to a teenage mentality when thinking about your cock?"

His lips pulled into a dirty smirk. "No teenage mentality could come up with the things I want to do to you, Dahlia."

I rolled my eyes. Again. I was getting a headache. It was throbbing right behind my eyes, and each throb said the same thing: self-inflicted.

I knew better than to bring a man—any man at all—into a bookstore.

"Can you attempt to take this seriously? Believe it or not, this is actually work." I trailed my finger across the spines until I reached the end of the historical section. I went back to add a few more books to the cart, but really, I needed Abby for that.

Ancient love was her jam, not mine.

"I fail to see how buying books is working."

Pursing my lips, I plucked a four-book, romantic suspense series off the shelf. "I need to replace the books in the bar. Therefore, it's working." I gave him a pointed look.

He stared at me flatly, his dark eyes just as plain as his expression. Except boredom. There was a hell of a lot of boredom there. "I don't think you want to revamp. I think it's just an excuse to buy books."

"I'd be lying if I said it didn't cross my mind." I crouched down to avoid meeting his eyes.

What? I loved books—any excuse to buy books was valid in my eyes.

New baby? Here, have a soft book.

Toddler's birthday? This cardboard book has fuzzy bits.

Reading age? Here's a picture or chapter book.

Birthday? Anniversary? Graduation? Wedding? *Here, have a fucking book.*

Books were always a good idea.

"If you didn't own The Scarlet Letter," Damien started, scooting down the aisle after me, "What would you be?"

"Professional reader," I answered automatically.

"No such thing."

"Fine, I'd be a librarian or an editor if you want to be specific, but they both get paid to read." I poked my tongue out at him. "What would you do if you didn't own your business?"

"I've never really thought about it." He rested his forearms on the handlebar of the cart. "I guess I've always taken it as fact that I'd own the business one day, so thinking of something I wanted to do was never an option for me."

"Why not? Couldn't one of your sisters do what you do? Or is it because you're the oldest?"

"Partly because I'm the oldest, partly because I'm male."

"Oh dear." I paused, a thick book in hand. "This sounds like we're throwing back to the chauvinistic conversation we had once before."

"You mean the comment you took and ran with."

"Semantics." I waved the book before putting it back on the shelf. "What does your possession of a penis have to do with your ability to run a business?"

His grabbing of a book with a shirtless man on the cover was about as subtle as a hungry newborn.

I'd also never seen a man so engrossed in another shirtless man. At least, not a straight man.

"Damien." I whipped the book from his hands and dropped it in the cart.

So, it was an impulse based on the abs. Shoot me.

He sighed, rubbing his hand down his face before he met my eyes. "My dad is pretty…traditional."

"Traditional." My voice was flat. I didn't need to continue this conversation to know where it was going.

"He's all for strong women, as long as they're lifting a laundry basket."

I snorted. "So, he's a sexist pig."

He didn't say anything. "He doesn't think women have places running businesses, from what I can gather."

"So, it doesn't matter if your sisters are more capable of running the business than you. He'd rather die than let them take it over." I tried for another snort, but it came out a tired scoff.

It all made sense now, didn't it? The borderline harassment that happened before and after my return from California. The insistence that he would get what he wanted.

But who was the driving force?

Damien or his father?

I walked away from him a few feet down the aisle to where some of my favorite books were. In silence, I picked up one after another of the engrossing romances, holding them in a tall stack in my arm until I couldn't fit another one there.

Two strong hands took several of the books off the top and carefully deposited them into the cart. Damien took the rest, stacking them gingerly beside and on top of one another.

Before he could return to me, I shuffled down a few steps and stared at the books in front of me.

There was a thickness in my throat—one that was linked up with the tightness in my chest. All the doubts from before came flooding back, slamming into me with such severity that I had to lock my knees to stay standing.

Everything I'd ever thought about him, every question I'd ever asked, every doubt I'd ever entertained, they consumed me. One after another, like waves crawling up a beach.

Slowly.

Ferociously.

Repeatedly.

"Is that why?" I asked softly.

"Is what why?" Damien stood next to me, staring at the side of my head.

"Why you tried to buy Scarlet. Why you wouldn't let up. Why you kept going on and on about it."

"Dahlia—"

"Is it why you're standing with me in the middle of a fucking bookstore like you give a shit?" I snapped my head around to look at him. My eyes burned, the stinging threat of tears just seconds behind my hard glare.

I couldn't even pass it off as anger. The fact that someone who acted like they cared about me was sounding like they didn't believe I could do what I do as successfully as him.

"You wanted to buy my business because I'm a woman."

"Stop." He took my hand and yanked it down, twisting me until I was looking at him.

A woman walked down the aisle, ignoring us completely.

"Dahlia." His voice was softer and gentler than I'd ever heard it, and his eyes—oh God, his eyes. They were raw and unguarded, full of feelings you couldn't fake. "Stop, all right? Stop and listen to me."

I blinked to fight back the tears. Why did I have to be a crier?

"My *father* wanted to buy your business for that reason. And yes—I kept going on about it because he did. I thought you'd be easy to break down. But what you don't know is that it's over. It's done."

"What?" I whispered.

"There will be no more attempts to buy The Scarlet Letter. You aren't going to sell, and I've told him as much. I gave up trying several days ago, so whatever you think, is wrong."

I swallowed.

"I won't lie and say that my attempts at spending time with you weren't because I wanted the bar. They were. One hundred percent. But now..." He ran his hand through his hair, still keeping his eyes locked onto mine. "Now, I'm here because I want to be. Look at me, Dahlia. Do I look like the kind of guy who browses the fucking romance aisle in a bookstore for fun?"

I traced my gaze up and down his body, shaking my head, hiding my tiny smile.

"I'm here because I'm not acting like I give a shit." His fingertips were soft against my skin as he crept his hands up to cup my face. "I do give a shit. I do care. About you."

I covered one of his hands with my own, my chest tight. "You don't agree with him? You think I can run the business?"

"Sweetheart." With our breath mingling and our lips a heartbeat apart, he said, "I think you could run the world if you put your mind to it."

26

DAHLIA

Any doubt I'd had just moments ago evaporated the moment I touched my lips to his. The kiss was light, tender but real, more genuine than any of the ones we'd shared up until right now.

It was almost the moment two equals met in the middle, differences stepping aside for the similarities to come together.

Tingles scattered through my body, but they all ended in one place.

My heart.

The fool in me fell a little harder.

"You really mean that?" I said quietly, pulling back and meeting his eyes.

His slight nod answered it. "I've seen men buckle where you held strong." His fingers swept across the side of my face and he tucked some hair behind my ear. "And I finally worked out why you fascinate me so much."

"Enlighten me."

"You're the most unpredictable little thing, and I can't get enough of you." He kissed me once more, slower and firmer than the one we'd just shared, but no less spine-tingling. "Now, can we please get this trip over and done with?"

And just like that, there was the Damien I'd come to feel so strongly for.

"You don't get a bookstore trip over and done with. It gets done with you." I grinned as I escaped his clutches and walked backward, almost into a person. "Oh my gosh, I'm sorry!" I said to the lone, elderly gentleman.

He smiled, holding up his hands. "Don't worry." Then to Damien as he passed, he said, "She's right, son. The bookstore tells you when your trip is over." He held up his left hand and pointed to his ring finger. In the worst stage whisper I'd ever heard, he added, "I've been married forty years. Listen to her. She's always right, even when she's wrong."

I cough-laughed into my hand, turning away, but not before I caught Damien's half-stunned expression.

Ah, yes. The being wrong thing was a new experience for him.

"Thank you, sir. I'll take that advice into account. Got any advice for when I mistakenly believe I'm right?"

Oh my God.

"You buy her a book, of course. Just avoid the ones with pirates. The role-play is questionable."

I darted around the end of the aisle, gripped a shelf, and let the giggles burst free. The man was in his sixties, no doubt, and there he was. Talking to Damien Fox about pirate role-play.

I couldn't control it anymore. When Damien joined me, a sore stomach, an almost-pee, and a few minutes later, he looked much less amused than I felt.

He swallowed hard. "I think this bookstore is done with me now."

I laughed all over again, this time using the cart to steady me on my feet.

"I'm glad you found that so amusing," he drawled, stepping up behind me. He gripped the sides of the cart handle and trapped me between him and it, pressing his body against mine. "I may be traumatized."

"You're the one who asked him for advice," I sputtered out. "Oh, grab that Danielle Steele! And the ones on either side of it."

He did as I said. "Any others?"

253

I pointed at book after book. He put each one in the cart, the only common thing was the fact he was always touching me. Whether he kept his hand on my back or pulled me with him, he never released me fully. That had to keep up for a good hour before we finally reached the final section with only a few shelves left to go.

"What kinds of books do your sisters read?" I asked, looking up from the back cover of a book by someone I'd never heard of.

The question was a risk. I knew that. But I felt like maybe this time, I'd get an answer.

"Did." He pulled one off the shelf—a James Patterson. I paused. "Did?"

"Did read, is the correct question," he said, flipping the book over.

That wasn't the answer I was expecting.

A chill ran through me. "Did read," I repeated softly, the implications of that correction aching through my heart. "Both of them?"

Slowly, he shook his head. "One. Penelope. The youngest."

"What about your other sister? Perrie?"

He shrugged a shoulder. "As far as I know, she's still alive."

Wow.

Ouch.

"I get the feeling this isn't exactly bookstore conversation," I murmured, putting a few first-in-series books into the cart.

"Not exactly. Then again, I'm not sure it's conversation for anywhere." He handed me two books. "If these were movies, they'd be great."

My lips twitched up, and we both held onto them for a moment. "Noted. But the books are always better."

"Yeah, yeah." He gripped the cart and steered it around. "You achieved the impossible. You filled the cart."

I linked my hand around his arm. "It was only impossible in your mind. It was totally realistic in my world, thank you very much."

"I underestimated you once again."

"You'd think you'd have learned by now."

"I agree." He laughed lowly. We stopped a few feet from the cashier, and he looked down at me. "Pick a book. Any one. I'll buy it for you."

My eyebrows raised. "Is this in case you tell me I'm wrong later on?"

More laughter. "No. It's a...just because."

"Have you ever bought a book before?"

"Don't make me take it back, Dahlia."

I leaned into him as I laughed quietly. "Anything?"

"Any book. Any story. In this store right now," he confirmed.

Honestly, anything that had interested me in the store was already in the cart. There was nothing I could think of that I wanted, except...

"There is one I'm desperate to explore, actually," I said slowly, meeting his eyes.

"Oh yeah?" He quirked a brow. "What's that?"

With hesitance trembling my fingers, I reached up to the side of his eye and brushed the tip of my forefinger down alongside the scar there. "Yours."

He stared at me for a long moment. The longest one, actually. It was unnerving and discomforting. The moment I was about to open my mouth and take it back was the moment he dipped his chin.

With the barest nod of his head, he opened the door for the one thing I wanted to know more than anything.

"All right." He took my hand in his, kissed my palm, and released me. "I'll tell you. Tonight."

Dammit.

"I have to work until close," I said softly.

He crooked a finger beneath my chin and tilted my face up to his. "Doesn't matter. Midnight or three in the morning. I'll tell you. You'll come to my house after?"

He was so tentative, his gaze so soft and almost…scared.

There was no way I could say no.

"Deal. I'll even bring pizza when I'm done."

The smile that crept across his full lips was so tempting to kiss. "Deal. Leave the pants at home, though."

"I can work with that." I kissed his cheek, his stubble scratching against my chin. "Now, I have to buy my books."

"I still can't believe you spent almost two thousand dollars on books!" Abby said across the bar, stacking glasses as she went.

"I can't believe I sell drinks cheaper than books," I replied, taking two stacks over to the glass washer beneath the bar. I had to stifle a yawn as I opened it. "It was straight-up heaven, Abs. There are so many books in my front room waiting to be ordered and organized to come here."

"Did you…Did you get any historicals?" she asked, sidling up to the bar with more glasses.

My wry smile was unmissable. "Yes, I got a few. I need you to take the card and go and buy some, though. They're not my thing."

She gasped, dramatically slapping her hand against her chest. "I can buy books for work? This is the best job ever!"

I laughed. "Yes, you can. But only historical romance."

"Can I buy the ones with the Scottish Highlanders with their thick, sexy brogue and all plaid everything?"

My side-eye was dubious. "Er, sure?"

"Yes!" She punched the air with her excitement.

I side-eyed her once more and set the glass washer going. "If you want to go home and bring up Amazon, you're welcome to."

"Nah, I'll help you finish up here," she said. Extra sad. Extra pathetically.

"Go," I sighed. "I can see you're dying to. I'll finish up here."

"No, I know you're going to see Damien after this. It'll take you twice as long without me." She reached over the bar for a cloth to wipe the top down with. "I'll help you."

I smiled gratefully.

"He's really called off buying the bar?"

I hadn't told her everything we'd discussed, for obvious reasons, but that was important she knew, so I nodded. "Just as I said earlier."

"Do you think he's spinning you a line?"

"No," I said slowly. "I think he means it. He doesn't gain anything from lying to me, Abs. I'm not going to sell, so that's the end of it."

"Hmm. I'll remain skeptical until you're married to him."

"Well, this escalated really quickly, didn't it?" I said it more to myself than anything.

"Do you really know what you're doing with him?"

"Yes. No. Possibly. It varies."

"Aren't you afraid he's going to break your heart?"

I took the cloth from her and wiped down the handle of one of the draft beer pumps, saying nothing.

"Dahlia."

I moved to the next.

And the next.

"Oh God."

"Oh God, what?" I gripped two handles and leaned forward. "How do you expect me to answer that, Abs? He's nothing like what you think he is. If you attempted a conversation with him, you'd see that."

She softened, sighing as she leaned on the bar. "I know. Fergus already told me all he knows about him. I'm just worried about you. After your dad, you're...vulnerable, I guess. I don't want you getting hurt because he's waltzed in here and swept you off your feet."

I smiled. "I know what I'm doing, okay?"

"You just said you didn't."

"I don't, not really, but pretending is fine." I cleaned the last handle. "I do know that he's not a bad person. He's fun to be around, and he's sweet, and he's sensitive, and he's just so…different," I finished lamely.

Dear God. I could hear myself and I sounded damn stupid.

"All right," was all Abby said. "I guess we should get done here then, right?"

I blinked at her. "That's it? You're dropping it?"

"Am I not supposed to?" She stared at me for a moment. "I mean…You seem happy. He's dropped his attempt to buy the bar, and you're still spending time together. I'm good to play the evil best friend if you want, but I feel like it's a further waste of my time."

"A further waste of…Never mind." Shaking my head, I dropped it. Abby had her reasons for just about everything and I wasn't going to argue it further.

If she was deciding to do a one-eighty on her feelings regarding him, I was going to run with it.

Abby laughed and smacked the bar. "Come on. Lover boy is waiting." She made smooching noises as she continued on her glass-collecting mission.

"I'm in charge here," I murmured, turning away from her. "I shouldn't have to take this crap."

"I love you!" she shouted, clinking glasses together.

Ugh…

SIN

27

DAMIEN

The silent hours that passed before the driveway crunched under the tires of Dahlia's Jaguar were long and painful. The echoes of the past had swarmed me, all the memories coming to the forefront of my mind as I waited.

The grandfather clock in the hallway ticked loudly. It screamed out every second, each more aching than the last.

For the first time in years, I wanted to talk about it. I wanted to talk about my past, about the decisions that the people in my family had made. About why my father held the belief that women were weak. About why I carried such a dull pain with me almost constantly. About why I sometimes struggled to sleep.

About the scar that hugged my eye, the same one Dahlia traced with her gorgeous eyes every time she thought I wasn't paying attention to her.

Unfortunately for her, I always paid attention to her.

It was addictive. Just like her.

"Hello?" Her voice tentatively sounded through my house.

"In the kitchen," I called back.

The sound of heels clicking echoed through the silence. She entered the room with a groan, slumping a small, black backpack-style bag onto the table in front of me. "I think there are matchsticks in my eyes."

"Busy night?" I asked, eyebrow raised.

"You could say that." She grabbed the backpack back to her. "Let me go change, okay?"

I smiled as she turned and disappeared before I had any say in the matter. She looked absolutely exhausted thanks to the dark circles that shadowed beneath her eyes, and that gave me pause.

Was tonight the right night to tell her everything? She needed to sleep. The heartbreak of my family would still be there in the morning.

The tapping of my fingers against the countertop was dull. Was I saying that because I was putting it off? Perhaps. It was anybody's guess. What I really needed was to get it over and done with.

"All right," Dahlia said, padding barefoot into the kitchen. "Let's go get comfy." She flounced off into the living room before I could say anything—again.

I followed her in there. "Are you sure? You look tired."

She spun, grabbed my hand and literally yanked me down onto the sofa with her. "I'm fine. You promised me."

"I'm not sure I said those exact words."

"Stop being awkward."

"Now you know how I feel every time we have a conversation."

She pursed her lips, but she was clearly hiding a smile by the twitching of them. "Stop it."

I laughed, but it was hollow. Hollow right down to my goddamn gut. "Where do you want me to start?"

"At the end. That's obviously the logical place."

She was using sarcasm to bait me into spitting it out. Could she see how this made me feel? I was thirty fucking years old, and here I was, feeling like a damn kid in front of a haunted house.

Hell, the woman sitting in front of me was younger than me, but she was stronger, too. She'd lost her dad just months ago and was able to deal with that pain already.

Me? Years later, and I was still fucking struggling.

Dahlia's indigo-blue eyes searched my face. Her soft, warm stare traced every inch of it until she lifted her gaze to mine. "You really have never spoken about it before, have you?"

"Never. Not once."

"Even when you were younger?"

"Nobody ever cared enough to listen." My words were bitter—twisted and angry. But the truth. So much the fucking truth.

"I care," she whispered, brushing her thumb over my jaw.

I knew it. I believed her.

"My parents were childhood sweethearts. Like yours." I pulled my gaze from her and rested it on the bay window. The curtains weren't fully shut so the light from the half-moon crept in, illuminating the room with the help of the dim table lamp. "They met in high school but broke up during college. They didn't exactly reconnect in the most normal way—my mom auditioned for a job at Goldies when Dad was first opening it."

"No way." A smile twitched her lips.

"Yep. I believe he said something along the lines of 'Fuck this, nobody else is seeing the woman I love up on a stage,' and married her. Just like that."

"He was different then, huh?"

"No doubt about it. My mom made him a better person. A few years after they got married, I was born. Mom had helped him run the business up until that point, so she found it pretty boring to be home with me all the time with nothing to do. I think that was when the problems started—she wanted to put me in daycare when I turned one, just for a few hours a week, but Dad refused. He believed it was her duty to stay home with me. He'd just bought another club and didn't have time to reintroduce her to all the ins and outs of the ones they owned. Professionally, it was getting better, but personally, it was turning to shit."

I leaned back against the sofa and ran my fingers through my hair.

"They fought pretty much all the time. For years. But neither left, because they loved each other, even if they didn't have a relationship. After I started school, my mom would take me to a 'friends' house. What I didn't know then was that she was cheating on my dad. He worked all the time and didn't pay her attention, so although she loved him…" I shook my head and laughed bitterly. "It was fucked up. He had her heart and the money, but they were both fucking miserable all the time. The guy she was seeing made her happy, and I was too young to understand it. Anyway, she got pregnant by him, and my dad kicked her out."

"Was it definitely not your dad's baby?"

I shook my head. "When I was older and asked Mom if there was a chance Perrie was Dad's, she said no, because basically, at that point, they didn't have sex anymore. There were no doubts."

"Wow. Did they get divorced?"

"No. Mom didn't want to marry this new guy. We moved in with him on the rougher side of town—or it was back then. She'd never intended for it to be serious, and the longer we lived with him, the more obvious it was that he was hoping my parents would divorce, Mom would get a good-sized settlement because of me, and then he'd marry her, divorce her, and get the money."

"What a dick."

That was one way to put it—and she hadn't even heard the worst yet. "Well, my mother wasn't innocent in it all. She fell down the social pole like a brick being dropped off a roof. That was her own fault. She should have guessed what he really wanted. Fact is, he wasn't a nice guy. He was abusive to her, both verbally and physically. He never touched me, but he made it known that he hated me, while he pretended to dote on Perrie."

"Pretended to?"

"She was his meal ticket. Looking back now, I think he intended to beat my mother into submission, claim full custody of her, and get the money that way." I scratched my jaw, anger nudging at my consciousness. "She couldn't leave, of course. She had nowhere to go, and the only money she had was the child support my father paid her. It was very little, just enough to get by on, because he knew what the other guy was like.

"I think Perrie was almost two when it all changed. I remember going downstairs for something. I might have been thirsty or just woken up by their arguments, but it was the first time I saw Roy hit my mother. I wasn't an angry kid. I never had been, but the moment I saw him hit her, I understood why people got so angry."

Dahlia's eyes widened, and she placed her hand delicately on her chest.

"I acted on stupid, childish impulses. I screamed, ran toward him, and hit him with the nearest thing I could find, which was a remote control."

"That's…different."

I shrugged, a slight smile on my face. "Like I said… it was impulse. And the reason for a black eye on his mugshot."

Her lips tugged up to the side.

"Now, I wish I hadn't done it." My smile disappeared, and I let out a long breath. "I should have called nine-one-one before he knew I was there, but I didn't. He grabbed me and threw me into the dining table for daring to touch him."

She drew in a deep breath.

I tapped a finger to my scar. "I was a scrawny kid. I flew through the air like a fucking bullet, and I still don't know how I didn't get blinded that day. But, the corner of the table cut right through my skin."

"Oh my God," she breathed, covering her mouth with a shaky hand. "Your sister?"

"Woke up when she heard me screaming. By that point, my mother, who was almost unconscious on the floor…I don't know. I guess her maternal instinct kicked in when she saw him hit me. Somehow, she got up and hit him with a glass vase from the coffee table. Knocked the bastard out cold." Chills ran over my skin, forcing all the hairs on my arms and my neck to stand on end as the memories flooded me.

It was all momentarily real—the anger, the pain, the adrenaline.

Until Dahlia touched my face, and it all disappeared.

"I'm so sorry."

"You didn't do it," I said wryly. "My mother called the police. Turned out Roy had been on the run from an incident several years earlier in another state and was living under an alias. He was arrested and convicted of a bunch of counts of abuse, attempted murder on my mom, and an actual murder charge from somewhere else. He'll never get out of prison, if he's even still alive."

"Wow. So, what happened? Did you move back in with your dad?"

I nodded, taking her hand as it fell onto my lap. "It was only supposed to be temporary," I said, threading my fingers through hers. "My parents hadn't been together for years, but Dad had never seen anyone else, they'd never divorced, and he had apparently realized that Mom needed something to do other than be a parent."

"What about Perrie?"

"He adopted her at Mom's request. It was a fight, legally speaking. I think Roy dropped his claim to his daughter in exchange for my parents paying his legal fees."

"Again, wow."

She didn't need to say that twice. "Yes. It all seemed better after that. A couple years later, my youngest sister, Penelope, was born. Nobody had to say it, but she was the angel. Dad loved her more than anything—something that made it awkward for Perrie. She'd tried to be perfect for him, but I guess that all my dad saw when he looked at her was a mistake. I held some childish bitterness toward her because if she didn't exist, my parents never would have broken up."

"Maybe they would have."

"Of course. But in my young mind, she was the cause of that. That changed over the years, though. The older

Penelope got, the more she was idolized by my father. I was pushed away, and he became crueler and crueler to Perrie. My mom suffered from depression because of what Roy had done to her, and occasionally, she'd spend time in the hospital to heal the wounds. Dad took some of the blame for her, realizing he'd pushed her toward him, even if he didn't know it then, but that didn't make it better for my sister."

My heart panged every time I said Perrie's name. I missed all the women in my family—I'd lost them all so quickly, but she was maybe the one I missed the most.

"I became Perrie's protector pretty quickly. She was tiny and quiet—as shy as one person could possibly be. I got into many verbal fights with my father over his treatment of her. He would tell me the same thing all the time. That, if it weren't for her, my mother wouldn't be crazy and I wouldn't have this scar."

"In the nicest way possible, your dad sounds like one of the cruelest men I've ever heard of."

I wished I could tell her she was wrong.

"He didn't—doesn't—deal with emotions well. It's where I get it from." I squeezed her hand. "Around the time Penelope hit her teens, my mom got better. It was as though she felt she could finally live again, and Dad let her back into the business. She looked after the girls at her favorite club, which was Foxies. She relished in it. With both our parents out of the house a lot, I did a lot of watching over my sisters. Which wasn't easy—I was working part-time for Dad since I'd just graduated, and those hours steadily increased until I was working almost as much as he was.

"Luckily, by that point, Penelope was sixteen and didn't need to be watched anymore. In theory," I added dryly. "If she hadn't been so perfect in the eyes of my parents, maybe they would have noticed that she was the biggest fuck-up of the three of us."

Dahlia's eyebrows shot up, but she didn't say anything.

"She could have shot someone in front of them and they would have blamed the gun." Once again, my tone was tinged with bitterness, but I didn't care. It was the fucking honest truth. "While I was busting my ass helping Dad run the business and getting criticized for bringing him coffee a degree too cold, and Perrie was working in the office, Penelope was out doing crazy shit. Drinking, drugs, hanging out with the wrong crowds."

"How didn't they know?"

"Rose-tinted glasses? Who the fuck knows? They blamed the smell of pot on me and the missing alcohol on Perrie. At least, Dad did. Mom ignored it entirely. She didn't want to rock the boat with any of us. In her eyes, we'd been through enough shit, and she pretty much stopped parenting us. I was in my early twenties at this time, so I guess it was easier to blame me for the pot."

"Did you ever tell them otherwise?"

"No. They couldn't punish me. I was over twenty-one and only lived at home because it was easier at the time. Plus, I didn't want to leave Perrie." I sighed and rested my head on my hand.

I was numb. All the emotion I'd felt earlier had disappeared. I was just cold and numb and unfeeling.

Dahlia blinked at me with her wide eyes, waiting for me to carry on. I didn't know if I could get the words out. They were fucking stuck, swirling around in the emotionless void that was my mind in that moment.

Why the fuck couldn't I say it? I'd put it off long enough. I just needed to say the words. Four words. Four fucking words that would open the floodgates to the rest of the story.

My sister committed suicide.

Why were they so hard to say? It was a fact. She did. Knowingly and selfishly, despite my parents' alternative beliefs.

Dahlia slid across the sofa, coming closer to me. She adjusted herself, swinging her legs over my lap and wrapping her arm around my body. The warmth of her as she laid her head against my chest was the comfort I needed.

My heart thumped a little louder against my ribs.

SIN

"My sister committed suicide." Finally, I said them. Flatly, coldly, uncaringly. "She was found in a motel close to the highway surrounded by drug paraphernalia by the motel manager after she hadn't checked out. She was dead and cold by the time she was found."

Dahlia said nothing. She only squeezed me a little tighter.

I closed my eyes for a moment, breathing in the sweet, apple scent of her shampoo. "The autopsy ruled it an intentional overdose. My parents fought the ruling tooth and nail—they insisted she didn't do drugs, that somebody had tricked her and either administered all of them to her, or it was accidental. They were insistent enough that the police reluctantly opened an investigation, although that might have been more to do with the fact my father threatened to out the chief's extracurricular activities to his wife than the LVPD actually wanting to investigate it."

"Your father blackmailed the chief?"

"Blackmail is a strong word," I said slowly. "It was more of a...casual mention."

She laughed silently.

"Anyway, it worked. They held off on a final verdict, initially, until they'd done more investigation, although the coroner was adamant nobody would accidentally ingest that amount of hardcore drugs. I think they investigated for about a week before security tapes confirmed that Penny was one hundred percent okay when she checked into the motel under an alias. She was alone, sober, and never left her room once she'd entered it. Nobody went in, either." I ran my fingers through Dahlia's dark hair. The softness of it had the strands slipping through my fingers like silk. "It was finally ruled suicide. I think they arrested the person who'd sold her the drugs, but it wasn't good enough. My parents refused to believe she'd killed herself."

"What about now?"

"My father refuses, still. Perrie and I found a diary in Penny's room that expressed the stresses she felt at having to be constantly perfect. She was seventeen, maintained a four-point-oh GPA, captain of the swim team, head cheerleader…But in the rest of her life, she acted out. She didn't care about anything, and she hated me and Perrie because we weren't pressured the way she was."

"Did you ever show your parents?"

I shook my head. "They had enough guilt. We felt it was better they never found out, and we burned it in the bathtub one night when we were both home alone. It was for the best. We'd all failed each other as siblings—we hated her for being perfect, and she hated us because we didn't have to be. All she wanted was to be us."

"That's so sad." Dahlia's voice was soft. "I bet you blame yourself, don't you?"

"It's hard not to. I was her brother—I was supposed to be there for her, but there was always a line between us. I think back now to how we all were growing up, and if only me and Perrie had been able to put aside our jealousy, she'd probably still be alive now. It was always us and then her."

There it was.

The guilt.

It ate me alive, snaking through my entire body like the disease it was. And it fucking hurt. What if I'd noticed? What if I'd not been so jealous? I was older than her by years. I should have been able to be there for her, but I wasn't. I was too caught up in being petty and jealous that I'd never thought for a second about how she felt.

"Don't." Dahlia looked up at me, taking my face in her gentle hands, and speared me with a firm gaze. "Don't you dare blame yourself for something you had no control over."

28

DAMIEN

Taking her hand, I kissed her palm. Her other hand fell to my chest where she flattened it against my skin.

"Easier said than done. There were many things I could have done differently, but she hid it all so well. The biggest thing I felt guilty for was taking the blame for the pot and not being honest. Maybe that alone would have changed things."

"Or maybe it wouldn't." Her soothing tone was like a balm to the ache in my chest—when she spoke, it didn't sting quite as much.

Because she got it. She understood.

"If your parents really didn't believe she was responsible for it, then they never would have. Isn't that obvious from the way they reacted to her death? All you tried to do was protect her. That doesn't make you responsible for the choices she made—or the way your parents treated you all." She held my hand to her face, brushing her soft lips over my knuckles. "They drove the divide, Damien. Not you. They pressured her to be perfect while treating you and Perrie as though you weren't worth it. And even then, you tried to protect them by burning her diary so they wouldn't know they were at fault."

I rolled my shoulders and sighed. "It doesn't matter. Things happen, and my dad will never apologize for it. My mom couldn't even if she wanted to."

Realization flashed through her gaze.

"Three weeks after Penny's death was ruled a suicide, she hung herself." Back was the hollow tone. It was fact. It was simply the way it was. I couldn't bring her back. "Our housekeeper at the time found her. She'd done it in the middle of the day when we were all at work. She left behind a note saying she didn't want to live in a world without Penny. I guess it triggered her depression and she didn't feel like she could carry on any longer."

"I'm so sorry." Dahlia wrapped her arms around my neck, holding me tight against her.

I snaked an arm around her body, pressing my face into her hair. At this point, it felt like she was more affected by this than I was. Like she hurt for me. I didn't want her to feel that.

"What about Perrie?" she asked. "Is she…?"

"Alive?" I leaned back, blowing out a long breath. "The last I heard she was alive. She got pregnant not long after Mom died. I don't think she could cope. Her biological father was an abusive piece of shit who had disowned her, her adoptive father didn't care about her, and her mom was dead. She pretty much went off the rails the same way Penelope did, but without the drugs. She drank and had sex with a bunch of guys, but there was one guy she was seeing pretty regularly. He got her pregnant, but a couple weeks after she found out, he died in a car crash. He was drunk driving because he was an idiot."

Her lips parted in shock.

All I could do was shrug. "Dad was of the mind that the best thing Perrie could do was have an abortion. She was only just nineteen, grieving the loss of her sister and mother, and in no state to be raising a child. Especially not alone."

Dahlia was almost hesitant when she said, "And you?"

I looked away from her. It was the one time I'd ever let her down, but it'd been the biggest one. And for that, I took full responsibility. I owned that guilt.

"Damien?"

"I agreed with him," I said quietly. "I didn't think it was the right choice for her. I felt like she would be better off not going through with the pregnancy, mostly because of her emotional state. She disappeared a week later."

"Oh," she said in a small voice. "Where is she now?"

"She's still here. In Vegas. I've seen her once since. A few weeks after she had the baby." I swallowed, the emotion making my throat raw. "I spent five minutes with them, and then she told me she never wanted to see me again. That I didn't care about her and the baby when she was pregnant, so I had no right to care now."

"That's really the last time you saw them?"

Slowly, I nodded. "I keep tabs on her. I tried sending her money, but she wouldn't take it. She sent it right back. She's broken all ties with us, and there's nothing more I can do. I save money each month for her daughter in a bank account. Dad doesn't care, but I do. It's the only thing I can do to make up for what I said a few years ago. Hope that she doesn't feel like the only way she can survive is by doing what Perrie does."

"Which is?"

"She's a prostitute."

Dahlia froze. Her mouth opened and closed a few times, but the rest of her never moved. Except her eyelids—she blinked so many times, a smaller person would have started flying.

"I don't understand." She finally relaxed, frowning up at me. "Isn't she a part of the business?"

"Yes. She owns ten percent, I believe, per my mother's will. She shuns it because she believes we disowned her because of the pregnancy. Problem is, the will was ironclad. It'll roll over to her daughter, whether she wants it to or not. My father attempted to have Perrie removed as a part-owner, but there's no way in hell to do it. My parents owned the business sixty-forty, and the ten percent my mother passed on upon her death belonged to her. He's powerless and it kills him."

"Why would she do that when she has a rolling income? I don't understand."

"Neither do I, sweetheart. Like I said, I tried. She made it perfectly clear what she wanted. I do what I can with what I have. If I had my way, I'd have her and her daughter living here with me."

She smiled sadly, touching my face once more. "Has anyone ever told you that you're a really good guy?"

I raised an eyebrow. "No, actually. That's generally the last thing people say."

"Then, they're idiots."

I raised my other eyebrow.

"No, don't look at me like that." She tapped my chest. "I will admit that when we met, I thought you were a bit of an asshole."

I snorted.

"All right, a lot of an asshole. A raging one with hemorrhoids, actually," she paused, and I cracked the smallest of smiles. "But, you were just annoying. Infuriating. I plotted your murder a few times." Another pause. "But you're not a bad person, Damien. That's evident by everything you're doing for your sister even though she doesn't want it."

"It doesn't make me a good person, either."

"Maybe not. But isn't it better to question whether or not you're a good person than knowing that you're a bad person?"

"Stop making sense," I said quietly, cupping her chin and tilting her face upward. My eyes searched hers, looking for the knowledge that I was guilty, that the blame of some of what had happened lay with me.

I searched.

And searched.

And searched.

I didn't find it.

It wasn't there.

There was no hint of blame for the child I'd been. There was no hint of it for the teenager I'd been and the adult I was. There was nothing but understanding—pure, real understanding of the pain I'd been through and the guilt I'd carried inside me for so many years.

SIN

There was nothing but Dahlia—of the woman who'd proved herself to be worth a thousand of me.

Yet, as I stared into her eyes, maybe I was worthy of her, too.

Maybe I was worthy of her love.

Because there was no doubt about it. This woman held my heart in the palm of her hand. I didn't know when it'd happened, when I'd fallen wholly in love with her, but I fucking had.

She had the power to create me or crush me.

Everything I was, belonged to her.

Mind.

Body.

Heart.

Soul.

There wasn't an inch of me that she didn't own.

Each one burned with the imprint of her existence. Of her heart and her soul—of the goodness that she embodied with every step, every smile, every blink of her goddamn beautiful eyes.

Fuck.

All the whole pieces of me, every last shattered fragment of me, loved her.

I loved her.

And there was no going back from this. Not now.

"You know," I said, my voice low and gruff as I held onto her like my life depended on her, "six weeks ago, I didn't know who the fuck you were. I didn't care. Now, all I care about is that I don't have to be in a position where I might forget you."

She stared at me—then, she leaned in and kissed me.

She didn't need to say anything.

Her kiss said she felt the fucking same.

———

The clock on the nightstand told me I hadn't had nearly enough sleep to face the day, no matter how soundly I'd slept in the end. Apparently, talking about everything had been the therapy I needed to sleep like the dead.

Having Dahlia Lloyd curled against me wasn't exactly hard.

Unless you asked my fucking cock. It was as hard as it could be. My hips were currently a few inches back from her since I had no desire to wake her up. She hadn't shown up to my house until the small hours last night, and we'd talked until at least four in the morning. It wasn't even nine yet.

She was exhausted.

The last thing she needed was my cock poking into her.

Unfortunately, that was the exact thing I wanted.

My cock inside her tight little pussy.

Goddamn it.

I rolled over onto my back and covered my eyes with my hand. She needed to sleep. She was tired. She had to sleep longer than four hours.

I would not wake her up. No way. I'd go and get coffee and leave her until she was ready to wake up.

Sneaking out of the bed with as much finesse as a rhino, I managed to get up without her stirring. She didn't even twitch, her breathing didn't change, so she was still asleep. The carpet prevented any wayward floorboards creaking beneath my feet as I headed for the doorway in my boxers.

One last check over my shoulder confirmed she was still asleep, and I couldn't look away. So, I didn't. I leaned against the doorframe and stared at her for the longest moment.

One of her long, tanned legs had escaped the confines of my white sheets, and her foot hung over the edge of the bed. Her other foot peeked out of the end of the bed, her scarlet painted toenails a stark contrast to the sterility of my room. Her hair spread across her pillow and the sheets like a dark sea, but it was her face that had me mesmerized.

SIN

The duvet was tucked beneath her chin, almost as though she were hugging it to her. Her face was devoid of makeup, yet her eyelashes were just as thick and dark as always as they fanned across her skin.

Other than the tiniest purse of her lips, the peace that radiated off her as she slept was palpable.

If my cock weren't so fucking hard, I'd be climbing back in here and holding her to me in the hope she'd pass some of it off to me.

Because although I'd slept well and I felt lighter from our talk, the ache was still there.

But, it was different.

I pulled the door so it was almost closed and headed for the stairs.

The ache wasn't so painful anymore. It was dull, an acceptance of what had happened. A realization that I needed to move forward.

That Dahlia was right.

No matter what I'd done, I wasn't to blame. I was a child, a teenager, a young adult. Parenting wasn't my job—keeping my family happy wasn't my job all those years ago. I was simply along for the ride, and in the end, the only people responsible for what happened where my parents and my sister.

Nobody made Penny do what she did.

Nobody made my mom do what she did, either.

They both made those choices.

My parents made the choice to treat us the way they did.

Nothing would change that. Nothing could change that. And more than that, no longer could I blame Penny for our mother's suicide.

She didn't make her do it.

She didn't make her tie that bathrobe belt around her neck and hang herself.

That was a choice made by one person.

Just like nobody forced Penny to take all those drugs.

One choice. It was remarkable how one choice, made in a split second, could destroy so many others for so long.

Downstairs was silent. There was still no movement from Dahlia, either, so I skipped the coffee for the utility room. My running stuff was hanging on the rack, so I pulled it off, along with my sneakers, and quickly changed into it.

I scribbled a rough note for Dahlia, just in case she woke up, and with my keys jingling in my hand, left the house. It was too far to walk to the cemetery right now, so I hopped into my car to drive the majority of the distance. There was a parking lot not far from there—I could jog lightly from the car to their graves in mere minutes.

I took the drive in silence.

Soul-crushing fucking silence.

It sucked the life out of me. I drove slower and slower until I rolled the car's wheels into the parking lot at something that couldn't even be described as a crawl. It took no effort at all to put the car into park and get out of it.

That was a fucking lie. Getting out of the car was achingly painful. Every part of me screamed at me as I forced myself from its confines and into the already-hot morning air.

Still, I fought it. I made one foot move in front of the other until I'd padded down the dusty road to the cemetery. It seemed quieter today. Almost as if the demons that usually surrounded me had given up for the day.

Had I finally made peace with what had happened? Was it really as simple as speaking about it and letting go of all the anger I'd kept cooped up for years?

Maybe it was.

It was working, after all.

The gate screeched through the silent, morning air as I pushed it open. The overgrown weeds that stretched up against the low, old brick walls were dry and gnarly. Familiar, too. I'd seen them so many times.

The damn things never died.

One crunched beneath my foot as I headed for where Mom and Penny's graves were. For once, the silence of the

276

air around me was welcome, because as I stopped in front of the two stones that marked their final resting places, the thought was able to hit me with perfect clarity.

I forgave them.

Both of them. I forgave them both for making the decisions they did.

With it all laid out, with my entire life condensed into an hour's worth of conversation, the reasoning for why they could have reached the point they did make sense.

They simply couldn't live the way they were anymore.

Was it selfish? Yes. They hurt the rest of us beyond belief. They'd escaped the pain, yet the rest of us were left to pick up the pieces and live with it.

I was hurt, but I was no longer angry.

I understood.

I kissed my fingers and pressed them against Penelope's name. The stone was chilly beneath my touch, shaded from the already-harsh heat of the sun. It didn't warm at all, staying just as cold when I pushed off the stone.

I'd lost my sisters. One was uncontrollable—but the other wasn't.

I couldn't bring Penelope back, but I hadn't done enough for Perrie.

And that had to change.

DAHLIA

I dropped the note back onto the kitchen island. Damien's blocky handwriting stared up at me, and a hint of worry tickled the pit of my stomach.

Was he okay?

I had no idea. The silence of the house offered me no clues. If he hadn't left me the note, I would have sworn he'd disappeared into thin air. Eerily still and overly clean, a shiver danced its way down my spine.

The coffee machine was my first spot. The combination of the noise and the fact I knew I'd splatter coffee on the countertop would be enough to eliminate the two things that were slightly chilling right now.

I relaxed the second the hum of the machine filled the air. At least, my body did. My mind was another story.

Where was he running?

Was he okay?

How long had he been gone?

How long would he be?

Did he sleep last night?

Did he have his phone in case I had to leave?

What would I do if he left?

How was *I*?

How were *we*?

What were we?

What was this?

Where was Perrie?

How did I find her?

The coffee machine stopped. The silence came back with a biting harshness, so I hummed to myself to break it.

Why was it so daunting, the quiet? My gut whispered it was because I didn't know how Damien was—it was taunting me. For all I knew, he was perfectly okay. He could have been buying breakfast at that moment.

The run was his routine. Totally normal. Perfectly fine. Yet last night had been none of those things. It'd been so far from routine or normal or fine.

Hell, if I felt the dull ache of sadness, he sure as hell had to, too. Right?

Unless he really wasn't human with a heart of stone and a black soul. Something I knew for a fact wasn't true. Okay, so maybe I'd expected a little more emotion last night as he'd told me everything, but just because I was a blubbering, hysterical mess when I talked about my mom dying didn't mean he had to be.

He was composed, but not heartless.

Restrained, was probably the best word to describe him.

I smacked my lips together and touched the top of my mug to my chin. Steam from the hot coffee wafted up right in front of my face, and for a moment, I stood there, doing nothing but stare straight ahead.

How was I supposed to handle this? Was I supposed to be proactive, or was the best idea to follow his lead?

I knew nothing about it. Nobody in my life had ever dealt with as much shit as he had. He even sounded like he was trapped in the family business. Maybe he'd grown to love it, but from what he'd said, it'd been thrust upon him without any care.

And what about his relationship with his dad? Was it a happy one? I knew he'd been forced into the attempts to buy Scarlet. Was everything I'd ever assumed about Damien because of his father's influence?

I'd thought that by finding out about his childhood and his family I'd have all my questions answered.

How wrong I was. How very, very wrong.

I had more questions than ever.

And I had no idea if I would ever get those answers, either.

———

I set my purse on my desk and sighed. My phone, tightly grasped in my hand, was still silent. There were no messages or missed calls, which I could only take to mean that Damien hadn't returned home since I'd left an hour before. Or, if he had, he'd not seen my note.

Or he was ignoring it.

Whatever.

The invoice from this morning's delivery was sitting on top of my keyboard, signed off by Abby. I hadn't seen her on my way in here, either, so as I finally put down my phone and picked up the invoice to file it away, I assumed she was likely sorting the order, far away from the drama queen behind the bar.

Not that I'd understood Fergus' rant in its entirety, but there was something about a giant penis, a text message, and his ex being an insult I didn't actually manage to decipher.

I'd patted him on the shoulder and moved on. He'd calm down eventually. Like…next week.

For now, I was still focused on Damien. Too focused, if I was being honest with myself. It was the day's miniature obsession, and considering I still had books to put on the shelves in the bar, it wasn't a good time to be obsessing.

I wanted to fix the situation he was in. The pain I'd seen in his eyes when he'd mentioned what had happened with his sister had actually hurt to see. In the weeks I'd known him, the most passionate emotion he'd ever shown was when he was buried eight inches inside my damn vagina.

Had he ever addressed his relationship with his sister? I didn't know what he meant when he said he had someone keeping an eye on her, but the fact was only one person should be keeping an eye on her, and that was *him*.

He wanted to. It was written all over his face.

But how did he cross that bridge?

I left that thought hanging in my office as I headed back toward the bar. It wasn't open yet, so I had plenty of time to get the boxes and put the books on the shelves.

"Hey," I said, walking out to the bar and spotting Abby.

She jerked her head up when she heard me. "Hey. When did you get here?"

"Not long ago. Were you sorting the order?"

Nodding, she put little bottles of tonic water into the fridge. "Makes sense. Are all those boxes books?"

"The ones on the tables? Yeah. They're all labeled, but I need to organize them. I'm thinking I might do them properly this time."

"Good thinking. Just don't mix the big books with the little books."

"Never. That was my mom's thing. It drives me insane when they aren't done by size." I put my phone down next to the boxes and opened the first one.

Taking every book out and putting them on the tables was a long, arduous process. The organization even more so—and unfortunately, the tediousness of the task opened my mind up to think back to the very things I was trying to avoid thinking about.

Perrie. Was she Perrie Fox? If Damien's father had adopted her, surely she'd have his surname. Or had she changed it after her estrangement? Maybe back to her biological father's?

The name itself wasn't too common. It was different— not like Abby's. If I asked someone if they knew an Abby, they probably knew five. Perrie was a different story.

"Hey, Abs?" I called, stepping back and admiring my handiwork on the first shelf.

"What's up?"

"Do you know anyone called Perrie?" I looked over my shoulder.

She stood behind the bar, frowning. "That's random. Why?"

That wasn't an answer. "Damien told me a whole bunch of stuff about his family last night. He and his sister are estranged, and—"

"You want to find her."

"Well, yeah." I picked up three books and set them on the next shelf carefully. "He has someone keeping an eye on her—"

"Slightly weird. Have you considered he might know exactly where she is?

No. I hadn't. "You might get an answer to that if you didn't interrupt me."

She poked her tongue out at me.

"For the record, no, I hadn't considered that." I paused. "But I think he's afraid to connect with her."

"Damien Fox? Afraid to speak to someone?" Abby snorted. "Try another line."

"It's a complicated situation. There's a lot of water under the bridge that probably won't be fixed with one conversation. It's not as simple as you might think it is."

"Whatever. I just don't get why you have to get involved. I know you and him are in this weird, hate-to-love relationship thing, but this is his problem, not yours."

"Scale back on the bitch pills," I told her. "And maybe it's not my business, but if I could help him fix it…"

"Fix what? Let's face it—it was probably his fault. He's not exactly the easiest person to get along with."

"I get along with him just fine."

"Now. You didn't before."

"I sometimes wonder how I get along with you."

She flipped me the bird.

"Girls!" Fergus flounced in, flapping his hands like tiny, awkward wings in front of his chest. "Don't fight. Tell me what's happening."

Abby relayed a very quick, very sarcastic recap.

"Perrie?" Fergus met my eyes. "I know Perrie."

"You do?"

"Sure. She did the books in the club I worked at."

"You stripped?" Abby's shriek sliced through the air.

"Surprise," Fergus said, barely glancing at her. He crossed the bar to me and sat on a table, then folded his arms across his chest. "Yeah, I remember when she 'disappeared' as it was put by Fox Sr. She was there, then she was sick, and then she was gone. Fox Sr. tried to play it off as her going away to college, even though he'd previously expressed his belief that his kids didn't need college degrees. Most people believed him, but the thing is, nighttime in Vegas is nighttime in Vegas. All you gotta do is know someone who knows a person who knows the butcher's cousin's ex-boyfriend and then, just like that, you have the truth."

"What was the truth?" Abby sidled across the bar.

Sure. Now she was interested.

Fergus hesitated, but I shrugged a shoulder. Chances are, it wasn't actually a secret anymore, and he probably knew more than Damien did.

"She was pregnant," he finally said after a moment of tense silence. "She was a lot younger than me, but there was a young guy at the bar who was close to her age and was friends with her. She got paid for what she did in the business, but she didn't actually need it to live, so she was able to get a small house in a rougher area of town. I think she worked some odd jobs, but she was young and pregnant and alone, and pretty soon after she had the baby, she was broke."

I picked up a book and stroked the cover. I didn't even know her and I wanted to hug her.

"What happened?" Abby swung out a chair and sat down.

"She tried to get a job, but she couldn't. Nobody wanted a teenage single mom with a baby only a few months old."

"She's a prostitute," I finished for him.

"What? They have all that money and the poor thing whores herself out?" my best friend sputtered out. "That's bullshit!"

"Damien says she won't take it." My finger brushed down the spine of the book I'd just shelved.

She snorted. "You really believe that?"

Knowing what I did? Wholeheartedly. "Yes. I know the whole story. He might not be an amazingly kind person compared to most, but he's not cruel or spiteful, either. She didn't want the help from her family, so she refused it."

"I heard the same thing," Fergus added. "I left not long after that, but I still see her around. Are you really trying to find her?"

I nodded.

"What for?" he asked earnestly. "Do you think you can fix the fuck-ups in that family? That's a tall order, Dahlia."

"I don't think I can fix anything." I met his eyes. "I just...you know."

"I can make a couple of calls and see if anyone knows where she is or how to contact her."

"Thank you. I just want him to find some kind of peace, and if this is what it takes..."

Fergus stared at me for a long moment while Abby chewed her thumbnail.

"You're in love with him, aren't you?" he said quietly, a knowing glint in his eye.

I shelved more books, turning my back to them.

This conversation was over.

———

"I am never pretending to be a straight guy ever again." Fergus slammed the bar's phone down on the table in front of me. "I'd rather sort those damn books until I'm covered in paper cuts."

"No, you wouldn't. The paper cuts last. Once you're done needing to be straight, you can be as gay as you wanna be again." I smiled. "I take it you got through to her?"

With his signature dramatic flair, he sighed and threw himself on the armchair in the corner. "Yes, darling. I got through to her. I could get through the door to Jesus' tomb if I really wanted to."

"No need to be cocky."

"I have a meeting with her in thirty minutes at Stanley's."

"The cocktail place?"

"Yes. And when I say 'I,' I mean you have a meeting with her in thirty minutes at Stanley's."

"I thought you were coming with me. You're the one who knows her! Damn it, Ferg, I don't even know what she looks like."

He sighed again. "I have a picture."

"I can wholeheartedly say that it's potentially not the kind of photo I want to see."

"Fine. I'll introduce you, but then, I'm leaving. And we're taking a cab because I'm not being stuck anywhere while you're in a cocktail bar."

"Right now?" I said as he stood. "We're leaving right now?"

"Yes. Stanley's is a twenty-minute drive without traffic. I have a plan, so let's move it, lady."

Groaning, I picked up my things. "Couldn't you have arranged a meeting for tonight?"

"Where's the fun in that? I thought you wanted to get this sorted out."

"I do. This is sudden, though. What is she expecting, an afternoon quickie?"

"Maybe."

"Wait, do we have to pay her for this time?" I questioned.

"Oh God," Abby said, catching my question as we walked past the bar.

"No time to chat!" Fergus grabbed my arm and literally dragged me through the quiet bar and out onto the sidewalk before I knew what was happening. "I'm not getting into it with her," he explained. "She asks too many damn questions, the little skeptic."

I laughed as he hailed a cab in a flash.

More likely, he'd booked it, because he was a diva and it was far too hot for him to stand on the sidewalk and wait for one.

"Okay, what's the plan?" I asked when we were both nestled into the backseat and on our way to the bar. "How are we approaching this?"

"We aren't approaching anything. You're approaching it," he corrected me. "I'm taking you, introducing you, and then I'm leaving again."

Well. He wasn't exactly supportive, was he?

"Gee, thanks. I appreciate that. Way to be a good friend, Ferg."

"You're the one who wants to get involved in things that aren't yours to get involved in."

I sighed. He was right, of course. It wasn't my business, but it was already well-established that I was very good at being in other people's business.

At least my nosiness hadn't killed anyone yet.

"Stop making sense," I said. "If you keep telling me all the ways I'm doing this wrong, then I'm going to not want to do it anymore."

"I fail to see how that's a bad thing. Nothing good will come of this, Dahlia. It's one thing to fuck a Fox—it's another thing to put your nose in their business."

"Then maybe Mr. Fox should have kept his nose out of my business and kept his son out of my bar. When you think about it, it's really all his fault."

"Boy. You could justify a bath to a shelter full of cats, couldn't you?"

"Yes. Yes, I could, and then I'd make someone else bathe them, because I'm not that much of an idiot."

"Suddenly, the reason for me having to call Perrie once I'd located her makes sense."

I smiled slowly and sweetly. He stared at me for a moment, but he couldn't keep it up for a long, and after a few seconds, dropped the act. His frown was replaced with a grin.

We took the rest of the ride in silence. Thankfully, traffic worked in our favor for the most part, so we arrived a few minutes early. This pleased Fergus—it meant he could do the thing he wanted most.

Steer me into a booth in the back of the bar with a drink so he could wait for Perrie. And that's exactly what he did, except my drink was water.

If alcohol went in my mouth, I knew I'd throw up.

I felt sick. The bile stung my throat, but the worst part was that it tasted like regret. This had all seemed like a good idea at the time, but now I was here, I had no idea what I would say to her.

Would she even speak to me? I wouldn't speak to me. I'd think I was an idiot who needed to be slapped in the face.

I was making a horrible mistake.

Fergus was right. This wasn't my business. I had it wrong. What if Perrie really didn't want to have a relationship with her brother? I wouldn't—I didn't—blame her. But a part of me wonders if Damien ever meant it, or if he said it because he had to.

Because of their father.

There was one thing that linked all the shitty things together, and they all began and ended with Benedict Fox.

I pulled my phone from my purse and laid it on the table. Aimlessly scrolling a news app was the only way I would be able to get myself through the next few minutes until I came face to face with Perrie.

I was stuffed in the corner of the bar. There was no exit. Sadly.

If there was, I'd have been out of here like my ass was on fire.

A few more minutes of mindless scrolling on my phone passed in silence. Hesitant laughter growing closer tightened my stomach with nerves. I didn't dare look up—I would only be looking at a stupid idea, and if I wanted to do that, a mirror was the preferable option.

"Dahlia?" Fergus touched my shoulder.

Damn it.

With a smile, I turned to him.

"Dahlia, this is Perrie. Perrie, Dahlia." He waved his hand awkwardly between us and stepped aside.

I stood to give the woman in front of me my full attention.

30

DAHLIA

She was Damien's opposite in everything but the eyes. Her blonde hair was light and cut just beneath shoulder length. The cut flattered her gentle features, and the color was just warm enough that it didn't look strange against her pale skin.

Her lips were lined with a matte pink, and they pursed as her dark, brown eyes danced over my face, examining me the way I was her.

"Dahlia. It's lovely to meet you," she said in a soft, lilting voice, offering me her hand.

I took it. "You, too." My smile held more than a hint of tentativeness, but she didn't smile at all.

Her lips stayed pursed, even as she sat down.

I didn't miss the dark glare she shot at Fergus.

He stood at the side of the table awkwardly as I returned to my seat, and then, after a moment of us both looking at him, clapped his hands. "Bye, now."

With those words, he disappeared. Quickly.

"You want to talk about my brother." Perrie cut right to the chase, folding her hands on the table in front of him.

"I'm sorry for the deception."

"Fergus already assured me it was all his doing." Her lips finally budged into something that was almost a smile. "If he hasn't changed in the past few years, I have no reason to doubt it."

"I'm almost entirely certain he'll never change."

"We're already finding something we agree on, so that's a good start."

Glad she thought so.

"What about my brother?" Any hint of warmth that was in her tone only a moment ago vanished.

How the hell was I supposed to start this? All the words I tried to say got stuck on my tongue. None of them seemed right to say to her. It was another confirmation that I was making a stupid choice.

"I'm sorry. I have no idea what to say. This was a good idea in theory, but now, not so much," I admitted, reaching for my water.

"Discussing my family is never a good idea, theoretically or otherwise." She pulled her clutch onto her lap. "If all we're discovering is that this is a waste of both our time, then you'll excuse me. I have to get my daughter from school soon, and I'd rather change if I have the time."

I took a deep breath as she stood. "Do you ever think about contacting them?"

Perrie stopped and, peering over her shoulder at me, said, "No. I have no reason or need to contact them. Listen to me, Dahlia. I don't know how you're involved with my brother and frankly, I don't give a shit. But if you have any sense, you'll run away now. Those men are nothing but poison, and if you let them, they'll destroy you."

"With all due respect, I think you're wrong," I replied softly.

"Have you met the ruthless bastard that is my father? Did he con you, too?"

"No, but he's spent enough time trying to harass me into selling my bar."

That made her pause.

She turned, head tilted, and came back to the table. "All right. I'll bite." She slid back onto her seat, but she kept her hand on her purse. "Tell me more."

I raised my eyebrows at the U-turn. But, hey. If this was the ice-breaker, I'd take it.

"My father died at the beginning of this year, and after a couple of months, yours apparently decided he wanted to buy my bar."

"I'm sorry. On both accounts." She tucked her hair behind her ear.

"Thank you. For both." I half-smiled. "He sent your brother to do the dirty work." I explained how I'd been in California and about our first few interactions.

Perrie shook her head. "Intimidation. I'm sorry. That's the way he does things. Like he thinks fear is a greater tool than respect. I'm ever more thankful I don't share his blood."

"I would be, if I were you," I admitted. "My point is, I recently found out the extent of his...I don't want to say control, but influence over your brother."

"Color me surprised," she said dryly. "Like I said, Benedict values fear over respect. I'm sure that Damien didn't necessarily want to be so aggressive in his attempts to buy it. Out of curiosity, were they successful?"

"Like hell they were."

Finally, she smiled. "Good. Now, tell me about your relationship with my brother. If you've gone to the trouble of seeking me out, I can only assume it's now personal."

"You'd be right."

"And if you're here, that means he finally talked to someone about our childhood."

I nodded. "Last night. He told me everything."

"Everything as it happened, or everything as he sees it?" she said bitterly. "We have two different views on my estrangement from them. The truth is their reluctance to accept the fact I wouldn't abort my daughter just because her father plowed his car into a tree and killed himself."

Well. That was a blunt way to put it.

"That's the story he told me. A little less graphically, but the same."

She paused. "Damn. There's one for the books. So, he sent you to check up on me? You're not as subtle as the investigator who shows up with a check every six months."

That was news to me, but also, another question answered.

"Actually," I said slowly, meeting her gaze. "He has no idea I'm here or that I even wanted to contact you."

She raised one dark eyebrow, a question in the slight movement. "Really." It was a statement. "That's interesting."

"Is it?"

"Yes. Because you're either stupid enough to fall for my brother and care enough to do this or he's manipulated you into believing what he says." She leaned back in the seat, studying me. "Thing is, you don't strike me as easily manipulated or stupid."

I wasn't. I was neither of these things.

So, I looked her dead in the eye and said four words. The ones I'd been avoiding.

"I love your brother," I said firmly. "He's not the man you've painted him to be. I thought he was, but he proved me wrong. He's nothing like your father."

She opened her mouth to argue, but I carried on.

"And I don't agree with what he said to you. It was wrong and cruel. He should have supported you regardless, but I also don't think he meant it. He misses you too much to have believed in the words he spoke to you." I wrapped my hands around the glass of water, the condensation coating my palms. "Now, you don't have to believe me. I'm not asking you to, I'm just asking you to listen to me. This is a man who keeps sending you checks and has a bank account for your daughter for when she's old enough to go to college."

Perrie blinked. "He has what?"

Shit.

"Shit," I muttered. "Damn it. I assumed you knew that."

"No." Her voice was a little over a whisper.

Ten points for me. Or not.

"He basically has a college fund for your daughter, in her name, for when she's old enough to need it. He cares about you. This isn't a man who believes you made the wrong choice. It's a man who, I think, was intimidated by the words he said." I reached for my purse and pulled out the silver business card wallet I used for my cards.

I dug for a pen and scribbled my cell on the front. She dropped her shocked gaze to it when I slid it across the table with two fingers.

"That's my personal cell. If you want to talk or you want to see him…Call me."

She took it.

I didn't think she would, but she did.

"Does he want to see me?" she asked me quietly, staring at the card.

"I think he'd move a mountain to see you if he could," I said honestly.

She nodded, each movement slow and if the clouded look in her eyes was anything to go by, full of confusion. "Thank you. I'll think about it."

I smiled. "You're welcome. Sorry this wasn't what you expected."

"Are you kidding?" She looked up. "This is the first conversation I've had in weeks that didn't involve my boobs or why I'm stepping on Barbie's shoes every five minutes. It wasn't enjoyable, but I've had worse." Her lips twitched sadly, but she tucked my card into her purse all the same.

It wasn't even sadness. There was something more hollow about the way she'd spoken. Something…defeated about her.

"Bye, Dahlia. Thank you." She tapped the table before getting up once again, but this time, she didn't stop as she walked away.

That air still followed her. That sad air that said she was stuck where she was, buried inside a life that she couldn't get out of.

And damn my feet for having a life of their own, because I jumped up and chased after her.

"Perrie!" I called her right before she could shut the bar door behind her. "Perrie!"

She stopped in the doorway, sunglasses in hand, and turned back to me. "Yeah?"

"Hold on," I said, stepping outside and moving so someone could walk into the bar. "Can you tend bar?"

She glanced away nervously before meeting my eyes. "I have before. Why?"

"On that card. If you're interested, I need another staff member. Someone just left and we haven't replaced him yet. Call the number for The Scarlet Letter and ask for Abby."

"You don't need to offer me a job just because you're sleeping with my brother."

"You're right, but I'm not." I pulled my own sunglasses from my purse, then touched her arm. "I'm offering you an interview."

"Why? You don't even know me." Her eyes were narrowed.

I slid my glasses over mine. "Because I believe you deserve more than the shit your life has thrown at you. Think about it."

Then, I left her standing in the doorway as I took to the crowd of people on the sidewalk and headed down to the nearest coffee shop to think about how royally I could have fucked everything up.

By the time my day was done, any concern I'd had for the apparently silent-Damien had long disappeared. If he was going to contact me, he would. Otherwise, I would give him the space he needed.

Not to mention I was still thinking about my meeting with Perrie. I hadn't stopped thinking about it all day long.

Maybe I'd overstepped the mark, but I had a feeling she was a lot like Damien. All they really needed was for someone to care about them. To take hold of them and say, "Hey, it's okay. I'm here and I can help you if you want it."

I'd been a fixer my whole life. I had to be a fixer—without me, I don't know if my dad ever would have survived my mom's death. I fixed all the things that were broken, like Sunday morning breakfasts, football games, and hell, I even started buying her hairspray just so it would linger in the house.

I didn't even use it. But it fixed that part of her that was missing.

This was a different desire to fix. I couldn't change the situation—I couldn't even slide into it to attempt it. All I could do was do what I was doing.

Stick my nose where it didn't belong.

I pulled up outside my house and killed the engine of my car. Tired was the word I could use to describe myself right now. I yawned three times as I made my way to the front door and let myself in. Fresh flowers sat on the side table to my right, so I knew the house had been cleaned.

I did most of it myself, but Mrs. Valerie had been employed by my parents for years, and I didn't have the heart to tell her I didn't need her to come in once a week anymore.

I sniffed the flowers as I walked past through into the kitchen.

And stopped in my tracks.

A giant bouquet of flowers sat in a crystal vase in the middle of the island counter. Shades of red, pink, and purple flowers burst out of the top of it, framed by green leaves and interspersed with sprays of white. Lilies and roses and other smaller flowers brightened my simplistic kitchen like crazy.

A small envelope was leaning against the vase. My name was printed on the front of it in Damien's blocky handwriting.

Had he hand-delivered these? And why?

I tore into that envelope like my life depended on it, almost dropping my phone and keys in the process. I set them safely on the counter before I pulled the notecard from the envelope because with how tired I was feeling, I knew I would actually drop them, and then I'd just be annoyed at myself.

DAHLIA,
WILL YOU HAVE DINNER WITH ME TONIGHT?
DAMIEN

PS: DON'T PANIC. DUSTIN LET ME IN.

I laughed as I read the last line. Actually, I laughed at the whole thing. All the conversations we'd had, and he finally asked…After entering my house with permission.

It was the little things, and even if I'd had the energy to be annoyed, I couldn't be.

I swapped the paper for my phone and texted him.

Me: *Thank you for the flowers. And yes, I will have dinner with you. Where and when?*

I'd barely finished making a coffee when his reply came through.

Damien: *My house, whenever you're ready.*
Damien: *Are you still at work?*
Me: *No. I just got home. I can be there in an hour. Does that work?*
Damien: *It does if you come without any underwear.*

Clearly, he didn't know how gross it was for women to not wear underwear. Besides, I had a better idea.

Me: *Sorry, no deal.*
Damien: *Why not?*
Me: *How can you take it off me if I'm not wearing it?*
Damien: *Hmm… Excellent point. And your shoes were delivered this afternoon…*

Well. That changed things.

Me: *I can make it in 30.*

SIN

Damien: *Imagine that.*
Me: *Want shoes, will rush.*
Damien: *See you soon.*

———

The only thing I hadn't considered when getting changed and packing my things for what would inevitably be an overnight stay was whether or not I was going to tell him that I'd found his sister.

Found her, spoken to her, and offered her a job.

When I put it like that, our meeting had escalated very quickly.

Now, it was too late to think about that. I'd either be brave and spit it out or be a chicken and not say a word until I had to.

I wasn't being a very successful adult today that much was for sure.

Damien swung his front door open before I could even knock. Instantly, his eyes dropped to the bag in my hand. "Overnight bag? Presumptuous."

"From the man who told me to come without underwear."

Lifting his gaze up to mine, he grinned. "I said it was presumptuous—I didn't say it was wrong." He took it from me and I followed him inside.

The house was filled with the scent of freshly cooked food, and I sniffed like an idiot as I tried to determine what it was.

"It's just steak," he said with a laugh. "Come on."

I took his hand. And noticed how differently we were dressed. He wore a light gray shirt and black pants. I wore yoga pants and a tank top that said, "Bitch, please, I ride a unicorn."

I grimaced. Was I supposed to dress up? He didn't say. Should I have assumed?

Damn it. Only idiots showed up to dinner in yoga pants.

Actually, no. That was a lie. All dinners should be eaten in yoga pants. He was the idiot for wearing real clothes.

There. That was better.

His fingers tightened around mine as he led me into the dining room. The only source of light was the candles on the table. Two were set at the end closest to us, and flowers to match mine—although smaller—were situated in the middle of the table. Two covered plates filled the spaces where we were to sit, and he even had a bottle of wine in an ice bucket.

"Whoa," I whispered. "What is this for?"

Damien looked down at me. "I never got to cook you dinner. So, I owed you, and I wanted to thank you for last night, so I did this."

"You cooked this? And set it up?"

"I may have had a little help in setting up. Apparently, my romance skills don't live up to my bedroom ones."

I bit the inside of my cheek. "I feel a bit underdressed."

He ran his gaze up and down me, sending a flash of heat searing through my body. "Hold on."

I spun on the balls of my feet as he swept past me and left me standing in the middle of the dining room. What was he doing?

What was I doing just standing here? Did I sit down? Pour wine? Sniff flowers? Follow him?

Dear God, this was the most real date we'd ever been on.

Had the others been dates?

Was this it? The real date? Was this the—

I needed to shut myself up and fast. I would be prepared and pour wine. Yes. *Be proactive, Dahlia, you donut.*

It was my favorite wine—of course—and it was so cold, it could have passed for ice itself. It was perfect, and I carefully poured two glasses. I was just setting the bottle back into the ice with several clinks when I felt two hands lightly grasping my hips.

"Here. Fixed the problem."

I turned, his hands stroking across my back and stomach as I did, and broke into a huge smile. He'd ditched the pants and shirt in favor of sweatpants. The only other item of clothing he wore was his underwear, given away by a bright-red waistband peeking out over the top of his navy sweats.

"You changed," I said dumbly.

"Now, you're not underdressed anymore." He laughed quietly, sliding his arms around my waist.

I slid my hands up his arms and tilted my head back as he lowered his to kiss me. Slow and gentle, it sent tingles over me, and my heart thumped so hard there was no way he didn't notice its fast beat.

"Need to eat," he said against my lips. "Or it'll get cold, and I'll have a burn on my thumb for no reason."

I pushed him back and grabbed his left hand. "Where?"

He waved his right fingers, amusement radiating off of him.

I rolled my eyes and swapped his left hand for his right one. Sure as hell, he had a small, flesh-colored Band-Aid on his thumb.

"It's slightly reassuring to know that you're not entirely perfect at everything you do." I shrugged it off. "Does it matter where I sit?"

He steered me toward one of the chairs. "You know what else is reassuring? Your concern for my thumb."

"Oh, please. I've had bigger Band-Aids on shaving cuts. You're just being a baby. Thank you," I added when he pulled my chair out for me. "Or is it like man-flu, but a man-burn?"

"Everything is worse when you're a man. The pain is so much worse than you can imagine."

"Then thank God you never have to go through labor. We'd never hear the end of it."

Damien's grin stretched right across his face, reaching his eyes. He held up his glass of wine, and I did the same. We clinked them, and he held my gaze for a long moment as he brought his glass to his lips.

A shiver ran down my spine.

Those eyes held a promise of what would happen by the time this night was out.

Was this a precursor for something that would be more normal in my life? Would these dinners happen more often?

Sweatpants at a dining table or virtually naked with take-out. I didn't care how or where it happened. I wanted more of these moments where there was nothing but us, guards down, smiles in place, feelings raw.

"So. How was your day?" he asked, pulling the cover from his plate and then mine.

"Long." Sure, it was evasive, but whatever. "Yours?"

"Enlightening. I spent much of my morning talking with my father."

"This doesn't sound like an enjoyable topic of conversation for dinner." I reached for my glass.

Damien watched me as I sipped it, a smile tugging at his lips. "Do you have something you'd prefer to talk about? The weather, perhaps? Or shoes?"

"I would like to know where my shoes are."

"Upstairs. Now, the weather?"

"It's hot. It's always hot. It's a moot point." I waved my hand. "Nice attempt, but I know you want to talk about your dad, so…"

"Want is a strong word," he said slowly. "I wouldn't say I want to talk about him."

"You brought him up and now you're stalling." I pointed my fork at him. "Get on with it."

His eyebrows arched, and he sipped from his glass to hide a smile. "I went to the cemetery this morning. I wasn't there long, but after my run, I decided I needed to speak with him, so I went to his house."

"That explains why you were gone so long."

"Sorry. It was spur of the moment, and I'd left my phone in the office here."

"Don't worry." I smiled. "So, you went to his house."

He nodded, chewing. When he'd finished, he continued. "I told him straight out that I was tired of pussy-footing around the subject. He either came to terms with what happened and stopped trying to work against me in the business, or I'd sell him the percentage that's mine and he'd be on his own."

I choked on the stem of broccoli I was halfway to swallowing. Thumping my chest, I forced the vegetable down before grabbing, watery-eyed, at my glass.

"That's an extreme reaction if ever I saw one."

It wasn't my most mature move, but I stuck my middle finger up at him. I could barely see and my throat was on fire.

"Shut up," I rasped. "Go back. You did what?"

"Are you done choking?"

"I'll choke you in a minute."

His eyes flashed with amusement. "I told him if he didn't fix himself up, he could buy back what I own and do it all himself."

"I thought it was just a family thing."

"No. I got ten percent when my mother died, and a further fifteen when I turned thirty last year. The twenty-five percent would cost him several million dollars."

"Wait." I wiped my mouth and set down my fork. "If he can buy out, why has he never bought out your sister?"

"He doesn't want her to have the money. He'd rather lose it, long-term, out of spite, than pay up and own the income."

"Sounds like a stunning way to go out of business."

"It'd be different if he were peddling newspapers, but he makes more than enough money." He leaned back in his chair.

Somehow, we'd both managed to make some headway with our food, but now, we were apparently abandoning it.

"Fair point. What happened after you made that threat?"

He stretched his hands above his head. "He said he'd call the lawyer for a valuation."

I blinked at him. "Would you actually do it? Sell to him?"

301

"Yes. But he won't buy it. He's bluffing his way through it, hoping that I'm doing the same thing. He doesn't have the patience or the will to run everything the way I do. We both know that."

"Are you aware this entire situation is slightly screwed up?"

He gave me a wry smile. "More than. Welcome to my life."

I had to laugh. "Was that all you talked about?"

"I told him I was going to find Perrie. He was more annoyed about that than my threat to leave him to run it on his own."

"Why?"

"Because he doesn't actually believe I'd leave him, but he believes I'll find my sister."

This was it. This was my moment.

I had to be honest.

"You'll find her. I'm pretty sure of it."

He tilted his head to the side, gazing at me intently. "Really?"

I nodded. "One hundred percent."

"You're sure."

"I know. Thing is…I already found her."

Damien stared at me. The flame of the candle flickered, casting an extra shadow across his face.

His expression was unreadable. His poker face was something else—not even his eyes showed any emotion. There was no way to tell what he was thinking.

I didn't want to know what he was thinking. I was now officially scared of what was going through his mind, and thanks to the regret coiling its way through me, I was regretting what I'd done.

He sighed. "I know. Fergus called me."

"Goddamn snitch!" I slapped the table, making the candles jump. "What the hell?"

"He didn't think you'd tell me by yourself, so apparently, he called me so I could bring it up if you didn't."

"I have no idea how I tolerate that man." All right, I'd been the one being a little sneaky, but still! He'd orchestrated it.

I grabbed my glass and finished it in three large mouthfuls. I was no longer scared—I was pissed off.

"If it makes you feel better, I was subjected to a ten-minute-long rant about why he could never be straight," Damien offered.

"I had it all afternoon. Try again," I replied dryly. "Are you annoyed?"

He frowned, his eyebrows pulling together in confusion. "Why would I be annoyed?"

"Because I found your sister and spoke to her."

"You mean she didn't run the moment you said why you were there? Fergus didn't get past the awkward moment you both sat down and stared at him."

That made me snort. "Yeah, I've never seen him run so fast. Forrest Gump would be jealous. Actually, Perrie was pretty interested in my ability to withstand your harassing attempts to buy the bar."

"Harassing."

"Yes."

"Now the fact you had an entire conversation with her makes perfect sense. You're on her side." His poker face was back in place.

I wasn't falling for it this time. I flicked a pea in his direction that he promptly swatted out of the air. "On the fact you've made a whole bunch of stupid decisions? Totally. Also, the fact you're an asshole. That's something I'll never change my opinion on."

"I'd be insulted if you did." He knocked his foot into mine under the table in a weird moment that felt completely natural. "What did you talk about?"

I took a deep breath and had a drink before I told him everything we'd discussed. I even apologized for bringing up the bank account, but he didn't really care.

Apparently, it was one more thing he didn't have to bring up one day.

Typical male.

"So, she's going to call you?" he asked when I was finished.

"Me or Abby," I said vaguely. "I might have accidentally offered her an interview."

31

DAMIEN

My eyebrow arched at her admission. The clink of my fork as I set it down on the plate echoed through the room. "You offered her a job? Why?"

"I offered her an interview." Dahlia fiddled with the corner of her napkin. "And I did it because by the sounds of it, if she's in the same…profession…nobody else has given her a real chance yet. If I'm wrong, then I'm wrong." She shrugged her shoulder, dropping her eyes down to where she was now rubbing the napkin between her finger and thumb.

I didn't know how to respond to that, but what if she called Abby and not Dahlia?

Had Dahlia told her about our…relationship, if we could call it that right now?

Did I want to call it that? Fucking yes—I did. I wanted a relationship with the gentle woman in front of me. I wanted her to stay with me, right here.

I cast my gaze over her beautiful face. Her brows were furrowed, and her lips were turned down the tiniest bit. I could feel the weight of her uncertainty as it sat heavily on her shoulders. She was regretting her conversation with my sister today. I didn't have to be a fucking mind-reader to know she was lost in her own thoughts about the decisions she'd made.

I wasn't angry.

I wasn't even close to it. I was shocked when Fergus had called me, mostly because I hadn't made the connection between him and Perrie. It hadn't even crossed my mind that Dahlia might want to try to fix things.

But it made sense when I thought about all the things I knew about her. She was a problem solver. In her eyes, this was something that she wanted, maybe even needed, to make right.

Her heart was in the right place, even if she felt like her head wasn't. Maybe it wasn't. Only time would tell whether the limb she went out on was the right one.

That didn't mean I wanted her to feel bad for the choice she'd made. She did it out of the goodness of her soul, something I was certain was pure. I don't believe she had a bad bone in her body or that she was capable of having such a thing.

I wiped my mouth with my napkin and stood. She didn't look up as I rounded the end of the table and held my hand out to her. Instead, she sighed.

"Dahlia."

She looked up at me through those long, thick lashes that lined her eyes.

I presented her my hand again. Wide eyes, brimming with sadness, met mine, but she put her hand in mine anyway. I gripped hold of her, pulling her up toward me gently.

I wrapped her in my arms and kissed the top of her head. "I'm not mad," I murmured. "How can I be? You did what you thought was best. Don't feel bad, sweetheart."

"But what if she doesn't call me? Now, you know, and what if—"

"What if she does?" I cupped her face and touched the tip of my nose to hers. "You did a good thing, Dahlia. Stop doubting that."

"I just—"

I pressed my lips to hers. She was only going to continue to doubt herself if I didn't. That wasn't something I wanted. It also wasn't something I seemed to be able to get across to her with my words. She was asking too many questions of herself.

My original plan was quickly back on the table.

"Come with me," I said in a low voice.

"Why?"

"Just come with me."

She didn't budge. "Where?"

"Don't make me throw you over my shoulder."

Stubborn as she was, she still didn't move.

I did as I'd threatened. Grabbed her by the waist and hauled her over my shoulder. She screamed, her nails scratching at my back as she did everything she could to grip onto me. All I could do was laugh at her—I'd warned her.

I clamped one arm around her waist and the other around her legs just beneath her ass to keep her still and close to me.

"Put me down!"

"Nope." I carried her out of the room and into the hallway, then to the stairs.

"Damien."

"Dahlia."

"Put me down."

"No."

She wriggled. I stopped, almost at the top of the staircase until she'd stopped.

"Could you not try to throw us both down the stairs?"

"No need to be so sarcastic," she muttered, stilling once again for me to walk. "Now put me down! I mean it!"

"Gladly," I said, reaching the bedroom. Just feet away from my bed, I stopped, gently easing her down my body until she was on her feet. "There. You're down."

She glared at me, but her blue eyes were too full of laughter for me to believe she was truly at me. "That was unnecessary."

"You wouldn't come with me."

"So, you made me?"

"I get the things I want. Like you. I wanted you upstairs, so I got you here."

"You told me you'd get my bar, too," she replied wryly. "You didn't."

"I'd rather you over the bar."

She brushed her fingers over my chest. "I think I prefer this way, too."

"Think?" I teased my lips over hers, resting my hands on her hips. "You think?"

"Little bit."

"Remember when I told you you'd be mine?"

She drew in a shallow breath. I slid one hand up her body to cup the back of her head. My thumb just brushed against her jaw, and I pulled her into me a little more.

"Dahlia. Do you remember?"

"I remember," she whispered.

"Was I right?"

Her fingers twitched, sending sparks across my skin. I'd never wanted to hear a fucking answer quite as much as I did this one. Nothing else much mattered other than what she was about to say.

"Mhmm." She peered up at me, barely tilting her head back. "You were right."

I covered her mouth with mine, taking it in a fierce kiss that made my heart thud against my ribs.

She was fucking mine.

Of course, she was. It was never in question, but I wanted to hear her say it. Something about hearing her say it was fucking intoxicating.

She was mine.

"Good," I breathed, breaking the kiss for a moment, pushing her back to the bed.

Her legs hit the bed. She stumbled back onto the mattress, and I leaned over her, pinning her down with my body, slipping a leg between hers, trailing my hand up the side of her body until I had my palm against her cheek.

Our breathing mingled when my lips hovered just above hers. I wanted her, but not in the ways like before. Not in the frenzied, desperate ways I'd fucked her before.

I wanted to fuck her the way I loved her.

Easily.

Deeply.

Dangerously.

Because that was the goddamn truth. The way I loved this woman was fucking dangerous. Nothing else would ever be as much of a risk to me as my feelings about her were.

I stared into her eyes. Her big, blue, intense eyes. Her lips were parted, her cheeks flushed as she caught her breath.

"I'm yours, too," I said hoarsely, running my thumb over the curve of her lower lip. "And I'm about to show you just how much."

I kissed her again. It was all I could do. I needed to kiss her so deeply all the thoughts that had been swirling around in her head were gone—even if just for right now when she was in my arms. I wanted to consume her the way she owned me.

Her fingers slid into my hair and grasped it, her nails slicing across my scalp. It was the strangest sensation, hurting while it felt good. Her body melded to mine and she moved with me as I went through the motions of removing her clothes, throwing each item on the floor until she was wearing nothing but her lace thong, white and bright against her tanned skin.

She sat up, grabbing the waistband of my sweats. Gladly helping me get her out of them, I kicked them to the side with my underwear and climbed back over her body. Her hardened nipples brushed over my chest. My fingers probed her thighs and hips and ass until her legs were wide open and I was between them, my cock hard against her underwear.

I reached between us for her pussy. The second my fingertips eased beneath the fabric, her hips rose, and I made instant contact with the wetness of her. She was ready for me, but I pushed a finger inside her anyway, and then another, slowly pumping them against her as she moved her hips with the rhythm.

Her gasps filled the air, echoed by tiny, occasional moans. I wanted to watch her come undone, but not like this. I wanted my cock in her, buried far inside her as I fucked her slowly, as she begged me for more and harder.

I moved back, leaving her gasping, and grasped the band of her thong. I pulled it down her legs, leaving her bare, and hesitated before I moved back in position.

Like she knew, she looked at me, nodding the barest amount.

She cupped my neck with her hands as I guided the head of my cock to her wet opening. Her legs were wrapped around my waist, and she tilted her hips toward me. She wanted this as much as I did, but it was her words, breathed against my lips, that got me.

"Thank you for trusting me."

The barest whisper, but the rawest thing I'd ever heard her say.

"I do more than trust you," I whispered right back. "I love you."

Whatever she was saying back was forgotten when I pushed inside her. All that existed then was she and I— maybe she spoke, maybe she didn't. I couldn't fucking tell anyone anything. All I knew that was there was nothing sweeter than the way she clenched her wet cunt around my hard cock and tightened her legs around my waist.

Nothing better than her nails in my back.

Than her gasps in my ear.

Than her low, deep moans that pleaded for more with every single one.

Nothing fucking better than the way she moved with me as I grabbed her ass and rolled to the side and hooked her leg over my hip.

She pushed me onto my back before I was even comfortable.

Straddling me, my cock still inside her, she moved. Slowly and torturously, she rocked her hips against mine, taking me deep inside her. She controlled every inch of me, from the way she clenched on me to the way she slid her hands over my body until she was leaning over me.

Her hair tickled against my skin when she dropped her head. I swept it up into one of my hands and held it encased in my fist at the base of her skull. My knuckles brushed her skin when her entire body moved with the way she fucked me.

One hand around her and one on her ass, I dropped my head back. She felt so fucking good on top of me. My cock throbbed as she worked it. The desire that flooded my body was hot and desperate, and fuck if I could hold on much longer.

I let go of her hair and grabbed her other ass cheek. She moaned as my fingers dug into her tight ass, but complaints died as she forced her mouth onto mine and I thrust into her.

I fucked her hard. Her moans teased over my lips. I swore into her ear.

She grabbed the sheets and dropped her head.

Cried out into them.

I groaned.

She turned her head.

I held her.

She whispered, "I love you, too."

epilogue

DAHLIA

One week later

"Well?"

Abby tapped her fingers against the desk. "She's not bad. Honestly, she's mostly rusty. She can't step right into the job Russell had because of training, but she should pick it up pretty quickly."

I leaned back in my chair and spun it side to side. I hadn't ever expected Perrie Fox to call me or Abby, but she'd called us both. Me to meet with Damien, Abby about an interview.

An interview that had just happened. Successfully, apparently.

"It's up to you. You're far more subjective on this than I am," I admitted, clicking my pen top. "But also, you're the one who has to work with her. I work the bar so rarely, it's a hobby more than anything."

Abby sighed. "I knew you'd say that. I feel like if I hire her, I'm doing both you and Damien a favor, but if I don't…I'm denying her the opportunity to better herself and denying myself a potentially excellent bartender."

"Did she ever mention…life?"

"No. Not once. Just flexibility because of her daughter and how she'd need a little time to schedule affordable childcare."

I was absolutely sure that childcare would no longer be an issue for her, affordable or not. Her phone call to me yesterday afternoon telling me she wanted to meet with Damien to speak to him had set a fire inside my guy.

I'd had to stop him from calling a realtor to buy her a house.

And he called me the fixer.

Pfft.

"Then it's down to you," I said to her, putting my pen down. "Honestly, you're the manager here."

"I wish you'd never put me in this position."

"Owner perks." I grinned. "Look, it could just be temporary, all right? You know I'm seriously considering purchasing the club Damien's father is selling. What if I said train her and then she can move there?"

"Why can't I move if that happens?"

"Do you want to move?"

"No."

"Then there's your answer." I loved my best friend, but my god. "I don't know what I'm doing yet. I still have to think about it. I'm not sure it's a good idea."

"As a rule," she said, stretching her arms above her head, "Buying things from your boyfriend is not the best idea."

"Technically, I'd be buying it from his dad."

"Still not a good idea."

"Maybe not, but after their fight, they straightened everything out. Besides, I'm not against this twist of irony."

And I wasn't. I was all for buying a Fox business after Benedict had tried to buy mine. As for the fight—Benedict had his lawyer instruct Damien's valuation. Damien had flat-out refused it, claiming all sorts of reasons, and had eventually gotten through to his father.

As I sat in front of my best friend, discussing this, Benedict was on his way to rehab in Lake Tahoe. Nobody believed for a second it would work, except maybe me. Then again, I was an eternal optimist. I believed he had the opportunity to change, so maybe he would.

Damien thought it was a deflector for the fact he'd stepped down from the business in everything but ownership. The official line was that he was sick and headed for some treatment—which wasn't a lie—but it also meant that all the things Damien wanted to do were going at warp-speed.

He was incapable of doing anything slowly. Combined with a potential reconciliation with his sister, it was a fucking shitshow, to put it lightly.

That was partly why I wanted to buy the club from him. Being an older bar, it was run-down and in need of renovation, but I was willing to make it work.

My father hadn't wanted to expand the business. It had always been his, but it was now mine, and I'd already made changes. I didn't want an empire like Damien had—I just wanted something that was mine.

And I wanted a family-friendly restaurant with reading areas and nooks and crooks. With book-themed tables and drinks menus and decorations on the walls. With fairy lights and music and happiness.

I wanted something that honored the relationship I had with my parents—and one that would honor the one I desperately hoped Damien would have with his sister and niece.

They were talking right now. As bad as it was, I could barely focus on Abby's words. Her predicament seemed so small given that she only knew such a small fragment of the story. I completely understood the position I'd put her in, but I hoped she'd choose professionalism over it all.

The way life had changed was so insane. I could barely fathom that two months ago, I was coming home from California on the warpath to the man I now loved. That'd he'd morphed from an arrogant asshole to a sweet and sexy man who held my pain as tightly as he held his own.

We were two broken hearts. We'd collided somehow, someplace, somewhere. We made sense.

I believed we always would.

"She's the best I've interviewed, and she wasn't even great," Abby said, breaking into my thoughts. "What if I trialed her? One week if she can get childcare."

"She'll be able to. Well, if her meeting with Damien goes well, but then I don't think she'd have called at all if she didn't want to make amends."

"Tough. I think a trial is the way forward."

I nodded and reached for my phone as it vibrated.

Damien: *Can you have kids in your bar?*

A smile stretched across my face.

Me: *Until later, yeah.*
Damien: *Will be there in a few...*

"What are you grinning about?"

I showed her my phone screen.

Her eyebrows shot up. "Damn. I guess it went well?"

"I guess so. At least well enough for him to bring them here."

"Did you meet the kid when you saw Perrie?"

Shaking my head, I stood up. "Nope. Just Perrie. I don't know her name and even her age is vague."

"So, you're really meeting the family today."

I glared at her.

"Kidding! You know I'm happy for you. That turd has kinda grown on me. His good looks help his cause."

"I saw you checking out his ass the other day."

"Again. It only helps him. As long he doesn't talk around me…"

"Funny," I said slowly, opening the door. "He feels the same about you."

Her laugh was infectious.

I walked through to the bar. It was the middle of the day, so it was as quiet as it would get. I didn't know exactly what it meant that Damien was bringing his niece and probably his sister here, but I hoped it was all good.

I hoped they'd rebuilt their bridges and burned all their walls down.

I hovered by the edge of the bar. It was, thankfully, Fergus' day off, so Abby went to talk to the part-time girl behind the bar. All that did was leave me alone to tap my nails against the end of the bar.

I didn't need to know everything, but I wanted to. All I needed to know was that he was okay.

I needed to know he had his sister back.

I watched the door like a hawk. Waiting and waiting and waiting until it opened and I saw three figures, two tall and one small, coming through it. The small person had her hand tucked onto Damien's, and she was staring at him in awe.

Perrie Fox tucked a strand of loose hair behind her ear. Today, she looked a million miles away from our initial meeting. Her hair was pulled into a twisted knot on top of her head, and she wore ripped jeans and a tank top proclaiming that she'd run for wine.

We were destined to be best friends from that shirt alone.

The little girl who held so tightly onto Damien had Perrie's blond hair. Her eyes were dark, too, the only familiarity to her uncle, but there was something about seeing the three of them walk to me.

There was an easiness in their relationship that made my heart warm.

Damien grinned as he caught my eye. I fought my smile, but it was damn near impossible. Especially when he picked the little girl up and perched her on the edge of the counter.

"Good?" he asked her. "Comfy?"

"Yes, and no," she replied in a small voice.

He whispered something in her ear and she giggled. I guessed it was a bribery for a soda since he motioned to Abby to come over.

"One hour and he's already the favorite," Perrie said dryly, meeting my eyes.

"He has that effect on some people." I shrugged my shoulder.

"And you weren't one of them," Damien shot at me.

I shared a smile with Perrie.

Then, she hugged me.

Tightly.

"Thank you," she whispered into my ear, squeezing me.

I swallowed hard, blinking back emotion. "It's my pleasure."

And that was no lie.

Perrie released me with an emotional smile.

The little girl on the bar groaned. "Oh no, Mommy. Is it your special time again? Do I get extra candy?"

Perrie coughed. "No, Lo, it's not. I'm happy. Why don't you say hi to Dahlia?"

She narrowed her little, brown eyes. "Do I gots to?"

"Do I have to," she was gently corrected. "And no, you don't have to, but I'd like you to, Lola. First, it's polite, and second, your Uncle Damien likes her very much."

Lola turned her attention from her mom to me. She examined my face for a moment before saying, "Are you going to be my aunt?"

"You bet," Damien said before anybody else could respond.

Abby almost dropped the glass of lemonade in her hand.

Perrie froze and then laughed.

I choked on my own damn spit.

"Okay. Uncle Damien, where's fizzpop?" Lola turned around, apparently unperturbed by his declaration.

"Right here, princess." He handed her the short glass with a half-cut straw in it—and a fucking strawberry sitting on the rim.

I peered around her and gave Abby a single raised eyebrow in question.

"She's cute," she mouthed, shrugging.

It was hard to argue with such truth. Lola was for sure the cutest-looking kid I'd ever seen. I didn't let just any kid sit on my bar, after all.

"Mommy," Lola said, "I need to pe—the bathroom."

Perrie lifted her down. "Where are they?" she asked me.

I pointed to the 'Staff' door. "Take her in there. You'll find it to the right, right before the staff room."

"Thank you," she said, her words weightier than just a simple thank you.

"Perrie," Abby said, darting across the bar. "Will you give me a couple minutes after? I'll wait in the staff room for you."

Her hands were resting on her bouncing daughter's shoulders, but her lips parted, and she paused. "I—sure."

I watched as she guided Lola to the back room and then met Abby's eyes.

She winked, following them back.

"What was that about?" Damien asked.

I turned. He was leaning against the bar, one arm on it, looking exactly like he belonged there. His signature black shirt clung to his body in the way I loved so much, but it was his lips that got me. Turned up to one side, the spark in his smirk matched the ones in his sinfully dark eyes.

"She's got a trial," I said, walking toward him. I stopped, smoothing out his collar. "Abby thinks she has a ton of potential. I think, with her experience, she could make a great experience for the new bar I intend to buy."

He snaked his arm around my waist. "You don't need to buy it."

"I do, and I want to. Don't tell me no. Historically, it hasn't worked out well for you."

He laughed, burying his face in my neck. "Damn it, Dahlia Lloyd. All right...Make your offer. I'll instruct it's accepted no matter what."

"Excellent. Fifty bucks it is."

"I'd accept that."

"I know," I said, amused when he pulled back. I ran my finger down the side of his face, over the scar he once winced about when I touched, and across the rough stubble that coated his jaw. "It'll be market value, don't worry."

"I'm not. Although I do find it highly amusing that you're buying a property that will, eventually, be mine again one day."

"Is that so, Mr. Fox?"

"Almost certainly, Ms. Lloyd." His lips were warm against mine.

"Your comment to Lola just then," I whispered. "Flippant or not?"

His lips pulled to one side, his eyes warm and raw. "Have I ever been flippant regarding my intentions with you, sweetheart?"

I couldn't fight my smile. God. Even when he was being the presumptuous man I'd once despised, I could only love him.

"I'm holding you to that."

"You do that. I'm entirely certain you'll marry me."

"Like you were certain you'd buy my bar?"

His laugh was wild and real. "No. Not like that." Still shaking from his amusement, he wrapped his hand around the back of my head. "Like I was certain you'd own me entirely when this was all said and done."

"And do I? Own you entirely?"

"Dahlia." Lips on mine. Fingers in my skin. Heart thumping against my chest. "You own me. Entirely. Always."

I smiled into his kiss.

That was a promise I could believe in.

I believed in love stories. In the predictable and the obvious. In the unrealistic and the unpredictable. I loved them. I lived them. They were my passion and my escape.

Now, I had my own, in the strangest of circumstances.

I didn't know which of those categories we slotted into. Perhaps all of them, depending which part you looked at.

All I truly knew was that we were crazy and unrealistic, until the moment we were predictable and obvious and real. We were opposites that attracted until we were similarities that combusted.

We were nothing until we were everything.

Then again, that was the way all good love stories played out.

Read on for information about LUST, Vegas Nights, #2, and a preview of the first two chapters.

L U S T

Book two of the Vegas Nights series.

Coming September 12th and available for pre-order
everywhere.

You've met one Fox sibling.
Now meet the other…

SIN

Detective Adrian Potter had a lot to answer for. I didn't care that he was tasked with shutting down the city's most prolific hookers.

I cared that he was stopping me from providing for my daughter.

He didn't care.
Not at all.
Until I broke down in the backseat of his car... And he let me go.

Adrian was a single parent, too. He knew how hard I had it. At least, he thought he did.
He had a job. He had people who cared. He didn't know just how lucky he was.

My name is Perrie Fox.
I was a whore of the highest value.

Until Detective Adrian Potter.

Until the tattooed, redemption-seeking detective etered my life, looking for his fairytale.

The cop and the hooker.

Happily ever fucking never.

SIN

1

PERRIE

Sometimes, a girl just didn't need a finger up her asshole. Today was that day.

Unfortunately, whether I needed it or not hadn't mattered to the selfish, married guy lying on the bed in the next room. He wanted his finger in my ass, so I had to deal with his finger in my ass.

Thank god I made him pay before I fucked him. I wanted to get the hell out of this room—and before he did. I'd been stiffed with a hotel bill before, which basically meant all the degrading bullshit I'd put myself through that evening had been for nothing.

I brushed my hair up into a ponytail. The band snapped against my fingers right as the sound of a phone ringing shrilly crept through the crack in the bathroom door. The sounds of a scramble ensued, followed by a very clear, very bright, "Hi, honey!"

Yeah. I'd be bright and happy if I were a guy who'd just got my dick sucked by a professional.

If I had business cards, that's what I'd put on them. Perrie Fox: Professional dick sucker. It had a ring to it.

As much as I wanted to stand here and cuss out the guy, I couldn't complain. One, I was as bad as he was. Two, he'd paid me enough to keep the roof over mine and my daughter's heads and feed us for the next several days. This was also my cue to leave.

I knew how it went. He'd speak to his wife for at least fifteen minutes, telling her all the things he'd done. Then, when she inevitably saw the credit card bill or bank statement—or she'd been online—he'd explain away the cash withdrawal as a little gambling he'd inevitably lost.

Welcome to Sin City. Not even Satan wanted half these fucktards.

I stuffed my heels in my purse and slipped on my flats. They allowed me to escape through the suite unnoticed. I didn't know which room the guy was in, but he didn't hear the click or creak of the door as I made my getaway.

Thank god.

I'd learned to read people in the few years I'd been doing this. It came in handy—if I had to approach anyone in a busy place, it made it easy to pick out who I could sidle up next to at the bar or the gambling table and get lucky with. I was rarely wrong. I couldn't afford to be wrong—if I was, by the time I'd realized it, someone else had grabbed the right guy.

Anyway, this meant I knew exactly what kind of man the guy I'd just disappeared on was. Aside from being a sleazeball cheat, he was one those. He'd ask for my number to call every time he was in Vegas since he was here for business.

The fact he'd told me, mid-screw, that I was the best hooker he'd ever paid for gave that away.

Unfortunately, I'd had virgins give me a better time, so he could suck it.

I certainly wouldn't be doing any more sucking for him.

I handed my ticket to the hotel valet. He'd already been slipped a hundred bucks by the guy, whatever his name actually was, so the valet retrieved my car and handed me the keys without a word. He knew exactly what I was. I wasn't exactly a stranger at any of the hotels in Vegas, but as long as they kept getting business out of me, they didn't really care that much.

Because, let's face it. This was Vegas. Hookers weren't exactly unique here.

Or, maybe they did care. Maybe they simply realized that for every moment they did care, there was someone else who didn't.

SIN

It was whatever to me.

I slipped the valet ten dollars and got into my car. It wasn't the newest car—hell, it was older than my daughter, so I stood out like a sore thumb at this high-end hotel, but no amount of luxury could disguise what I was, and it was just that simple.

No matter how you looked at it or even considered the fact my family owned half the strip clubs in Las Vegas. I always was and always would be a whore, because they were all but dead to me.

Stuck in traffic, I tapped my fingers against the top of the steering wheel. The minutes were clicking over on the clock, and I was ever more aware of the fact that if those minutes ticked over the hour, my sitter was going to cost me even more money. Which was a joke in itself, because my daughter, Lola, would be asleep. And if she wasn't, I needed a new damn sitter since it was a quarter to midnight.

Thankfully, I managed to escape down a side road and made it home minutes before the clock hit twelve. I hastily paid my sitter, bid her goodnight, and locked the door as she left. I watched through the window as she got into her car and drove off down the street into the darkness.

I rolled my shoulders. I felt dirty—dirtier than normal. There was no other reason than the one that had caused my absence from my house that evening. The man who'd defied what I'd wanted and done whatever he wanted, regardless of how it would make me feel.

I should have been used to it.

Really, it should have been something so normal to me after all these years.

Yet, it wasn't. It never would be. I was, after all, the embodiment of the seedy underbelly of the city that could be so beautiful.

I was the lie in the fancy dress, the deceit on the arm of the rich businessman, and the humiliating truth of what really went on between the sheets.

327

Tonight, not even scalding hot water of my shower could wash away the regret.

The humiliation.

The dull ache inside.

It never would.

***

I hit 'send' on the email seconds before I heard the elephant-like stomps as Lola made her way down the stairs. My seven-year-old daughter was many things—bright, inquisitive, imaginative, but quiet was not one of them.

"Mommmmmmy!" she shrieked, skidding to a standstill in the doorway next to me.

"Right here," I said, clicking off the browser screen.

"Oh." She turned to look at me. "Is it breakfast time yet?"

I glanced at the clock. "Almost. Ten minutes, okay?"

She sighed dramatically and threw herself onto the sofa. Her braid was half undone, and her flop through the air allowed the loose strands of hair to circle her head like a halo. "This is so unfair!"

"Welcome to real life." I snorted and walked into the kitchen.

"Oh, Mommy! You don't know. I'm starving! My tummy is eating itself. Nom nom nom nom." She made chomping noises and clapped her hands together to coincide with each one. "I won't survive."

"That's slightly dramatic, given that all you want is a bowl of cereal."

"And an apple, some grapes, and a juice."

"A bowl of cereal is all you're gonna get if you carry on speaking to me like that." I swear, seven-year-old attitude was going to kill me one day. I didn't much care about how bad teenagers were. They were old enough to know better.

Lola, however, seemed to have one setting: Full attitude. There was no 'off' button. Sadly.

One day, maybe evolution would get around to installing that off button on children. Preferably with 'sleep' and 'mute' ones to cover all the bases.

I'd just pulled a bowl from the cupboard when I felt a small hand tugging on the bottom of my ratty, old NKOTB shirt that I'd worn to bed last night.

"Yes?" I said, looking down at my daughter's angelic face.

"Mommy, please may I have an apple, some grapes, and a juice with my cereal?" She blinked her dark blond eyelashes, staring at me with those big, brown eyes that got me every time.

"Of course. Go sit at the table, okay?"

"Okay. Thank you!" She ran away, and the scrape of a chair against the hard flooring in the next room made it clear that she'd actually done as she was told.

Wow.

There was a first.

I fixed her breakfast and took it in for her. She'd switched the TV on and was jabbing at the DVD player controller to start the disc. A tiny growl escaped her mouth, and when her lips curled back, I could see her teeth clenched in frustration.

"Here." I set the breakfast down and took the controller. "You just gotta wait, Lo. See? It's not ready yet."

"I know that, but it just takes so long." She groaned, picking up her spoon. "Mommy, why is it so slow?"

Probably made by a man, I wanted to say.

"That's just how it is," was my actual response. "Don't forget you're sleeping over at Felicity's house tonight. She's coming with her mom to pick you up at two."

"How many hours is that?"

I glanced at the clock. "Five."

"So, when the big hand is on the twelve and the little one is on the two?"

"Exactly right, chickpea." I chucked her under the chin. "Are you excited?"

"Mhmm," she said around a mouthful of cereal. Milk dribbled down her chin, and she reached up to wipe it away. "Yuck."

"You're a messy eater." I threw her a cloth, turned on her DVD, and headed back into the kitchen.

"I'm seven, Mom! I have to be messy. It's in the rulebook."

"I don't think there are rulebooks for children except the ones their parents make," I called over my shoulder.

Her sigh was so loud I could hear it perfectly. "Obviously, you don't know about this one. It's a secret."

"Oh, fair enough." Shaking my head, I hit the button on the small coffee machine in the corner.

It looked like I was gonna need it.

———

I adjusted the top of my stocking, the elastic snapping against my skin as I released it.

Sitting on the edge of my bed in front of my mirror, I looked like the complete opposite of the thing I was. All right—so my dress was bunched around my hips, but still.

My hair was perfectly curled, hanging around my shoulders in big, loose ringlets that framed my face well. I'd perfected it over the years, knowing exactly how to style it so I showed off my features the best I could.

My make-up may as well have been applied by a professional. My slick, dark pink lip followed the curves of my mouth, while my bright-blue eyes were extenuated by the darkness of the smoky powder on my lids and jet-black mascara curling my lashes.

I stood, pushing the skirt of my dress down. Falling to mid-thigh, the floaty skirt highlighted my curves in a way I knew would tempt any red-blooded man to look my way at the very least.

If only I wasn't so hollow inside, I might actually think I looked beautiful. As it was, I was nothing more than a plaything to whoever picked me up tonight.

I was an expensive plaything, but a plaything all the same.

I swallowed that feeling and slipped my feet into a pair of heels. There was a way out this life, I knew that, but there were so many bridges to cross. A hateful family and a father who wasn't really my father were my obstacles—ones I would probably never be able to get past.

I'd made my bed when I got pregnant, and their insistences upon an abortion I refused to have was when I laid in that bed.

This was my life. I accepted it—I had no choice.

I'd given myself no choice.

I went downstairs, locked the door, and got into my car. Thinking about the 'why' always got me. Why did I do this? Why had my life gone this way? Why was I allowing it? Why couldn't I do better?

Maybe one day I would understand that the 'why' didn't matter. I was here, and it was my job, and I had to get on with it. No matter how badly I wanted to change things, unless someone was willing to take that chance on me, there was nothing I could do about it.

Not a damn thing.

2

PERRIE

The smoky air of casino surrounded me within minutes of me stepping inside it. It was thick and choking, but it was almost normal to me now. Sure, I'd need to scrub it off my skin when I got home, but that was my routine anyway. It'd just need a little more washing to get rid of the smell.

I ordered my drink at the bar and looked around the room while I waited. The smoke wasn't as thick here, so now only could I breathe again, but everything was clearer.

Scanning the men sitting alone, I picked out the three who looked as though they would be the easiest targets. One of them I recognized, but the other two just had that look.

They glanced around constantly, almost as if they were looking for someone to catch them doing something they shouldn't be.

Those were the ones looking for someone like me.

"One strawberry margarita. Fifteen bucks." The bored-sounded bartender slid a red margarita toward me.

"Virgin?" I asked pointing to it.

He stared at me. "No."

"I asked for a virgin one."

He sighed heavily, taking the glass back. I rolled my eyes and leaned against the bar when he turned around. There was nothing like manners, was there?

I tapped my fingers against the bar so he knew I wasn't happy and focused my attention on a man sitting a few feet away from me at a blackjack table. He looked antsy, and he kept glancing at me like a piece of meat.

The next time he caught my eye, I smiled.

He paused, holding my gaze for a second too long before turning away.

"One virgin strawberry margarita," the bartender said, shoving it toward me.

"Are you sure?"

"Take a sip and find out," he said dryly.

I did just that. No tequila. "Perfect. It'd be better served without the attitude, though." I set my purse on the top of the bar and pulled out my wallet. "How much?"

"Fifteen dollars."

"Are you in the habit of charging the same for non-alcoholic drinks as you do for alcoholic ones?"

"Fifteen dollars, ma'am."

"The drinks menu at the end of the bar says twelve," a deep, husky voice said from beside me. "And this is on me. I'll have a Coors, when you're ready."

I swivelled around and the second I laid eyes on the person the voice belonged to, I stilled.

He wasn't like the guys who usually bought me drinks, that much was for sure.

He had dark hair cut close to his head, and a thick stubble of the same color coated his strong jaw, breaking way for thick, full, pink lips that were currently pursed in mild annoyance. His eyes were a stunning blue with a hint of green at the edges of his irises, and the dark lashes that framed his eyes only served to accentuate the brightness of them.

He slid those eyes to me. "Sorry, do you mind?"

"Mind what?" I blinked.

His lips curved into a smirk, and he scratched at his jaw. His white shirt was rolled up to the elbow, hugging sizable biceps and revealing dark ink on his forearm.

"I kinda jumped in here when he was telling you the wrong price, even though you looked like you had it handled."

He was hot, inked, and was asking if I minded that he'd saved me from throwing my drink at the bartender.

Have mercy.

Not that I would have thrown my drink at him.

Well, maybe. I'd learned a thing or ten from watching Real Housewives.

"No. Actually, thank you. I hadn't looked at the menu for the pricing, I just assumed from experience that a drink minus tequila would be cheaper," I said.

"And it is." Hot Guy handed the bartender money to pay for the drinks with a, "I'll have the change back," and a nod.

Well.

He received his change and made a show of counting it in front of the guy before pocketing it. "With an attitude like that, who can trust him?"

"Good point." I smiled. "Again, thank you. I appreciate it."

"You're welcome. I watched you for a moment and thought your husband might come and rescue you."

I stared at him. "My husband? Oh—I'm not married." I awkwardly waved my left hand at him to prove it. "Single, actually."

"Single?" His eyebrows shot up, and amusement curled his lips. "Huh. I never would have pegged you for a single person. So, my next question is: are you here alone, or with friends?"

"Alone. Yourself?"

"Couple friends somewhere around here. My best friend is getting married, so we're here for his bachelor party this weekend. I'm not really a gambler," he added. "How come you're here alone?"

Questions. I liked questions. This meant he probably knew exactly what I was and was talking to me for one reason and one reason only.

And, hey—saving a lady from a rude ass bartender trying to overcharge her was a good way to start a conversation.

"My daughter is at a friend's house, and there's only so much silence one person can take on a Saturday night."

"Do you gamble?"

I tilted my head to the side. "You ask a lot of questions."

"I'm an inquisitive person." He grinned, leaning against the bar. "And a beautiful, single woman in the middle of a casino in Las Vegas drinking a virgin cocktail invites a lot of questions."

It did?

"It's more common than you'd think," I said cryptically. "To answer all your questions, I'm single because I haven't found the right man yet—"

"Ooh, cliché."

"But true." I sipped my drink. "I like the atmosphere in casinos because I don't go out often, and I'm drinking a virgin cocktail because I'm not a big drinker. My daughter will come home tomorrow morning and the last thing I want with a hyperactive seven-year-old and her encyclopaedia of questions is a hangover."

He laughed. And god, it was a nice laugh. Just as low and husky as his voice was. "That makes a lot of sense. I don't understand it, but hey." He swigged from his beer. "So, do you just stand here all night?"

"I people-watch."

"What do you watch them for?"

"My own amusement."

He laughed again. "What are you, a body language expert?"

I perched on the bar stool behind me and clasped my drink. "No, I'm just one of those weird people who can sit alone for hours and watch other people have fun."

"That sounds dreadful."

"Clearly, you don't have children. Otherwise, you'd know that's what I do every second of my life."

He reached behind him for a stool and pulled it under him to sit down. His dark jeans stretched across thick thighs that had to be just as muscular as his upper body was.

He didn't look like a guy who skipped leg-day.

"Actually, I do have children. Well, a child. My son is eight," he answered awkwardly.

"Ahh, so are you married?"

"As far from married as one person can get. He's with his mom for the weekend."

Hmm. "For the weekend? So, you have custody?"

He nodded. "So, I understand where you're coming from about having a break." His smile was wry. "I love him, but there's only so much baseball even a grown ass man with a love for the sport can take."

I laughed and set my drink on the bar. "I feel the same way about Moana."

"Thankfully, princesses aren't an issue in my house. Marvel, however…"

"Don't start dissing Marvel. They brought me Chris Hemsworth as Thor."

He sighed. "Always with Thor. My sister and mom are the same."

I shrugged, leaning over to sip my drink. "Then, they have good taste."

"Debateable." He swigged from his bottle again. "So, people-watcher. What can you tell me about the people in this bar? Who are the people to avoid?"

"To avoid?" I laughed. "Well, anyone with a bulge in their pocket and a cigar in their mouth."

"That sounds stereotypical of the mob."

"You'd be surprised," I said dryly. "I don't know who you should avoid, but…" Glancing around, I picked a relatively obvious target. "That woman there, by the slot machines. Wearing the purple scarf."

He craned his neck, leaning into me a little. "Oh, yeah. I see her."

"She's what we call a lurker. Most of the machines are rigged to pay out every, say, twenty coins," I said in a lower voice, "so, she hovers, figures out the pattern, and as soon as you give up, jumps on your machine."

He snapped his fingers. "And steals what should be your winnings."

"Exactly. There are a few in every casino. They amble from machine to machine, just waiting for the big win.

Actually, wait. That lady in the blue dress? She sat down real quick. Watch her."

"All right." He kept leaning over until his fingers brushed the top of my back.

A shiver tickled down my spine, but I ignored it.

We both drank and watched her in silence as she played the machine four times before she got the jackpot. The lights and celebratory sounds went crazy.

"Well, hell," Hot Guy said. "That's impressive."

"Yep. And very time-consuming."

"Isn't it illegal?"

"Probably not. Morally wrong, possibly." I turned my face and he was right there.

Too close.

"Oh, sorry." He sat back, withdrawing his feather-light touch from my back. "Who else?"

Dear god, if this guy ever took me to his room, he better pay me a ton of money or be a damn good fuck for the amount of time I have to put into this.

"That guy in the black and gold shirt. Which should be a crime," I added as an afterthought. "He's here with what I think is his mistress. Or a hooker."

"Unless he's paying her to be his mistress."

"Hence the hooker comment." I'd been there. "He's wearing a ring and she's not, simply."

"How the hell can you see that?" His eyes widened.

I shrugged a shoulder. Because I was good at putting men into boxes? That probably wasn't a good answer.

"The way she's dressed, she'd have a rock the size of a cliff on her finger if they were married," I said instead. "Look—she's going over there."

The woman in red sauntered across to the table he was sitting at. Slowly, she slid her arm across his shoulders and bent forward, giving him a full view of his chest. She kissed his cheek before perching next to him, still with her hand on his back.

When she flicked her hair over her shoulder, my stomach clenched with recognition.

She was no mistress. She was a bought and paid for whore pretending to be his mistress.

"What do you reckon?" Hot Guy asked me. "Mistress or whore?"

"Paid to be a mistress," I answered. "She's quite obvious. A real mistress wouldn't be so in his face."

"You seem to know a lot about this."

"I grew up in the…hospitality…business." Strip clubs counted as hospitality, right? "So, I'm used to the different people. I've seen all kinds."

"Hmm." He finished his beer and put the bottle down. "Do you think he picked her up here tonight?"

I shrugged. Probably, but I wasn't going to tell him that. "She could be an escort from an agency. That's pretty common."

"How many prostitutes do you reckon are in this casino right now?"

Boy, that was a loaded question.

One that made me slightly uncomfortable.

"You know…We've been talking this whole time and we didn't actually introduce ourselves." I spun on my seat to face him.

A slow smile spread across his face. "You're right, we didn't. Shall we start over?"

"Let's cut to the chase." I put my glass down. "You don't really care how many prostitutes are in this place, because you know exactly who you're talking to. If not, surprise."

"I did know."

Thank god for that. "So, kindly, if you're not going to make my night useful, it was fun chatting with you, but, you know. No hard feelings." I stood up.

Once again, he scratched his jaw, lips still curved. "Maybe I am going to make your night useful. You still didn't tell me your name."

SIN

"Liane Carter," I lied smoothly, holding my hand out to him.

He took it in a firm grip, standing in one quick movement. He pulled me close to him, dipping his head to my ear.

"Nice to meet you, Ms. Carter. My name is Detective Adrian Potter, and I'd like you to come with me, please."

Oh. Fuck.

"Now, we can do this one of two ways." He released my hand and touched my waist, making it look to anyone else that we were a couple. "You can put your arm through mine and we can leave quietly into my unmarked car."

"I presume the second option includes handcuffs," I muttered.

"You presume correctly. For the record," he said, bringing his mouth closer to my ear, "you are under arrest for solicitation of sexual services. You have the right to remain silent, but anything you say may or may not be used against you in a court of law. Do you understand?"

"Yes." The word was no more than a whisper.

"How are we doing this? Are you leaving in cuffs or out of them?"

"I'll go quietly." There was no use me fighting. He'd caught me red-handed, and hey—I'd made a rookie mistake. I'd outed myself first.

I was an idiot.

Plain and simple.

"Take my arm," he instructed.

I did as I was told. All I could hope was that I could get a phone call and ask Felicity's mom to keep Lola for a little longer.

He'd already said I was under arrest, and that meant I was spending my night somewhere other than my own house, and it wasn't even as though I had spare money to pay any kind of bail.

Panic flowered in my chest. I had no idea how I managed to walk calmly beside Detective Adrian Potter as he lead me out of the casino and the hotel, but I did. Nobody even gave me a second look.

Would they have if they knew what was happening? If they knew that panic from seconds ago was now a borderline anxiety attack?

My chest burned. Nausea rolled through my stomach, and my hands trembled with the fight to keep it all inside. Even my eyes stung, and it took all I had to blink back the tears that threatened.

I'd gotten away with it for so long, I should have known that one day I'd get caught.

Detective Potter handed his ticket to the valet without a word. I looked down at my feet and tried to focus on my breathing.

In. Out. In. Out. In. Out.

It was barely possible, but by the time a sleek, black car rolled up in front of us, I almost had my breathing back under my control.

"Your keys, sir."

"Thank you." Detective Potter took the keys from the valet and opened the passenger door for me. "Liane." He smiled and motioned for me.

This was the weirdest arrest I'd ever experienced.

"Thank you." I forced a half-smile and got in the car.

He slammed the door behind me and, when he went to the driver's side, the valet caught my eye.

He offered me a sympathetic smile.

I barely shrugged my shoulder in response. Not only would I have to pay to presumably bail my ass out of jail, I'd have an astronomical valet parking fee on top of it.

Awesome.

We drove away from the front of the hotel. I kept my head down, staring at my purse instead of out of the window as the silence weighed down on me.

We drove for hours, but at the same time, by the time we pulled into a semi-deserted parking lot with dim lights, the clock had only ticked over five minutes since I'd gotten in.

Detective Potter killed the engine and got out. I didn't have long to wonder what was going on, because he yanked open my door, took hold of my arm, and half-pulled me from the car.

Then, he put me in the backseat.

The childlock clicked on when he shut the door.

Now, I felt like a criminal.

Seemed a little extreme for someone who only trying to bring a poor, unfaithful bastard an orgasm, but whatever.

He fiddled around in the front seat for a moment before he said, "Name?"

"I already told you."

"Your real name."

I sighed. "Perrie Fox."

He paused for a moment. "Related to Benedict and Damien?"

"Unfortunately," was my answer.

He tapped his pen against whatever he was writing on before turning and looking at me. "Color me surprised."

"Like I said: unfortunately, we're related."

"Uncle? Cousin?"

"Adoptive father and half-brother," I answered. "And it's unfortunate no matter the relation."

"Hm." He turned back in the seat properly and proceeded to ask me questions.

Age? Date of birth? Address? Phone number? Was I with an agency or lone? How long had I been doing this? How often did I do this? Did I have another place of employment? Did I have a criminal record?

I answered every last thing he asked me. The only problem was, with every question, my earlier anxiety returned. Every answer I gave made my heart beat a little faster and my breathing came a little harsher.

This time, it was uncontrollable. Nothing I could do would stop it. But it wasn't because I was being arrested—it was because I was alone, and because of that, what would happen to Lola?

Felicity's mom could take her one more night, but what if I couldn't bail myself out or I was offered a fine and then jail if I couldn't pay? I didn't know the penalties or sentences for being a prostitute.

I'd been a stupid idiot who'd assumed I'd never get caught.

Now, I had been, and I had no idea what would happen with my daughter.

"All right, Ms. Fox. Thank you." He slapped something shut and put it on the front, passenger seat. "Seatbelt on, and if you continue to come quietly, I won't need to put cuffs on you."

Gripping the seatbelt, I asked, "Will I get a phone call? I just—like I said, my daughter is with a friend, and I—I'll probably need to call her parents."

He looked at me in the rearview mirror, his blue eyes dazzlingly bright despite the low light of the parking lot. "That wasn't you spinning a line?"

Oh god, he thought I was lying. I was never going to be able to handle this.

I inhaled shakily until my entire body burned with the pressure of it and shook my head. "No, I…"

The emotion took me. This time, there was no fighting it. Panic flushed through my veins with the sick force of adrenaline, and the tears I'd successfully held back stung cruelly as they fell down my cheeks. Every attempted breath hitched, closer to hiccups than an actual attempt at calming myself down.

My ears even throbbed as blood rushed through my body. The swishing pulse of my own heartbeat pounded through my mind. Somehow, through it, I heard the opening and closing of doors, but my face was in my hands and I couldn't breathe or think or process or—

"Breathe into this," a softer, but still husky, voice said to me. "Here. Breathe on my counts."

Paper covered my mouth. Fingers brushed against my cheek as they held the bag in place and slowly counted me down from full-scale panic to hysterical crying to, finally, subdued tears that wouldn't stop falling.

"Here. Tissue." He handed me a small, pocket-sized packet of tissues.

Gratefully, I took them. I had no idea what I looked like, and there was nothing this packet of tissues could do to fix the inevitable mess I was in, but I had wipes in my bag. Whether I could use them or not...

"I'm sorry," I whispered, blowing my nose. "I'm just worried."

He said nothing.

"I, um, I have some facial wipes in my purse. Do you mind if I get them?"

"I would advise you do before going out in public again." He reached between the seats and grabbed my purse from the floor of the front seat.

The man could stretch.

"Here."

"Thank you. I didn't want you thinking I had a gun or anything." I pulled the packet from my purse, along with my compact mirror, and examined the damage. Black streaks across my cheeks, lipstick smudged...Yeah, that was about right.

"Do you have a gun?"

I shook my head, cleaning my right eye. "I couldn't hit a dartboard with a meteor. I definitely do not own a gun."

He chuckled quietly. When I was done cleaning my face, he held up a small bottle of water. "Water?"

I stared at him.

"You're looking at me like I have two heads." He was clearly attempting to control his laughter. "It's only water. I promise I didn't poison it. It's sealed, see?"

"No, I...Weird situation..." I trailed off. Gathering myself with a quick, jerking shake of my head, I said, "Yes, please. Water would be great."

He handed me the bottle and I opened it—it was actually sealed—and drank. My throat was raw from my attempt at controlling my breathing, so even though the water was warm, it was soothing all the same.

"Feeling better?" he asked, eyes fixed on me.

"Yes. Thank you." I recapped the bottle and cleared my throat. "Can we just go and get this over with?"

"Good idea."

He got back into the front seat, and I put my seatbelt on like he asked. I trained my attention on the bottle in my hands. I didn't want to watch my journey to the police station. Plus, the longer I looked out of the window, the longer the journey would take.

How many ways could I explain this when I called Felicity's parents? I could say it's a family emergency—a recent reconnection. A sick grandparent from out of town? I didn't want to lie about that kind of thing, but at this point, everything was a lie.

The only truth in my life was my daughter, and all I was doing was tainting her perfect life with my bad choices.

This was one step too far, and if I ever got out of this on the other side, something would have to change.

Like it was that easy. Like I could make my life change in a heartbeat. I didn't want my family's dirty money—they weren't really my family anyway.

But if it meant Lola couldn't get hurt...

"Here."

I looked up. He'd pulled up at the side of a road just feet from the hotel.

"Did you forget something?" I asked, looking from the hotel to him.

He reached over to the folder and ripped out the sheet. "You're free to go, Ms. Fox. Unless you need a ride home."

My heart thumped. "I don't understand."

The sound of the sheet crumpling into a ball filled the car, and he dropped it on the floor in front of the empty front seat. Turning back to me, he rested his elbow on the back of his seat and his hand on the back of the other.

"Listen," he said quietly, his gaze holding mine steadily. "I'm a single parent, too. I get it. If I arrest you right now, am I helping you? No. I'm making your life harder. Despite the luxury your family lives in, clearly, you don't live in that, or you wouldn't be whoring yourself out, would you?"

I opened my mouth to speak, but I couldn't disagree, so I settled for saying nothing.

"So, tonight, you're free to go. Go get your car, go home, then tomorrow, get your daughter and do the thing you're best at—being her mom. Me throwing you in jail tonight is a waste of everyone's time."

I wet my lips with my tongue. "I...I don't know what to say," I whispered.

"Start with thank you." His lips pulled upward.

"Thank you." I clutched my purse to my stomach as he got out of the car to let me out.

I couldn't believe it. He was letting me go. This was insane.

He opened the door and stepped aside, holding it for me to get out. I stepped out onto the curb, straight into his outstretched arm.

"If I see you again, I won't be so nice." His tone was light enough, but there was a firmness in his gaze as it met mine that told me I'd gotten lucky tonight.

That, next time, I'd be screwed.

"I understand." I hooked my purse over my shoulder.

He closed the car door. "Goodnight, Ms. Fox."

As fast as I could, I ran to the valet, paid him, got my car, and got the fuck out of there.

NOW AVAILABLE FOR PRE-ORDER EVERYWHERE. COMING 9/12/17

ABOUT THE AUTHOR

Emma Hart is the New York Times and USA Today bestselling author of over twenty novels and has been translated into several different languages. She first put fingers to keys at the age of eighteen after her husband told her she read too much and should write her own.
Four years later, she's still figuring out what he meant when he said she 'read too much.'

She prides herself on writing smart smut that's filled with dry wit, snappy, sarcastic comebacks, but lots of heart... And sex. Sometimes, she kills people. (Disclaimer: In books. But if you bug her, she'll use your name for the victims.)

You can find her online at:
www.emmahart.org
www.facebook.com/emmahartbooks
www.instagram.com/EmmaHartAuthor
www.pinterest.com/authoremmhart

Alternatively, you can join her reader group at
http://bit.ly/EmmaHartsHartbreakers.

You can also get all things Emma to your email inbox by signing up for Emma Alerts*. http://bit.ly/EmmaAlerts

*Emails sent for sales, new releases, pre-order availability, and cover reveals. Each cover reveal contains an exclusive excerpt.

BOOKS BY EMMA HART

The Vegas Nights series:
Sin
Lust

Stripped series:
Stripped Bare
Stripped Down

The Burke Brothers:
Dirty Secret
Dirty Past
Dirty Lies
Dirty Tricks
Dirty Little Rendezvous

The Holly Woods Files:
Twisted Bond
Tangled Bond
Tethered Bond
Tied Bond
Twirled Bond
Burning Bond
Twined Bond

By His Game series:
Blindsided
Sidelined
Intercepted

Call series:
Late Call
Final Call
His Call

Wild series:
Wild Attraction
Wild Temptation
Wild Addiction
Wild: The Complete Series

The Game series:
The Love Game
Playing for Keeps
The Right Moves
Worth the Risk

Memories series:
Never Forget
Always Remember

Standalones:
Blind Date
Being Brooke
Catching Carly
Casanova
Mixed Up

Made in the USA
San Bernardino, CA
15 October 2017